Serabelle

TAVI TAYLOR BLACK

Black Rose Writing | Texas

The author grants the final approval for this literary material.

First printing

This is a work of fiction. Names, characters, businesses, places, events, and incidents are either the products of the author's imagination or used in a fictitious manner. Any resemblance to actual persons, living or dead, or actual events is purely coincidental.

ISBN: 978-1-68513-406-8
LIBRARY OF CONGRESS CONTROL NUMBER: 2023949101
PUBLISHED BY BLACK ROSE WRITING
www.blackrosewriting.com

Printed in the United States of America
Suggested Retail Price (SRP) $21.95

Serabelle is printed in Adobe Jensen

*As a planet-friendly publisher, Black Rose Writing does its best to eliminate unnecessary waste to reduce paper usage and energy costs, while never compromising the reading experience. As a result, the final word count vs. page count may not meet common expectations.

Praise for
Serabelle

"A compelling story wrapped in stunning, lyrical prose that is perfect for fans of Kate Morton's, *The House at Riverton.*"
–Shanessa Gluhm, author of *Enemies of Doves* and *A River of Crows*

"Tavi Black designed her second novel, *Serabelle*, around such complex emotions as lust and patriarchal entitlement, pitted against female accession."
–Anita Gail Jones, author of *The Peach Seed*

"Evocative and finely drawn, *Serabelle* is a must read for lovers of historical fiction."
–Ellen Birkett Morris, author of *Beware the Tall Grass* and *Lost Girls: Short Stories.*

"*Serabelle* is an affecting story of a teen servant striving to belong in Gilded Age Bar Harbor. Fans of Joy Jordan-Lake's *Under the Gilded Moon* and Shana Abe and Joy Callaway's *All the Pretty Places* will surely enjoy this read!"
–*Book Life Review*

"Tavi Taylor Black has crafted a gorgeous tapestry of intricate relationships and lyrical prose, offering readers a vivid portrayal of the Gilded Age and its enduring inequities. *Serabelle* a moving, exceptional historical work with memorable characters and important themes that will hold readers until its final page."
–*Reader's Favorite*

"It was we, the people; not we, the white male citizens; nor yet we, the male citizens; but we, the whole people, who formed the Union. ... Men, their rights and nothing more; women, their rights and nothing less."

—Susan B. Anthony

Serabelle

Chapter 1
Want to Know a Secret?

Serabelle Cottage, 1913

Mabel Rae spied glimpses of the rocky Maine coastline from the horse-drawn buggy, her eyes blurred and watering after a grueling trip from New Jersey into the far reaches of New England. The driver, who had gathered his passengers at the Bangor rail station, halted his rig in front of a massive wooden gate, practically yanking Mabel out of her seat with his rough, calloused hands before moving south with a young male bank teller and a woman in suffrage white and gold. The three had spoken politely if perfunctorily about the woman's work during the two-hour, jostling trip. Through vast stands of pine and maple and birch, over the long expanse of a wooden bridge from the mainland, Mabel's mind had conjured images of the summer cottage where she had been hired on—pounding ocean beyond a stone facade, tranquil green lawns, and marble statues.

The Ainsworth-Hunt cottage stood on the east side of Mt. Desert Isle, just north of Bar Harbor proper. The driver dropped the girl's threadbare bags and climbed back onto the bench, slapping the reins roughly against the horses' necks. Their hooves flung mud at her long skirt, splattering the shabby fabric, and she cried out, powerless to stop the spray. As she stepped back, her worn boot slipped on a stone in the muddy wheel ruts, forcing her ankle to twist to the side. She landed with a thud on her behind like a woman she had seen in a cartoon mocking suffragists.

Mabel tested her ankle. It would bruise but did not feel like a serious injury. She picked herself up, brushed at her skirts, and glanced about, down the lane of oak trees newly starting to leaf out, their green buds bright against the pristine morning sky. Her hands and her clothes were soiled beyond saving. Her ankle ached. An unfavorable start to what would be her new life.

She considered the iron knocker of the main gate with a quick glance at the smaller, less ornate servants' entrance to the north, her stomach fluttering. The main gate towered above her; the tips of her fingers barely reached the iron handle. Mabel stood at a loss: should she announce her presence or simply enter the grounds? She longed for her mother's guidance. Having every faith that Mabel could do the work, her mother had secured this job at the cottage. They both knew it was time for Mabel, at seventeen, to make her own way. Her mother's parting words were, "Mabel, I beg of you, heed your attitude with Mrs. Ainsworth-Hunt. Her family owns a railroad. A *railroad*. This is an important family, my darling. Tend to your pride."

An engraved metal plate arched high over the oak gate. Mabel was not an excellent reader, but her father—a sailor who seemed to live outside the constraints that ruled land-bound society—had insisted that she learn basic spelling and writing. Mrs. Rae blamed the child's father that Mabel often acted as if she did not understand she was the daughter of a servant, that she would grow up to be a servant herself.

Mabel stood back and craned her neck to the sky, mouthing the word over the gate: *Serabelle*.

Acid threatened to rise into her throat, but she swallowed, forcing it down. Alone in the world for the first time, she would not let her nerves get the better of her. She walked through the gate, certainly knowing enough to recognize the servants' quarters when she spied the tall yellow house to her left. But she continued toward the main house's massive columns and stone portico, her impulse toward grandeur. The second butler, coming off his all-night shift, answered the door with a sigh, checked out her mud-stained clothing, and rerouted Mabel down the gravel path to the servants' house to meet the people who would surround her—those who, by all accounts, should become her friends.

Though dawn had newly broken, the yellow house bustled with men in canvas trousers who shoveled gruel into their mouths. A young woman with a bonnet hanging loose down her back served up a strong-smelling meat. Only one young man, a dark-skinned stable boy who sat at a small corner table by himself, looked up as Mabel entered with her worn bag. Mabel glanced from face to face, trying to gauge whom among these starched folk she might trust.

"New chambermaid," the second butler announced and wearily took his place at the table.

The stable boy stood in one brisk motion and relieved Mabel of her bag. "I am Willie," he said. "Welcome. Welcome. I will show you to your room."

"You will do no such thing," a proud-looking woman announced from the cast-iron stove in a far nook of the kitchen. "Sit down, Willie. You will not be getting a peek into the girls' quartahs. Rebecca, take Mabel upstairs."

"I didn't mean any disrespect, Ma'am," Willie protested.

"Rebecca," the older woman ordered again, "you heard me."

Mabel, limping slightly, followed the rotund maid up a narrow set of wooden stairs. "Let me give you a word of advice," Rebecca said, pausing mid-stride to look over her shoulder. "Always do as Beverly asks."

"Beverly?" Mabel asked.

"The woman at the stove. We call each othah by our Christian names here. Mr. Hunt—well, you will find out—he insists. You will get used to it."

Mabel nodded, keeping further questions to herself, though she felt her stomach flip, nerves jangling down her arms.

The maid continued her climb, talking with short bursts of breath the whole time. "Beverly's tone may be harsh, but, honestly, with all these wild men on the cottage grounds, she must set firm lines. You will find we are quite outnumbered."

Rebecca led Mabel to a stark room, nearly empty save a graying hand-tatted rug and an oval washbasin. Over one bed, a large wooden cross hung: a distraught Jesus with carved blood droplets oozing from punctures through his wooden flesh. Mabel inhaled, taking in the scent of sap and salt and aging wood. She laid her bag at the foot of the other bed.

◆ ◆ ◆

The first few nights at the cottage were lonely for Mabel. The room was drafty and plain, much colder than the room she and her mother had shared. Their quarters had been in the attic of the main house in Newark, above the kitchen, which kept the room snug and warm at all hours, almost unbearably stuffy in the spring and fall, in the days before and after the cooks moved outdoor to the summer kitchen.

Mabel wondered if she might ever feel comfortable in this wild northern land where the sun stayed up until nearly ten p.m. in the summer months (or so she had been informed by Rebecca, who chatted constantly). In the first few days of her employment, Mabel washed dishes in the servants' kitchen, removed linens from beds in the main house, visited Cook to bring a pot of lunch to the staff, and watched the butlers, grooms, and maids come and go. Her ankle healed quickly. She had wrapped it the first day in cloth and hoped no one would notice her limp, but Beverly immediately asked if something was wrong with her leg, as if inspecting a new horse. She gave Mabel a salve to rub into her ankle—comfrey, she said, and arnica.

Though much of the work here was similar to what Mabel had done in Newark, she had always had her mother to follow up behind her, to check her work, and to hurry her along. The staff at Serabelle seemed to number in the dozens, though only fourteen people lived in the yellow house. Mabel felt intensely forlorn in those first days, extremely different, though why she felt that was unclear. Was it the accents or their mannerisms—their flat, expressionless, slow responses?

The other servants acted as if they had lived on the grounds their whole lives—though Serabelle had been built in the last twenty years—since cottagers had made Maine a summer destination, since New Yorkers and Philadelphians and Bostonians began traveling via rail and steamer to Eden and Somesville instead of Newport. Mabel noticed how the household staff moved with ease and practice. At mealtime, each man came in from his work in the stable or the main house, sat in what seemed to be his spot, grabbed a particular plate (a large blue one for the head chauffer; a tiny fellow from the barn used a brown dish with a crack right down the center as if it might split in half at any moment) or cup. Routine, familiarity.

Mabel did not know which plate or cup to use, did not have the same lilting accent, did not cut off her 'er's, did not add an 'a' sound at the end of her words, so that "buggy" became "BUG-ay," "far" became "FAH," and "center" came out like "CENT-ah." Their voices sounded as though air had been caught in their noses, as if they could not move their breath to their throats, from where it lodged in their foreheads.

"Why are you staring at me like that?" Willie, who sat in the same corner by himself, asked the second day. "Never seen a negro man before?"

Mabel looked away, embarrassed. "Of course I have. That is all I lived with in New Jersey." Most servants on the estate where Mabel had grown up (other than Mabel and her mother, both auburn-headed and freckled) had been negroes, children of freed slaves who had migrated north and had chosen domestic work over factory labor. Somehow, the lack of color here in Maine unsettled her, though she could not have voiced the reason why.

"You only lived with negro men?" The gardener laughed, a hulking man who ate out of what looked to be a serving bowl.

Mabel reddened as the five or six men who had come in for lunch turned their focus to her. "I meant in New Jersey, most of the staff was negro. You are all so..."

"So what?" The gardener growled as if he thought Mabel might insult him personally. "Han'some?"

Beverly, who had been overseeing Mabel's work, came up behind him and snapped threateningly with a dish towel. "Leave her alone, Gardener."

Mabel moved closer to Willie, lowering her voice. "Well... I have noticed that you don't make the same sounds with your voice like the other people here. I was wondering if it is because you are, you know, a different color. I mean, none of the other people I worked with... the negroes didn't speak like the staff here."

Willie smiled. "I'm not from 'round he-ah," he said. "I'm from away," he said, echoing the colloquialism of the locals.

"I'm from away, too," Mabel said, laughing, though she could not mimic the accent. Yet.

The rowdy chatter of the stable boys covered their conversation, though Mabel felt the eyes of the gardener still watching as she spoke to Willie. Cool March air entered as the men came and went, taking the edge off the stove's heat. Beverly moved to shut the door and called Mabel over to help. They were not done serving.

◆   ◆   ◆

On a blustery April day, a month after she had been hired on, Mabel swept half-heartedly at green velvet curtains in the parlor. Heavy salt air made the fabric stick together, encouraged dirt to gather in the folds. Though Serabelle was solid, the sea had crept into the house's structure along the foundation, quickly aging the building. The cottage stood erect, stone walls battling against the surf, a cold expanse of dark rooms hunkering over rocks, white gables floating above the eaves.

A strong wind hammered at the windows all spring. Locals promised it was the sign of a great fishing season, but for the cottage staff, it was a nuisance. Gardenias had blown out of their pots before even coming to bloom; lawn umbrellas tumbled end over end across the yard. Even inside the house, Mabel felt frazzled and wind-tossed. She tucked her ginger hair up under her bonnet and continued cleaning.

Alistair entered the parlor, his eyes on an article in *The Bar Harbor Times* until he realized the maid was in the room. Her legs were spread apart, and she ground her weight into the floor. She stood like a woman in a Vermeer painting but smaller—not round or robust in any way. A tiny girl like her did not stand a chance against all the dust in a seaside mansion.

The first time she met Alistair Hunt, Mabel had sense enough to bow her head. He wore dark burgundy leather shoes, polished to a shine. She could see the reflection of her bonnet warped in the folds of the shoe. Most men towered over her, made her feel small, but Mr. Hunt was barely a head taller. When she looked up at Mr. Hunt, he was pursing his lips as if he had just tasted his favorite food.

"Good day, Mr. Hunt," she said.

"Call me Alistair," Mr. Hunt said. Eyebrows raised, he waited for her response.

"Yes, sir," she said, like her mama taught her, polite, even humble. Mabel was convinced she would not be working at the cottage for long. After seeing how remote and distant from any city (or even what one would call a town) Serabelle was, Mabel immediately decided that she had erred in accepting a post in New England. She had always dreamed of heading west, to California, maybe to San Francisco. Here at Serabelle, however, she was about as far east as you could travel without actually crossing the rollicking ocean and heading back to her ancestral Scotland. In those first weeks, Mabel could not picture herself lasting more than one season on this homogeneous and, for all accounts, quiet estate.

"Hard work?" he asked her now in the parlor.

Mabel looked up, startled. "Yes, sir," she said.

Alistair moved close to the maid, intrigued. Unlike other cottage owners, he took an interest in the hired staff. Alistair considered himself a convivial person, truly sociable. He knew his servants' names, remembered their interests, and sometimes even knew their birthdays. And to be modern, he insisted that the servants use their Christian names, a choice that often flummoxed guests and outraged his wife. Mrs. Hunt, though, finally conceded, as the mixture of surnames and first names quickly became confusing to the point of ridiculousness, particularly when one footman in the Boston household had the surname of "Stevens" and a butler was called "Stephan."

"How did those curtains get so dirty?" Alistair asked. "Someone not doing their job?"

"You see here?" Mabel pointed at the gold brocade trim. "All these little fancy things gather dust. Mix that with a bit of salt air, and you have nothing but a mud cake on your hands."

"That fancy trim is Julia's touch. I never would have gone so ornate myself."

"I didn't mean to say—"

"You did not say anything." Alistair touched the brocade, letting his fingertips caress the fabric. He stared at the freckles that dotted her arms. "Look at that mess of dog hair on the curtain, on everything." He shook his head in disgust. "You like dogs?"

"It does shed," Mabel answered, noncommittal.

"That is a lot of extra work for you, cleaning up after the dog."

"I don't mind."

Alistair studied Mabel's expression. She *did* mind. He could tell that she minded very much cleaning up after a dog. Possibly after anything or anyone.

"Want to know a secret?" Alistair looked toward the door. "I cannot stand that damn little dog of Julia's, always yapping at me. I imagine running over it with the Olds."

Mabel dropped the curtain and walked to the next window, her pulse thrumming in her neck, a smile teasing her lips. Alistair followed.

"What if I threw the little thing in the ocean?" he pressed on, wondering if she would break custom, if she would treat him as a confidant.

"Sir, I do not think you should be talking to me about such things," she said, disappointingly.

Wind jolted the window. Menacing clouds tumbled into shore.

"Listen," Alistair said, "I am having some guests over tonight for drinks." There was nothing better for Alistair than getting to know a new person, really getting to know them. And what better opportunity than when someone was living in your own house? He was not able to study any of his friends' behavior, not intimately. Sure, he watched their expressions from across the room at soirees, at the club, but wasn't everyone hiding something behind their social persona? Was not each person different when they were at home and relaxed?

Since Alistair had given over the running of the railroad to his managers three years ago, he had lost the opportunity to observe people daily. If Alistair were honest—and he would never be quite this honest with himself—he would admit he never truly *ran* the railroad, but instead inserted himself and his opinion constantly, thereby mucking up the works to the extent that his managers were relieved when he retired.

"You will serve," he said to Mabel now, relishing the idea of getting to know this girl and learning why she seemed so strangely dissatisfied. "It will be fun."

✦   ✦   ✦

Rebecca carried a heaping laundry basket on her hip, walking at a clip towards the yellow house, despite the overflowing basket of sheets and pillow covers. Beverly led the charge, keeping up a steady stream of orders and directions for Mabel regarding sweeping and preparing of fireplaces— directions that Mabel later wished she had paid attention to.

"Do you understand the steps?" Beverly asked gravely. In nearly every aspect, the older maid was solid and sturdy, except for short wisps of brown curly hair that escaped like springs from under her bonnet, framing her face, softening her expression—from afar, one might even use the term cherub-like to describe her round face.

"Yes, but Beverly, please, I am trying to tell you," Mabel panted, attempting to keep up with the other two, "Mr. Hunt has asked me to serve at a party this evening, and I don't know what's expected of me."

Rebecca and Beverly both halted at her words.

"I can't believe she gets to serve," Rebecca complained as the three of them moved into the kitchen of the servants' quarters in the fading afternoon light. "I've nevah gotten to serve drinks at a dinner party."

"Mrs. Hunt will not be present this evening. You would not be involved, regardless." Beverly waved a dishrag toward Rebecca as if at a hungry squirrel. "Mr. Hunt requested Mabel, so that is that."

"He has never asked for *me*."

"Leave it be, Rebecca." Beverly stood with her hands at her hips. "I don't have time for this. I've got to take Mabel over to the house and show her our system. You finish this laundry."

Beverly and Mabel walked to the main house along a gravel path that was hidden by a line of evergreens. "Is she always like that?" Mabel asked.

"Always." Beverly chuckled.

✦ ✦ ✦

At the gathering, the men were all dressed exactly like Mr. Hunt: black suit, dark tie, white shirt. Mabel couldn't tell one from the other. Eight or so men milled about the parlor until she couldn't be sure who was who. Mabel started to think of them by their ordered drinks: "Manhattan" or "Extra dry martini." She was glad the butler was there to pour, as she had no idea what was in the fancy unlabeled bottles or how to make anything more than a whiskey.

The butler, a slim and efficient man, swiftly added ingredients to a shaker or straight into glasses, sliding them across the bar without so much as a glance at Mabel's face. He made no effort at sociability, despite how closely they worked. Beverly was the sole person truly nice to her—she and Willie, the stable boy, practically as new to the cottage as Mabel.

The men at Mr. Hunt's party talked of inheritance taxes, government overreach, and regulatory laws—all conversations Mabel couldn't follow, though she understood that these were powerful men, owners of newly built factories. Listening in, she learned that most of these men were at odds with Mr. Hunt regarding the debate over automobiles on Mt. Desert Isle.

"Dammit, man, we rusticators made these poor old natives prosperous! We built up this land to the fashionable place it is today," a mustachioed man argued. "It is imperative for peace and quiet—the reason we all come here—I am, frankly, completely discouraged that they will now allow automobiles into the town of Bar Harbor."

"Now, Mr. Deasy, let us not be common. Tell me you do not love the feel of that power under your arse." Mr. Hunt laughed heartily at his own colorful language. "Tell me you would not like to drive over Eagle Lake Road? I can take you out now. Leave your livery here in the stables." Mabel noticed that he had not used the man's Christian name, and she felt, without knowing, that Mr. Hunt meant this as an insult.

"Rest assured, Alistair," Mr. Deasy retorted, pointedly ignoring Mr. Hunt's provocation. "We will take this back to the legislature within the year."

"It is over, Luere. I can never again be arrested for driving my Winton."

Many of the men laughed—one of them recounting the tale of Mr. Hunt driving from Somesville down to Town Hill with his chauffeur early last season, hats off, cravat whipping in the wind, the raucous motor waking the old and infirm who slept late on the Sabbath. In deference to Mr. Hunt's position, the local constable tried to arrest his chauffeur Josiah, but Alistair would hear nothing of it. "I will take my punishment due," he insisted. "My noble man here insisted we turn back, but I forged on. He is but an innocent."

Alistair laughed now, recounting the hours spent in what he called "the pokey," a cell with a floor of dirt, crusted and oily along the outer edges. "I met a local boy, a ne'er-do-well youngster used to know my son, it seems. We talked of his family, the Wicks, who own that Crow's Nest cottage, falling on bad fortune. He admired my cufflinks. Constable Jenkins gave me a lecture about civic obedience. Cost me twenty whole dollars in fines, it did. Highway robbery," he joked.

"Let us hope, at least," Luere Deasy went on, trying to steer the conversation back to the debate, "that at a minimum, Mr. Dorr gets his road built. We must keep these beasts off the main throughways."

Mr. Hunt, as if tiring of talking with Mr. Deasy, signaled to Mabel from across the room. She handed off drinks from her tray and hurried over.

Alistair slid his arm around her waist when she drew close, a bold and startling move. "Look at this one," he bragged.

Mabel had never received this type of attention from a man before. In Newark, there had been a crush, brief flirtations with one of the boys at church, but Mr. Hunt's focus felt different, so completely adult, as if she had finally crossed into maturity.

Mr. Deasy, taking the bait, looked Mabel up and down, eyes lingering on her waist. "She new?"

"Brand spanking."

Mabel went tense under his arm.

"Lucky," Mr. Deasy said. "Alistair, remember that cousin of mine who went homesteading all those years ago out in Oklahoma?"

"Short fellow? Knew him at Deerfield, two years ahead of me."

The man seemed to take pleasure in Alistair calling another man short. "Yes, that is right. I guess he might be about as tall as you," Mr. Deasy guffawed, all disagreements forgotten. "Well, he grabbed a nice tract right outside of Norman in the '89 stampede. Had to scare off a bunch of darkies by threatening a lynching, but he got the property all right. Beside the point, that bit, ha ha." Deasy finished his drink in one swallow. "He is still out there. Ended up taking on a fine young gal like yours off one of those orphan trains to keep him company; that was my point. His wife being taken down by the palsy. Been bedridden for years now. That and eight children about the property." The man smiled broadly at Mabel. "He needed the girl's help, you see. All those offspring."

Mr. Hunt kept Mabel close to him all evening, only releasing her so she might fetch the others' drinks. At one point, he had her sit next to him on the big, overstuffed couch. She felt her face reddening, but none of the men reacted. They went right on with their stories about acquired property and how they had dominated over the landscape, over people.

Then the butler pulled her aside. "You bettah be careful, you," he said through his thin lips. He did not even use her name.

Mabel felt her dander rising. "Careful of what?"

"Mrs. Hunt will get rid of you the moment she hears of your behavior."

Mabel lost grip of the calm, quiet demeanor she had tried to put on these first few weeks. "And how would she hear about it?" she hissed.

The butler had not yet looked in her face, but now, his eyes snapped upward, his pale, almost colorless irises startling her. "I have a duty to my employers."

"But I have not done anything."

"You are encouraging him."

"I do not mean to," Mabel said, unable to articulate how good it had felt to have the attention of these influential men, to be seen. But she also knew that the butler could have her fired instantly. "I was… he's my boss. What can I do?"

"Stupid girl. You will learn." The butler returned to the bar, leaving Mabel to fume over the insult.

◆　◆　◆

In the maids' kitchen, a pan had burned a dark ring into the birch countertop. Crumbs littered the table, and a thick film of dirt had been scuffed into the pine flooring, coloring it with a maple tinge. A smattering of dishes lay here and there on the table and atop the bread box. The reek of sour milk wafted up from the sink drain. Mabel had offered to do the tidying this morning while Beverly and Rebecca prepared for church. She had not told them yet that she was not going. They would fight her on it. Since her arrival at the cottage, no one had bothered asking Mabel if she wanted to attend the Eden Congregational Church on Sundays. She only ever went to church because it was expected of her—the quiet of the vestibule made her uncomfortable. She hated how everyone whispered as they entered. Even her mother had dragged her to a Catholic Church in Newark after they arrived in America when she was six. Somewhere back in her mind were memories of a cold stone structure on a hillside in Scotland, strong incense, and Latin phrases floating in the chill air.

As there was no mention of Catholicism at the cottage, Mabel did not bother with the distinction. Denomination made no difference to her. She didn't feel a great obligation towards any god, though a girl like her—even one as bold as she—would never dare speak her thoughts. Mabel found it ridiculous to believe that someone or something so huge and omnipresent as God could care about every human pettiness.

Mabel placed the plug in the sink and ran dish water, her knuckles turning pink under the icy flow. Her ribcage shook. This morning, a fluttering in her throat felt grand as she considered what she was about to do.

Over the past month, Mr. Hunt had grown more and more friendly. By now, he had become bolder: stroking her neck, smelling her hair, running his hands across her shirtwaist whenever they had a few minutes alone.

He asked her questions—questions no one in her life had bothered to ask: "What is the one thing you would like to do before you die? Where would you like to visit? What is the subject you think of most?" Mabel hardly knew how to answer. She did, of course, confess to him her desire to see California, but Mr. Hunt laughed. "Why, that is easy enough. That is a mere train ride away. Think big, Mae. Think Africa! India! The Orient!"

When Mabel served the family dinner at the banquet table, his eyes held the sparkle of crystal goblets. She blushed and turned away, afraid that Mrs. Hunt would see.

Now, she struck a match, held the stick to the gas burner, and then placed the kettle atop the flame. Light from a hurricane lamp flickered on the table, throwing early morning shadows onto the wall in front of her. Mr. Hunt had asked her to stay home from church today. He had come to her in the laundry room and spoken to her softly.

The kettle whistled on the stove. Mabel grabbed the handle. She looked up quickly to ensure no one had entered the room, swung the kettle over the sink, and poured. Mabel bit her lip and stuck her left arm under the stream of boiling water. The skin of her forehead pulled tight, and she felt a flush creep across her face before she cried out, dropping the kettle into the half-filled sink. Water splashed at the edges of the porcelain, and the kettle rocked about before settling upright on the bottom of the sink.

"Lord, child. What have you done?" Beverly was quickly beside her, inspecting her forearm.

"It hurts," Mabel cried.

Beverly rushed to the icebox and sat Mabel at the table. Blisters formed on the pale surface of her skin, bubbling up white and fluid. Beverly rubbed a pat of butter across the burnt skin and shook her head. "Get some bandages," she ordered Rebecca, who came and stood over them, fussing and clucking. "We will get her wrapped up befah we ah off."

"I don't think I should go," Mabel said without looking up.

"Oh, no?"

"I probably couldn't sit still for that long with this thing burning."

Beverly frowned and took three breaths before answering. "I s'pose not."

◆   ◆   ◆

Mabel watched the servants' figures grow smaller and smaller as they made their way to the church. Rebecca's solid form shuffled on the dirt path as if it were a burden to pick up her feet at all. Her shoulders were hunched, giving her the appearance of an old spinster, though she was a mere twenty-two. She wore a knit bonnet that she bleached weekly, white as the virgin's headdress. Every other day of the week, it hung from the corner of her bedpost, underneath the carved wooden cross nailed to the wall.

Two weeks ago, Mabel heard a scream in the night. She flew out of bed and across the room they shared. Rebecca moaned and flailed her arms about. "I am struck. I am struck," she cried. From the pale light of the moon, Mabel saw a spot of blood on Rebecca's forehead. She ran for a towel and blotted Rebecca's skin. It was but a small cut. On the pillow, the wooden cross lay next to her head. It had fallen from the nail.

"I think it is a sign," Rebecca whispered. "God is trying to tell me something."

"Like what?" Mabel asked. She did not believe in omens.

"He needs my attention. I will be a bettah Christian from now on."

◆   ◆   ◆

Beside Rebecca, as rigid as the majestic oaks that lined the street, Beverly's back was stiff and haughty over quick, precise steps. She wore a cream-colored chenille dress on Sundays, cleaned and pressed for church, her chin held carefully parallel to the ground. She looked neither side to side nor up or down, keeping her eyes straight forward, towards the church. Beverly's husband's long strides kept him ahead of the women. Every few minutes, Josiah stopped and let them catch up, turning his thick head towards his wife with a blank expression. The cook had already gone ahead; she liked to sit up close, absorbed for the hour and a half in the preacher's fine words. The first butler and the stable boys would come along behind, to sit near the back of the church. The gardener was nowhere to be seen.

◆   ◆   ◆

Mabel crossed the wide expanse of gravel between the servants' quarters and the main house. She moved with broad, confident steps as if propelled by a strong wind, though the day had begun with an uncustomary calm.

Alistair opened the door and took her tiny chin in his palm. Her hair was swept back into a loose bun, and she wondered if she smelled like the sea, dank and salty, from hanging clothes in the yard all week. Alistair pulled her inside. The white bandage wrapped around Mabel's arm peeked out from under her shawl, but he didn't reveal that he noticed.

"Julia will be gone until evening." He led her into the parlor by her shoulders. "I told Beverly to keep everyone else out of the house. Let us take our time."

He removed her shawl and threw it across the settee, leaving her standing in the middle of the room, in her rag of a dress. She stood stiff as a starched blouse, feeling as if she should fluff the pillows or straighten the afghan as he rifled through a collection of celluloid discs.

"Four minutes of play." He held up a disc. "Have you ever heard Puccini?"

"What?" she asked.

"Listen." Alistair dropped the needle gently on the phonograph and held his arms wide. "*La Bohème!*" he shouted over the soaring violins. "His best opera."

Mabel squealed as he grabbed her and swung her about the room. She winced when he touched her forearm, but the joy, the novelty of being in Mr. Hunt's arms, overshadowed her pain. The music swept around their bodies and carried them past the settee, across the polished floor to the bookshelf, and over the Oriental rug that Mabel had spent yesterday afternoon beating out on the back lawn. Her feet lifted off the ground at the turns, and her arm throbbed with the strain. Alistair paid no notice of her injury, holding her roughly, her hand swimming inside his thick palm. Dark, fine hairs covered the back of his fingers.

"I could eat you up, little girl," he whispered into her hair. "Where did you come from?"

"Newark," she said awkwardly, unsure what he meant.

The singer's voice soared above their heads and filled the room with a passionate vibrato in a language she had never heard. Mabel didn't know that anyone could sing that high, that powerfully, but she believed in the confidence, in the righteousness of the singer. Though Mabel didn't understand a word, as she spun around the room in the arms of this man who was sweating under his tight collar, she understood for the first time the urge to dissolve inside another human being. Alistair Hunt was not stately or even handsome. He didn't possess chiseled features or a slim waistline, but he had liquid eyes like sea glass and a tender, salty smile. His nose, if a bit red in the afternoons, was as button-like as a child's. Her eyes welled up, and her stomach contracted. Alistair drew his face close, as if he might lick the falling tears from her cheek.

Chapter 2
Mark My Words

Thursdays were not the easiest day in the cottage, but to Alistair, something was attractive about being free of the servants—and that freedom lent a wild frisson to the day. Dishes lay on the dining table after dinner, no one willing to transport them to the kitchen, though Alistair vaguely remembered his daughter Sarah being responsible for such when she lived in the house. An abandon to Thursday nights suited Alistair, the thought of the staff rowdying it up, getting into trouble, and looking for small adventures.

As full dark came over the cottage grounds, Alistair left his bedroom and wandered into the kitchen to find the second butler at the table, a novel spread out before him, though surely the print was too small for such an old man to make out the story with a lone candle to light the prose.

"Why, Wilson, how is it you sit here on your night off?" Alistair slapped the butler on the back, frightening the old fellow. The man jumped in his hard, wooden seat like a seal on the rocks, sliding part way down upon landing. Alistair wondered if he might slide right under the table. He had the urge to prop the butler up under the armpits as one might a toddler, but the man quickly righted himself.

"Sir, but you scared me mightily." The old man cleared his throat and fiddled with his clothing, making Alistair wonder whether he might have wet himself.

"A reader, are you? Good for you. Must have been absorbing; you did not even hear me coming."

"Truth be told, sir, I think I had drifted off. Not much of a story, I am afraid. All these new dime novels are filled with smut. What happened to all the Stephen Cranes? Where are the Melvilles of this generation?" The old man shook his head. "Forgive me. I know a youngster like you probably likes this kind of thing, but I must be selective with my time, if you understand what I am suggesting."

Alistair, suddenly forgetting what he had come to the kitchen for in the first place, pulled a chair out across the table from Mr. Wilson. The old man reminded him of his grandfather, who would have—had he still been alive—been nearly one hundred years old. Mr. Wilson was not like the other servants. At least, that is what Alistair told himself to explain why he had never called him by his Christian name. Since joining the staff some years ago, the second butler had always referred to himself as Mr. Wilson, and Alistair never attempted to correct him, to make him conform to the ways of the household. There was something dignified about the man. And this reading business confirmed those feelings. It seemed he was an educated man.

Alistair changed his mind about sitting and walked to the hutch in the next room, returning with two whiskey glasses and a bottle of Old Foreman.

"So, why sit here in the kitchen all alone on your night off?" Alistair poured a glass for Mr. Wilson, who looked quite perplexed. "Would you not rather spend it with some friends, someone special?"

Mr. Wilson picked up the glass, raising his eyebrows as if to ask permission. Alistair nodded at him, encouraging, though the butler sadly raised it to his nose and sniffed instead of drinking.

"Sir, I am not sure you would understand," he mumbled, as if embarrassed to suggest Mr. Hunt didn't know something. He glanced at his glass, set it on the table, and looked as if he had lost his courage but was forging on, nevertheless. "I have spent a good deal of my time in this kitchen, or in kitchens like this, my whole life. I guess you could say this is where I am comfortable."

Alistair nodded and threw back a splash of the whiskey. "Surely there is somewhere you would rather be?"

"Perhaps in bed with my wife?" the man joked, coloring.

"That is more like it!" Alistair said. "Would not have to be your wife, you know."

The old man looked Alistair in the eye for the first time. "Call me old-fashioned, but that does not seem right, bedding a woman who is not your wife."

Alistair stared back, wondering whether he was being admonished or if the old fellow was simply stating his opinion. He searched the stern face, the sunken eyes. Oh, he was being admonished, all right.

Fighting the urge to put Mr. Wilson in his place, somehow wanting to allow this old fellow his dignity, Alistair commented instead, "Well, I guess you have earned the right to be stodgy. I bet you once had a wife that was a looker."

The butler's eyes softened while he thought back. "Esther was lovely. Like a young Clara Barton. Married nearly fifty years, we were."

Alistair nodded. Not what he would call a looker by the comparison, but he was not going to voice that observation.

"'Til the consumption got her," the butler continued. "One too many of these cold northern winters, I suppose."

The talk of death and disease was too much for Alistair. Romantic sweetness, he could indulge for a while, but not this morose talk of dead women. "Is there nothing else you would rather do than sit here, something with the living? Go sailing? Take a hot-air balloon ride? Board a train somewhere?" Alistair couldn't understand the impulse to stay put in a kitchen, even his spacious and well-appointed one.

The man spun his still-full glass around in his hand, chuckling. "I suppose there is one thing I have always wanted to do."

"Well?"

"It is silly."

"You are talking to me," Alistair said, hands wide.

The butler smiled as if he appreciated Alistair's good humor about his own wild behavior. "Yes, sir, I do believe I can tell you." He still took a moment before he confessed, looking around the room as if someone might overhear him. "I have heard you many times talk about your trips to the mines. I have always wanted to do a little prospecting myself, take up a hard hat and pick and dig at the earth. Like looking for a prize." Mr. Wilson smiled. "Of course, I have no need for a gem even if I laid my hands on one, but I like the idea of finding something. For someone with no athletic ability, I imagine it might feel like winning a medal."

Alistair stood, hands on the table. "Really?" he asked. "Digging in a mine is what you would do before anything else? Well, hot-diggidy, that is easy enough to arrange, Mr. Wilson." Alistair paced the room, excited. "A man after my own heart," he said, then stopped and turned. "You might have told me this years ago. You could have accompanied me on a trip." Alistair paced the length of the kitchen, tapping at his nose. "Not too late. Not too late at all."

The butler's eyes followed Alistair's movements around the room, a small smile teasing his mouth. The fellow finally lifted the glass to his lips and took a tentative sip. Alistair came around and patted him on the shoulder. "We will make a trip happen, Mr. Wilson. Mark my words. You will find your gem yet."

✦   ✦   ✦

By June, Mr. Hunt was meeting with Mabel several times a week, never twice in the same place. Last week, he had followed her into one of the spare bedrooms in the east wing overlooking the harbor. When she returned to the room to clean, Mabel tucked the corners tight and sat on the bed's edge. Her mother had taught her to bounce a coin off the sheets before covering them with a blanket. Tight, her mother said. Tight means true, and true is how you want to live your life. No wrinkles, no room for filth. A practical woman, she taught Mabel to be efficient and modest at all times, though she certainly understood her challenge with her daughter.

From the time Mabel learned to speak, she developed the ability to debate, often confounding her mother into compliance. Mabel argued she *should* be able to bathe in her own clean, hot water, rather than her mother's leftover bathwater, so that she not get even filthier from all that floating dirt; Mabel *could not* possibly carry the wood inside as she might get a sliver that might bleed and then stain her dress, making more work for her mother; if Mabel ate the bean-hole beans, then she might vomit, which could make other servants ill—or maybe someone would vomit just because she had vomited. Then mother would have to clean up the mess, and was it not better if someone who *liked* bean-hole beans ate them instead?

Never had she accepted the truth in words—Mabel demanded proof of all statements, catching her finger under a heavy lid rather than heeding her mother's warning. She had been told how she grabbed at scissors as a toddler, saying: "I can do! Self, self!" She was born that way and couldn't help her urge to fight.

So, of course, Mabel never bothered to bounce a coin on the bedsheets. In the eight months she had been at the cottage, no one other than she and Mr. Hunt had used this room or any of the rooms in the east wing, though she changed the linens weekly. Mabel imagined spending the night here. She could see herself choosing an undergarment, silky and delicate, from the bureau. Dressing gowns hung in the immense closet on padded hangers with satin ribbons. Ten, twenty, thirty different gowns to choose from. One in every color. She flopped back onto the bed and thrummed her fingers on the soft cover. The silver wallpaper was bordered with a strip of cherubs floating in space, some with wings, one playing a harp. She ran her hand along the curved wood of the headboard and pulled a tasseled pillow from underneath her head. She flung the pillow onto the chair next to the bed.

That chair had been a witness to their love. Mabel rolled over and fondled the soft velour upholstery. So fine. She swung her legs off the bed and kneeled on the seat, running her hands up the cherry wood of the sides. The chair saw how he had loved her, how he had kissed and fondled her body. She had been scared at first, though thrilled by the touch of his warm hands inside her bodice, then against the bare skin of her ribs. Her whole body felt electrified, like the energy Mr. Hunt had described to her. He had watched the workmen in Boston string wires and tubes through their estate to light up every room.

Eyes closed, every part of her felt on edge, each finger, each nipple, each knee, each elbow as he explored her like one of his mines, as if he might unearth a fresh gem. Her body was alert in a way she had never thought possible. As Mr. Hunt had thrust himself into her, she had felt a jolt, the pain intense and localized between her thighs. The ache quickly turned into something curious, friction-filled, while she finally gathered the courage to open her eyes to spy the creased, leathery skin of Mr. Hunt's turtle-like neck. She nearly burst out laughing but quickly stifled the sound, sensing that a laugh would not be welcomed at this moment as he slapped his rather rotund belly against hers. Never had she been this close to the flesh of a man. This was the sex act. So far, she had learned that everything leading up to it was better than the actual insertion. Mr. Hunt pumped and grunted during fornication, compared to the sweet words he had petted her with before: beautiful, sweet, young, fresh, soft, gorgeous.

The chair had held their clothing side by side, patiently, until they were finished. Mabel dug her fingernails in at the top, making a slight indent through the varnish. This was their room, their chair.

Mabel sidled to the door and looked down the long hallway. Beverly would be cleaning the dining room now. Rebecca would be in Mrs. Hunt's room. Mabel didn't hear a sound except for the constant crash of waves below the far window. The maids' policy was to keep all doors open while they cleaned. No secrets, no suspicious behavior allowed. She swallowed hard and quietly closed the door, taking a letter opener off the bureau. The opener had a wooden handle carved into the shape of an abstract face, a foreign design she had never seen before. The polished wood felt slick in her palm. She wondered what faraway place the opener had come from— maybe some savage land Mr. Hunt would take her to one day.

Mabel turned the chair away from the wall and sat on the edge of the bed. She glanced at the door once more and poised the letter opener on the back of the chair. Her hand shook. The varnish gave, soft and tacky under the hard metal tip. The wood underneath resisted the pressure, but Mabel dug in, carving her initials, MR, next to his, AH. She kept her ears alert, ready to spring at the slightest sound. The opener bore into her hand, etching a red line down the center of her palm, but she continued, quickly drawing a heart in between the letters. She brushed at the flaking varnish and surveyed her work. Now it was her chair, their chair, forever.

Mabel wiped the end of the letter opener and placed it back on the dresser next to a fountain pen set and a crystal vase. She turned the chair back to the wall and swept the floor, removing the telltale varnish specks. The hallway was still empty when she opened the door and moved into the next room. Waves collided on the rocks below.

◆   ◆   ◆

Alistair Hunt married Julia Ainsworth of the Worcester Ainsworths in 1876. It was deemed all around to be a match well made, but there was some debate as to whose fortune was the largest, the Ainsworths' or the Hunts.' Alistair had not fallen passionately in love with Julia, but in those early days, her innocence seemed endearing. And his father liked Julia's family's railroad fortune. "We are cast from the same lot—that being *a lot of money*," his father repeated at their engagement soiree, believing his witticism to be incredibly clever. The Hunts, in general—owners of bauxite mines in Virginia who had eventually moved into aluminum production— were not known for their tact.

Alistair's mother, too, liked Julia, liked the fact that her family was willing to give Alistair a title at Boston & Lowell Railway, albeit however ornamental. Her son had managed to disappoint his father in every position given to him at the mines. Truth be told, Alistair was not particularly interested in running the day-to-day operation of either mines or railways. However, the core of these businesses—minerals and travel— fascinated him. So much so, he found himself taking a jaunt up to New Hampshire when he should have been at a board meeting or sinking down a mine shaft to observe an impressive vein of ore instead of meeting with investors. Alistair's father-in-law eventually became impatient, too, remarking on Alistair's whimsical, unpredictable nature.

Alistair's lust for life—an enthusiasm that could not be contained, which might have been infectious had it not been so alarming to those trying to run a successful business—was exactly what Julia lacked. As a freshly budded young woman, Julia was fascinated by his robust enthusiasm. And what man could resist such unabashed adoration? Had Alistair been a thinking man rather than an excitable one, he might have realized that Julia's awe would wear off like the sheen on a new automobile—that once a couple settles into married life, there must be more to a foundation than superficial admiration (and, of course, the promise of a management position).

The newly united families summered at the cottage and traveled back to Boston when the weather turned. Serabelle—part of Alistair's family's slow creep north—seemed as unruly and exotic as Julia's husband, up in the untamed wilds of coastal Maine. The Atlantic pounding at the shore, the brutal onset of winter, making the roads nearly impassible by November, were as unpredictable and, quite honestly, as frightening as Alistair's antics as he approached her bed chamber. Julia had imagined that lovemaking would be a gentle and emotional act, but Alistair never lost his enthusiasm. He fairly attacked, making those sessions less about enjoyment than survival. A few weeks into the marriage, Julia wondered if the two of them might be irreversibly incompatible.

At her first gentle admonitions, Alistair seemed unable to curb his eagerness, but as the months wore on, she finally insisted. "Alistair, I will not have you mount me like a rabid dog. Try to calm down. I would appreciate it if you thought to stroke me gently." Not enjoying being corrected in the realm of seduction, Alistair pouted, rebuked like a bad pet. Eventually, he stayed away from her bedroom altogether.

Despite their rough beginning, the couple knew the routines and habits of society and went about their lives in Boston. Alistair traveled or worked in the railroad office. Julia became involved in various clubs and charities, her favorites the Woman's Christian Temperance Movement and Protestants against Poverty—these were easy stands to take, unlike the confounding suffragists. In principle, Julia understood she should be able to vote, but their loud-voiced mannish protesting turned her stomach. Julia found comfort in the church and in the lives of the celibates, though she was not Catholic. She wondered whether she should have converted and chosen a future as a nun. Had she understood sex before she was married, perhaps she would have.

But of course, there were the children. Once Rupert and Sarah were born, the family settled into summers at the cottage. Julia grew to love the brutal landscape, those months on the coast—seagulls and waves, wind in the pines, and the occasional sounding of a boat's horn.

But the northern sun and a lifetime of insincere acquaintances had burned the lines of a permanent scowl into the corners of her mouth. Now that her children were grown, Julia devoted herself to her causes. But even the sense of righteousness derived from these measures could not compare to the relief gained from her powerful belief in a blissful afterlife.

+ + +

All three of the maids sat in the parlor with Mrs. Hunt on Wednesday evenings after supper, reading passages aloud from the Bible, a ritual they all took up after Julia's daughter Sarah married and left the house. Beverly sat straight as a board with her ankles crossed, as if she too were the woman of the house. Rebecca slumped over her bulky thighs, and Mabel shrank into herself, making her body as small and invisible as possible, wondering why Mrs. Hunt had not taken up a cause like women's right to vote. The lady of the house where Mabel spent her childhood had held meetings and fundraisers, getting even Mabel's mother involved. It seemed all of Newark society had been abuzz about the suffragist parade in Washington, D.C., this past March. Two of the ladies who frequented the Newark house had even been arrested.

But here at Serabelle, there had been no mention, as if the world had left Maine behind to talk only of automobiles and liquor and God.

Tonight, Beverly read from Jeremiah: "'For I know the plans I have for you,' declares the Lord, 'plans to prospah you and not to harm you, plans to give you hope and a futchah.'"

Mabel tried to pay attention, but her mind drifted from suffragists at the Newark estate to her family's house in Scotland. She remembered sweeping its dirt floor with a child-size straw broom behind her mother, the dirt kicking back into her face, the honey-like smell of heather wafting through open windows. They had always been cleaning, the two of them.

Hard as she thought, she could not conjure up an image of her father in that mud and brick house. With her mother, Mabel had strolled through fields surrounding their hovel out back to hang laundry that absorbed the sweet odor of the purple flower that soaked up the intense solitude of the wind. Those last fall days portended a desolate winter, months of huddling inside the house—Mabel knew that was the reason they had to leave. Muthill, the village where they had lived, held no promise at all.

Beverly's voice droned on: "'Then you will call on me and come and pray to me, and I will listen to you.'"

A slam made them all jump. In the doorway, Mr. Hunt bent to pick up a book he had dropped. "Excuse me," he said. "Continue." Mrs. Hunt turned fully around and glared at her husband. "Go on, Beverly."

Mabel avoided Mr. Hunt's eyes, though she felt them boring into her, making sweat form on her upper lip. She thought of her mother, excited the day she acquired the Newark estate job.

"'You will seek me and find me,'" Beverly said and then glanced up to see if Mr. Hunt was still in the room.

"Pay no mind to him," Mrs. Hunt ordered, petting her dog Chou Chou, who had climbed onto her lap. "Alistair, either sit down and listen to the lesson or take your book out of here. You are making Beverly nervous, loitering in the shadows."

"All right, I will listen." Mr. Hunt crossed to the sofa and sat between Rebecca and Mabel. The dog yapped.

"I do not understand you." Mrs. Hunt motioned for Beverly to keep reading.

Mabel scooted to the far end of the couch. She kept her head down and pressed her hands hard onto her twitching legs. Her mouth dried up; no trace of moisture remained. Her tongue felt as rough as pine bark.

Beverly began again. "'You will seek me and find me when you seek me with all your haht.'"

Mabel felt a tickle in her throat and tried to clear it.

Beverly continued: "'I will be found by you,' declares the Lord, 'and will bring you back from captivity. I will gathah you from all the nations and places where I have banished you,' declares the Lord, 'and will bring you back to the place from which I carried you into exile.'"

The tickle would not clear. Mabel swallowed. Her throat was parched. She rubbed her tongue in between her lip and her gums. She stretched her neck out like one of the harbor seals who swam close to shore, searching for signs of fish. Mabel opened her throat for air. She couldn't help herself; she coughed with a loud hacking, so forcefully she felt her supper might rise up from her stomach. They all looked to her.

She threw her hand over her mouth. "Excuse me," Mabel said.

"Yes, this is what the Lord Almighty says," Beverly read. "'I will send the sword, famine and plague against them and I will make them like figs that are so bad they cannot be eaten.'"

"Amen," Mr. Hunt shouted and clapped. "Bad figs! That is fabulous stuff, fabulous." He laid a hand on the girls' thighs on either side of him. Mabel coughed again and wiggled free of his grasp.

"Alistair, do not you have anything better to do?" Mrs. Hunt complained. "You are disturbing the girls."

"Better?" He laughed. "What could be better, my dear, than to spend the evening in such delightful company? What could make me more joyous than to hear words from the good book?"

Not one person in that room thought Mr. Hunt was being sincere.

Chapter 3
Lovely, Darling

The door to Mrs. Hunt's anteroom made a loud creak when it swung open, echoing across the empty suite. Darkness amplified Mabel's footsteps, her quick breath, every sound she made. She had told Beverly that she was fetching laundry she had left hanging on the back line. It was the height of summer, a Friday night, and the Hunts were out at the Kebo Valley Club, an exclusive membership club Mabel had seen from the outside—the tennis courts in the back, the long expanse of golf greens and croquet fields, the shingle-style arch of the gatehouse building.

Mabel had helped Rebecca by ironing Mrs. Hunt's slip earlier in the evening. She had pressed the billowing emerald ribbon to tie around the matron's waist and the crisp white gloves that came to Mrs. Hunt's elbows. She had watched as the Hunts climbed into the auto together, driven by Josiah down into Eden, where locals zipped around in their rough, newly acquired Model Ts while cottagers clung stubbornly to their horses and carriages.

Mabel shut the door behind her and walked through to the bedchamber. She sat at Mrs. Hunt's vanity, wiggling down into the cushion until the metal ribs poked at her skin. She lit a candle and opened Mrs. Hunt's ebony makeup case, running her hand over the shell inlay, taking a soft brush out of the bottom. And she imagined. What would it be like to live here, not solely to live, but to own all these delicate items? With a quick glance behind her, Mabel dipped the brush in a round canister that released the smell of violets, then shut her eyes, lifted the handle, and blasted her face with powder. She smeared her eyelids with a sparkly gold paste and chose a subdued pink lipstick. Gulls cried out over the ocean. She rubbed a dark rouge along her cheeks and smacked her lips together.

"Lovely, darling," she whispered.

Mabel rifled through Mrs. Hunt's jewelry box and lifted a strand of black pearls with a gasp. She had never seen anything so gorgeous. Mabel fastened the pearls around her neck with shaking hands and turned to study her reflection. With her gaze on the pearls, she believed could pass for Mr. Hunt's wife. Her neck was smooth and dignified in the dancing light. But when she raised her eyes and leaned closer to the mirror, the freckles on her nose glared through the makeup. Pink lipstick clashed with her red hair, and Mabel knew she still looked like a child. She dropped her chin and stared down at the slight paunch of her belly. A child who was going to have a baby.

She had not yet told Mr. Hunt she was pregnant. She had not told anyone. Mabel rubbed her hand across her swollen breasts. They would know soon. And then what? Mabel lifted a bottle of lotion, inhaling the deep scent of jasmine—strong enough to make her gag. She tried the next bottle—a gentler orange blossom that she rubbed up and down her arm; the burn had healed, leaving a small pink scar. Mr. Hunt certainly seemed to be enamored with her; he had whispered as much while they were making love. She knew for certain he hated his wife. Enough to divorce her, though?

Mabel held her breath when she heard footsteps in the distance. Clod, clod, clod, clod. They stopped in the hallway. In front of Mrs. Hunt's quarters. Mabel inhaled a quick sip of air, filling her lungs. A light rap on the outer door and a creak as the doorknob turned. Her eyes darted to the candle, and she blew hard, putting the fire out for a second before it burst back into flame. The burnt odor of carbon stung her nose as steps clunked into the room.

"God almighty!" Rebecca screamed, looking through to the bedchamber.

Mabel bumped her elbow against Mrs. Hunt's face powder, and the tin flew, lid off, sending puffs of dust through the candlelight.

"You," Mabel breathed. "Gosh, look what you made me do."

"What in the world?" Rebecca squealed. "Are those Mrs. ... Oh, Dear Lord, do not tell me you are wearing Mrs. Hunt's pearls. I saw a light. I thought she had come home. What're you thinking? What is all ovah your face? Oh no. Oh no. Get out this minute. Are you trying to get us all fired? I'm going to get Beverly."

Rebecca stomped out of the room. Mabel reached up to feel particles of powder that clung to the pearl necklace. She unclasped the necklace and wiped each bead blindly. In the quiet of anticipation—of waiting for her punishment—Mabel dropped to her knees and began cleaning the floor with her dress.

◆ ◆ ◆

The three maids gathered around the old pine table in the servants' kitchen. A soft glow emanated from a lantern in the center, throwing flickers of light across their solemn faces. Beverly's hands were folded into a prayer position, and she stared hard while Mabel studied the table carved with names of servants who had worked at the cottage—for most, the lone word they had known how to spell. Proof of existence.

"How dare you, Mabel?" Beverly demanded.

Mabel bit the nail of her forefinger, refusing to answer.

"Anyone else would fire you for this."

Mabel snapped her head up. "You cannot fire me. Mr. Hunt loves me."

Both Rebecca and Beverly inhaled sharply. "Has he touched you?" Beverly demanded.

"We are in love."

"Ha." Rebecca laughed.

"Be quiet." Beverly turned back to Mabel. "Do not tell me you let that man near you."

"He does not love his wife. She is awful to him."

A harsh beam moved across the kitchen floor as a servant outside passed the window, lantern in hand.

"Let me tell you a story—about a girl around your age Mr. Hunt took a liking to three years ago." Beverly pointed to the name "Shauna," carved in small awkward letters in the table. "Mrs. Hunt found out about their frolicking, and Shauna was fired. No one within a hundred miles would hire such a shameful girl when Mrs. Hunt was through with her. Shauna had to leave town. You know what she's doing now? She works in one of those houses in Portsmouth. Do you know what houses I am talking about?"

"It is not like that with us."

"What makes you different?"

"I am with child."

Beverly slammed her hands on the table. "Lord Jesus, no."

Rebecca screamed, and Beverly slapped her.

They all fell silent. Overhead, the men moved about in their rooms.

Rebecca rubbed her cheek. "Why did you slap *me*?"

"Quiet down, Rebecca."

Mabel spoke softly. "When I tell Mr. Hunt, I think he will want to marry me."

"O, child." Beverly shook her head and patted Mabel's hand. "Don't you know? That man would never marry you. You are a maid, Mabel. He is of a different set. *He has a wife.* Let me think." She sat contemplating while floorboards creaked above their heads.

Mabel stared at the ceiling.

"We are going to fix this," Beverly finally said. "You probably don't deserve it, but I'm going to take care here. You just don't know any better, I think. Now, don't breathe a word to anyone, and for pity's sake, do not go getting into Mrs. Hunt's things."

✦　✦　✦

Beverly's husband, Josiah, was a large, hulking man who had arrived with the livery team years ago, but being naturally mechanical, he had taken an interest in the special-order Winton Quad when Mr. Hunt smuggled it onto the island in 1908. Josiah had stayed on as the sole mechanic and driver on Serabelle. He not only knew the intricacies of the Winton and the newer Oldsmobile Limited Touring Car but had learned to repair the steam engine on Mr. Hunt's yacht, moored at the marina two miles south towards Eden. When Josiah was not working, he played cards with the other servants in the spare bedroom. Though the women were excluded from card games, Beverly trudged upstairs every few days to pick up the bottles and food scraps the men left lying about. A Victrola sat in the corner, and on any given night, the sound of hymns, low and hopeful, floated down the stairs. Beverly liked to play "Nearer, My God, to Thee" before she cleaned the mouse droppings scattered across the less-than-sanitary room. The men's slovenly habits mostly kept the mice out of the pantry, anyway.

"I'm gonna ask you a question, and you need to ansah me with not too many questions," Beverly said as she and Josiah settled into bed.

He raised his eyebrows.

"Who on the staff do you think would be willing to marry young Mabel?"

"Mabel? She in trouble?"

"Ayuh."

"Who with?"

"Can't say, but she might be in need of a husband."

"I see."

They both stared out into the dark night. The wind had not let up and rattled at the single panes in a staccato rhythm.

"I seen Gardener eyeing her," Josiah finally answered. "He owes me a bit a money."

"From those cards, I would dare say."

"This something worth losing a good sum over?" Josiah asked.

Beverly chewed at her bottom lip. "I think it is."

"Okeh, then. I'll ask."

Chapter 4
Let Us See What We Can Do

Willie readied Mr. Hunt's stallion to ride out to the Bay Trail that wound along the water on a worn dirt path. Once he had led the horse out past the main cottage, Fierce Competitor pranced, fidgeting in the Atlantic wind as if readying for a race. Willie carefully guided a dun-colored mare behind the stallion. She was pregnant, and he likely should not even ride the girl, but Clarissa had not been out of the stables most of the week. She had frisked about in her stall, practically begging for a ride out on the trails.

Mr. Hunt strutted past hollyhock beds and dahlias, down the long gravel path of the Italian-inspired garden. Taking the reins from Willie's hand, he mounted Fierce in one leap, catching his outside foot into the mount and swinging his right leg over the saddle in a surprisingly fluid motion.

Outside the garden gate, the Atlantic wind picked up force over the ocean and whipped Mr. Hunt's normally slicked-back hair into his eyes, rushing color to his cheeks. "This wind could make a man crazy," Mr. Hunt yelled, forcing his horse into a gallop, powering into the blast. The stallion dropped his head and dug in. Willie stayed close behind, despite Clarissa's delicate state. He refrained from spurring her on with his heels, but Clarissa was ready to go, almost keeping pace.

They went as far as the marina and then turned around, trotting in silence. Gulls circled overhead and dove for herring and clams. Far out into the bay, towards Rodick Island, a harbor seal squawked.

"Arousing, this weather," Mr. Hunt shouted over his shoulder.

"Exciting," Willie agreed.

"Let us stop here for a rest."

"Yes, sir."

Mr. Hunt dismounted on a curve a few paces before the cottage wall. Willie took the reins of both horses and climbed a short hill. He tied them to a nearby juniper, patting the horses' flanks while they cooled, whispering in their flattened ears.

"Willie," Mr. Hunt yelled. "Come down here. Grab a breath of this air."

"Yes, sir."

Mr. Hunt ran his hand over the boy's tight brown hair, fingers rubbing deep into the scalp, and Mr. Hunt stared out at his yacht anchored in the harbor. Willie had never been out to the yacht (nor would he ever be), but he wondered what it might be like, walking along the deck of such a large boat, feeling secure in its ability to traverse the waters below. Willie had only ever been in a rowboat, rickety and serene on a pond in Northern Maine.

Waves rocked the larger vessel below in looming swells, bringing the bow ten feet into the air before the stern kicked off the tail, tipping the balance. It would be rough out there today.

A beech tree behind them rustled with the scurrying of a squirrel. Not another person was on the bluff. Ants trotted across the dirt path at their feet, in twos and threes, carrying crumbs back to their nest. Fishing boats in the distance headed in to drop their morning catch at the wharf.

"Do you know how to fish, Willie?"

"Yes, sir."

"Fishing is a good, practical skill. You seem like a sensible boy—an outdoorsman, so to speak."

Willie recalled that trip to Northern Maine in the rowboat, his father taking a rare break from his job as a Pullman porter to bring Willie fishing when he turned ten. They had ridden the rail, just the two of them, with his father in uniform. They had been treated with what seemed like real respect in the station in Bangor. In Boston, his father kept his eyes down to the floor and said "yessir" to any white man who came close, but he held his gaze straight ahead while they were in Maine. He talked to locals face to face, who looked more fascinated than disgusted by the two of them. On that trip—the only one he and his father had ever taken alone—Willie had fallen in love with the whole state. He never forgot that feeling of being looked at, if not as an equal, at least not as less-than-human, and he swore he would live up in Maine someday.

In Boston, a few years later, he met Mr. Hunt while working at Ellis & Sons Mercantile. Despite the fact (when Willie was twelve and barely able to scratch out his own name) that he had been encouraged to sign a Lincoln-Lee pledge swearing he would abstain from drinking liquor, Willie fetched Mr. Hunt's whiskey week after week from the back room. He figured selling the stuff was not the same as imbibing, so he bagged up bottle after bottle despite the reproachful scorn of the other assistant, a burgeoning prohibitionist. Mr. Hunt took a liking to Willie. They had chatted and joked all through the winter months, and when Willie mentioned his love of horses, Mr. Hunt offered to bring him up to Maine the following summer. Much to Willie's surprise, Mr. Hunt made good on his promise and, with a proud grin, delivered a train ticket one Saturday.

"My son does not fish," Alistair said now. "He does not really know how to do anything useful. Rupert is not even much of a rider; he lacks agility. I blame myself for that—I do not know how to do much of anything either, other than play cards, collect stones, and ride horses."

"You are an excellent rider, sir."

"Is that so?"

"Yes, sir." Willie smiled. Mr. Hunt was a funny man, needing Willie, a groom, to tell him he was good at something.

Willie remembered the first time he had walked down the path from the stables, through the Asian garden, onto the sweeping back lawn. Looking around to see if anyone was watching, feeling slightly uncomfortable near such a grand cottage, as if he were doing something wrong by standing there, Willie unlatched the back gate and stepped onto the path over the bluff. He had never seen anything so stunning. It took his breath away. He stared out into the horizon, feeling as if he might be able to step right out onto the blue line, floating out over the high cliffs to become a part of the ocean.

"Maybe I have still got some mettle." Mr. Hunt clapped Willie on the back. "Well then, let us see what we can do."

Helping Mr. Hunt back onto his saddle this time, Willie cupped his hands and offered a low step. Mr. Hunt took off immediately down the path, urging his horse into a canter. By the time Willie was on his mount, Mr. Hunt had chucked his heels deep into his horse's flanks, prodding him into a full gallop. He leaned into Fierce's mane and shouted, "Hah! Hah!" into the wind.

Willie eyed the path now for the patch of rocks ahead. Mr. Hunt cleared them and took a sharp left onto the cottage property. The gate where they had come out was closed; Gardener probably shut it behind them out of habit. The clopping of the horse's shoes echoed off the stone wall. Gardener stood from where he was kneeling as Mr. Hunt urged the horse into the air, trying to clear the rock wall a mere ten feet from where Gardener stood, but the leap was too soon, too shallow.

Willie rounded the corner to the property and watched Gardener back up, out of the way. Fierce Competitor's head flew over the wall, and his front legs cleared. Mr. Hunt stood in the saddle as the horse whinnied. It appeared he would make the jump until the horse's back right leg caught the edge of the wall. Willie and Gardener watched it happen in slow motion. Momentum kept the horse's body going forward as his back legs crumbled, forcing the belly out over the top of the front legs. The horse tucked his head and rolled onto his side. Alistair fell to the left, smacking his shoulder and head on the ground before the horse landed with a rocking thud on top of his leg. Mr. Hunt's thigh bone snapped.

✦   ✦   ✦

Mabel was hanging linens on the clothesline when Rebecca ran from the house. "The Master is down. Lord have mercy, the Master's down. He has fallen." Tears welled in her eyes, and she clasped her hands under her chin in prayer.

"What in the world are you talking about?" Mabel shouted over the top of the line. She dug a clothespin from her apron and secured a pillowcase.

"Mr. Hunt. He was struck down on his horse not half an hour ago. The doctah's with him now."

"Struck—" The word had not passed her lips before she dropped her basket of linens and ran for the main house.

"You cannot see him now," Rebecca shouted at her back. "They won't let you see 'im."

Hushed sounds of scuffling shoes and low voices emanated from the guest room on the ground floor. The doctor kept Mr. Hunt on the first floor instead of authorizing the long haul to his quarters up the stairs. Julia Ainsworth-Hunt sat in the living room, holding her embroidery on her lap, staring at the ornate cross pattern without picking up the needle. She looked up briefly as Mabel ran past, then back down to her needlework. When she was done, the cross would be surrounded by yellow and red roses, a crown of thorns drooping over the top. This was the last in a series of fifteen pillows Julia was creating for the church bazaar. Her designs sold out every year. Sometimes Rebecca would lend a hand, but she could only entrust her maid to work the simple stitches; she did not have the finesse for fine needlepoint.

Julia sighed and looked towards the long hallway to the west. Mabel would be going to see how Alistair was faring, she suspected. She heard a rapid knocking on the guestroom door, then Beverly's sharp reproach. Julia pulled her lips into a tight smirk. She had left orders that no one was to be admitted except herself and the children—if they came. They probably would not come.

·   ·   ·

Beverly pulled Mabel's hand away from the door. "Stop it at once!" she hissed.

"I need to see him." Mabel tried to free her arm from Beverly's grasp. The noise of their struggle amplified in the tiled hallway. Willie watched with interest from his squat against the far wall.

Mabel managed to knock once more before the door opened. A large woman with a mule-like face stood in the doorway, a nurse's cap pinned crookedly to her gray hair. "What's all this racket?"

Mabel tried to peer around the woman's bulk, but the room was dark. "I must see Mr. Hunt. Is he all right?"

"No one comes in."

"Tell him it is Mabel."

The woman shook her large head. "I have my orders."

Beverly put her arm around Mabel's shoulder and tried to pull her back, but she wouldn't budge. "Child, don't make a fool of yourself."

"Please," Mabel begged the nurse. "Tell him. He'll want to see me."

The nurse stood with a stony face, a hint of pity behind her eyes. "Hold on. I'll ask." She closed the door.

"I told you to behave yourself, Mabel. You know the consequences," Beverly said.

Willie cleared his throat, and they both looked over when the nurse reappeared. "I'm sorry, honey. He doesn't want to see you. Now go on."

Chapter 5
Serve Him Right

The sound of rustling trees dominated the afternoon. Mabel and Rebecca trod across the mud-caked road; a few leaves had fallen in the high winds and lay smashed and hardened over, frail veins popping out of yellowed skin. It was not yet August, and already the leaves were pale. An occasional auto or buggy rode by, and the maids waited along the side of the road, hair covered by bonnets. One of the ties on Mabel's bonnet was stained with apple juice. Unlike Rebecca, Mabel cared little for her things, for her cheap clothing; she knew she ought to, as she was unlikely to acquire more. If things changed for her, though, she would certainly learn to take care of fine clothes. When Mr. Hunt had paid attention to Mabel, when he had focused on her—complimenting her skin, her shape, her eyes—she had believed she was worth something.

Past the rock wall that rimmed the edge of the property, down the steep slope of land, the Atlantic Ocean lapped and sang and beat at the shore. Out past the granite and sand, lobstermen pulled up traps, and fishermen headed into the docks to sell their morning catch. On the horizon, a tanker disappeared into the distance. Even inland, down the road and along the tree-lined street, the smell of ocean permeated, rendering the air thick with salt, coating throats and nostrils.

It had been a strange summer, a whirlwind of activity and excitement, a blessing Mabel felt she somehow deserved, was destined to live out. Mr.

Hunt's attention waned and waxed, but Mabel clung to the good moments as to a lifeboat, waiting for the day she would be rescued, sure the hour would come. Separately, she and Mr. Hunt were less than remarkable: he, short and squat, hairy and ruddy-cheeked, she, mere bones and freckles. But together, they were beautiful, complementary. Together, they made sense.

If she could talk to him privately, she knew she could persuade him to divorce his wife, but Beverly had kept them apart. Mabel had not even had a chance to tell him she was pregnant. Beverly and her ideas about what was proper. Beverly was wrong, wrong, wrong. Mabel unclenched her fists and continued walking into town next to Rebecca, sent to pick up the embroidery thread for Mrs. Hunt and some salt for the cook.

"And then, do you know what that blue jay did? I looked through the kitchen window and…" Rebecca turned to Mabel. "Ah you listening to me?"

Mabel continued to look off at the horizon. "Yes."

"What ah you looking at?"

"Hmmm?"

"I guess you have other things on your mind. Now with the…" Rebecca lowered her voice, "baby and all. Is it true you're going to marry Gardener? I heard Beverly and Josiah talking. It's really the best solution. But he's awfully surly, as far as I can tell, the way he shovels food in his mouth. He doesn't even go to church…"

"Stop, Rebecca."

"But are you scared of him?"

"No, I'm not scared."

"He's awfully, um—big. And he drinks so much alcohol. You know it is illegal up here? He could get in a lot of trouble."

"I don't know anything about liquor laws, and I don't care a lick about Gardener, Rebecca. Do you not know? It's Mr. Hunt who matters."

"But Beverly said that other girl…"

"That was a long time ago." Mabel waved her hand at Rebecca. "This is about things you do not understand."

"I guess not."

The girls walked on towards town, keeping their thoughts to themselves. Mabel remembered her afternoons in the east wing with Mr. Hunt, his teasing bites on her neck. A chill ran through her insides, and her stomach muscles contracted. Beverly was mistaken, she thought. All those intimate moments, all that skin, must have meant something.

"I turn to God when I don't understand what's happening," Rebecca blurted.

Mabel didn't answer. She tried to hold on to her pleasant thoughts, but Rebecca insisted on breaking through.

"When I pray, it's as if a cool breeze washes over me. Suddenly, there's no longer a need to understand what's happening. I accept things. He always makes me feel at peace."

At the edge of town, on West Main Street, people milled about, carrying parcels wrapped in brown paper and tying up teams of horses. Women in neat white dresses with purple sashes approached the maids, handing them a flyer. "Hello, girls. Can you read?" one of them asked gently.

Mabel nodded, mouthing the slogan on one of the women's sash: "Votes for Women."

"Exactly," the kind woman said. "We think it's important that, as half the population, we be allowed to express our opinion."

"Oh, Lord," Rebecca said, refusing the pamphlet. "You're one ah those suffragettes the Mrs. is always warning about. Oh no, go away." Rebecca waved her hand at the woman like a magician trying to make a rabbit disappear.

The woman seemed prepared for this type of reaction and gave a patient smile. She was not at all the type of brusque woman portrayed in advertisements and radio programs. Mabel recognized the woman behind her—the woman who had ridden in the buggy with her from Bangor.

"Well, hello again," the woman said, approaching Mabel. "I hope you've settled in well. We're having a meeting next Thursday for household staff if you'd like to attend. I think you'll find it illuminating."

Mabel nodded and tucked the pamphlet in her basket at the bottom, under the lining.

Across the road at the American Express Company, goods were loaded up, sent off, and delivered to cities far and near, to buggies or trains, to steamers that would travel across to other continents. South of town center, in front of Sherman's Printer & Stationer, a group of negroes gathered, laughing and checking each other's baskets of goods. Miss Sherman came out and shooed them from the front of the store, and they shuffled over, down the block near the milliner's shop.

Mabel spied Willie among the negroes and waved. He nodded tentatively at her, barely perceptible, though his eyes remained riveted. During their busy workdays, the two barely saw each other—Willie always out among the horses, riding with Mr. Hunt, sitting with other negroes from town during the church service. The two of them sometimes managed to speak briefly during meals, Willie telling Mabel about his family, his grandparents traveling north from Virginia to Boston, then eventually to Lowell, Massachusetts.

"My daddy works for the railroad," Willie had said. "He wanted to get me a job too, but I always liked real horses better than iron ones. Our neighbors had one I used to take care of."

"I find railroads fascinating," Mabel had disagreed. "All that power, so much distance."

Willie shook his head. "Too loud."

"Too steely cold?" Mabel guessed.

Willie smiled as Mabel was shooed back to the stove by Beverly, as if he had been happy to be so understood.

Mabel turned to Rebecca now, motioning at her to stay. "What're you doing?" Rebecca asked. "You can't go over there."

Tuning out Rebecca's protests, Mabel walked toward the group of negroes; Willie's gaze had shifted to the ground. Talk fell silent when Mabel broke into the circle. "Hi Willie," she said. No feigned question.

The men who had previously been laughing and joking with Willie bit their lips and elbowed the boy, mute and impatient.

"Hi, Mabel," Willie said.

Everyone stood for a moment, gazes landing on the dirt or buildings surrounding them, on passing carts. Mabel stood waiting, not really having anything to say, drawn by some urge to escape Rebecca's prattling.

"Is there something you wanted?" Willie finally asked.

"Not really," Mabel admitted. "Just curious what you all were laughing about."

There was an awkward silence, filled by the sound of a cart full of feed rumbling by, the horse's hooves clomping loudly on cobblestone, the load heavy with grain, heading away from the station towards one of the livery stables along Cottage Street.

"Ma'am, we was talking about your Mr. Hunt," one of the negro women finally said. "We was teasing Willie here, saying he coulda stop his fall, had he wanted to."

Mabel started at her calling him "your Mr. Hunt." Did everyone know? She scanned their faces, dark with pink accents, the whites of their eyes bright against black. "Willie couldn't have done anything to stop it. Could you, Willie?"

"I don't think so," he said without conviction.

"But you were with him?" Mabel asked.

Willie slowly shook his head. "I was behind him."

"Why did he fall?" Mabel asked.

"Well," Willie began, then looked at the others in the group as if trying to discern who might gossip, who might understand. "He tried a tricky jump. Fierce Competitor wasn't quite ready for it."

Mabel nodded, accepting this explanation, which was more than anyone else had given her. "Did you see him take the fall?"

A couple of the fellows in the group wandered off, pulled by their own errands or bored by the conversation. On the other side of the street, Rebecca stood, raising her eyebrows at Mabel, giving fitful little waves, trying to get her attention.

"He was on the other side of the gate by the time I pulled short. I saw the start of the tumble, saw Fierce's leg get nicked." Willie hesitated. "Then I heard the snap."

"Snap?"

"Of his leg when Fierce landed. It was something awful. Never heard anything like it."

Mabel took in her breath at the thought of that sound—did it crack like a tree branch? Or like a wishbone from a bird? Was the sound muffled from all that horse flesh on top of it, encased in muscle and skin? Or did the sound echo out over the landscape, ungodly and prescient? Mabel might have asked some of those questions had it not been for Rebecca, who stepped purposefully toward Mabel, causing an empty buckboard to swerve to the left, a narrow miss. The driver raised his hand at Rebecca as his horses stomped, correcting themselves. The man cursed at Rebecca's thoughtless dart into the road, one that might have thrown a passenger or two, had there been any.

Last week on Hancock Street, a young boy had been trampled under the wheels of another man's buckboard. A screaming set of rusticators who had been heading up to Jordan Pond House for popovers and tea witnessed the whole sordid event. They climbed out and stared, pointing but not moving toward the boy—perhaps for fear of getting bloodied. Or from a lack of understanding of how to help? Because they panicked?—until the driver hollered at the group of them to fetch the doctor. Of course, the boy didn't survive—the rear axle had caught on his belt, dragging his head under the wheel.

Drivers were on hyper-alert around the whole town of Eden. The boy had been the only son of T.L. Roberts, who rode the sprinkler tanker up and down the dusty roads in the dry summer months. Locals had whispered to each other that a boy whose father ran a team of horses every day should have known to watch out, but, well, life was ironic like that sometimes.

"Mabel!" Rebecca cried as if somehow Mabel was at fault for her near accident. She stood a league away, down near Sherman's. "Mrs. Hunt expects us back."

Mabel gave a little formal nod to each of the negroes in the group before rolling her eyes and grimacing comically, the same expression the cook on the Newark estate used to give after the madam of the house came in to give some instruction.

"I am being summoned," Mabel said in her best acting-for-the-stage voice. The group broke up in laughter at her antics, exactly the reaction she was going for. "See you at supper, Willie."

"Goodbye, Mabel," Willie said softly, with no little amount of affection.

✦   ✦   ✦

Mabel sat on the bed in the spare room—hers and Mr. Hunt's room—in the east wing. It had been a month, and still Mr. Hunt refused to see her. She had been to the door night after night, requesting visitation, believing it was the nurse that kept them apart. But this last time, she heard Mr. Hunt's voice. A stale odor, like Gardener's compost piles, wafted from the depths of the room. "No," he said. "Go away."

Beverly was right; she had been used and disgraced. What could she even offer a bastard child? What did she know of children? Mabel edged up to the window and threw open the curtains, letting in a beam of sun that splashed across her white skirt. White like the suffragists, she thought, but representing bondage, not liberties. She cranked open the pane and leaned into the vast, empty space. The sky was cloudless but not blue—a color she couldn't name, a gray just short of white. Mabel gathered her skirt and lifted her foot up onto the window ledge. The charged air assaulted her skin, mocking her, making her aware of how small, how inconsequential she was. A life full of servitude. That's what she was facing. A child of hers would be damned to the same life. Mabel hoisted herself out onto the narrow stone ledge. This house corner was nearest the beach, jutting out towards the endless ocean. Below her, a low stone wall and then relentless waves battered the rocks. Elements receded with the undertow, the shore eroding at an imperceptible pace.

Mabel had a sudden urge to jump, to make all her problems, her lack of esteem, her predicament—her pregnancy—disappear. No need to find a solution. No need to bring any of this to a conclusion. She looked down at the grass and the shoreline beyond. A jump from here would have to be aimed away from the house to make it past the wall and the lawn, down onto the ragged, threatening rocks below. She would have to use every piece of strength she could muster to not be slammed against the house by the wind, not to land on the narrow strip of grass three stories below.

Mabel crouched down and unlaced her right boot. She carefully unfolded and tugged it off her foot, sobbing with the effort. Still holding onto the window frame, she threw the boot out towards the horizon. The little black shoe tumbled once, twice, turning in the air with laces ajumble, whipping freely about, until it took a sharp dive at the edge of the lawn, hitting a mulberry bush and bouncing in ever smaller arcs until it came to a halt at the edge of the cliff.

"No," she cried.

A spray of mist off the water splashed fifty feet below the lawn, white and teasing. One perfect leap, and it would be all over. No more humiliation, no more pain, no more praying to an unknown God. Mabel shivered as she pictured Mr. Hunt finding her broken body on the rocks below. That would serve him right. She let go of the window and swayed in the opening, sobbing. Her leg would be bent at a sharp angle, her head sagging off to the side with blood trickling out from behind, where it smashed on a pointed granite boulder. Mr. Hunt would cry, "Why?" But he would know. Her serene face, beautiful in death, would haunt him for the rest of his life.

Mabel doubled over and pulled off her other shoe. She felt brave now. She drew her arm back and chucked the boot with a great upward arc, testing the angle. The wind picked up with a sudden burst and spat the boot back at the house. The dark leather shoe made a dull thud as it hit the foundation below.

She couldn't even get a shoe over the cliff. She couldn't even do that right. Mabel wailed into the misty afternoon, into the bottomless ocean beyond.

"If you are done with this, might I use it?"

With a yelp, Mabel grabbed the jamb and looked down. The gardener stood on the narrow grass strip in front of the wall. He held her boot. Mabel didn't answer. She had never spoken more than a couple of words to the man everyone simply called Gardener. He was tall with brilliant red hair and the cocky stance of an Irishman. He was in his thirties and a drinker—that much, she knew.

"I think my bride-to-be is in need of a pair," he yelled.

Mabel slunk back into the room and slammed the window shut.

Chapter 6
Is That a No?

Gardener knelt in the front yard outside the main house, though there was barely a weed to be seen. He waited for Mabel to come fetch her shoes. Surprisingly, he found himself nervous about being with the girl. Though he didn't frequent the cat houses, he was no stranger to them. In fact, he had just once been with a woman who wasn't a professional—an actress who had come through town and was trying to prove something to her boyfriend, one of the other actors. Gardener guessed now that she had chosen him because of his size—because he might be willing to fight if the boyfriend came knocking, which he did.

From his crouch, Gardener watched balls of clouds roll across the sky. The air was cool on his neck. It was certain to be a long, cold winter. He hoped he wasn't making a mistake with Mabel, but it would be good to have a wife here over the off-season while the Hunts were away. She had spirit; he liked a girl with a bit of fire. And there was no doubt Mabel was not a prude, given her circumstances. Though he didn't know for sure, Gardener imagined it was Mr. Hunt that Mabel had gotten into trouble with. He remembered the other one they had sent away for the same thing. She had been foolish. Shauna—that was her name—had believed that Mr. Hunt would make an honest woman of her. What malarkey. Gardener wondered how she had ever gotten the idea into her head. Shauna was a curvy gal, pretty to look at, and with a mouth as filthy as the men who ran the betting tracks. She probably did fine in her new job.

Gardener had tried to engage Shauna himself, but she kept teasing him, kept flirting here and there until one day she was gone. This time, Gardener mused, he would be privy to what Mr. Hunt had known. Clearly, the man had an interest in Mabel—who wouldn't? She was full of life and fire and had a little wispy body, though she must've been nearly eighteen.

Gardener pulled at the grass and waited. He picked up his shears and walked to the shrubs, clipping and trimming minuscule branches, pretending to prune, though the yard was nearly immaculate. He pruned every few months, and it wasn't time, but Gardener could think of no other reason to hang around in the front yard. Even though he spent so much time with this land, at this cottage—years—he still didn't have the right to admire his own work. He would be reproved by someone, if only the other servants, for standing idly.

The sun had dropped below the line of trees across the road before Mabel stepped out into the yard. When she saw Gardener, she jumped, letting go of her skirt ends she had gathered to cross the gravel.

"You," she said accusingly.

"We gotta speak a word," Gardener replied gruffly, still holding his pruning shears. Mabel's eyes fell on the sharp tool until he walked over and placed it in a bucket by the drive. "Follow me," he barked as he walked around the edge of the cottage, bucket in hand.

She followed him back to his tool shed, commenting on the garden as she walked. "You really do know how to tend the flowers; that's something."

"After you," Gardener said, holding the door to his gardening shed open.

"Could we not speak outside?" Mabel asked.

Gardener smiled at her protest. Yah, she would be a challenge. "I'd like us to have some privacy."

"I'm sure you would," Mabel said and stepped cautiously into the shack, her stockinged feet dirty from treading across the yard.

Gardener became suddenly aware, self-conscious for the first time, that the room smelled slightly of manure and whiskey.

"Could you please open a window?" Mabel asked. "I need some air."

"Have a seat." Gardener gestured toward a bench.

Gardener felt intensely how large he must look inside the tiny shed, how massive and powerful, as if he might burst out of the four walls at any moment, like ruptured stitching. He did as she requested, opening a tiny window on the far side of the shack; then, in one smooth motion, before he lost his nerve, he dropped to one knee and took Mabel's hand. She looked puzzled, truly taken aback by his actions, as if she had expected him to maul her—or at least try to paw at her somehow.

"Mabel... Mabel..." Gardener stumbled, searching for her surname. He continued without it in a soft voice, as he imagined a gentleman would speak. "Mabel, would you be my wife?"

"I do not even know you," Mabel whispered.

He stared at her, confused, waiting for more. Surely, she would not refuse him.

"We have never even had a conversation before," she continued, hedging. "Do you think we should...?" But the moment was lost.

Gardener stood. "Foolishness," he said, losing his nerve. "You're knocked up, yah? You need a husband to make you legit? I'm offering. Take it or leave it."

Mabel looked as if she was fighting off a wave of nausea, as if even the idea of him made her ill. "Why would you do this?"

"Propose?"

"Yes," she said.

"I owe someone a favor."

"Not because you love me."

"Like you said," Gardener reminded her, "we don't even know each other."

"Do you consider me damaged—this way?"

"Only if you don't offer me the same 'delights' you gave the master."

Mabel hung her head. "How did you know?"

"Obvious."

"How?"

"I hate to be the one to break this to you, honey, but Mr. Hunt is a randy bastard who's done this before. I guess he figures it's his right as the cottage owner. You're nothing more than a piece of property to him."

"And what about you? Would I be more to you?"

"That depends." Gardener smirked.

"On what?"

"On your attitude." Gardener could wait no longer. He reached across Mabel's lap and grabbed behind a worn piece of canvas for his flask.

"My attitude." This was more of a statement than a question from Mabel.

"Yah," he said after a good swallow. "You're with me or not. Up to you. We can be friends, or we can be enemies. You ain't gonna win, though, if you decide to battle. I'm sure Beverly made the choices clear. You're looking at your sole option at this point." Gardener turned around in a circle, raising his arms so that his hands touched the rafters. "Hope you like what you see."

Mabel's face contorted, and suddenly, she leaped up and flung open the door, making it outside barely in time to vomit at the base of an Alba bush.

Gardener leaned out after her and chuckled. "Good, natural fertilizer."

Mabel looked up, a thin stream of spit hanging from her lip.

"Is that a 'no'?" Gardener asked.

Mabel wiped at her mouth with the back of her hand. "Do I have a choice?"

Chapter 7
Breach Birth

Summer came rapidly to an end. Though the Ainsworth-Hunts traditionally headed to Boston after Labor Day, this year the family would extend their stay by three weeks because of Mr. Hunt's injury. Eden and Bar Harbor's society counted on the Ainsworth-Hunts to close the season in style with a Labor Day weekend gala. Guests came from as far away as Philadelphia, with the most prominent of Boston's and Worcester's cultured making the trip up by automobile for the first time. Even those who had fought for the prohibition of autos on Mt. Desert Isle were secretly intrigued by the idea that they might drive their cars all the way. Even the traditionalists were tiring of the long railroad trip followed by a steamer ride to Bar Harbor.

Mrs. Hunt sent out notices and planned the menu and décor while her husband healed. Servants prepared for the coming event, cleaning every corner of the main floor and polishing each piece of silver, each metal banister. Stable boys bleached planks in the barn. On a Wednesday evening in mid-August, Beverly sent Mabel out to call the men to supper, as the meal had been sitting on the stove for a half hour, and she had seen neither hide nor hair of her husband or any of the stable boys. They always came for food. As Mabel approached the stables, she heard murmurs over an agonizing cry. Mabel rushed to the wide door of the stable. Lanterns hung from corner posts, and the men circled around a mare lying on the hay-covered ground inside a stall. Mabel recognized the local vet kneeling behind the mare. His hands were up inside the horse, through her hind quarters.

The mare, Clarissa, let out a mournful whinny and thrashed back and forth across the stall. The vet's face was mashed up against her rear end, and his arms moved inside the cavity, up to his elbows. Josiah helped George and Theo, two stable boys, try to restrain the horse. Willie crouched at her head and whispered, stroking her face. There were tears in his eyes.

"It is not good. Breach birth," the vet said and craned his face away from Clarissa. He pulled his arms out of her body and wiped his bloody arms across his apron.

The stable master, a crusty man who had been at the cottage for over a decade, crossed into the light. "Think we can save 'em?" he asked.

"Possibly."

"What do you need?"

"I'm going to have to open her up. I can't get a grip enough to turn the foal inside. It's taking a chance, but if I don't try, they'll both die."

"I'm here, Clarissa," Willie whispered.

Josiah turned to Mabel. "What're you doing here?"

"Beverly sent me to get you all for supper."

"Tell her we'll be up."

Mabel turned reluctantly, fascinated and horrified by the traumatic labor of the horse. She stared at the mare's face, unblinking eyes, bared gums, and strained muscles. Mabel didn't know if she could do it. What if, in her labor, she had trouble like this? Who would stand at her head and whisper sweetly in her ear?

"Go on," Josiah said and nudged her out the door.

Finally, an hour and a half later, the men walked into the servants' kitchen, covered with hay and dirt and sweat that dampened their foreheads. Several men had blood spattered on their clothing, and Beverly ordered them to clean off before they sat at her table. They begrudgingly walked to the laundry and to their bedrooms, returning in clean clothes, scrubbing their hands and faces in the kitchen sink.

"That's better," Beverly said as she served them. When they had settled down, she asked, "How'd it go?"

Mabel listened from the top of the stairwell.

"The foal will make it. The Doc opened up the mare's stomach, reached right in, and took him out."

"And the mare?"

"Prob'ly not," Josiah said.

"Too bad. She was a beaut, ayuh," Beverly said, handing them each a slice of bread. "Where's Willie?"

"Wouldn't leave her," the stable master said. "That boy has taken quite a liking to the mare."

The soup was thick and the bread hard, but the men made quick work of it. The air inside the house was filled with stable smell—hay and manure mingling with the sharp tang of overcooked mutton and tomato. Silverware clinked against glass plates; mugs slammed against the table. Mabel waited until the men had finished their supper before she slipped out the back door and into the stable.

Willie lay next to the mare, his dark arms wrapped around Clarissa's neck, fingers entwined in her mane. Blood soaked the hay strewn across the floor, and Mabel could see the hastily stitched seam on her abdomen where the vet had opened her up. Willie's cap was tossed into a corner, his hair bushy and his eyes red. He sat up as Mabel approached, though Clarissa lay still, her eyes open but glassed over, as if she had already moved on.

"She lost a lot of blood," Willie said. His voice was husky and sad.

"They say she might not make it," Mabel whispered.

"No."

"She looks bad."

"I know." Willie continued petting her mane. "I wish there was something I could do."

"Seems to me there never is anything we can do for anyone else."

"What do you mean?"

"I mean, we're all on our own." Mabel took in the barn's smell, the heavy scent of afterbirth. "Maybe you have someone to look after you for a while. Maybe you can be friends… or more, or family. Well, I guess people get married, but still, it's no guarantee. Life doesn't keep any promises. Everyone's on their own in the end."

"That's a pretty sad view of things," Willie noted. He was quiet, watching the mare's ragged breath.

Mabel walked to the corner and sat on a pile of hay bales. "Looking at her trying to give birth but not being able to… I saw her eyes tonight. She was so frightened, and if something that big and powerful can be frightened, what chance do I have?"

"You've got Gardener."

"Really, Willie, do you think so?"

"I don't know."

"Gardener has his own concerns, and my well-being isn't one of them. He doesn't care if I have this baby, if I die in childbirth."

"That can't be true."

"I'm afraid it is."

Willie reached across and laid his hand over the nose of the foal, trying to nuzzle Clarissa's teat. "Clarissa is going to die."

"I know. I'm sorry, Willie. I know you love her."

Clarissa let out a soft whinny.

Mabel cleared her own throat in answer. "Does everyone know why I'm in trouble?"

Willie cast his eyes down. "Yes."

"Willie, what do you think a life is worth?"

"Whose?"

"That's exactly what I was thinking. Some lives are valuable; some are not." Mabel thought of the pamphlet she had been handed in town the other day. She had taken it out of the basket and tucked it inside her bodice, only to unfold it later that night in bed, by candlelight.

Twelve reasons why women should vote, it said. Mabel read down the list, clinging especially to the words, '*Because 8,000,000 women in the United States are wage workers, and the conditions under which they work are controlled by law.*'

"Clarissa," Mabel said to Willie. "No one here except you really cares that she's dying. She's not valuable. If she had been a stallion… if there was something wrong with Mr. Hunt's stallion, do you think they would've left him to die?"

"Not likely," Wille admitted.

"That's what I thought. In this world, females don't count for much. We aren't even allowed to vote." Mabel sniffed and tried to hold back her tears. "I can't figure out why Beverly thought my life was worth saving. Other than my mother—who might never even see me again—who would really care if I was dead?"

"I would."

Mabel looked at Willie's face, sad and soft, his look distant. "You're being kind. I don't think you'd miss me."

"I'm telling you the truth." Willie stood and walked over to Mabel. He took both her hands tentatively in his, as if asking permission. He had never touched her before. Ripe with the scent of blood and dung, his face was suddenly flushed with life, his eyes sparkling. "I would hate it if you died. You are one of the nicest people I ever met."

Tears rolled freely down Mabel's cheeks, and she found she couldn't speak. What would someone who came upon them think? A young, pregnant maid holding hands with a negro stable boy? They stood still, freezing the moment in time, looking into each other's eyes, until Clarissa made a soft hiccup. As if he had read Mabel's thoughts, Willie dropped her hands and lay back down next to the horses. The baby made a bleating sound, nudging its mother. Clarissa did not move.

Chapter 8
The Spectacle

Close to the date of the gala, Alistair began walking with crutches. He practiced at night, through the long corridors of the cottage, so as not to be seen stumbling. By day, the grand ballroom was opened and aired, scrubbed, and polished clean. Parquet floors gleamed with a waxy shine. The butler helped hang fabric from the ballroom ceiling, creating a soft, billowy effect throughout the immense space. Mirrors sparkled, free of all streaks and splatters. On the morning of the event, Gardener grudgingly cut flowers by the bushel and arranged them in massive displays. The cook had spent a week preparing food for the lavish banquet that would precede the dancing. Mabel set the good silver on the sideboard.

The evening of the gala blew in strong and bold, a preview of the stormy season to come. No calm fall days would follow this year, no Indian summer. The autumn of 1913 would bring an early frost, strangling and killing crops, marking a quick end to the fishing season. Guests arrived at Serabelle wrapped in shawls and mufflers pulled from winter stashes. The hall closet overflowed with fur coats and knitted scarves. Those who had traveled from Massachusetts arrived with valises and trunks.

Willie, George, and Theo, the stable boys, greeted the guests who arrived by automobile, while Josiah, the sole staff member who drove, hustled back and forth, parking cars in the field south of the cottage. With the ban against autos newly lifted, it seemed half of the cottagers—most of those who had opposed lifting the ban—were eager to show off their shiny, loud acquisitions.

The stable master himself dealt with those who arrived by horse and buggy. When the line of buggies and cars backed up, Willie allowed guests to leave their teams and cars in the drive, in triple rows and randomly strewn, some with wheels upon the lawn. One rowdy partygoer drove his Studebaker into a garden of fading lilies. Those drivers who arrived with their masters' autos were asked to park the cars themselves, but eventually, even they couldn't get around the blocked drive. Chauffeurs walked off to wait in the kitchen of the servants' quarters, or in the barn.

"What's going on out here?" Alistair yelled from the stoop.

"I can't control them, sir!" Willie answered, frantically bowing and nodding at the guests as they passed.

"Where's Josiah?"

"Out in the field, sir. He can't keep up."

"Do not be daft. You take the cars, then."

Willie looked at him, panic in his eyes. "I don't drive, sir."

Alistair hobbled down a step. "For God's sake, Willie, learn. I cannot have my grounds destroyed, and Julia will have your head if the guests have to wait. Get on it."

"Yes, sir."

Willie wound the starter of a Ford Model N, knocking his thumb when the crank reared back, but his reflexes were good, and he quickly hopped into the driver's seat. He had been in the Winton with Josiah before, when they drove the women to market. Willie knew where the gas pedal was. He remembered, from watching, which one was the brake.

The car jumped forward when he pressed his foot down. Willie cranked the wheel left and let off the gas, letting it sputter to a stop off the gravel drive. He hopped out to the laughter of Theo and George, who had stopped to watch. This time, Willie cranked the engine up again and eased his foot down on the pedal, holding the steering wheel steady between his hands. George and Theo cheered as the car puttered off at a snail's pace towards the lot, past a frantic Josiah, waving his hands at Willie.

Josiah met Willie on his way back to the driveway, ready to read him the riot act until Willie explained. Josiah brought him to the next car in line, a Holsman Runabout. He set him in the cab, giving him instructions and orders on how to safely deliver the vehicles to the parking area, briefly explaining the differences between the electric and gasoline engines. "It's not a game, Willie," he sternly reminded the boy.

By the fifth car, Willie felt like he had the hang of driving. The shaking, jerky sensation felt the opposite of a horse's soft, warm ride, but it was not nearly as disagreeable as he had anticipated. He started accelerating and driving with one hand, taking the corners hard. Driving, he thought, might be better than riding the horses at full gallop. He made a vow to follow in Josiah's footsteps, to learn more about the maintenance of automobiles.

Night began to fall when Willie realized he didn't know how to turn on the headlights. He parked one last car before flagging Josiah down. They passed each other quickly, able now to keep up with the flow of guests. Willie rounded the corner of the property at a speed that he knew was too fast, too uncontrollable in a shiny Cadillac Tulip Roadster, glossy red with black tufted leather seats. Willie clung to the wheel, pulling it tight to the left, so as not to lose control. He saw the outline of the stone wall closest to the house and the glow of the cleared road. Willie spied a movement in front of him, but he couldn't make out what it was. A rabbit, maybe? A cat? He slammed on the brake, causing the car to swerve and the wheels to squeal out a god-awful sound. Willie released the pressure on the brake and heard a thump as the car came to a halt. Panting and sweating, he hopped out to see what he had hit.

Lying in the middle of the drive, its hips smashed into the gravel, was Mrs. Hunt's dog, Chou Chou. The dog didn't make a sound. Its tan fur was smeared dark with blood, and its tiny front paws stretched out in front of the body, as if he were still trying to run. Willie whimpered and turned away from the tiny mound of fur. He would probably be fired.

He stood in the road and waited for Josiah to tell him what to do.

+   +   +

Inside the cottage, the party was in full swing. Local musicians strolled the dining room while members of the Boston Symphony Orchestra, who had been hired for the weekend, warmed up in the ballroom. Plate after plate of local oysters were served on ice. Dishes of warm lobster tail soaked in butter were placed before the guests who sat along the massive banquet table. The courses began with soup of ground chestnuts (hard to locate so early in the season), followed by quail stuffed with dates and rice. Guests found their glasses continually filled with Spanish wine or French champagne. Dessert was a dollop of raspberry sherbet with a drizzle of dark chocolate syrup. Many drunken revelers dribbled and dripped on their fine clothing, but they laughed off their spills, making their way to the powder rooms to wipe the mess.

Mabel joined the staff delivering food to the dining hall. The smell of briny oysters made her stomach turn, so she asked if she might pour champagne instead. She made her way through the crowds in her special gala uniform, and though the material was black, it was becoming impossible to hide her condition. Mabel had begrudgingly agreed to marry Gardener but had been unwilling to set a date. Beverly urged her every day, eventually threatening that if she did not choose, Beverly would do it for her.

Mabel had not seen Mr. Hunt since the accident. He had kept himself shut up in his study or in his recovery room on the first floor. Mabel occasionally walked by the room in the daytime, hoping to catch a glimpse of his stout form. Perhaps if he saw her, his heart would melt, as it had that day in the living room with the Puccini. Mabel had planned what she would say to him: "Do you not remember, Mr. Hunt, the room in the east wing? The way the velvet chair held our clothing, how you cradled your hand behind my neck, how you ran your fingers over my freckles?" Mabel blushed thinking about those days. They seemed so far away now, so distant that, had she not been pregnant, she would have wondered if she had concocted the affair completely.

Mabel scanned the crowd for a sign of Mr. Hunt but could not find him. Guests called and gestured for her to refill their glasses. Her worn black boots crunched over broken wine glasses throughout the hall, and the careless guests asked for new ones. Mabel delivered the alcohol with a smile and bent to pick up broken shards. She placed her tray on the sideboard and carefully cupped her hand to hold the pieces of glass.

"What are you doing down there? Serve the guests," Julia spoke to Mabel's back.

Mabel straightened from her crouch. Mrs. Hunt crossed her arms and scrunched her face into a bitter scowl. Rebecca stood behind Mrs. Hunt, awaiting orders, her expression nearly echoing her Mistress's. Rebecca would stay with Mrs. Hunt throughout the night, shadowing her, trying to anticipate her every need.

"Ma'am, there's broken glass," Mabel said.

"For pity's sake, do not be so clumsy."

"I didn't…"

"Can you not see that there are people who need a drink?"

"Yes, ma'am."

Mabel picked up a remaining piece of glass and watched Mrs. Hunt retreat into the crowd, her cream-colored silk dress swaying. Rebecca waddled behind her, smirking, trying to imitate her mistress's manners. Mabel dropped the glass into a basket by the sideboard and picked up her tray. A tiny shard stuck to her palm and, with the pressure of the tray, cut into her skin, leaving a nick that trickled blood. Mabel winced when she felt the prick and set the tray back down, bringing her palm to her mouth.

"Get to work, Mabel," Beverly commanded as she passed by with a tray of shellfish.

Mabel glanced at her hand and fingered the cut. She grabbed a cloth napkin and wrapped it around her hand to resume her duties. Men raised their glasses as she passed, and tipsy women tried to hold themselves and their cups straight as she poured. Behind her, Mabel heard another glass fall to the floor. She moved back and forth, grabbing new bottles from the kitchen, and glancing out into the hallway each time she neared the door. Mr. Hunt had yet to make an appearance.

✦　　✦　　✦

Josiah slammed on the brakes when he rounded the corner and saw Willie standing in the road, hand raised to shield his eyes from the headlights. "What the—" Josiah said, seeing the dog's body.

"Willie, did you run over the dog?" he shouted out the car window.

Willie rushed to his side. "I didn't know it was… I couldn't see—"

"Is it breathing?"

"I don't think so."

Josiah climbed out of the car and walked to the body, brushing his hand across Chou Chou's muzzle. "Right. He's pretty well gone."

"What am I going to do?" Willie cried.

"You ah going a carry the body to the barn; then I'm going a find Mr. Hunt."

"Right now?"

"After we get these motorcars parked. Most ah the guests are here, I would guess. It'll start slowing down in the front."

"Should we wait until tomorrow?"

Josiah looked back at the house, the first floor aglow from the party, the upper floors dark. He shook his head. "Better you face it now," he said.

"What if we got rid of the body?" Willie tried. "No one would ever know."

"Park the car, Willie."

✦   ✦   ✦

Alistair strode around the main ballroom with the musicians, swinging his crutches with a loping gait. He had lost weight with his ordeal and knew he looked good—light and slim as a boy. Julia had popped her head in, letting him know it was almost time for the guests to enter the ballroom. They had planned a grand reveal, an opening of the ballroom doors while Alistair stood on a dais in the center. The platform had been specially constructed with a bar attached to the side where a boy, hired in town, would grab it and run along the side, rotating the entire platform.

Surrounding Alistair on a lower stage, just beyond the boy's track, sat the orchestra. The musicians and Alistair were dressed in pure white, while Alistair's suit was trimmed in silver brocade, his tie and cummerbund a brilliant azure. He had a top hat and a cane designed to match the suit, and he planned to sing as the orchestra played "Au fond du Temple Saint," a favorite from the opera *The Pearl Fishers*.

Alistair had no great operatic voice, though he believed himself to be a superior singer. He often wandered the rooms of Serabelle, belting tunes slightly off-key, with a shaky timbre and rough edges. Julia had warned he was about to make an ass of himself in public—she had fought against the spectacle, but he would not be dissuaded. Though he would inevitably sing at any of their yearly galas, his performance was usually towards the end of the evening, after most had gone home, when only the inebriated or insomniac were left to witness the event.

The orchestra struck the first chord, and the doors swung wide. Julia and the servants had gathered guests outside the ballroom, and a cheer rose as soon as the music built to a crescendo. Then Alistair belted out a courageous note well beyond his comfortable projection range. "Au fond du Temple Saint—"

Guests cringed at the door, dumbfounded and amazed at the sight of Alistair on the pedestal, his lapel shining with the silver trim. Footlights reflected off his spangled top hat. Alistair continued as partygoers were ushered inside. Slowly, as the professional that Alistair had hired to sing harmony stepped up behind him, the platform began to rotate, and the crowd gasped, laughing aloud at the pomp of the show, commenting, "only the Hunts." The laughter grew louder, and guests shouted over Alistair's performance, requesting more alcohol. A few who had already overindulged joined in the singing, figuring if Alistair could do it, so could they. Eventually, the whole crowd was humming or singing along with the orchestra, a great drunken cacophony.

A concerned look grew across the harmonist's face as Alistair jumped in and out of key. He finished his song with a shrill A sharp that he held for ten seconds, his face turning bright red with the effort until he followed the harmonist down to the D. Alistair took a deep bow, his face beaming. The crowd roared and clapped and laughed at the insanity of their host, at the unpredictable time they would always have at the Hunt's end-of-season gala. The harmonist promptly left the stage.

From the doorway, Josiah listened to the end of Mr. Hunt's performance, shaking his head; the man was reckless, for sure. Maybe such recklessness came with freedom, he thought, and everyone knew that freedom came with wealth. Josiah watched the guests walk into the ballroom, all clean and straitlaced. He studied their faces and saw mostly amusement or joy in them. One or two looked bored, and a few grimaced at the sounds of the performance. No reveler's face held the kind of determination, anger, or pride you could find in any of the servants' features. If you stripped everyone down and dressed them in gunny sacks, rich and poor alike, you could still tell who had been ordered around their whole lives and who among the crowd carelessly owned power. Mr. Hunt hopped down from the platform. Applause followed Josiah back out the door.

Chapter 9
Pure Evil

When the guests had finished their formal dinner, staff laid out small finger foods, hors d'oeuvres, and delicacies on the banquet table. Dishes overflowed with mixed berries and nuts, cucumber sandwiches, and pâté. Sausages cut into bite-size pieces lay next to cheeses from local Maine farms and three kinds of relishes. Mabel thought that the cook had done a spectacular job—she had never seen so much food, such variety in one place. Mabel watched the guests gobble it up, shoving tidbits into their gaping mouths without comment. Dishes of caviar—a tiny silver spoon set inside black eggs—anchovies, pastries, and chocolates washed down with a coffee or tea. At some point in the evening, each servant smuggled at least one bite of some rare food. Except for Beverly. She wouldn't deign to cheat her employers in such a manner. Rebecca ate at the insistence of Mrs. Hunt, who became tired of the girl trailing at her heels.

"Please, Rebecca, go eat or some such."

"Ma'am?"

"Wait for me in the dining room. I will come get you if I need something."

As Mabel came through the banquet room where butlers were changing over the service, she watched Rebecca fill a plate with cheese and chocolate, pausing here and there to shove an olive or a date in her mouth.

"What are you doing, Rebecca?"

"Mrs. Hunt told me to eat."

"I'm sure she didn't mean in the main dining room." Mabel nodded at the newly laid spread. "She'll have your hide."

Rebecca froze. "She said wait here. Oh, she meant—" Rebecca dropped her plate and ran through to the kitchen.

Mabel smiled and picked up Rebecca's plate, taking a small cake from the center. She looked to the door to ensure she was alone and then dropped the sugary pastry on her tongue. The cake had a sweet, velvety filling that swooshed through her mouth like cream. Mabel walked to the display and grabbed another pastry covered with almonds and a flaky crust. She wiped her mouth and took a third, a dark chocolate cake, slightly bitter, that melted in her mouth, sucking on it like a hard candy until only the flavor of chocolate remained. Mabel even took a swig straight from a new bottle of Chablis she had been bringing out to the guests.

Behind her, the sounds of the orchestra swelled. Mr. Hunt was singing in that rough voice of his, the voice she had once found so charming. She tilted her head back and took another swallow. The wine burned down her throat, and she immediately felt better, a sense of satisfaction rising at the idea she had gotten one over on the Hunts. As Mabel released the bottle from her lips, wiping her mouth with the back of her hand, the cook's assistant, the second chef, walked through the swinging door that led to the kitchen. She eyed Mabel suspiciously and shook her head. "Disgraceful," she said and shooed Mabel out into the hallway.

◆　　◆　　◆

Willie had left the body of the little lapdog in the barn on a pile of hay near where a roan mare was boarded. The horse stood in the far corner of her stall, alert to sounds of revelry. She gave a soft whinny as Willie came in with the dog. "Keep still, girl," he whispered. "A big ole party, that's all."

The barn was filled with neighs from the cottage's horses, disturbed by the strange teams that had been brought in and watered, placed in empty stalls in the back. Willie set the dead dog on the hay and walked into the roan's stall. He gently put his face to her neck. They had become closer since Clarissa's death. Though Willie felt protective of Clarissa's foal, Trouble, the truth was he bonded more easily with the mares. They had a different energy—softer, more loving—than the stallions. Willie wondered whether his days at the cottage were over because of this one mistake—if all his concern over the horses, all his love and care was for nothing. Maybe Mabel was right—maybe some people didn't count, no matter how good they tried to be.

"I have to go park some more of those autos," he said to the mare, "but I'll be back later tonight."

✦   ✦   ✦

Mabel felt a warm glow in her blood from the wine. She walked the ballroom with a coy smile, offering drinks. Alistair had finished his solo, and the crowd mingled on the dance floor. The orchestra continued, picking up their pace into a swinging version of "Golden Arrow." Partiers began dancing as applause quelled from the opening number. Mabel watched a guest snicker and roll her eyes when Alistair passed on his crutches. That woman's disrespect emboldened her, and Mabel crossed the room, stepping directly in his path. Mr. Hunt had not spoken to her since his accident. She was determined that he not ignore her tonight.

"A glass of champagne, sir?" Mabel thrust the tray under Mr. Hunt's nose.

The smile on Mr. Hunt's face faded, and he turned away, but Mabel stepped around, following him to the south. She thought of those bold women with their pamphlets, pushing to have a voice. "For your victory, sir."

Nearby guests urged him to take a glass, but he gazed over and past the tray, refusing to look at Mabel's face.

"Your guests want you to celebrate such a fine performance," Mabel said with a smirk. "They appreciate talent when they see it."

A few of the guests giggled at Mabel's comments.

"Do, Alistair. Take a glass. Let us drink a toast to your 'talent.'" Mrs. Hunt walked up behind Mabel.

Reluctantly, Alistair grabbed a glass from the tray, pressing the weight of his arm on the edge so that the entire tray tipped. Mabel reached up with both hands to steady the bottles, and her hand touched Alistair's as he, too, tried to prevent them from falling. He looked at her with what she thought might be fondness—a brief acknowledgment of what they had shared—as the remaining four glasses tumbled to the floor, shattering on impact. A woman next to them screamed as a shard lightly touched her ankle.

Before bending to gather the glass, Mabel searched Mr. Hunt's face. He gave her one of those salty smiles she remembered from the early days, so brief, but she had seen it.

"What a mess." Mrs. Hunt scowled at Mabel.

"Never a dull moment with you, Alistair," a man beside him said.

"Here is to Alistair," said another man, "the life of the party."

"That girl is a menace," Julia said.

"Why do you keep her?" a neighbor asked.

"I do not know why we do." Julia turned to her husband. "Alistair, can you answer that? Why do we keep this clumsy girl on the staff?"

Mabel squatted on the floor, her legs slightly parted to allow for her growing belly, picking up glass once again. She kept her head down and concentrated on what they were saying about her.

Mr. Hunt didn't answer.

"Look at her, Alistair. She is a wreck." Julia would not let it go. "Tell me, my dear, why I should not fire her tonight?"

"That is no concern of mine," he said, though when Mabel looked up, she swore she saw a hint of regret on his face before he raised his glass. "To the Ainsworth-Hunts," he cried above the music. "And to Serabelle."

✦   ✦   ✦

The Hunts' son, Rupert, entered the ballroom on a wave of applause. He and his wife had gone to their room upon arrival and didn't join the party until hours later, missing Alistair's performance.

Inside the ballroom, gilded mirrors that had been shipped from France hung upon walls of carved mahogany. Gas lantern sconces flickered with constant motion, the back and forth of air as guests moved and breathed and danced through the space. Tropical ferns and potted palms adorned the room's corners, kept miraculously alive through no small skill of Gardener during the less-than-balmy coastal summer.

"Glad to see you are up and around," Rupert said, finding his father and clapping him on the shoulder.

"You might have been concerned before, when I was bedridden for a month."

"Pop, you know it is not that. I told Mother I was entrenched in a big case."

"A lawsuit is more important than your father?" Alistair tried to catch his son's eye, but Rupert looked over his shoulder as they spoke, as if searching for someone more interesting.

"You broke your leg, right? You do not have leukemia," Rupert pointed out.

"It would take a deadly disease to get you here?"

Rupert laughed him off. "I am here; am I not?"

"What did you think of the song?" Alistair asked.

"Stellar," Rupert said automatically like a lawyer accustomed to flattering his clients, habituated to appeasing. "One-of-a-kind performance."

Alistair stared at his son, knowing he had missed the whole thing. The boy had always been an uninterested snoot, yes. But a liar? That was new. Alistair lifted his drink in salute.

✦　✦　✦

The ballroom became stuffy with hot breath, words, and laughter rising over the symphony's music. Alistair walked into the night air, inspired to see his stallion again; despite the fall, Fierce had served him well. He had carried him and run with him for years, all sleek muscle and silky black fur.

So that the stable master could see when he brought in arriving teams, lanterns hung from every other post. All twenty-five stalls were occupied while buggies of those who refused to bring their autos up north despite the changing laws lined the exterior. Alistair walked through to the back of the barn, relieved for the moment to be far from stifling conversation about autos on Mt. Desert Isle. He and the locals had finally won—and judging by how many people had driven automobiles to the party this year, the political tide was quickly turning. Alistair guessed those stuffy supporters of Mr. Deasy who had tried to keep the island pristine and free of autos would come around soon enough. There was no slowing progress and no denying convenience, even up in the wilds of Maine.

Alistair wondered at those men who clung to their old ways, resisting change. The world *was* change, as far as he could see. People were moving faster and farther; humans were developing and exploring more than ever. And was that not a good thing? Railroads were being built. Mines were being dug. Women were getting out there and fighting for votes. Good for them! Negroes owning businesses, why not? He never understood holding ideas and possessions close to your chest. Was it not more fun to explore the unknown rather than holding tight to what you already had?

Alistair walked the length of the stalls, proud of his cottage, proud of his estate staff. The stable master had done a good job taking care of the animals. A lesser professional would have kept the teams together, hooked up to their buggies, but the stable master hung the outside of the stall with numbers that he matched to a particular buggy. Put away, the horses were not as restless.

His crutches clomped against the hard ground, and the hay clung to his dress shoes. Horses whinnied as he passed, bumping their noses up against wood stalls or hanging their necks over to see if he held a treat in his hand.

Alistair made a sound with his mouth, a double-clicking with his tongue that Fierce Competitor recognized immediately. He whinnied in return. Oh yes, Alistair wanted to get back onto that horse. Alistair, replaying the fall in his mind, remembered Gardener standing by the wall, watching him tumble, knowing that Fierce would not clear. Knowing he had shut the gate.

Outside the stables, servants' shadows slunk back and forth. Noise from the party was a constant hubbub of activity, laughter, and music, somehow soothing from this distance. Alistair hobbled up to Fierce on his crutches, holding his hand until the horse nuzzled his palm. He put his face to the horse's mane and tugged on the tough hair, leaning his crutches against the side of the stall.

"That's my fella," he said. "That's right."

Alistair heard Josiah's voice outside, raised as if he was chastising someone. He hopped closer to the door, on one foot, without the aid of his crutches, and leaned against the door frame. He spied something to his right on the hay. Blood. Alistair turned his full attention to the object and saw it was his wife's dog.

"What is—?" he yelled.

Alistair hobbled over and knelt next to the stiff body. He felt for a pulse in its furry neck, but the animal was clearly gone. He stood and hollered for Josiah, who immediately entered the stables, followed by Willie, who stopped short when he saw Alistair next to Chou Chou.

"Josiah, what happened here?"

"The dog, sir," Josiah said with his head bowed. "He got undah the wheels of a car."

"Whose car?"

"One of the guests', sir."

Willie had not moved from the door, his body visibly shaking as the discussion continued.

"Which guest?" Alistair demanded.

Josiah continued to answer for the two of them. "I'm not sure whose cah it was, sir."

Alistair looked from Josiah to Willie. "Who was driving?" Neither Josiah nor Willie seemed to breathe. Alistair waited. "Well, who?"

"I was," they both said.

"Come now, you could not have both been driving the same car."

"Josiah, no." Willie stepped forward. "I was driving, sir. I didn't mean to. The dog ran right out in front of me. I tried to miss it."

"Why would you do that?"

Willie held his breath. "Sir?"

"Why would you try to miss it?"

"Sir?" Willie looked confused.

"I should think you would have done it on purpose."

Josiah cleared his throat and shuffled his feet.

"I did not—" Willie said.

"I knew I liked you, son." Alistair clapped Willie on the shoulder. "Get me my crutches, there. We must tell Julia." Alistair strode out of the stables, stopping when he realized that Willie was not following him. "Come on, Willie. You are giving her the news."

Willie looked to Josiah, who pushed him forward. He squared his shoulders and followed Mr. Hunt.

"Wait," Alistair stopped mid-path. "Bring the dog."

"Sir?"

"Grab the body. It will be more dramatic that way."

✦ ✦ ✦

Julia found her maid in the kitchen. Four or five servants lounged at a table, eating and laughing, halting when she entered. "Rebecca, come with me," she barked and retreated out the door.

"I'm sorry, ma'am," Rebecca muttered.

"Stop talking," Julia said. "I want you to track down my husband. He has not shown his face for an hour, and he is not in his recovery room."

Rebecca curtsied.

"One more thing," Julia said. "If you should find him in some, shall we say, compromising position, under no circumstances will you give me the details. Do you understand?"

"Ma'am?"

"Do not tell me where or how you find him."

"Yes, ma'am."

"Go on."

No one watched the small, husky girl in the maid's uniform hustling from room to room. She was invisible, as insignificant as a mosquito. Rebecca moved quickly through the crowd, halting when she spied Mabel in the ballroom, holding another tray of drinks. Mabel stood haughtily, laughing and joking with the guests as if she belonged with them. Rebecca had mentioned to Beverly earlier that she thought Mabel was nothing but trouble; she didn't respect the commandments and didn't seem to care that she was pregnant with no husband.

But Rebecca was wrong about Mabel's indifference. At that moment, though Mabel indeed circled the ballroom with a jaunty smirk, she stewed internally over her snub by Mr. Hunt. Would she be fired after all? Sent back to New Jersey in shame, to her mother with a bastard child in her belly? Mabel poured champagne and decanted wine, secretly aching for a moment alone with Mr. Hunt, hoping he might look her in the eyes and remember.

Rebecca moved on to the library. She cranked the doorknob to the right, peering discreetly through a crack in the door in case Mr. Hunt was somehow occupied. The room was dark, and it took a moment for her eyes to adjust. Figures moved in the shadows, silhouettes near the desk by the far window. She didn't call Mr. Hunt's name; she didn't make a peep. The two men moved and whispered and didn't seem to realize that the door had opened. They took a tray from a cabinet, and one of them lit an oil lamp. Young Master Rupert and another fellow she did not recognize. They held what looked like a rock up to the light, spinning the green object in a circle. Rebecca quickly pulled her head back out into the hallway. She took a lesson from Mrs. Hunt. Whatever was going on, it was better if she did not know.

Rupert looked up, alert as the door clicked shut. He held his finger to his lips and crossed quickly to the door, swinging it open with a wild fling. The hallway was empty. Laughter floated from the ballroom. Rupert stepped a few paces into the hall and scanned up and down until he was assured no one was nearby. He re-entered the library, hitting the lock as he closed the door behind him.

With a shaky breath, Rebecca emerged from the broom closet underneath the stairwell, surprised by her instinct to dash into the closet when she heard Mr. Rupert's steps crossing the library. She didn't want to get involved in anything. She simply wanted to do her job and live a pious, god-fearing existence. No trouble. Unlike Mabel, Rebecca wanted peace.

♦   ♦   ♦

Julia sat on a divan in the corner of the ballroom, surrounded by a group of women involved in the church bazaar planning committee. They spoke of the success of this year's event, two weeks previous, how Julia's pillows had sold out in hours. They tsked about the bevy of automobiles on the roads since the new law had been passed, though five out of the six women had arrived in motorcars. The one who arrived by buggy had been picked up at the *Sieur de Monts* steamship dock, or she surely would have come by automobile as well.

"The island will never be the same," a dowdy widow remarked.

"We might as well have kept vacationing in Newport," another commented, sighing.

One of the livelier women, Mrs. Helen Bates, who had come down from Portland, where her family had settled permanently, lowered her voice and showed the ladies a pamphlet. "Look," she said, passing it around. "I have begun working with an anti-suffrage organization that believes we must organize ourselves or else we will be run over by those with louder voices."

Several of the women scanned the pamphlet, nodding. "Let me read you this passage, which I find particularly convincing," Helen said once the booklet had reached her hands again. "'Opponents of suffrage believe that political life with its antagonisms, its jealousies, its excitements, its strivings would be inimical to the repose of life, which is essential to woman's nature if she would bring to her task that poise of nervous and physical strength which ensures the best development of the race which she bears.'"

The women heard gasps of shock in the foyer, imagining falsely that those gasps had something to do with their whispered comments on suffrage. On the far end of the ballroom, music continued, but nearest the door, conversation had ceased—only low whispers and expletives could be heard. Julia stood and craned her neck to discover the source of the disturbance, hoping one of the inebriated guests was not making a scene.

"I will be right back," she muttered to the ladies and walked toward the entrance.

Dancers in the ballroom stopped when they heard Julia's shriek. Musicians halted mid-chord. All guests turned to the foyer.

Willie stood with Chou Chou in his arms. The dog's hindquarters were wrapped in a stable blanket, but blood had soaked through. Chou Chou's eyes were open, and his tongue lagged out of his mouth like an uncooked sausage.

"I didn't mean to," Willie said with tears streaming down his cheeks. "Ma'am, I never would have—"

Willie cringed when Mrs. Hunt screamed a second time, unsure what he should do with the dog. The scream faded into a sob. Julia saw the grinning image of her husband behind Willie as her sight grew cloudy. "Evil," she said, a dizzy air coming over her. She grabbed for something to hold onto, fanning the air impotently.

An unwitting guest caught Julia as she fainted.

Chapter 10
Water Trapped Inside the Stone

Alistair rolled off his bed in the recovery room and stuck his feet into fur-lined slippers. He wrapped his terry-cloth robe around his shoulders in the cool morning air and crossed to the door. "Nurse," he said through the door, "coffee."

Alistair clapped his hands, the fog of sleep lifting as he remembered last night's victory. Ah, how the guests had talked about Julia's fainting and falling apart over that little dog. She had had to be carried to her room and never returned to the festivities.

A momentary twinge of remorse flooded his soft, fuzzy morning brain, remembering the early days of their courtship when Julia openly admired his daring and *joie de vivre*. He recalled how they had strolled along the Charles River, how he had, on a whim, rented them a double scull at the Riverside Boat Club. He nearly capsized the boat, trying to pull out of a current that pinned them to an archway under a bridge. Julia had giggled that day, watching him. She didn't panic—or scold him as she would now.

His vision of young Julia faded as the cloud of their current relationship rolled in. The warmth of those memories couldn't undo all the scorn and derision she had laid on him in the years since. Ridiculous, she had called him. Godless. And worse.

Alistair rubbed his thighs, bringing his attention back to his body. His leg, his whole body, felt loose and strong again, nearly fit enough to ride.

His performance was a success. And his son was here. Perhaps Rupert would stay a few days and explore the new Emery Path on Flying Squadron Mountain with him. Last night, he had promised his friend George Dorr, who was personally supervising the construction of the trail, that he would make the journey over to the wilds of the island and traverse the series of stone steps his friend had ordered carved from the mountain. He was about ready to make a trek of that magnitude.

Alistair took the tray from the nurse when she came to the door. He dressed while he drank his coffee, humming the tune from his performance aria. Oh, a success indeed. Another fabulous party for the Ainsworth-Hunt cottage.

He found Rupert and his pale wife in the dining room.

"Joining us for breakfast, father?" Rupert asked, glancing up from his paper.

"Not for me. Staying trim. I am thinking about riding out on the bluff; what do you say?"

"Have fun," Rupert answered.

"How long are you planning to stay this time?"

His wife smiled and looked at Rupert. "Dear?" she asked.

"A day or two," Rupert said.

"Then we best recreate now. What do you say, Rupert? If not a ride, how about we explore Dorr's new Emory Path? Or could we drive down to the croquet field at the Kebo Valley Club? Your old man needs to get a little exercise."

Rupert's wife looked passively at her husband, as stoic as always. Melinda was one woman Alistair had never been able to draw out. She was more neutral than icy, as implacable as a marionette (and as stick-like too).

"I cannot today," Rupert said. "I have a meeting."

"A meeting? Up here?" Alistair asked.

"A consultation, so to speak."

Even Melinda raised an eyebrow, as if she might be curious herself for once. Alistair, however, would not let it go. "How does that work?"

"I met someone at the party last night who needs some advice."

Melinda kept her body still and her mouth closed, but her eyes moved back and forth between father and son, as if she were watching a tennis match.

"Well, maybe this afternoon, then—" Alistair said. "Perhaps I can show off the newest gems in my collection. I have added some beauties since you last cared to look."

"You know what?" Rupert said, pushing away from the table. "I have a few minutes. Why don't you show me now?"

Alistair swung his crutches up under his arms and moved towards the door. "Great idea, son."

From the center drawer of his teak desk—a magnificent piece brought over from Siam on a trip he had taken three years ago with a hunting buddy—Alistair pulled a key. Siam was deemed too tropical for the ladies, too uncivilized, so Alistair had sent his wife gifts, several items for the household he thought Julia might enjoy, none of which she did. Was this ingratitude the catalyst of their rivalry? Or had a seed been planted long before? Either way, the desk had been relegated to his library. Other items such as vases, letter openers, and statues were spread throughout the cottage. Not one item remained in Julia's private rooms. She did not have a taste for the exotic.

Rupert watched his father carry a tray from the hutch after he had opened the lock. How ridiculous, he thought, to keep the key in the most obvious of places. He had found it easily last night at the party. Why bother locking the hutch at all? The shelves were filled with racks, black-velvet-lined trays made of a dark hardwood Rupert could not name. He knew next to nothing about nature, in fact. He could not tell a birch from a maple if the skin was on it. No, not skin… bark. He would not even know a tree if it still had its bark. Bark, like the yelp of a dog. Rupert thought of homonyms, synonyms, and double entendres. Language and numbers interested him. And money. Money, of course, was mostly interesting as a gauge of how successful one was in life. And to be successful, you must accumulate as much money as possible—by your wiles and wits, by work, and by negotiations. By thievery, if need be. As long as you were smart enough to get away with it.

"Now, look at this," Alistair said, picking up a white opal the size of a robin's egg. "Straight from Australia. My man picked this up for me himself—superior quality." Alistair hobbled to the window without his crutches and opened the shade. "We need more light to view these. Light that lamp," he said. "See all those blues and purples and pinks? That is from the amount of water trapped inside the stone. The higher the water content, the more colors you will see. The less water, the more monotone. This one: the color, the sheer size of it, quite rare."

Rupert held the stone up to the window and squinted to see if he could detect water. "Then it is valuable?"

"Of course. In the past, I have shown you the micas and the serpentines. But I know my son; the gems make your eyes sparkle. I figure I better stick to those, or you might lose interest." Alistair lifted four more trays out of the way without unstacking them until he found the markings he was looking for (he had created a private cataloging system related to color and rarity). He chose a dark stone, about half the size of the last, and held it up to the light. "If we are talking numbers, take a look at this. Black opal," he said.

Rupert reached for the stone.

"Do you see that red?" Alistair continued. "Talk about rare. This beauty was found in Nevada, of all places. Until a few years ago, we thought opals only came from Australia. In 1905, the first opal was unearthed in Nevada, a small black one, but it started a bit of a frenzy. I have been to the Royal Peacock Mine myself—they had nothing near that size when I was there, but they let me dig around in the dirt. I picked up a few pea-sized specimens; very exciting when you see that sparkle in the ground. You take a pickaxe to the earth, gently tapping away the dirt. Nothing like that anticipation when you are holding your breath, wondering how big your find will be. In fact, I am going to bring Mr. Wilson out there next spring."

"Who?" Rupert asked.

"The night butler. The old fellow."

Rupert turned the black opal around. "Why in the world would you take a servant to a mine?"

"Because he is interested! Have you ever talked to the man? Funny fellow. His dream is to dig in the mines, so why not give him a chance? I never unearthed a big one myself." Alistair gestured at the rock in his son's hand. "Had to pay quite dearly for that baby—found at the Bonanza Mine down the road. Did you know the Loughead family started that mine—I am talking the Lougheads who built the Model G flying boat."

Rupert shook his head. "Hmm?"

"Those Lougheads out in California. Those brothers out there are making loads of advances in flying technology. I heard last week that they have an idea for a twin-engine ten-passenger seaplane. What do you think of that? Airplanes that land on the water. First, the Wrights, then the Lougheads. Makes me wish I had a brother; maybe I could have done something."

Rupert held up the stone again, attempting to steer the conversation back to gems. "So, this black opal's worth more than the white, even though it is smaller?"

"I would not say that. The clarity is better on the white, and it is almost twice the size. Crystals are set closer together there, so you get more refraction, caused by more compression. I feel you cannot compare the two; they are in different spheres, so to speak."

"But if you had to put a price on them, say, if you were to sell them both?"

Alistair put his hand out for the black stone and held it up next to the white opal in the light coming through the window. "Not that I would sell them," he said, "but I would put the black opal at three thousand, perhaps, and the white opal, maybe forty-five hundred? That is a guess, of course, judging from what I paid and how the market has changed over the last ten years. Although exciting, the discovery of opals in Nevada has lowered the value of the stones."

Rupert nodded and turned towards the racks, running his finger along the black velvet lining of the tray holding ebony and smaller black opals. "What would you say is your most valuable gem altogether?"

"I am glad you asked." Alistair rubbed his hands together and walked to the corner.

A white alabaster pillar, Greek ionic style, held a flowing ivy plant in a heavy stone pot that Alistair picked up with a groan and placed awkwardly on the floor, his bum leg sticking straight out for balance.

"I had this specially constructed," Alistair pointed at the top of the pillar.

Rupert moved close to his father, who removed a small cork disc from the surface of the platform. A sunken dial lay flush to the top of the pillar; Alistair turned the dial—right, then left, then right again—to align with numbers etched into the metal. Rupert could not make out the combination; his father's hands moved too quickly. Alistair pulled on two notched handles on the plaster's underside and lifted the pillar's top off, setting it next to the cork cover. Rupert peered inside the column. It was lined with a sable-colored velvet, like the lining of the trays. Halfway down, in the center, sat a glass case with a purplish gem inside, sparkling, though there was very little light in the cavernous hole.

"May I?" he asked his father.

"Go ahead."

Rupert lifted the small glass case up to the window. The gem inside, lying on blue silk, was nearly the size of a golf ball. When he held it up to the window, a beam of sunlight—pushing through the cloud cover as if its sole intention had been to reach the stone—burst onto the surface, exploding the refractory rays into a rainbow of colors. But Rupert had been wrong: the gem itself was not purple; it was pink.

"What is it?" Rupert asked.

"What is it?" Alistair echoed. "What is it? My boy, sometimes I do wonder where your head is. What sparkles like that? Are you not my son? Have I taught you nothing about gemology? It is a diamond, Rupert."

"But this stone is pink."

"I should think you knew my taste by now; I would not be interested in any old diamond. This is the rarest of the rare. A pink diamond. Forty-two carats. I guarantee you have never seen the like, and probably never will again. An emerald cut."

Rupert's mouth salivated, a hint of moisture as if anticipating a delicious taste. "Why an emerald cut?"

"Because not only is this a rare type of stone, but it is rare in its clarity. Look closely—you will not find any bubbles or scratches. A stone of inferior quality would have had to be cut with more facets to bring out the brilliance. My lady here does not need any help."

"Where did you get it?"

"This sweetheart is not merely an 'it.' She is one of a kind. I got her where everyone goes for diamonds." Alistair threw his hands in the air with a flourish. "Africa, my son. Africa."

"You went to Africa? When?"

"Last winter, to the wilds of German East Africa, on safari."

"Really." Rupert kept his eyes on the diamond.

"I used to believe that diamonds were an overrated gemstone. After all, coal takes as long to form as diamonds, for Christ's sake." He tapped Rupert's chest. "I bet you did not know that. As a geological aficionado, so to speak, I used to be unimpressed by the ever-luminous diamond. Until, of course, I went to the mines. Until I was encircled and enraptured by the witchy facets of her. The mine owners took me to their back room, into the vault, and there she was, not two weeks old, as far as unearthing goes. As if she had surfaced particularly for me. I had to have her."

Rupert finally peeled his eyes from the gem. "Why keep it here? Why not put it in a bank?"

"Two reasons." Alistair took the case from his son and held it to his cheek. "I need her close so I can look at her. What is the point of owning something this gorgeous if you are going to keep her hidden away? Second, you think I would trust those dimwits at the Maine Savings Bank? Maybe a bank in Boston, but then, she would be way over there, so far away from me."

"Seems risky," Rupert said. The sun had ducked back behind the clouds. Now the sky seemed to be forecasting imminent rain.

"At the moment, you are the only other person who knows it is here. Not even your mother knows."

"No one?"

"Well, the stonemason down at the statuary made this safe, so he knows I have something valuable, but he does not know what."

"Surely you have the diamond insured?"

"Yes, but my agent does not know exactly where I am keeping it. I am very careful, of course, with whom I share my information. I am having another display case made as well. A Frenchman I know is working on a thing called safety glass—hard to break. He is going to make me a glass case so I can display it in the parlor."

"Display it? Are you crazy?"

"I figure I am better off keeping it out in the open, where I can keep my eye on her. The complete case will travel with us to Boston in the winter, along with the rest of my collection. I do not want to be without it."

"What would you put the value on this one?"

Alistair cleared his throat. "A smidge under eighty thousand."

Rupert swallowed. "Did you get a good deal?"

"I paid what she was worth."

Alistair placed the stone back into the pillar and closed the top, cranking the dial and placing the cork and the plant on top.

"Why the sudden interest in my collection?" Alistair asked.

"I have always been interested, Father. I simply do not know very much about gems."

"You might have asked."

"I am asking now," Rupert said.

Chapter 11
Like a Good Tiding

The ladies at the Gala were right, Julia thought as she rubbed the thick pancake makeup from her skin: she should consider an anti-suffrage meeting. She had seen the suffragists in Bar Harbor with their white dresses, their sashes, and loud mouths. Watched them recruiting household workers, any old woman who walked by. Asking for trouble.

In the mirror, she saw that mascara had bled down into long black streaks over her face, giving her the appearance of a criminal staring out past steel bars; the prison of her life, she thought, manifested on her face. Julia wiped at the makeup until her face was clean, until she looked upon the wrinkled, plain face of an old woman. Nothing more.

There was a cold stone this morning where her heart used to be; she was sure of it. How would she ever recover from such a shock? Julia walked to the corner of her room where she had had Chou Chou's body placed, on the pink silk that used to be his bed, over a bucket of ice. The butler had wanted to take the dog out back and bury him, but she could not bear it. She wanted to be with him for one more night, stroke his soft, tan fur (where it was not caked with blood), and whisper to him.

Julia reached over to pet Chou Chou, but he did not feel like the dog she knew. His body was cold and stiff, and Julia let out a whimper that did not sound unlike the one that Chou Chou might have made.

"I know he did it on purpose, Chou Chou," she growled. "I am so sorry you're gone. You did not deserve to die."

Julia clenched her fists, her long nails digging into her palms as she let out another sob. There was a knock on her door.

"What is it?" Julia dabbed at her tears with a hankie.

"It is me, Mrs. Hunt, Rebecca. I wanted to see if you needed anything."

"Come in, dear," Julia said, with an edge of sadness in her voice.

Rebecca clomped across the room and started to speak. When she saw the body of the dead dog, she let out a cry. "Oh, I'm sorry, ma'am. I didn't expect to see him there, all messy, I mean, all so squished… sorry, ma'am. It's that he is so… dead."

Julia let out a long sigh. "I know. I know. It was shocking to me, too."

"Can I do something for you, ma'am? Can I bring you some tea?"

"Come sit," Julia said and patted a chair in the corner. "I do want to ask you a favor."

Rebecca bustled over to the chair, as if happy to be away from the bloody body of the dog.

Julia looked Rebecca straight in the eye, hoping to intimidate her maid into telling her the truth. "Now, I know that all you servants talk."

"Ma'am?"

"I mean, you gossip about everything; am I right?"

"I do not like to gossip, ma'am. Maybe some of the—"

Julia nodded as if it would be expected that her maid would refrain. "But if you wanted to, you could hear the gossip?"

"Oh certainly, ma'am."

Julia stood and paced, the long gauze of her dressing gown sweeping in dramatic arches as she pivoted. "I need you to find out whether my husband killed Chou Chou. I am sure he is behind it. You must find out." Julia stormed up and down the room, flipping the drapery out of her way.

Rebecca nodded her head. "Yes, ma'am."

"Can I count on you, Rebecca?" Julia pivoted her head. "I need more than a 'yes, ma'am.'"

"You know you can count on me, ma'am. I won't let you down. If there's information to be found, I'll find it." Rebecca's hands shook as she clasped them in front of her.

Julia held her maid's gaze, wondering how effective she might be. Rebecca was loyal, but Julia needed more than loyalty in times like these. She needed a staunch ally. "Go now, Rebecca. See what you can do."

◆　◆　◆

Julia lit the lantern on her mantle. She enjoyed the soft glow of the fire rather than letting in the sun that threw constant, harsh light across surfaces, corners, and over her skin, revealing the flaws in life. Even worse, Alistair had wired the house in Boston for electric lights. Julia could never get accustomed to the sudden onset of intense light. These new inventions scared her. But Alistair, who would not be outdone by his neighbors, needed to own or install all the latest scientific advances. He was so thrilled the day he brought home a phonograph, new on the market. Honestly, Julia had never even heard of such a thing. Who knew where he got his information? When he first brought her into the parlor for a demonstration over ten years ago, she recoiled at those voices from the box, echoing through the walls as if ghosts were in the room. It was hard to comprehend all these new discoveries.

Alistair was so protective of his purchases that he had tried to fire Rebecca, *her* maid, when she bumped into the phonograph in the parlor, scratching one of his cylinders. But Julia had come to her defense. The hiring and firing of servants was tedious. Finding good, trustworthy staff members was nearly impossible, especially up here in the far reaches of the wilderness. The locals here were daft in a way she found hard to tolerate, with their strange speech and lilting accents. Rebecca might be simple, but she understood Julia, and she behaved properly. She had had Rebecca with her for a decade—the girl was barely an adolescent then, the daughter of her mother's maid. You could trust a girl who had been brought up to know her place. She would never be one to join some movement to give women a voice.

Now this Mabel—this improper, impregnated little minx—what was Julia to do with her? Did they all think she did not know? Did they think she was ignorant of the goings on in her own house? Pale light from the lantern flickered across the room.

Some guests must have stayed the night: a few stragglers' voices could be heard downstairs, still hanging around. Alistair would be among them, she knew. She would never understand how she ended up with such a man. Their union was a testament to the folly of youth, to how thoroughly one can change over a lifetime. A profound sadness came over her, familiar and encompassing—melancholy that she had such hatred for the father of her children—that he had grown to despise her too.

Julia pulled the curtains; a beam had begun to creep across the floor. The sun seemed too bright, too cheerful for such a morning, as if it were mocking the death of her beloved dog. She stood a moment, hesitating with her hand on the curtain, looking out at a car pulling up from the stables. There was that negro boy again, still working, so casually, as if he had not held a dying Chou Chou in his hands a few hours ago. He stepped out of the vehicle and spoke to the owners. Julia recognized the Millers—she did not remember adding them to the invitation list—they were probably thrilled to have made it inside this year. The man drove his own car; Julia guessed they didn't have a driver on staff.

Behind the Millers, Mr. Wilson trudged across the gravel, appearing out from behind the hedge that hid the lower floor of the servants' quarters, walking right across the front yard. Julia supposed she didn't mind if he did so; the old man was dressed neatly. He moved over the wide expanse as Julia imagined a gazelle might move, in starts and stops, looking around him every few steps, ears alert, eyes wide. He jumped nervously out of the way of the Millers' car as they zoomed past. She enjoyed the quiet dignity of that man, how he kept out of everyone else's business. Julia was sure he would not be a source of gossip, though she would bet that he was still privy to all the secrets the walls of Serabelle kept hidden inside.

Too often these days, she found herself thinking about the servants. Really, it was Alistair's fault. That ridiculous little girl. The maid was clearly in love with her husband, whether it was reciprocated or not. She couldn't be sure, but he certainly hadn't done anything to put the girl off, and now, she seemed to be strutting around the cottage with a sense of entitlement, emboldened by his idiocy. It was for Julia to knock the pomp out of her, let her know her place. Easier, really, than trying to find some other girl. They would leave within a week for Boston, anyway, and most of the servants would be left behind.

Beverly, that trustworthy and devout head servant, had told her that Mabel would marry the gardener. Well, what did she care? Fine, she had said. As long as they continued to do their work. She had let Beverly know that the little maid had received her last warning this evening when she spilled the tray at the party. If she got in Julia's way again, she would be forced to fire her, no matter the bother. It might be best, though, to put a good scare into the girl before they departed, to show her the reality of the situation.

Julia made her way over to the cushion where Chou Chou's body lay. She preferred to have the room dark, preferred not to see the ghoulish, flattened form that he had taken on. Julia knelt beside the dog and lightly put her hand on his head.

"My little dear," she said. "You have been a friend to me like no other, making me laugh with your wet little kisses upon my nose. You have followed me around like a good tiding, and I shall miss you more... I am going to tell you the truth, Chou Chou..." Julia sobbed as she whispered the next sentence. "I will miss you more than I miss my own children. They never cared for me even half as much as you did."

Julia listened as the front door closed once again behind the departing guests. There had been voices in the parlor, muffled constant drones highlighted by an occasional cackle. She could not abide such vulgar noises and wondered who possessed such a laugh. Alistair must be down there clowning, no doubt.

Julia turned her attention back to the dog. She stroked his head, recoiling slightly when her hand hit the sticky blood on his neck. "You need not worry, little one. I will get revenge on that man for doing what he did. He *will* pay."

Chapter 12
The Thrill of Getting Away With It

Rupert met Forrest Wicks at the Eden Tavern at ten thirty a.m., not too early for the regulars, but certainly before Rupert would see anyone he knew (not that anyone he knew would frequent a tavern). You couldn't be too careful. Rupert had gone as far as to dig out some old clothes that he found in one of the spare rooms—clothes that were not those of a gentleman, that might help him pass as a local. He wore canvas trousers the muddy brown of the stables and an equally nondescript coat constructed of a fabric that scratched his skin whenever it touched past his undergarment. He had no idea whose clothes he wore, could not imagine who had left such rough items in his parents' house, but he had often had the suspicion, even growing up at Serabelle, that he did not know half of what was going on in those rooms. Such a sprawling house, and so many servants.

Rupert's stomach was uneasy to the point of gurgling. A thrill ran through his blood, turning his limbs to ice and his lips frigid, yet it felt refreshing, like a mountain spring. Rupert wondered if he had ever touched or seen a mountain spring, other than in picture books. That must have been where the thought came from—the Swiss Family Robinson, or some such. How he had loved those adventure books when he was a child. Unlike other boys he knew, he had never had the urge to act out what he read in books—swinging on vines or fighting with swords. He knew he was not nearly coordinated enough, so eventually, his tastes ran to the mysteries, the novels with plot twists and detectives who could, through logic alone, figure out who had committed the crime. Rupert felt now as if he might be a part of some such novel, as if he were finally about to live out a fantasy. Meeting in a common bar, dressing under cover—it was all extremely exciting.

Forrest Wicks was a tall but very slender man, as if he were made of matchsticks. His hair was the whitest blond, but he often kept it covered, as if he were ashamed of the luster of his head. His lips were equally bright, and his eyes were a dazzling hazel. The first time Rupert met Forrest, he had thought what a stunning girl Forrest would have made—at least facially. To this day, his body was still that of an adolescent boy who had not quite grown into his height—a flat, almost hollow chest and spindly arms. Forrest moved with the awkwardness of a praying mantis, and he kept a constant grimace on his face, as if he desired to cover his beauty with a fierce expression.

Rupert knew Forrest from prep school, though they had not been friends. Forrest was with the kids who smoked cigarettes in the woods behind the dorms—a troubled boy whose parents had reportedly squandered their fortune so that Forrest was forced to work in the cafeteria to help pay his tuition. Though Forrest was skinny, he was tough. In all honesty, Rupert had always thought of Forrest as dirty. He remembered seeing grease under the kid's fingernails, as if he somehow could not come clean. Rupert had not seen Forrest since graduation—until the gala the other night.

At first, Rupert could not place him; the man seemed out of step with the other partygoers, a skinny reed in a thicket of bushes. Rupert had watched him across the dining room, shoving food into his mouth at an alarming rate. At first, Rupert had wondered if the man was hired staff, but his clothes were fine, his skin white and unmarred. And then Forrest had turned and looked him full in the face, and it clicked. Forrest smiled an honest grin and waved to Rupert, crossing the room and speaking with his mouth still full.

"Well, there you are. I was wondering if you would be here tonight," Forrest muttered, his cheek stuffed, still chewing.

"Here I am."

The men shook hands. "Forrest. Forrest Wicks."

"Prep school," Rupert said. "Been a long time. What brings you to my parent's cottage way up here?"

"I guess you do not know, but my parents bounced back from their little financial disaster—I am sure you will remember I was on scholarship at Exeter—and they have reacquainted themselves with society, so to speak." Forrest swallowed the food. "They are friends with your parents, I do believe."

"Do you live around here?"

"Part of the year. The parents bought Crow's Nest, a hop down the road, a couple of years ago. I come up for much of the summer with them."

Rupert then talked a bit about his life in New York. "So, what is your occupation now?" he asked.

"I would not call it so much of an occupation as I would a..." Forrest looked around the dining room corners and lowered his voice to a whisper. "Well, a curiosity, shall we say?"

"And what is that?"

"I am interested in fine objects. I have developed an eye for appraisal, that sort of thing."

"Fascinating," Rupert said and considered how he would get out of the conversation, thinking you could not scrub the man's rough edges away with polish.

"I hear your father has quite a collection of fine objects," Forrest said.

"My father?"

"Stones, gems, that sort of thing."

"Oh, yes, father certainly has all that."

"Worth a good lot, I would wager."

"I do not know."

"Could we look at the collection? Is it here, in the house?"

Rupert stopped scanning the room and looked at Forrest. "I suppose you should ask my father."

"What's the fun in that?"

"What do you mean?"

"No adventure in asking permission." Forrest shrugged.

"Are you suggesting—"

"Would not hurt to take a peek, would it?"

Rupert was quite startled at Forrest's forwardness. Not one bit of subtlety about the man. "Right now?"

"Rupert, when's the last time you did something just for the thrill of getting away with it? Like when we were kids?"

Rupert tried to remember acting in such a manner as a child. His father had never watched him, had never paid attention. Hell, unless Rupert wanted to go rock hunting or horse riding (neither of which interested him), he could not get his father to say "boo" to him. Rupert had thought, each time he won an award and was selected for a committee or a panel, *that* would be the thing to make his father proud, but no prize had done the trick—none had turned his father's eye to his accomplishments.

Rupert grinned at the thought of Alistair finding them looking at his rock collection. Would he be insulted or pleased? Would his father consider any attention he paid to the subject good?

"Well, perhaps a peek," he said and led the way to the library.

✦　✦　✦

Forrest was already seated at an oversized wooden table in the far corner of the tavern. His hair was covered in a dark wool cap, and he lifted one of his fingers in response to Rupert's appearance. Forrest did not even look up from his beer, and Rupert wondered how the man knew it was he who had walked through the door. A few fellows sat at the bar with their backs turned. Only the bartender looked up. The burly man in a dirty apron eyed Rupert briefly before returning to the bar and the rag he used to wipe a spill.

Rupert waited to let his eyes adjust to the dim room. A dozen or so tables were ringed by benches and stools. Bottles lined the back of the bar that ran across the room's width. There were no windows. He walked across the room and slid onto the bench across from Forrest, pulling his hat down over his brow. "I do not believe anyone saw me," he muttered.

Forrest did not answer, and Rupert could not read his expression, as the light was dim and Forrest kept his head down, looking at a beer he held between his rough hands. Rupert could see that, unlike at the party last night, there was the familiar ring of dirt under Forrest's fingernails, as if he had intentionally dug his hands in the earth. Rupert wondered what he could have gotten up to in the last twelve-plus hours to allow such a change.

The tavern was silent but for the soft clink of glasses behind the bar and the occasional sound of a throat being cleared. Forrest made a gesture over to the bartender, a quick nod that Rupert assumed the man would not catch, but within a minute, two glasses appeared on their table, and the bartender poured brandy.

"A gentleman's drink," Forrest said, holding his glass up for a toast.

"It is a bit early," Rupert replied. "And is this place legal? Maine is a dry state, right?"

Forrest gave him a reproving look and sipped his brandy. Rupert quickly followed suit, ashamed of his timidity. How was it that this ruffian could make him feel inferior? He winced as the liquid burned his throat. He was not a good drinker on the most festive of days.

"So, what is it you want to talk about?" Rupert asked.

Forrest slugged down the rest of his drink, obviously comfortable in his role as the mysterious figure. "That was quite a collection we looked at last night. Tell me this. Did you have fun sneaking into the library? Taking out your father's gems?"

"A bit of a thrill, I must admit."

Forrest spoke in a near whisper. "How would you like to up the ante, so to speak?"

"In what way?"

"See if we can palm some of them."

"Steal?" Rupert's voice rose to a panic.

"Calm down," Forrest ordered. "Are you going to deny that you have been thinking the same thing since I guessed what that collection's worth?"

"I would be hesitant," Rupert said, his stomach turning. Why would he steal from his own father?

"That is the point; is it not?" Forrest said. "Seeing what you are capable of, testing your own bravery."

Rupert sucked on his teeth, making a high-pitched sound.

"Let us start small," Forrest said. "No harm in that, so you can get your feet wet. Let us only take one. One little gem. How about that emerald we looked at? Worth a few thousand." Forrest let the thought settle with Rupert and then continued. "Tell you what: you go in, open the cabinet, and simply borrow it. See how it feels. Keep the emerald for yourself for a few days—do not even bring it to me. See if he notices. You can even put it back if you do not feel right. Start there."

Rupert considered what Forrest said. That would be easy. He could do that. "Then what?"

"I would need to know the schedule at Serabelle."

"I could not tell you," Rupert admitted. "Honestly, I am not around enough."

"Start paying attention to who is coming and going at any given hour, when the best time to strike is. Then, we need to plan your role and eventually talk about the strategy for sales after the event."

"Wait. My role, I assume, is to give you the information. I will not be there."

"You must be. Who will let me in?"

"Could you break in?"

"And draw attention to the theft? Why bother when I have you there?"

"It will be too obvious. I never stay at Serabelle long; more importantly, I am the only one who knows where the key is."

"So, you will make me a key. To the house and to the cabinet. I will do it after you have gone back to New York. But I will still need to know the schedule, the habits of your parents and the servants."

The door to the tavern opened, letting a stream of light into the dark room. Two men in work clothes wandered in, sitting at the table next to theirs. One of them waved to Forrest, and Forrest nodded back. Rupert ducked his head.

"Am I wasting my time with you?" Forrest asked.

Rupert did not answer. He fondled his glass that held the brandy he had yet to finish. The image of a gravestone came strongly to Rupert's mind, sudden and looming. His own headstone that he understood to be up here in Maine, at the small cemetery south of Town Hill. A large piece of gray granite, but the face of the stone was blank. There was nothing to be said about him, nothing to be set into his grave. No identity, no significant accomplishments. No loving son.

"I mean, are you still as big a sissy as you were in prep school?" Forrest asked.

"What?" Rupert stood and shoved his drink away. His heart beat in his throat, and tears automatically formed in his eyes. He blinked them away.

"Sit down," Forrest said firmly.

"I do not have to take this," Rupert said.

"No, you do not," Forrest agreed. "You can leave. But then you will have proved my point. You *are* a sissy."

Rupert sat back down. Either way, he made an ass of himself. If he agreed to the crime, he was being swayed by a bully, a petty thief. But worse, if he walked away, the bully was right. He was a coward. Rupert wiped his brow. How did he get himself into this? Why did he come here? What if he went along with the plan? Would Forrest take off with the gems?

Forrest waited a full five minutes before he spoke. "Have you grown into a brave man who makes his own decisions?"

Rupert stood. Enough. "How do I reach you?"

"Leave word here," Forrest said with a grin, "when you want to meet."

Rupert walked towards the door but stopped halfway across the room. "You may never see me again," he said in Forrest's direction. The men at the table next to Forrest looked up. The bartender raised his eyebrows, wondering why he should care whether he saw the man or not.

"Oh, I will see you. One way or another." Forrest laughed.

Rupert shivered, wondering whether that was a threat. He turned and walked into the daylight.

Chapter 13
It is My Fault

Gardener straightened from his crouch where he had been weeding in the rose garden at the south end of the grounds. He kept all the gardens in pristine condition, day after day, fertilizing, weeding, watering, and trimming. Yet rarely did anyone wander through the maze of plants. The beauty of the gardens was his alone to savor. His handiwork in the rose garden, his twenty-nine breeds—some of them developed and pollinated by his own hand—were a matter of pride. Gardener had developed a particular fertilizer that the roses drank up: a mixture of fish bones he dried and ground, along with vegetable scraps he composted in a wine barrel next to his gardening shack. The cook gave him waste every evening, and he rifled through, picking out the right morsels for his concoction. After twenty years of working with the soil, Gardener knew instinctively what foods gave nourishment his plants needed.

The roses were not the only flowers Gardener tended to. He had begun a wildflower garden based on the untamed, overflowing, natural style of the fields he had seen growing up in Ireland. The patch of ground he had seeded near the north end, around the corner from the short-cropped lawn below the east wing, had the appearance of a randomly strewn, unkempt field of daisies and marsh marigolds, columbine, and black-eyed Susans. Yet, Gardener had meticulously groomed and replanted these flowers, ensuring that no one area held too much white or too much yellow: no color dominated. Violets played along the edges, near the short grasses, while buttercups encroached on the stone pavers he sent straight down the middle, dividing the high wheat grass that tickled the chins of the sunflowers. Gardener controlled the layout of the fields with a master's hand—the type of control that was not obvious to the untrained eye. But if you searched with a magnifying glass, you could not find dandelion or milkweed among the thriving plants.

In the front of the cottage, past the bordering stone wall, low northern white cedars lined the circular drive to the inside, while a strand of fragile, young, white birch ushered guests in along the outside of the drive, standing like pale soldiers until the driveway branched off, the left fork towards the tall yellow servants' quarters, the top of which could barely be seen behind the spreading arrowwood bushes. The main driveway continued with a solid hedge of shrub honeysuckle, masking the laundry and utility sheds set back near the servants' house. The hedge took a sharp left two hundred yards before the house, opening onto sweeping green lawns.

Julia Hunt had insisted on two Roman-style statues, one of a man about to throw a discus and one of a woman in flowing robes, to be placed on either side of the main entrance to the house. Gardener had cringed as they were placed. In his view, the ridiculous statues pulled the eye from the simple beauty of the hydrangeas near the steps and the short sweetgale he had planted along the west side of the driveway interspersed with orange jessamine, imported from Asia, one of the few nice choices Mr. Hunt had made on his trips abroad as far as Gardener was concerned. Not that Gardener knew anything about art or décor. He knew plants, though, and the bamboo Mr. Hunt had insisted he plant had been nothing but trouble. Those roots spread faster than the plague. He had had a hell of a time containing them.

The year Mr. Hunt returned from Siam, he had instructed Gardener to make an Asian garden, past the stables and the field, south of the rose gardens. That year—what was it, three or four years ago now?—the household's focus was completely Asian. The dishes the Hunts used, and the food they asked to be served, all had an Oriental flair. After the original rush of having a pagoda built, Buddhist statues installed, mini shrubs, and flat sand and rock gardens designed, Mr. Hunt came out to the garden almost every day. He had even learned some prayer that Gardener overheard him chanting in the pagoda, in front of a shrine. Mr. Hunt rang a bell and crossed his legs while sitting on a straw mat. Gardener had never seen such nonsense, but he chalked it up to the eccentricities of the rich.

Now, several years later, no one came out to the Asian garden, save a few guests wandering at the yearly gala.

Gardener wiped the dirt from his knees and walked to the stone bench under a gallica bush, brushing a few brown, curled petals from the seat. The young one, the Hunts' daughter, Sarah, used to run along the paths of the rose garden when she came to the cottage, but she had grown up as snooty as her mother. Gardener remembered the year she stopped coming by to visit. His tool shed was set at the edge between the rose garden and the stables, nicely camouflaged from both sides by a lattice fence where he had trained an autumn sunset to branch up and through the wood pattern on one side and an altissimo, bright red and hearty, to grow up facing the stables.

Sarah was a bouncy child, as bubbly and friendly as her mother was dour. Unlike her brother, Rupert, she loved the outdoors and desired to learn everything she could about plants from Gardener, wanting to know what it took to become a great horticulturist. Yes, that is what she had called it. Gardener chuckled. Even the young children of the rich were pretentious. In the years before her adolescence, Gardener spent a couple of hours every day with Sarah, letting her use his tools, pointing out how he cut back each bush, trimming at the Y, culling after the season was over to ensure that next year's crop would be even more bountiful. She would smile and finger the pointy thorns, her blue eyes echoing the color of the ocean, her straw-colored hair whipping across her cheeks. He had loved her as a child, an avuncular love revealed in trying to teach his kin a useful trade. But Sarah would never need a trade. He should have known that.

The summer the girl turned thirteen, she stopped coming to the garden daily. He waved to her as she rode onto the grounds in the buggy—at that time, the chauffeur was a man named Howard, an old hackney driver who died the year before Josiah came on. Gardener had liked Howard—

probably better than any of his other co-workers. He had been as crabby as one of the old apples that fell to the ground in the field next to the cottage, but Gardener could see a lot of humor behind the man's biting words. Howard's legs were bowed into a permanent 'O,' so he moved like a toddler when he walked. He kept his upper lip curled under, baring his teeth in a manner reminiscent of a storybook pirate. Gardener didn't know exactly why Howard had not followed his father and grandfather into the fishing industry, but he guessed it was because of his deformed legs. The awkward curve must have made it difficult for him to get his balance on the deck of a boat.

Sarah ran Howard ragged her thirteenth summer. Gardener had no idea where she was off to all those early summer days, so when she finally managed to wander out to his garden, he asked.

"Well, young miss," he said familiarly, "what has kept you so off and busy that you can't stop in for a visit with yar Uncle Gardener?"

Sarah looked haughtily at the servant. "You are not my uncle."

Gardener stood with his spade in hand, taken off guard. Sarah's face held an expression he had never seen before, a sour scrunching of her brow, the mirror image of her mother's disdainful glare. Gardener wanted to tell Sarah not to make that face, that the skin might remember the creases, that lines would etch themselves permanently into her face. It was not too late to learn another look, another expression.

"Miss Sarah, I was missing our teaching sessions, that is all. You have not been 'round much this summer."

"Mother says it is not proper."

"I see."

"She says I should not be playing in the dirt anymore; it is time I start acting like a lady. She also said I should not associate with a grown man like you."

The words felt like a blow to Gardener, like the girl had stepped up and pummeled his gut with all her might. He was too surprised to speak.

"Besides, Gardener, you are not my teacher or my uncle," she continued. "You are our servant."

Gardener had turned on his heel then. "True 'nuff," he said into the wind. He had not had another discussion with the girl since. She grew up and went off to school, got married, and moved to England without another thought, he was sure, about him or their time in the gardens.

After brushing petals off the marble bench, Gardener ambled to his tool shed. The sun was hidden behind a low cloud cover that threatened rain. The grass had held onto its morning dew well into the day, and Gardener's knees were soaked from kneeling. His trousers clung to his skin, and he shivered, the sweat from his efforts cooling him. The wooden door creaked on its hinges, and the misty light revealed orderly shelves and tools hanging along the far wall. Gardener stowed his bucket in the corner and removed his gloves, pulling on one fingertip at a time, the leather making a soft pluck with each yank. He had paid for the gloves with his own wages. They had been pricey—a special order from the feed store—as his hands were larger than the gloves the store normally stocked. The Hunts might have paid for them, he knew, but Gardener hated to ask those two for anything. And knowing the gloves were his, not the cottage's—not the Hunts'—somehow made Gardener proud, made him care for the gloves as he did not care for any other item. When he finished, he oiled the brown leather every night and darned the fingers himself when a hole was worn through. He had borrowed the thread from that maid Shauna, though she had been reluctant even to speak to him.

Gardener placed his gloves on the shelf next to where his rain gear hung and took a seat on a wooden bench—the same bench that Mabel had sat upon when he was foolish enough to get down on one knee—carved by his own hand from a fallen pine at the edge of the property. The bench was rough-hewn and still had bark attached around the circumference of the seat, but it was wide enough to hold his bulk, and sturdy, with four thick, square legs that measured exactly the right height so that Gardener's thighs were perfectly parallel to the ground when he sat. On any given day, they could find Gardener sitting on his bench, sharpening tools or cleaning off dirt, drawing plans, or charting growth in his logs. He kept meticulous records of how each plant fared over the years, what every strain of rose preferred as far as sun exposure and watering cycles. The logs were private;

he had thought once—an idea too horrible to contemplate for long—that if he died and his notebooks were discovered, not one person would ever understand or appreciate his system.

Gardener grabbed one of his notebooks and a lead pencil from atop the counter that ran the full length of the far wall. From inside a wooden crate, hidden behind a canvas tarp under the counter, Gardener pulled his metal flask. Sitting heavily on the bench, he took a long, slow drink. He didn't like thinking about the girl, Sarah. What he had felt for her, what he had experienced when he was twenty-two, was the closest thing he could imagine to a father's love—with a person, anyway. He felt like a father to his plants, watching them grow and bloom, coming back year after year. If he did his job and cared tenderly enough for his wards, they would thrive; they would grow and make him proud. Gardener's plants were his joy.

He opened his book and made a notation next to his drawing of the rugosa rose. Because he did not know how to write, Gardener had created his own system of notation. He drew raindrops in a square next to a drawing of a plant to note how many minutes of watering for each plant each week. He kept track of the date by the moon's cycles, drawing the phase at the top of each page. His records were not precise by any scientific means, but to Gardener, they made sense. He could look back and reference what type of fertilizer was used if a plant was not faring well. The book had notations for fish bones or composted vegetable matter. He drew a circle for full sunlight, half filled in for partial shade.

There was a knock at the door of his shed. Gardener put the cap back on his flask and hid it quickly under the canvas flap. Rarely did anyone come looking for him out here. Maybe the cook, occasionally, with the day's scraps, or the butler, if he had heard a request from the Hunts. But mainly, he was left to himself, to draw in his notebooks, to take a drink.

"Hello? Gardener?" an authoritative voice yelled.

Mr. Hunt. Gardener cleared his throat and stood. "Ya?"

"Gardener, I would like a word with you."

Gardener swung the door open, nearly smacking Mr. Hunt in the face as he hobbled back on his crutches. "Sorry," Gardener muttered.

"You might warn a man," Mr. Hunt barked and pointed to the entrance with a crutch. "May I?" he asked.

Gardener moved aside without a word. Mr. Hunt plopped himself down and leaned his crutches against the workbench. Gardener stayed near the open door and eyed his boss. This was new.

Mr. Hunt took a big sniff of the air and pulled the corners of his mouth down. "Working hard?"

"Ya."

Mr. Hunt nodded, probably waiting for a "sir" on the end, but Gardener didn't give in, though he knew the conversation would go easier if he did. Mr. Hunt looked like he was considering a reprimand but had decided to let it pass. "What are you working on?" he asked.

Gardener nodded an unspoken thank you. "My records."

"Records?"

"Growth records, notes." Gardener nodded to the notebook lying on the floor at Mr. Hunt's feet.

"Let me see."

Gardener thought Mr. Hunt would pick the notebook up, but he sat, staring at Gardener. *Good lord*, Gardener realized. *He's waiting for me to pick it up and hand it to him.* Gardener wouldn't do it. He turned his head and looked out the door at the autumn sunsets hanging over the trellis. The flower was at its peak this week. It would not get brighter or cleaner than it was right now. Gardener felt the sudden desire to know how to paint. He wished he could capture that yellow rose's clarity and perfection.

"Let me see," Mr. Hunt repeated insistently.

Gardener sighed. He crossed the distance between them in four steps and bent to pick up the notebook. He raised his face to Mr. Hunt's as he handed the man his records, knowing that it wouldn't matter, that Mr. Hunt wouldn't understand his system.

Mr. Hunt smirked. "Is that whiskey I smell?"

Gardener straightened, blurting out, "Sir?" before he could think about it.

Mr. Hunt smirked. "Have you had a little nip this morning, Gardener?"

Gardener averted his gaze.

"I know whiskey when I smell it."

The heavy perfume of the rose garden swamped the room, as if the winds had shifted, carrying all the olfactory gifts of the garden to this one central spot. Gardener wondered how Mr. Hunt could smell whiskey over the thick scent of flowers. There was no way to answer the man. Gardener wondered if, after all these years, after his labor and meticulous care, he was to be fired.

Mr. Hunt fingered the notebook and flipped it open, scanning the pages. He chuckled at the drawings and markings. Mr. Hunt looked up and searched Gardener's face, but Gardener couldn't hold his gaze. Mr. Hunt threw the notebook on the countertop.

"Whiskey," he said again.

Gardener caught Mr. Hunt's eye. Fine. He'd take his punishment. He would take his notebooks and his knowledge, and he'd find another cottage to appreciate his skills, what he had learned. He had heard the guests—from a distance—at the parties. They had commented on his work, always complimenting Mrs. Hunt for her taste, as if she had anything to do with it. Someone would want him.

"I hope you have got some for me." Mr. Hunt raised his voice and clapped his hands together.

Gardener's eyes grew wide a fraction before he realized what Mr. Hunt wanted.

"So?" Alistair said. "Do I have to ask again?"

"No," Gardener said and reached past Mr. Hunt and behind the canvas, removing the flask. He handed it to Mr. Hunt.

"Do you not have a glass?" Mr. Hunt asked jovially.

Gardener looked around and rifled through his shelves, finally coming up with a jam jar in which he kept a book of matches. He grabbed a rag from a stack and wiped the insides clean.

"I would prefer if you use water," Mr. Hunt suggested. "You do have water here?"

Gardener nodded and stepped outside with the glass. Through the small window of the shed, Mr. Hunt watched him bend to the hose and spray. Gardener finished rinsing the jar and climbed back into the shed, wiping the vessel once again, pouring in a good slog of whiskey when it was dry.

Mr. Hunt held the glass up. "To your roses," he said and slung the liquid back into his throat. "Ugh," he grimaced, wiping his mouth. "What is this rotgut?"

Gardener smiled. "A friend got a still."

"How do you drink this? I will have to get you some decent whiskey, so you will know at least once in your life what a quality drink tastes like." He held his glass out for another shot. "But, since this is what we have now… Can you believe that Maine still has those silly prohibition laws on the books up here, that what we are doing is illegal? You know groups are working to make it a dry country? Ridiculous. First, it is the automobile, then it is a fresh round of laws against liquor. Good to know you have another source if things go truly south."

Gardener poured. He knew about those laws, had lived in Maine his whole life. He was born shortly after the laws were created in the fifties, though they had never really been taken seriously by anyone he knew other than his devoutly Catholic grandparents. Uncles and neighbors stumbled out of Portland's illegal, yet popular, saloons named The Whistling Betty or McGlinchy's.

"Drink with me this time," Mr. Hunt insisted.

Gardener raised the flask to his mouth and took a drink.

"Great God, you must have an iron stomach." Mr. Hunt's cheeks glowed red, and his voice grew excited. "I have not had hooch like this since I was a boy. What fun," he said. "Makes me feel like a kid, hiding out in a shack like this, out back in the gardens. This is what we would do, you know, as kids—go to a friend's house, usually Freddy Gentry's, and head to the tool shed. We would steal some liquor from his parents' cabinet. We would take about half a bottle, then fill the rest with water so it did not look like any was gone. What a riot. The parents never knew. I have to say, though, I do not think my kids were ever bright enough to pull off something like that. Not adventurous enough, anyway, if they were smart. Rupert never had a rebellious bone in his body. Wanted to study all the time. I bet you were not like that. Well, I can see that, with your hiding of the whiskey and your chicken scratch. No studying for you. Who knows what you are up to…?" Mr. Hunt took a breath and held out his glass for more.

Gardener poured.

"We did not get this kind of rot gut from Freddy's parents. No, they had the good stuff. That is where I learned the difference. The hooch came from the cook. Freddy's family cook was a drunk if I ever saw one. What a riot that man was—he was what the Indians called a *berdache*. Never seen such a thing in my life. Could not tell by looking at him what he was, man or woman. He swished around the kitchen with these big, long lashes, but boy, could he cook. Guess that is why they kept him, even if he was womanly. Drunk every night, too, but up every morning at five, so nobody cared. We kids would ask him for the hooch, and he would give it up—of course, he sold it to us. Probably made a profit now that I think of it."

Gardener took another drink and studied Mr. Hunt's face. He was animated and loud, clearly having fun. What was the man getting at? Why was he here? Was he simply ribbing at him before the axe fell?

"Ever know a man like that, Gardener, one of those *berdaches*?"

"Nah."

"Funny to watch, funny to watch."

When Mr. Hunt stopped talking, they could hear the light twitter of robins and buzzing of the hummingbirds out in the garden. Gardener stood with his head hung, looking at his feet, waiting.

"Well, let us get to it," Mr. Hunt finally said. Gardener looked up at his boss. The red of his cheeks had faded, but his nose was now aglow, like a clown. The man's eyes had the soft, foggy gaze of inebriation, though his words did not slur. "Remember the day my horse fell?" Mr. Hunt patted his leg.

"Yah," Gardener replied. Of course, he remembered.

"You shut that gate; did you not?"

"The gate?"

"When Willie and I went for a ride. We left the gate open. When we came back, it was shut."

Gardener set the flask on the counter and walked to the door. He probably had shut the gate—if it was open, that is what he would have done. Sure. Mr. Hunt was looking for someone to blame. Why not say 'yes,' even if he did not exactly remember? What would it cost him? Better than having to find a new place to work. He had it good on Serabelle, had his own domain that he controlled. And soon, he would have a pretty little wife.

"I 'spose so," Gardener finally said.

"I thought as much," Mr. Hunt said. "Now tell me you are sorry, and we will have another drink to celebrate."

"Sorry," Gardener said, giving up all pride.

"You should be. Cost me a couple of weeks in bed." Mr. Hunt hopped back over to the bench but didn't sit down. He grabbed the flask and poured another drink, handing the whiskey back to Gardener. "Salute," he said and drank the whiskey down. "Gets easier as you go," he said with a laugh. "Now, I feel better. How about you? I guess you will know that if I leave the gate open, in the future, you will mind your own business. Right?"

"Right," Gardener said and took a drink.

"Well, we should do this again sometime. I will bring the good stuff." Mr. Hunt picked up his other crutch and stepped out of the shed without another glance at his servant. He strode to the main house, back to his good liquor and his fine furnishings.

Chapter 14
The Doll

The Ainsworth-Hunts spent the evening in the parlor playing whist, but Rupert was jumpy the whole time, hoping his father would not guess his intentions. If this was what duplicity felt like, Rupert doubted he was cut out for deception. Despite his nervousness, however, he couldn't deny a trace of power was also involved, a feeling that energized him. He couldn't remember the last time a jolt had run through his limbs this way—perhaps in his solo court case, right before he was to make an opening argument. He came through that well enough, if not brilliantly (in fact, he soon decided that litigation was not his strong suit).

"You are staying longer than I expected you to, dear," his mother commented. "Not that I mind. It is quite wonderful to have my son around." Julia did not mention Melinda, though the two ladies cohabitated easily enough. No one took exception.

After the ladies retired, Rupert and Alistair stayed in the parlor, Rupert fiddling with his father's pewter chess pieces, Alistair clipping the ends of two cigars, then handing one to his son. They raised their glasses of brandy in a silent salute, to one another, to themselves, to their lives—to nothing at all. Rupert fiddled with the cigar, letting it go out after one puff. He was not a connoisseur of such things, but he had learned to fake it. He had had to hide his revulsion in many a salon, learning early on that plenty of business deals were made over the clear glass of a snifter behind a wall of cigar smoke.

Rupert took a sip and lounged across the chaise, fingering the dark velvet. The room was toasty warm from the fire that a servant had started. Rupert thought it was a bit early for the fireplace, but his mother had been cold and had ordered a young maid to bring wood in. She had dropped a piece of wood on the Persian rug, squealing as the log hit her toe. Mrs. Hunt scolded the maid with a threatening voice: "That better not have dented the parquet." The girl tried in vain three or four times to light the fire, her face blanching further with each failure. With amusement, Rupert watched the freckled girl's shaking hands and nervous twitches until he noticed how his father watched the maid. The way his mother scowled. Finally, the old second butler had been called to light the fire.

Rupert wiggled his toes and considered removing his tight shoes to toast his feet. He twirled the cigar and stared at the candles flickering on the chandelier above.

"Tomorrow, then, if you are not leaving, let us try to make it to the croquet field," Alistair said. "Unless, of course, you have another meeting."

"I do not," Rupert said hesitantly.

"I can see you are champing at the bit to join me," Alistair teased. He walked in slow circles around the parlor, trying out his unsteady gait without the crutches. "It is the least you can do to join your old man in a game. After all, I have been through quite a trial, what with the horse taking a fall."

"I understand."

"I finally figured out what happened, by the way," Alistair said. "In case you are wondering how such a skilled horseman could allow that to happen."

"I *was* wondering," Rupert said. He had not been wondering.

"It was the gardener's fault. He admitted as much. He closed the gate. Fierce was planning to trot right through an open gate. That was the way we left it. You expect on your own property to have things remain as you leave them. But, as you can see, we have servants you cannot rely on. That idiotic gardener shut the gate behind us. If I did not know better, I would say he did it on purpose, to foil me, the big, dumb oaf."

"I remember him as such," Rupert said offhandedly.

The fire threw bursts of light across the room, dancing with the chandelier's light. They had lit no wall sconces in the room this evening, as Julia found the fireplace and chandelier sufficient. Rupert thought maybe, for once, his mother was right.

"If we must, Father, I will go play croquet tomorrow," Rupert said, though it was no secret he found croquet, like most sports, to be a silly waste of time: what was the attraction in following a bright red ball across the grass? As if anything promising could come of the game. As if the world would change—in any way—depending on who won or lost.

"You could show a little enthusiasm," Alistair said, staggering to the sidebar and pouring himself another drink from the crystal decanter. "Just pretend, for Christ's sake, that you care about your old man."

"That is uncalled for," Rupert mumbled.

"What? When have you ever wanted to do something with me? When have you ever taken an interest in the things I care about?"

"Me?" Rupert sat up. "When have you cared one lick about what I do?"

Alistair spun from the bar. "You do nothing but work, Rupert."

Mr. Wilson came to the parlor door, called by their raised voices.

"And when was the last time you asked me about my work?" Rupert continued, despite the presence of the old man.

"What is there to ask? You file some papers and go fight it out with other lawyers. You do not even ever go to trial, do you?" Alistair sneered. "At least *that* would be exciting."

"Nice to know what you think of me," Rupert said and slammed his glass on the side table. He stood and threw his cigar into the fire.

"Stop being so dramatic. You would benefit from an activity or two— get your head out of all that legal mumbo jumbo. Have some fun, for Christ's sake. Go out and live a little." Alistair raised his glass and did a faulty pirouette on his good foot, landing halfway around in a wobble that almost threw him off balance. "Whoa," he said. "Look at that. I almost fell turning around in a circle." He set his glass down and walked over to his son. "When is the last time you turned around in a circle, Rupert? Really. Try it. Take a couple of spins and see how you feel. Might loosen you up a little."

Rupert scoffed. "I am not going to spin, Father."

"One little circle."

"I do not want to."

Alistair put his hands on his son's shoulders and leaned close to his face. "For me, Rupert, spin around. One time."

"Let go, Father. I will not spin around in a circle for no reason."

Alistair sighed. "Then, because I am asking you to."

"That's no reason." His father looked so sad that Rupert almost relented.

Alistair dropped his hands and walked over to pick up his drink. He poured the liquid up to the brim and then attempted to pick up his crutches with one hand, but they clattered to the floor. "Mr. Wilson," he yelled. "Mr. Wilson!"

The old man stepped silently into the room and took the glass from Mr. Hunt's hand, bending to retrieve the crutches while holding the drink aloft. "Sir, can I carry your beverage to your room?"

"See that, Rupert?" Alistair said, his back to his son. "Here is a man who is trying to help me. He is not even family." Alistair stopped before he reached the door. "Mr. Wilson," he said. "Spin around in a circle."

The second butler spun on his heel without hesitation, landing perfectly where he had started.

"How did that feel, butler?"

"Quite good, sir."

"See, Rupert? See?" Alistair said, his back still to his son.

✦   ✦   ✦

After Alistair was carried off to his room, Rupert sat in the parlor, quietly letting the candles burn out overhead. He watched the cream-colored wax puddle in trays under the candles, building up in steep piles until the wicks reached their ends. Within five minutes of each other, all eight candles sputtered out. Not one drip poured past the trays to the carpet below. Rupert had watched a trickle that seemed like it might spill over the edge, but the wax hardened into a tear under the lip. Not a speck let go. That was some engineering, Rupert thought. The man who designed this chandelier. To know your subject in that manner was mastery.

Rupert believed he was an expert in his craft, yet received little recognition. To his great satisfaction, he had settled every case he had ever taken on. He never had to go to trial after that first unsatisfactory attempt, never felt that he had lost. He had gotten his clients the maximum of what they could hope for, financially, anyway. So, a handful of people were grateful to him, but that was it. He would never achieve notoriety this way. Maybe his father was right: perhaps he should take his cases to trial, make a name for himself.

The papers loved a good, scandalous case. Like the last client he had helped: a woman whose husband had been killed by a construction beam. The man was a fruit vendor. He had been carting his load of peaches down a busy street when the board swung wide on its winch and clobbered the man—his head ricocheted like a tetherball. The peaches were saved, but he was not. The woman was left with three small children.

Rupert was not in the habit of taking on poor clients—he always insisted on a thirty percent down payment—but the woman was a distant cousin to his wife. Melinda had insisted, and the case was a sure win. The construction crew had been hired by a wealthy merchant who traded in imported marble, and there had been no lack of eyewitnesses. If the woman had not been intelligent enough (or lucky enough) to track down a decent lawyer, she certainly would have been swindled out of her settlement. But with Rupert's help, she was looking at a tidy sum. In fact, she would be much better off now that her street vendor husband was dead.

He should have told his father about that case and the good he created by purely doing his job. That was exciting. He had had to meet with the merchant and his lawyers—some of the best in the city—and though he was not in court, he had to argue for his client. Rupert stood uneasily, woozy from the bit of alcohol he had ingested. Alistair would never know this, because he didn't ask. His father would interrogate any old stranger—

household staff, party guests—but when it came to his own son, Alistair had absolutely no interest.

Rupert closed the damper on the fireplace and rang the bell for the butler.

"Yes, sir?"

"I will not be needing you for the rest of the evening. I am putting the fire out, so you can go to bed."

"Sir, I do not sleep. I am available in case someone needs me during the night."

"You do not sleep?"

"At night, sir. I sleep during the day."

When Rupert was a child, there was no night butler, as far as he could remember. Or maybe he was asleep before the first butler retired. He had seen this man around before when he came to visit, but it was hard to keep track of all the comings and goings at the cottage. "How long have you been at Serabelle?"

"Sir, over ten years now."

"Did someone else do your job before you?"

"I do not believe so, sir."

Rupert felt justified that he was right, that he was not completely daft. "Where will you be? In case I need you?"

"Simply ring the bell, and I shall appear."

Rupert sighed in frustration. "That is not what I asked."

"I will most likely be in the kitchen, sir."

"Most likely?"

"I will be in the kitchen, sir. Unless someone calls for me."

"Fine. See that you stay there."

Mr. Wilson hesitated too long for Rupert's taste before answering, "Yes, sir."

Rupert followed the butler into the hallway and watched until he disappeared into the dining room. Rupert tiptoed to the foot of the stairs and listened for any sign of activity. All was quiet. He moved past the stairway into the hall that led to his father's recovery room. He heard his father's heavy snore behind a far door. The man was like an animal. Rupert had often wondered how he could be related to such a feral little man. Rupert was tall like his maternal uncles, if a bit pudgier. Julia's side of the family was light-complexioned, and both Rupert and his sister carried their Anglo-Saxon genes. Rupert, though, had Alistair's dark, wavy hair.

The house made creaking and moaning sounds as Rupert walked the halls. He had never loved Serabelle, had always found the place too cold, devoid of life. His house in New York was a five-bedroom brownstone, large and well-appointed but not too large for him and Melinda. Unlike this sprawling cottage, it would be impossible to get lost. When Rupert was a child at Serabelle, he would play up in the east wing, throwing items out the window of the guest quarters, trying to see whether he could smash them on the rocks below: watermelons, books, vases, and plates. He kept a log of what happened to each item, having just learned how to write.

Rupert laughed, remembering when he stole his sister's favorite doll and threw it on the rocks. He had rushed down to see how the blond porcelain head had fared—from the window, it had appeared that it had smashed into pieces—but when he arrived on the shore, the doll was gone. The tide was extremely low, and Rupert could not imagine a wave coming up so quickly, so high. He walked the shoreline, jumping from rock to rock, searching for some sign of the doll. Gulls screeched over the tops of wet rocks, slimy with seaweed, crunchy with barnacles. It must have been a mighty wave, he thought.

His sister had wailed that night, looking for her doll, but he had not confessed—he was not the type to have a guilty conscience. But he had not slept either, thinking of the doll—not because he felt bad for his sister, but worrying that another, even bigger wave might come out of nowhere and snatch him off the rocks, off the lawn, even out of his bed.

The next day, like some sort of miracle (or nightmare), the doll had turned up on his sister's bed, her head mostly glued back together, part of her scalp covered over with a cloth. She looked like a diseased little girl, with sections of her hair missing and cracks on her face. Someone had tried to scrub her clean, painting over the scuff marks, but she still bore the signs of one who had been through an ordeal. Rupert screamed when he saw the doll sitting there, wide-eyed and accusatory. How had it been resurrected?

Had the wave returned and deposited the doll in his sister's room? These were the first thoughts of seven-year-old Rupert.

He clearly recalled trying to make sense of its appearance. He didn't remember when he figured out that a human had taken the doll, but it must not have been long after that day. Rupert wondered now if it had been his father who had foiled his experiment, who had ruined his fun—if Alistair had been against him even then.

Rupert wandered up and down the halls, from darkness to light—the wall sconces here were lit. He moved upstairs, past his mother's room, stepping into his anteroom to change into his slippers. He heard his wife's shallow breathing in the bedchamber, though her lamp was still illuminated. Rupert slipped back out and tiptoed through the halls, taking in the dank smell of the walls. A house like Serabelle never dried; it was too close to the ocean. The cottage had taken on the characteristics of a boat, with swelling floors and salt-worn walls. Though Manhattan, where he lived now, was technically an island, it lacked the briny, grimy, oceany smell that Acadia imbued in its residences.

Rupert took his time winding down the long front staircase, listening for any other movement, before making his way to the library. He stepped inside the dark room and locked the door behind him. Was he really going to do this? His heart pounded inside his chest. It certainly was thrilling. No one would expect that he was capable of such a thing. Even his wife, he knew, might wager that Rupert lacked the guts to pull off a heist.

He pulled the key from the desk drawer, noting with his fingertips exactly where it had been placed and which direction the tines were facing. He had not lit a lamp and could barely see what he was doing, but he made out the edge of the glass on the hutch. Quietly lowering the wooden blinds behind him for privacy's sake, he ran his fingers over the shellacked door and found the keyhole. Rupert held his breath as he fit the key into the lock. It clicked open, and he swung the door wide. He squinted, trying to read the trays, remembering that the emerald was on the second shelf, in the third or fourth tray, but he wasn't positive. He pulled out a stack. The wood felt slick against his sweaty palms. Rupert set the trays on the desk blotter, knocking over a crock of quills with his elbow. He stood stock still.

To him, the noise had sounded as deafening as the peal of a church bell. He waited for the sound of footsteps outside the door. None. Rupert patted his hands around the desk, soft feathers tickling his fingertips.

Rupert's eyes began to adjust to the darkness as he finished placing the feathers back in their holder, but he would need more light to find the emerald. He cursed his poor planning and felt along the edge of the desk for a carton of matches. As suspected, a stack lay next to the cigar box in the front. Rupert struck a match on the flint and searched the desk for a lamp or a candle. He let the match burn almost to his fingertips before dowsing. It would be difficult to search the gems this way. Last night, they had carried in an oil lamp. Had he returned it to the mantle? Rupert reached for another match and held it high, crossing the room slowly until he spied the lamp. On the third match, he lit the wick and carried the light back to the desk.

If he were privy to what Rupert was up to, Alistair would have mocked his ineptitude in planning the theft. Rupert also realized that of all people, his father would approve of his adventuresome spirit in taking on this challenge. What requital Rupert would feel in deceiving Alistair, the man who had done nothing but whine about his disappointing son. He had tried to be interested in the rocks. When he was young, Rupert asked his father questions about how the rocks were formed, about chemistry and color, and his father answered him. Still, he also wanted Rupert to go outside and dig on their various outings, not understanding his son's resistance to the filth. Rupert wanted facts and theories. He considered himself a naturally curious person, but somehow, over the years, he found himself despising geology, even gemology, mainly because his father enjoyed it.

Rupert had to admit that his father had done a good job with the care he took in sorting, in labeling. It was too bad they had not seen eye to eye in this realm, at least. Rupert intuited that his father would not leave the gems to him in his will. Alistair was the type of man to will the collection to a charity or some such out of spite.

In the third tray, Rupert found the emerald. He held it up to the lamp once more and turned the stone in the light. The green was as rich and dark as the best-kept lawn in the afternoon haze of August and as brilliant as a full moon over the ocean. Yes, this was the stone. Rupert slipped it into his pocket and put the stacks back together. His palms were no longer damp, and his heart had calmed to an almost regular pace. He replaced the trays in the cabinet, straightening them into a perfect row. He shut the door with a click, placed the key back in the desk drawer and carried the lamp to the mantle, pocketing the burnt match sticks before he blew out the flame.

Rupert listened again for any sign of life in the hallway before carefully unlocking the door. He felt for the gem once more in his pocket. Forrest was right: it felt good. This was the bravest thing he had ever done. He straightened his lapel and took one last look around in the dark.

Chapter 15
Shenanigans

Five days after the gala, most of the household had returned to normal. Maids and cooks had washed and stowed away the party finery, stable boys had cleaned up visiting horses' manure, and cars were re-washed and tuned.

In the yellow house, dark pine floorboards of the spare bedroom creaked loudly as the men rose from their regular Thursday night card game to grab a beverage or to use the outdoor privy. The cook's bedroom was directly under the men's game room, so this first week after the gala, Beverly reminded them to tread lightly as Cook was still sleeping off her weeks of toil.

"Ante up," Gardener barked at the smallest of the stable boys. Theo had only come to a couple of poker nights, intimidated by the older, more experienced staff. The twenty-year-old pip-squeak of a boy was an expert rider—in fact, he had been in training as a jockey before his parents lost their fortune in a poorly judged business venture. Theo was still uncomfortable around the rough and uncouth estate staff. Willie had taken pity on him, though, and encouraged him to come play poker with the rest of the men.

"Hold your horses," Theo said, staring hard at his hand.

Gardener looked around at the other men, raising his eyebrows at the young man's audacity. He tilted his chair back on two legs and tapped at the table, folding his cards into his palm. "Horses are your game, not mine. Make a move."

The men around the table chuckled.

"Fine," Theo threw in his penny.

Gardener took a drink from a flask and wiped his lips with the back of his hand. They played out a couple of hands, the first going to Josiah, the second to a butler from a neighboring cottage, and the third to Gardener, who gave a loud "whoop" as he raked the change toward him.

"Keep it down, Gardener, or Cook will have your head," Josiah reminded.

"Cook can kiss my ass."

"Very nice," Theo muttered.

"What did you say?" Gardener asked.

Theo looked to see if anyone would answer for him. "That's awfully ungrateful of you," he finally said, his voice as small as his frame, "after everything Cook does."

"You little—" Gardener put his hands flat on the table.

"Have some respect," Theo said.

"I'll show you respect," Gardener growled and leaped across the table, overturning his chair with a loud bang. The rest of the chairs scraped back, and there was a scuffle as Gardener grabbed Theo's shirt, managing to gather skin in the process. Josiah lunged at Gardener, trying to pin his arms, but the big redhead shook him off.

"Let go," Theo cried.

Willie stepped in front of Gardener, smacking his mammoth hands with a chopping motion.

"Stay out of it, Willie," Gardener yelled.

Willie, wide-eyed, kept chopping. "Let him go."

Josiah tried once again to restrain Gardener. Downstairs, the women heard the commotion and stood waiting, ready to move should the fighting continue. From the main house, Mr. Wilson watched shadows in the third-story window. There were days when he felt he was living a spirit's existence, where he merely watched what was happening in the material world. Nights, alone in the house, he would bring an occasional glass of milk to Mrs. Hunt and whiskey after whiskey to Mr. Hunt, but he had no other human contact. He watched the scene in the game room as one would watch a play. Shadow theater, with small silhouettes attacked by a larger shadow. The big and powerful picking on the defenseless young. No wonder the youngster did not like to join in the card games. Mr. Wilson often saw Theo treading across to the barn by himself in the evenings, a book tucked under his arm.

"Gardener, stop bullying everyone!" Willie cried.

Gardener released his grip on Theo and turned toward Willie. He sized up the boy, nearly as small as the jockey. Willie was young and fresh-faced, a darkie to whom he and everyone else at the cottage had taken a shine, not a high hat who fell on hard times like the other boy. "What do you care?"

"You scare people. It's not right," Willie said.

"Who cares what this milksop thinks?" Gardener asked, gesturing to Theo. "He don't belong here anyway."

"You don't just scare Theo," Willie shot out. "You scare everyone, especially the women."

"I scare the women?"

"Yes," Willie said, unblinking.

Gardener sat down in one of the upright chairs. Theo ran to the door, though he stayed to listen, fascinated that Willie had the same thoughts as he did. The other men righted the chairs and cleaned the spilled cards and beer. In the kitchen downstairs, the women went back to cleaning dishes. Gardener reached for his flask and took another swig. "To hell with it," he said. "Let's play cards."

Willie swallowed hard and took a breath. "I want to finish talking about this, Gardener."

"Nothing to talk about, boy."

Willie winced at 'boy' but continued bravely on. "There is."

Gardener looked over at Willie, shaking his head. "I said—"

"I know what you said, but I want to finish the conversation about the women."

"Drop it, Willie," Josiah said.

"No." Willie lowered his voice to make sure the women couldn't hear. "Gardener, we can talk about this alone if you want, but I hear you're going to marry Mabel, and personally, I don't think…"

"That's enough!" Gardener slammed his hands on the table.

Theo jumped, but Willie didn't flinch. He set his shoulders and lifted his jaw. The rest of the men sat open-mouthed.

"Leave it alone, Willie," Josiah repeated.

Willie exhaled through his nose like one of his horses, a short whinny. "Mabel is scared of you."

In a flash, Gardener grabbed Willie by the collar and shuffled him out the door, past Theo, and into the hallway. In the main house, Mr. Wilson lost track of what was happening. He had expected the fight to come to blows, suspected that it was Gardener causing all the trouble. He could tell his silhouette not simply by his size (after all, Josiah was a big man, too) but by his sloping nose that flipped up like a shoehorn at the end.

"You better mind your own business." Gardener tightened his grip until he was almost holding Willie off the floor. He spoke in a soft hiss, close to Willie's left ear. "You think the *women* are scared of me? Take a lesson. You don't want me on your bad side, Willie. I'll make you wish you never even looked at me, let alone had the nerve to say my bride's name."

Willie smelled the liquor through Gardener's skin, seeping out through his pores.

"I'm gonna put you on those stairs now, Willie. And you even think about turning around to look at me, you're going flying. I don't ever want to catch you looking at me or at Mabel. Don't try to talk to her, or get any other kind of ideas, neither. Mind your own damn business, Willie, or I'll have you strung up. Mabel ain't no part of your business." Gardener placed Willie on the first step and released his grip. "Get moving," he said.

Willie stepped slowly down, fighting the temptation to look back. There was a divide even here on this cottage, where no one had mentioned the color of his skin all summer and where he had felt safe (if not completely accepted). An "otherness" to Willie that Gardener had called out. Would he have threatened to "string up" any of the white stable boys?

"Move it," Gardener hissed and touched his boot to Willie's back. "Now."

In the room behind him, Willie knew they were all listening, holding their breath. If he caved in, no one would have a hope of ever standing up to Gardener, no one but Josiah. And his pride flared up over the stringing-up comment. Willie didn't budge. He managed to crank his neck halfway around when he felt the blow. The kick lifted his whole body like a kite in the breeze before he tumbled down the narrow stairway. His heel caught on the third step as he descended, causing his lanky body to flip head over heels down the remaining treads until he settled with a thud on the landing. At the top of the stairs, Gardener stood in the shadows until Willie moved again; then, he stepped back into the card room.

"Willie will not be joining us for the rest'a the evening," he said as he sat down.

Theo ran from the room.

One by one, the staff slowly got up from the table, shaking their heads at Gardener. From the main house, Mr. Wilson watched the party disperse. It was an early one tonight. Now, he feared, there might be trouble elsewhere on the property. The good thing about the card room was it kept all the men in one place, where he could keep an eye on them. On nights like tonight, when the card games did not last, he might find one of them creeping into the house or causing a ruckus in the stables. Mr. Wilson felt responsible for the cottage in the nighttime. He did not want any shenanigans.

On the landing, Theo helped Willie to his feet. Rebecca had rushed from the kitchen when she heard the tumble. She screamed and stood frozen on the stairs. Beverly pushed her way past Rebecca and held Willie's face in her hands. Without hesitation, Willie noted, at touching his tight, foreign hair. She scanned his head and cheeks for bruises, turning him this way and that, nodding her head at the scrapes along his forearms, the lump already forming on his brow.

"What kind 'a nonsense are you all up to this evening?" she asked the boys. "Can we not have a peaceful night?"

"It was Gardener," Theo protested.

Rebecca clucked from her position below, and Beverly shot glances back and forth from her to the young men. "Now, no sense pointing fingers, Theo."

"But he—"

"You heard me," Beverly said and turned to Willie. "Get on down to the kitchen, and we'll deal with your cuts. Rebecca, move."

❖   ❖   ❖

White-painted clapboard surrounded the walls of Eden Town Hall. Pine floors squeaked as women trod over them. The entire building was filled with the warm, pleasant odor of moist wood. Benches made of oak, tables filled with papers and notices—all the product of trees, of pulp. The whole of New England seemed to Mabel to be full of the smells of wood and sea: birch and maple, fish and kelp, and salty air. And on top of that smell in the hall rose the heat and must of dozens of women, powdery and stale simultaneously.

Mabel nodded shyly as she accepted another pamphlet from the hand of a smiling, white-clad woman. "Welcome," the woman said, no trace of the strange northern accent. "Go ahead and take a seat. The meeting will start soon."

Toward the front of the hall where a dais, a rickety-looking set of boards slapped together, had been set up, a couple of maids Mabel recognized from a neighboring estate were seated close together, laughing anxiously. One of them smiled at Mabel, who sat near the back. Would she get in trouble for being here?

A nervous buzz rose above the growing crowd of women as maids and cooks, laundrywomen and schoolteachers filled the benches. The day was cloudy; a hazy beam of the day's waning light streamed through the front doors, though much of the light was blocked by white paper shades set into the north wall. Mabel felt the impulse to wander over and pull up the shade, but perhaps the organizers didn't want people looking in. She shifted in her seat, hoping her condition was not immediately obvious.

The cacophony crested and hushed as the woman from Mabel's buggy ride from Bangor walked to the dais. A polite applause followed her, but the woman waved away the accolade.

"Come now," she said. "Let us wait to applaud until our actions have produced results."

The doors behind them shut with a bang, though no one turned around, their attention caught by the woman at the front. Her stature was stiff and confident, but not haughty.

"Some of you know who I am," the woman continued, "but not all of you. I am Cora Crawford, and I am from Philadelphia. Let me say how proud I am of all of you for coming out tonight. It takes real courage to stand up for yourself. This is a grand first step. But you all know it does not stop here. It starts here. Tonight, we will to arm you with knowledge, but we will also listen to what you have to say.

"When was the last time someone asked your opinion on something other than what to have for supper? When was the last time you were consulted regarding your knowledge of healing, of growing, of household accounts? I guarantee that many of you here have been overlooked, overshadowed, and ignored by brothers, husbands, or employers who likely knew less than you did."

"Amen," someone shouted from the back.

"That is right," Cora Crawford said. "And the time has come for that to stop. For women, who are nearly half of the population, to stand up and be counted as citizens of this country!"

Mabel watched the faces of the surrounding women, amazed at what she was hearing. Did all these women feel the way she did? Despite the standard of decorum on Serabelle, were there other maids on Mt. Desert Isle who wanted more? Did the women in this room all want to count for something? Looking around at nodding heads, hearing murmured assents, Mabel knew she was not alone.

Cora spoke for half an hour and then opened the floor to questions, which turned out to be affirmations and stories about how the women had been wronged in their jobs, lives, and families.

"So, what can we do with these feelings?" Cora asked. "Where can we move this anger and resentment?" She did not give anyone time to answer. "I will tell you where. Towards helping change legislation. Voteless persons cannot choose representatives to make laws for them. A vote is a weapon; without it, a woman is defenseless, exploited, and handicapped. The vote is an instrument for getting the kind of government you want. I repeat, women without votes are handicapped before the law and politically. It is time for us to let our voices be heard!"

With this last statement, a cheer rose from the small crowd of women.

"Tonight, the hour is late," Cora went on, "and we are less than fifty in number. But I can tell you that I have spent the last few months, as have many others, up and down the states of New England. Mothers, daughters, sisters, and cousins are ready to rise up and demand that they be counted. As many of you know, nearly ten thousand of us marched on Washington, D.C., this spring, and we will not let that momentum be wasted. We will march again! We will not give up until we have the right to vote."

Mabel rose with the rest of the women in the room, nodding and smiling, awaiting instructions. What came next, Cora explained, was recruiting, then more meetings, more marches, then petitioning. There were women in place for that last step, but they needed numbers for marching, for making the face of suffrage known. Mabel wondered if she could do any of that, considering her fragile state, both in body and position. But she thought she might try.

As the meeting broke up, there were shouts outside on the steps. The hall doors were thrown open to find another group of women with pamphlets of their own and hand-lettered signs saying: "Petticoat Rule" and "We do not need the Vote." The two groups met on the steps of the Town Hall, the charge out the door led by the woman from Philadelphia. Mabel hung back inside, recognizing several women from the Hunts' party in the opposition group.

Voices were raised in fury as the two sides addressed each other. "Go home!" some anti-suffrage women chanted, and "Do not put us at risk." Though the crowd with the two groups combined could not have numbered more than eighty, still, the constable arrived with deputized men on horses, billy clubs in hand.

"All right, ladies," he announced. "Break it up."

Mabel watched through a window, peering past the blind, afraid she would be seen. Though she had not been forbidden to attend meetings, she knew her participation would be frowned upon. Beverly would say she had caused enough trouble already.

Mentioning several of the ladies' names, the policemen asked them to calm down and be reasonable. Mrs. Bates, one of Mrs. Hunt's acquaintances, stood up front and proud in the anti-suffrage group. "Go on home now," the constable said to both groups.

Mrs. Bates nodded knowingly. "That is exactly what we are saying," she confirmed, though her sign said nothing about voting or staying in the home but was a temperance message: "Liquor equals Alcohol, Alcohol equals Poison. Why drink Poison?"

The protest group seemed to be interested in making both points. Their signs read: "Alcohol is a Food, Rich Food for the Undertaker and the Poor House" and "Women are Too Pure for the Dirty Pool of Politics."

The constable addressed the suffrage group: "Okay, Ms. Crawford, you have said your piece, and we have not stopped you." He knew Cora's name and where she and the other organizers were staying. "It is time you and your friends went on back to the Breakwater Hotel. Best to leave in the morning. We are not looking for any trouble here."

Ms. Crawford smiled knowingly, as if she had been through all this before. Mabel was amazed at how calmly she spoke. "I don't plan to leave right away, I'm afraid. We certainly don't want trouble, however. I'm always happy to meet with any of these ladies in a civilized manner. I would love to explain to them our point of view."

The constable frowned at her. He stepped back and raised his billy club, swinging it around in the air. "Everybody out. Get on back to your homes."

The crowd scurried apart then, and Mabel ran from the hall into the road. She kept her bonnet down and her coat draped over her shoulders. When she dared glance up at the edge of the property, she saw Mrs. Bates looking at her, a question in her eyes. Mabel swallowed hard and hid her face. It was past time to return to Serabelle.

Chapter 16
A Damaged Woman

Willie brushed at a tawny mare's coat with a vengeance that made her whinny. He couldn't believe he had to settle for letting Gardener bully him. After the fight, Willie had stormed around the stables for the next few days, fuming at his inability to stand up to the man. Even Theo had been unable to offer any consolation.

Willie threw down his brush and stepped out of the stall. Outside of the gala preparations, his workload had been lighter since Mr. Hunt's injury; the horses didn't need to be ready at a moment's notice. And neither did Willie. He didn't know how he had managed to escape the wrath of Mr. Hunt when he fell or when the dog died, but he had. The man seemed to truly like him, and for that, Willie was grateful. The stable master had told stories of working for horrific families, men, and women who enjoyed doling out punishment like it was medicine. All in all, the Hunts were not cruel to them; they mostly left the servants to run the household. And the fact that the Hunts were in Boston half of the year was a relief.

The old stable master had a makeshift office in the back—a desk constructed of two sawhorses with a couple of planks on top. Willie stuck his head around the corner. "I'm going to take a walk," he said.

The stable master looked up from the bridle he was repairing. "That right?"

"I need to get out of here," Willie pleaded.

"So, I guess I'll stay here and make sure everything gets done while you're out taking a leisurely stroll." The man was not known for his indulgences.

"I'll finish when I get back. I don't have that much left today," Willie said. "They are all fed. Princess is groomed. I'm almost done brushing Faith. I can finish her this afternoon."

"I didn't know that was how we were doing things now, you telling me the schedule."

"We aren't..." Willie clenched his fists and looked down at the floor. Theo and the other stable boy, George, were down at the far end, baling hay.

"Get back in there an' finish with Faith." The man turned his attention to his broken bridle.

Willie walked back to the stall, leaned on the door, and spoke to the horse. "Looks like we're both trapped here." Faith didn't respond, but she looked him in the eyes and bared her teeth, pulling her great lips back in a silly grin. Willie laughed.

He had to remember how good he had it now, how much Mr. Hunt seemed to like him, how much he enjoyed the horses. Willie's nerves calmed to think back to his life before Serabelle, particularly the early days in Boston when he worked at the general store. Not every customer was as kind as Mr. Hunt. Some refused to let a negro boy pack their groceries. He had heard a woman complain in a whisper, "I will not have my food diseased by a nigger boy."

Willie finished brushing out Faith's coat. It was not so bad, really, to be here, to be carrying out his responsibilities. He was proud to be good at his job. It was only... Mabel did not... Willie pushed thoughts of Mabel to the back of his mind. He got nothing but riled up when he started thinking of her tiny nose, her ruby-colored mouth, and then there was that big lug Gardener and the way he treated her, the way he treated everybody. Willie brushed roughly at Faith until she whinnied again.

"Sorry, girl," he said and finished up. A ride would do them both good.

✦ ✦ ✦

Willie stopped the stable master as he strode by with the repaired bridle. "What is it now, Willie?" the man asked impatiently. "Always something with you young fellas. You're like unbroken fillies."

"I've finished brushing Faith," Willie tried, smarting at the comparison. "And?"

"She's awful frisky. I thought she might like a ride. It's been a while since she's been taken out. Don't want her to forget how to behave."

"Willie, what did I tell you?" The man shook his head. "Finish up your duties, then maybe this afternoon—if Mr. Hunt does not come out—you can take her. Don't make me tell you again to finish."

"Yes, sir." Willie sighed.

✦ ✦ ✦

At lunchtime, Willie foreswore joining the rest of the stable crew in the boss's office, as usual. "I'm going for a walk," he said—a statement rather than a request—without looking at the stable master's face. The man would have to accept it. If he didn't want to sit and eat, the boss could not make him.

Willie swung his arms wide and flapped them up and down his sides, trying to shake the stiffness out of his joints, the ugly thoughts out of his head. A heaviness had fallen over him of late, a darkness he could not slough off. He traced his original steps from last summer, the first time he was on the cottage grounds. A sixteen-year-old Willie walked through the garden and out onto the back lawn. The air was still, stagnant in place, as if he must push it aside like a piece of fabric to move through. He stood on the bluff and took a full breath, but the air felt like a savory pudding sliding down into his lungs. He tasted the salt, could almost imagine that he was breathing in the whole ocean—seaweed, fish, seals, mollusks, and all. That summer, he thought he would be happy if he could spend the rest of his life right there.

Trying to bring back some joy, to remember what he loved about being here, Willie walked out on the bluff where stone steps had been carved into the hillside down to the shore. He knelt and ran his fingers across the cool, smooth basalt, black and sea-worn. He caught his breath when he saw a movement across the rocks. A flash of light fabric, and then she turned, looking up at him. Mabel.

Her bonnet was off and hung from her waist, and her hair was up in a clip, though pieces had fallen around her face, framing her eyes with wispy tendrils. She had removed her shoes and walked barefoot on the rocks with her skirt tucked around her waist so that her legs were showing up past her knees. Willie had never seen a woman—other than his mother—with her hair down and her legs showing, especially not a white woman. His knees trembled, but he forced himself to walk toward the shore, towards her.

Mabel didn't look embarrassed for him to find her this way. She ran her hands up over her head and smoothed down the tendrils, pulling some hair back into the clips on the side of her head. Willie wanted to tell her not to do that—that she looked perfect the way she was, but he found he couldn't speak.

"What are you gaping at?" she finally said.

Willie opened his mouth and a guttural vowel emerged.

Mabel smiled and looked back out at the ocean. "The air is heavy," she said.

Still, Willie couldn't find his voice. Sweat broke out on his forehead and under his thick, tight hair. He felt liquid dripping across his scalp and thought he might faint.

"It's too sticky today. I'm thinking of diving in." Mabel turned to him. "What do you think?"

"No," Willie managed, a little too loudly, almost panicky.

Waves slammed the rocks under their feet. At low tide, you could walk on the pebbled shore below them, but at this hour, a swimmer ran the risk of being crushed against the rocks. "I was joking," she said. "I wouldn't really jump in from here."

Willie's heart began to slow. He laughed at his panic, at his reaction to her presence in this state. His body had never reacted to a woman in this way. Sure, he had fantasies about imaginary women, about what a girl's body might look like, but that woman had always been negro in his dreams. He had once seen a dirty magazine one of the other stable boys brought out at night. But here were Mabel's legs, and they were so real. And here was her neck, little, tiny ears, the backs of her knees. Willie stared. She was so pale.

"My goodness, Willie." Mabel laughed. "You would think I was an apple pie sitting on the window ledge to cool."

"What?" he said, startled.

"And you outside, trying to figure out how you'll get a slice before supper."

Willie felt his face flush as he started to understand her comparison. He peeled his eyes away from her legs.

"Do you not know I am a damaged woman?"

"That's not true."

Mabel held her dress tight against her belly. "Look, Willie. Look at me. I'm not married. Some would call me a disgrace, a trollop—or any other name they could find."

"Don't say that."

She paused a minute, let him settle down. "Willie, take off your shoes."

"What?"

"Off," she commanded.

He did as she wished. Mabel edged toward the front of the rock.

"Don't," Willie looked up nervously from where he stood, rolling up his pant legs.

"Come to the edge with me, Willie."

He cast his shoes aside and followed willingly. Three feet below, the waves slapped and smacked at the shore. He would follow her in if that's what she wanted.

Mabel boldly took his hand in hers, then crouched into a squat. "Let's put our feet in the water," she said. "I want to touch the ocean with my skin.

I want to imagine for a moment it is possible to get out of here, float away like a piece of kelp." She smiled at him. "Like a sea otter."

Willie let out his breath, glad he would not be dying this day. He helped Mabel sit and dangle her feet over the edge, a jolt of pleasure singing through his body as he touched her. She squealed when the cold water hit her feet. Willie sat down next to her and watched glee spread across her face like the glow of a fire.

"Don't marry Gardener," he blurted.

The smile left her face at the mention of his name. "I have to."

Willie looked up to the sky, as if the clouds or the sun could give him the strength to say what he wanted. "No, you don't. It's not the only answer."

Salt air lay thick on their shoulders. Gulls circled overhead, looking for shellfish, their wings disappearing into the white of the clouds, then suddenly outlined when the birds crossed over into a patch of blue.

"I'll marry you," Willie whispered.

Mabel burst out with a laugh and clapped him on the shoulder. "Oh, that's so sweet, Willie. You're a true gentleman."

"I mean it. I will. There must be somewhere that we could be together. If not here, there has got to be somewhere in this world where we could live?" he asked desperately. "I'm strong. I'm smart. I could provide for a baby."

Mabel looked sadly at him. "It's too late for that, Willie. I've already accepted. Beverly's planning the wedding. The Hunts have been informed. It is too late."

Mabel kindly did not add the obvious, that there was no such mythical place where blacks and whites could live together as a married couple.

"It's not too late until you take your vows," he pled. "Gardener doesn't love you."

Mabel's face fell into a blank stare. "That's true, Willie, but Gardener doesn't have to love me. Who knows what he wants, why he's bothering with me? I suppose it makes him feel powerful. I bet he thinks he'll be able to order me around as if I was *his* servant." Mabel kicked her heels lightly against the rock.

"Why do it?"

"I get the feeling, Willie, that no matter what I do or choose in life, it doesn't really make a difference."

He did not know how to answer that.

"I went to a meeting the other night," she confessed. "I had this idea that I could make a change. Then I listened to the speaker, and I learned that change takes time. And that you need many people and probably a lot of power. I don't have any of those things." Mabel stared out at the ocean, breathing deeply. "If I marry Gardener, it's easier for everyone involved. I think Mrs. Hunt was about to fire me before Beverly told her I was marrying Gardener. Everyone sees this as a good solution. The truth is, Willie," Mabel bit her lip, as if figuring out if she should confide any further in Willie. "I've been trying to figure a way off this estate, but I need something else lined up first. I can't get fired with nowhere to go."

Willie looked at the horizon, remembering the feeling he had minutes before, relishing this estate, this view. "Do you not like it here?"

"I'm not sure what I like right now." Tears welled in her eyes, the reality of her situation settling on her. "You're going to think I'm ridiculous, but I actually thought Mr. Hunt would divorce his wife to be with me."

Willie tried not to look shocked. He had suspected that it was Mr. Hunt that had made Mabel pregnant, but had also assumed that she was not a willing participant, that Mr. Hunt had forced himself upon her.

"I know, silly of me," she said.

They sat quietly, Willie trying to align his feelings for Mabel with the knowledge that she had willingly had an affair with a married man.

"I've got to get back to work," she finally said. "Beverly will be looking for me." Mabel stood and patted Willie on the shoulder. "Thank you for trying to cheer me."

"Sure," he said.

"And the proposal. I believe *you* are the nicest person *I* have ever known."

Chapter 17
Literally

Forrest sat at the same table where they had held their last meeting. The bartender looked up in the same manner, then back at his same (Rupert imagined) bar towel. Three men sitting on stools with their backs to the door might have been the same customers; the dim light glowed as before. Rupert felt for a moment that he was in a dream, as if he had never stepped from the bar. He reached into his pocket and felt the emerald. Yes, today was a new day. He was a different man, not scared or timid, or predictable.

Rupert strutted to the table with renewed confidence. He had to show Forrest, this petty thief, who the real man was.

"Do you remember the tennis court at Exeter?" Forrest asked without further greeting.

Rupert settled into the booth, his grin fading to a wary look. "Yes."

"I recall you were assaulted by the ball, hard on the cheek. The sound it made was so loud. Now, tell me, is this an accurate memory, or did I make this up?"

What was he getting at? Rupert sat silent, the blood draining from his face. "I do not know," he answered.

"Did you not get pummeled in the face by the tennis ball?"

"I did once."

"Then the memory is true. Good."

"I do not remember you being there," Rupert barked.

Forrest motioned for the bartender, who appeared in the same sudden manner with the same golden brandy. "So, where is it?" Forrest asked when the bartender had retreated. Rupert reached for his pocket, but Forrest halted him. "Not here," he said. "I merely wanted to know if you had it on you."

Rupert felt nervous again, unsure of himself. He really had no idea how to conduct himself in such a situation. He watched Forrest look around the tavern with a sloppy grin and sneaky eyes, as if he had remembered a private joke.

Then Forrest leaned in over the table, keeping his voice quiet. "Just so you know, it is not a good idea to keep anything like that on you, in case your old man's looking for it."

"I thought you wanted to—"

"Not here," Forrest leaned back and lit a cigarette. "Tell me about your wife."

"My wife? What about her?"

"I saw her at the party. She's a pretty little thing."

"Leave her out of it," Rupert squared his shoulders, trying to pull his body up tall and somehow look threatening.

Forrest slouched back against the dingy fabric of the booth. "I meant it as a compliment." He took a drag of his cigarette and exhaled into the space between them. "You know I was married once?"

"I did not," Rupert said, still on edge.

"She was a whore."

"Oh my," Rupert blurted, giving Forrest the exact reaction he was going for, he realized.

"Not figuratively. Literally. That is where I met her—in a whorehouse. I thought I would make an honest woman of her, but you can never trust those types. Whoring was in her blood, I guess."

Rupert sat wide-eyed while Forrest forcefully ground his cigarette into a glass ashtray. A few more men had entered the tavern as it was getting on to afternoon. His fears of running into anyone he knew were unfounded. No one he associated with—especially now that he had been in New York for so many years—would be caught consorting in such a place. The volume had risen with the dozen or so locals who now sat and drank, played darts, or bet on snooker.

Forrest leaned in again, his hand pressing against the sticky surface of the table. "I want you to walk out the back door and put what you have in your pocket on a ledge behind the chokeberry bush growing up next to the building. It will be to your right, immediately after you walk out the door. Put it there and walk away. I will be right behind you."

"I do not think I want to—"

"I was not finished," Forrest hissed. "There is a little warehouse outside Town Hill, off Bass Harbor Road; you know where I am talking about?"

Rupert nodded.

"Sunday, meet me in this bay." He had written a number on a cocktail napkin. "At noon. I will give it back to you there. We do not want to raise suspicions; I need to know you are serious. Now, by the time you meet me, I want to have a full report of the comings and goings of the household staff, which doors are unlocked. Can you remember that?"

"Of course," Rupert said defiantly, insulted that Forrest was speaking to him as if he were a child. He pulled out a map he had drawn of the room layout and handed it over to Forrest, who nodded and stuck the map inside his coat.

"I am going to need a lot of details. Do not forget anything. Go home tonight and pay attention. Ask someone you trust about the schedule. Is there someone you trust?"

"I do not know."

"Forget it. Do not ask." Forrest waved him off. "Pay attention."

Rupert waited, but apparently Forrest was done with him. He half-rose, then hesitated. "I changed my mind," he said.

"What?" Forrest sat up, infuriated. "I thought we had a deal."

"We do. I decided I want to be a part of it. It will be better; I know where everything is." Rupert was about to tell Forrest about the pink diamond but decided not to. He wanted to have something Forrest did not know. He felt emboldened.

Forrest's body relaxed. "Whatever you want."

"And I will not give you what's in my pocket."

"Then the deal is off."

Rupert waited, but Forrest did not budge.

"Listen," Forrest finally stated. "I need proof that you are serious. I will get it appraised so I know you are not deceiving me. After all, I am taking the biggest risk here."

A group of men at the dart board burst out in a loud groan, joshing and ribbing a man who had made a bad shot. Rupert jumped at the noise. What was he doing? He didn't have the nerve for this kind of thing. He circled his head, stretching out the tense muscles of his shoulders and neck. That was exactly the point. He wanted to do something so completely out of character, some act that no one would expect he'd have the guts to do. This was it. His father and his stingy manner, always wanting to be the center of attention, never giving, always taking—he deserved this.

"It was a thrill; was it not?" Forrest asked quietly.

Rupert gave a slight assent.

"Be bold, Rupert." Forrest paused a moment, making sure he had Rupert's attention. "I remember the other boys calling you names. All those days, you went to class when others skipped out, fishing down by the river, carousing like boys are supposed to. You did not kiss the girl all those times, though she would have eagerly been kissed. Now is the time to be vindicated, Rupert. Show the world you are no pushover."

Rupert looked down at his hands as Forrest spoke. Those memories were vivid to him, too. The embarrassment he felt when he did not fit in, did not have the nerve to break the rules at prep school—it all came rushing back, making his face flush with blood, alive with the hot, fiery shame of adolescence.

He reached into his pocket and grabbed the emerald, slamming it onto the table.

"Here," he exclaimed. "We will do this, but we will do it *my* way."

Forrest quickly covered the gem with a napkin and slid it towards him. Only the bartender had seen the sparkle of green, but he was used to minding his own business.

Chapter 18
The Commandments

Rebecca moved slowly down the back staircase to avoid Mr. Hunt. She had spent the last few days listening for gossip, unable to bring herself to ask too many questions of the staff. She certainly hated to hear that the master might be responsible for the dog's death; though she didn't doubt Mrs. Hunt—would never dare doubt Mrs. Hunt—the idea that anyone could be so cruel, so intentionally mean as to kill a dog, seemed impossible. Mr. Hunt surely was unpredictable, but a killer? She shivered.

Mrs. Hunt was becoming impatient with her. How was she to find out? Rebecca walked the first-floor hallway, nodding to Mr. Hunt's nurse, who shuffled back from the pantry with a snack. It would be hours, Rebecca was sure, before Mr. Hunt was back in his room, now that he was feeling better. She had seen him follow some pretty young woman into the library on the night of the gala after Mrs. Hunt had been carried upstairs. He was a hateful man, really—and unholy, breaking all the commandments—or nearly all the ones she could think of.

Rebecca stopped and recounted the commandments as best she could: *Thou shalt have no other Gods than me; Remember the Sabbath; Do not take the Lord's name in vain; Honor thy parents; Thou shalt not commit adultery.* Rebecca flushed, just thinking of all these sins, and barreled on. *Thou shalt not murder*—who knew what Mr. Hunt was capable of?

Thou shalt not covet thy neighbor's wife. The neighbor Rebecca pictured was the old widow who lived in the estate south of Serabelle. She saw the old woman some days from the top floor, out in her garden in a slip of a nightgown, full jewels laid atop her wrinkled skin. Diamonds and rubies glinted around her neck and wrists, dangling from her ears. Once, Rebecca had seen the old lunatic wearing a tiara. The widow occasionally joined Mrs. Hunt for tea on the patio, bringing along baskets, hearty looking odd-shaped fruits she said came from Asia. She would wear pants and big floppy hats, inappropriate dress for a lady of any age, Rebecca thought. (Mrs. Hunt felt the same—Rebecca had heard her say so.) These old wealthy people could get away with practically anything. *Oh, Lord,* Rebecca thought. If Mr. Hunt was coveting that neighbor, she didn't want to know about it.

Rebecca splayed her fingers out: three more to go. She should know all the commandments off the top of her head. How could someone obey laws she couldn't remember?

Thou shalt not steal; Thou shalt not... bear false witness.

The last commandment came to her as she exited the kitchen's back door, taking the path around the back of the main house to the servants' quarters, hurrying in the growing dusk of the evening. From the corner of the property, she saw the two figures atop pedestals guarding the front patio.

No false idols. She had moved beyond thinking about Mr. Hunt's place on the scale of righteousness and on to considering her own transgressions. Rebecca wiped her brow, relieved. Once, she had used the Lord's name in vain. Not intentionally, but she had been frightened by a hornet's nest— that was in the days before she had been struck by the cross over her bed, though, before her commitment to being a better Christian. What else? She recalled clearly watching her childhood friend Sally flick silky blue ribbons tied to her braids, wishing she had the same, coveting. Rebecca had begged for her own ribbons, pure vanity. She had no need for such things.

Out of the corner of her eye, she saw a light bobbing and weaving in the evening sky. From where she stood near the house, the light seemed to rise from the ground, growing bigger and brighter. It took her a minute of squinting before realizing that the light was Mabel holding a lantern, coming up from the pathway that led to the shore. The fire lit her face from underneath, giving her an unworldly glow. Rebecca waited for Mabel at the edge of the lawn, motioning for her to come quickly.

"What in the world are you doing out here by yourself? In the dark?" Rebecca cried.

"I needed some air." Mabel panted. "What has happened?"

"What has happened? What has happened?" Rebecca echoed, practically hysterical.

"Were you looking for me?" Mabel asked.

"You should not be—"

"Is Beverly angry?" Mabel cut in. "I already finished helping Cook with the dishes."

Rebecca felt panicked for Mabel, for the blasé way she strutted around these grounds. "I don't know."

"Then what do you want?"

They heard the crank of a car engine, men talking over the whir. Though the woods were sparse around the estate, it was dark on the north end—large, threatening pines guarding spindly white birch. Fallen leaves and brown pine needles crunchy underfoot—she had once chased a pillowcase borne off the line by the crazy winds they had had this year. Even at its edge, the woods seemed mysterious and full of activity, a world of dark movement and rich, loamy smells. Who knew what the woods held? Luckily, the days were long in summer, and Mrs. Hunt would often retire before the sun had fully set.

"Tell me," Mabel said.

"I need to ask you something," Rebecca breathed. "It's very important."

"Go ahead."

Rebecca took the lantern from Mabel's hand and wedged it between some rocks close to the house. She lowered her voice to a whisper, stepping out of the circle of light. "You know that Mrs. Hunt's dog was killed?"

"No," Mabel said.

"I thought everyone knew."

"I didn't."

Rebecca sighed. "So, you don't know who did it?"

A slow, insolent smile spread across Mabel's face. "How did it die?"

Rebecca leaned close to Mabel's ear and whispered beneath her bonnet. "Crushed by an automobile. Run over. Flat."

Mabel caught her breath.

"What?" Rebecca asked.

"It was a long time ago..." Mabel left off, as if wrestling with what she would say, but then she blurted, "Mr. Hunt once told me he wanted to kill that dog. He even mentioned running him over with his car."

"Lower your voice," Rebecca said in a panic. "He said that to you?"

"Yes, he did." Mabel nodded.

"You're not making that up?"

"No," Mabel said, insulted. "I thought he was joking. He *said* he was joking."

"Good gracious," Rebecca said and waddled off towards the servants' quarters. "Gracious, me."

Mabel bent and picked up the lantern. Firelight danced into crevices of the rock, accenting the light-colored mortar and the pieces of mica embedded within the rock. Mr. Hunt had told her the name of the shiny little flecks. She had liked the sound of the word. They made radiotelegraph parts from mica, he had said, during one of his rambling monologues. He had often talked of rocks as he removed her clothing, contrasting the feel of her skin to the hard surfaces of the gems he collected. Mabel had picked up a few words that she liked from all this conversation: shale, slate, hematite, onyx. Her favorite, though, was opal. He had compared her freckled skin to the stone and explained how every color of the rainbow was held within so that—depending on which direction it was turned—many colors sparkled, each from a different facet. When Mabel flushed, he said, her skin glowed like a pink opal when they joined together.

Mabel walked around to the back lawn with the lantern. Most lights were extinguished inside the house now, but she knew Mr. Wilson would settle in the kitchen after he got Mr. Hunt to bed. Earlier, Mabel had heard Mr. Hunt's drunken voice over the drone of the radiotelegraph, bragging to some guests about this latest acquisition. She had to admit that the radiotelegraph was an amazing invention. More shocking even than the phonograph were the radio waves that sent signals from miles and miles away. Wireless, he had told her. If he was on his yacht, they could send each other messages. Mabel had wanted to understand how the box worked. Mr. Hunt was surprised by her interest and told her at first that it was not for her to figure out, that she would never need to understand such things. But Mabel insisted, had pursued her line of questioning until the invention made some sort of sense.

When Mr. Hunt brought the radiotelegraph home, the two of them still enjoyed their trysts, but she noted Mr. Hunt was talking less and less. He became rougher towards the end, not bothering to peel off her clothing with gentle phrases but rather pulling up her skirts and having at her quickly. He would pat her on her rear end and send her off to fetch him a drink. Their affair moved rapidly through several phases, but it was all Mabel knew of love, of passion. She guessed that this was often the case, that a man's physical need for a woman was a stronger bond than his words. In this manner, she held on too long to her belief that Mr. Hunt had feelings for her. How had he managed to be so tender, to say such romantic and kind things, and then to shut all that off? If only she, too, could extinguish the emotions that made her run off into the night, climbing over dangerous rocks, thinking once again of flinging herself into the ocean below.

Mabel reached the small lawn below the east wing. She blew out the lantern and wandered in circles, looking up at the window of the room she thought of as theirs. She briefly wondered if she had made up all those tender moments. Several times over the last month, she had checked for her initials in that chair, solid evidence. No, their affection had not been invented. Never in her life had Mabel even considered suicide until that day in the window. Now thoughts and ideas of killing herself and her baby plagued her, followed her around in the quiet hours of the night. What was it that kept her alive?

Overhead, stars fought through the mist of gloaming, standing out in contrast to the inky night sky. Mabel tilted her head back and breathed in the sharp, crisp air. It was cold for September, even in Maine, but the night was beautiful, filling her with the belief that there might be something in this world worth living for. What if someone understood her and comprehended how she wanted to learn, see, and experience more? Willie might, but he didn't seem to understand they would never be allowed to be together.

She couldn't bear the thought of spending every one of her days right here, working as a maid. Was there no other answer? Must she stay in the role she was born into? She turned and stared out at the ocean's edge. What about those ships she watched daily coming and going in the harbor? They were headed—some of them—to exotic lands, like the place where Mr. Hunt had purchased the letter opener she had used to carve her initials. Why could she not go on one of those boats, see the world? Why had she been born a woman if she had these longings? Why had she been born to poor immigrants if she had the desire for learning?

Mabel liked reading, had enjoyed her studies when she was a girl. She made a better student, she knew, than she did a maid. Though her body was sturdy and taut, she was often distracted by an errant thought, one that would lead her down a winding path of ideas and images and take her mind off her work. She found herself staring into space, halting a mundane task.

Mabel thought of those women in town at the suffrage meeting. Those women seemed worldly and smart. They wanted things for themselves. They read and thought and organized. Maybe, there was a way for Mabel to be like them.

❖   ❖   ❖

In the servants' kitchen, Mr. Wilson put his teacup in the sink and said, "Good evening," in a hushed voice.

Rebecca thought Mr. Wilson was as much a gentleman as anyone she had ever worked for. "Have you seen Willie?" she asked.

"I am sorry, no," Mr. Wilson said. "I suggest you check the stables." He stepped softly across the kitchen and out the door, ready to start his shift as the others were all finishing up. Rebecca didn't know how he did it, barely speaking to anyone all night, always alone in that huge dark house. She would go mad.

Rebecca knocked quietly on the door to the poker room on the third floor, but no one answered. She knew there would not be a game tonight, on Friday, but she thought she might try to see if Willie was there before checking the stables. The room and the hallway were the black of darkest evening. She heard a scurrying of rodents and—what was that? A flapping of wings. Could the room have bats? Rebecca shut the door with a bang.

She felt her way down a flight and stepped into the room she shared with Mabel, fumbling around on the nightstand to find matches and a candle. The room lit up with a soft, comforting glow. She sat on the edge of her bed and slowly unlaced her shoes. Looking up at the cross hanging over her bed, she said a quick prayer and got up, walking to the front window. Over the hedge, in the front drive, the chauffeur Josiah stood talking to departing guests. A man and his wife were clearly drunk, stumbling as they paced the drive. The wife, wrapped up in a mink coat, hung on her husband's arm and laughed with a shriek at whatever Josiah said. He gestured toward the stables, and the woman tilted her head back, her red lips forming into a pucker as she let out a howl.

At the far end of the estate, a car putted around the corner and, with a jerk and a sputter, came to a halt ten feet from the couple. Willie stepped out of the car. Rebecca sighed again, knowing that she had to go talk to him. She had no excuse; Mrs. Hunt would drill her first thing in the morning. She stuffed her feet back into her shoes and gave a third sigh, this one loud and ending with a whimper, as if she were making a point to someone.

Rebecca found Willie in the stables, petting one of the big horses. She kept her distance, speaking from the doorway near the lantern. One of the other stable boys nodded at her—Theodore, his name was, though they had never been formally introduced. She had been ill the day the little man had first joined them; she had gone to bed without supper and was too embarrassed afterward to ask for an introduction. He was quiet—she wondered if he was shy. There was talk of him coming from the upper crust, acting as if he were too good for the rest of them, always walking around with a book under his arm. But Rebecca, glancing quickly at him as he passed, thought it possible he was shy. She knew that feeling; though she was mainly outgoing, when it came to the opposite sex, she was awkward and jittery.

"Willie," she shouted.

He looked up but didn't answer, giving her a chance to continue, but she shook her head. Willie closed the stall door behind him, whispered something to the horse, and then walked to the front. "What is it?" he asked.

"I need to talk to you." Rebecca cleared her throat. "Alone."

"No one can hear us." He nodded at Theo, who was in the last stall at the far end of the stables.

Rebecca checked the drive. She was uncomfortable standing half in, half out the stable door, with night creeping in around her and the cool late September air sending a chill through her bones. Rebecca wrapped her shawl tighter and stepped out of the light. She wanted to hold onto Willie's arm for security and stuck out her hand but then thought better of it. How could she explain touching him? He followed her into the yard.

"Willie," she whispered, moving close enough to see his dark face. He glanced at her, then turned his head away, looking towards a copse of trees to the south. "Did you," Rebecca took an unsteady breath, "run over Mrs. Hunt's dog?"

Willie snapped his neck, staring back at Rebecca. "I thought that was over with."

"I must know. Was it you that killed him, or was it someone else?"

Were Willie's hands shaking? He wiped his mouth nervously. "What do you care?" he asked.

"Mrs. Hunt cares," Rebecca said, raising her eyebrows meaningfully.

"Why, so she can fire me?"

"No," Rebecca said and dropped her gaze. She wrung her hands together, realizing she should not be telling him anything. She wasn't very good at this sort of thing. "Willie, I don't know what to do. I must know the truth, and I don't know how to find it other than to ask. I'm not sneaky enough otherwise. Will you please tell me if someone else was the mastermind?"

Willie didn't answer, though he laughed when she said the word "mastermind."

"You won't be fired," she said hopefully, then added, "at least, I don't think so."

"It was my fault," he said defiantly, lifting his chin to look down his cheeks at her. He turned on his heel and stormed away.

"Wait," Rebecca said, "I need to know more." But he had reentered the stables and heard the ribbing of the other boys. She stood out in the yard alone, not even thinking about the dark at that moment.

Chapter 19
Do Not Be Stupid

The Acadia Storage Warehouse was a mile from Red Rock Corner, just as Bass Harbor Road turned into Sound Drive. As Rupert turned off onto Gilbert Farm Road, there was a clear view of the hulking buildings past empty fields and dirt roads. He pulled his father's Oldsmobile into the parking lot. No other vehicles were in the lot at this hour, and Rupert wondered if Forrest had yet to arrive. He let the car idle while he checked his pocket watch.

The buildings were constructed of worn planks that had aged to an algae green with the moist air of the coast. A whitewash had been applied to the lower portion, giving the buildings the appearance, from a distance, of floating above a mist. The red tile roofs looked like they would outlast the rest of the structures.

Rupert held the scribbled directions close to his face. His eyes were giving him trouble of late, and he found it necessary to move the bar napkin back and forth to focus. He already knew that the bay was 5A, as he had looked at the number a dozen times over the last twenty-four hours. Still, double-checking reassured him, like rereading a brief before heading for arbitration, ensuring he had all the details and facts before he was hit with questions. Rupert stood by the car and pulled out a notebook where he had scratched some notes. He wanted to review these as well, the details he would share with Forrest. After this meeting, after he spilled the habits of the household, there would be no going back. This meeting would define his fate, his success or failure at adventure, at revenge.

In the left column, he had listed the servants; on the right, some ideas about each person. Rupert read them over, hoping he could speak to Forrest without the aid of his notes. From even that one instance of being in court, he knew that a speech made without notes sold better to the jury. It seemed sincere—or true. And true is what he was always going for. The power of being a lawyer was to create the truth, not discover it. A lot of people did not realize that—that the truth was malleable.

He reread the notes. The second butler, always present at night. Usually in the kitchen. Aloof but probably aware. Beverly, the head servant, overly watchful of other staff, retired early and up at the crack of dawn— even before it was light outside. Rupert had stayed up the whole night, watching quietly as the house went to sleep and then came back alive. He had thought he would need a bit of sleep before the meeting, but he was wide awake, his nerves on edge.

Beverly had been the first person in the main house, even before the cook. He heard her and the second butler exchange a few words before the old man shuffled out the back door. Beverly stoked the fire in the kitchen, pieces of wood banging up against the back of the stove as she chucked them in.

Rupert kept looking over the list. His mother's maid was of no concern. She trailed after his mother like a hound. Rupert had a flash of his mother lying on the floor last week, the bloody dog in the arms of the stable boy. He tried to pull his thoughts into focus, though a chill ran across the back of his neck, thinking of the accident. He was not good with blood. The chubby maid was no problem. If she wasn't with his mother, she would be in the servants' quarters.

The other maid, though, the little freckled one. Mabel. He knew her name, though he preferred not to use it. She might present more of a problem; he couldn't track the girl. She was all over the place, and he hadn't managed to nail down when she left at night or how she slipped into the main house without him seeing. Suddenly, she'd been standing over him in the parlor, asking if he wanted coffee this morning. He thought he might have fallen into a daydream when he first saw her face floating above him, all sweet with rose-colored lips. He didn't know how to keep tabs on a girl like her.

The stable boys were easy. They stayed outside, taking the long path behind the back of the house for lunch and supper. After they brought in the horses in from the pasture in the evening, the boys would often cross the front yard if there were no guests at the cottage. The sole person who seemed to come out at night was the small one, the little guy with glasses. He had snuck across the front yard, rather than taking the back path, and found a place in the hay, settling back to read by lamplight. Rupert watched him for a few minutes from the library, then followed him quietly. There was nothing much to see; the boy clearly enjoyed reading. Rupert hadn't known that servants could read.

Last Thursday night, he heard a ruckus in the servants' quarters and went to investigate. He walked across the yard, pretending to go out for a stroll. He brought his walking stick and top hat, tapping the stick lightly on the gravel as he walked, keeping his eyes straight toward the main gate but using his peripheral vision to peruse the action at the yellow house. Several scruffy-looking men holding lanterns entered the servants' gate. They nodded quickly in his direction and shuffled inside. Dusk settled on the day, and the smell of honeysuckle was overpowering, as if the flowers had waited for the light to fade before releasing their perfume. As Rupert watched another lantern approach from the direction of town, he stepped behind a large pine and planted himself there until the lantern drew close. The man holding it entered the servants' gate as well. Rupert watched this happen twice more before he slipped back toward the cottage in the growing dark. Rupert stumbled over a pothole, barely regaining his balance before he hit the road. One of his knuckles grazed the dirt, and he nearly cried out.

Back in the safety of the main house, Rupert climbed to the third floor. Melinda had settled in beside his mother in the parlor, working on needlepoint. His father was off that evening at some lodge meeting. From the west side, Rupert watched the yellow house. A bedroom on the third floor in that house was lit up brightly, and though the shades were drawn, he could see multiple shadows. The men must be having a party, he thought. This might be a good night to complete the deed, but he didn't know if it was typical, if the servants always had a party on their night off.

The gardener might pose a problem if it was during the day. He spent all his time in the yard, in the garden, or in his shack. But at night, Gardener didn't budge from the yellow house. If Forrest struck in the middle of the night, the man wouldn't make an appearance.

Rupert jumped in the parking lot when he heard a door slam. He looked up from his notepad but saw nothing. Behind him, a few cars passed on Bass Harbor Road, and a truck covered with a tarpaulin pulled down the road that led toward the warehouse. He closed his book and returned it to his pocket. The truck was heading this way in a cloud of dust. It wouldn't do for him to be seen. Rupert hustled down a row between two buildings, searching the sides of the bays for the right number. There were no windows in either building, causing the place to look sinister, forbidden. Like a prison. Every thirty feet, a large door with a handle was set into the walls, but none of them were open at the moment. Rupert heard voices in the distance, perhaps at the far end of the building.

When he came to 5A, Rupert stopped, wondering if he should try to lift the large door. Behind him, in the parking lot, the truck had stopped, and men piled out of the back from under the tarp. They were rowdy and wore the caps of laborers. They carried wooden crates with something inside that rattled, like glass bottles. Bootleggers, he thought and had a moment of panic. He didn't want trouble with bootleggers. Rupert turned his back so they might not see his face and tapped lightly on the door to 5A.

"Hey."

Rupert swore he heard the sound right next to his ear, but when he looked up, Forrest was leaning out of a smaller, average-sized door next to the large bay that Rupert hadn't noticed—it blended in, was made of the same wood as the siding on the building. The handle, from the outside, was a simple, flat, wrought-iron ring below a keyhole. It gave Rupert a nauseous feeling, somehow, this camouflaged door.

"Get in here," Forrest spat, eyeing the workers headed their way.

The hallway was dark and quiet as a graveyard. Rupert recognized the odor of concrete permeating the dirty, empty space, delivering the scent of dust and neglect up to his nostrils, though he couldn't imagine how he knew the smell. He stumbled along in the dark after Forrest, not wanting to fall behind in the disorienting blackness.

Suddenly Forrest threw open another door, and a soft, orange light lit up a space crowded with items in each corner: shelves crammed with what looked like lamp parts, gas cans, tools, and gadgets. But the center of the floor was spare, save for what looked like a series of paint stains. One corner held a pile of rags, a step stool, and two broken oars. Rupert couldn't imagine what this space was used for, what Forrest was doing here.

"Is this yours?" he asked, stepping inside.

Forrest slammed the door behind him without answering. Outside, the group of men from the truck passed by the roll-up door, laughing and talking. Men with no worries, Rupert thought. Did he ever behave in that manner, joking and laughing with his co-workers or friends? He didn't think so.

"You have my stone?" Rupert asked.

"I have it," Forrest said with his back to Rupert.

"Are you going to give it back to me?"

"Do not worry," Forrest said, laughing. "We will get to that."

Rupert couldn't tell what Forrest was doing, but he seemed to be fiddling with something on the bench. His arms moved up and down with small jerks as if he were adjusting an object, a lever. Rupert tried leaning around to one side to get a peek, but Forrest moved with him, blocking his view from every angle, sensing Rupert behind him as if he could see through the back of his skull.

"What are you doing?" Rupert demanded.

"Me?" Forrest turned. "Oh, nothing. You will see." He blew out the lamp on top of the bench, so half of the room fell into darkness. Another light, closer to Rupert, remained on, throwing its light across the paint-blotted floor. An orange glow bounced off the polished surface and lit Forrest from under the chin, shadowing his eyes, the tips of his incisors bright when he turned and opened his mouth.

"What did you find out?" he asked.

Rupert began to tell him about the schedule at the cottage, wishing he could sit but unable to find a suitable place in the small bay. He looked about him distractedly, his exhaustion from not sleeping suddenly coming over him in a wave. He spoke in fits and starts about the servants.

Forrest interrupted him. "Whose car is that you came in?"

Rupert looked up as if startled from a daze. "My father's, why?"

"You should not have parked it out front. What if someone recognizes it?"

"Where else would I park?"

Forrest looked at Rupert with exasperation. "In the back."

"Why did you not tell me that before?"

"I did not think I had to." Forrest turned his back again and stepped into the shadows, quickly reappearing after he had taken something off the bench. "What will you tell people if questioned about what you were doing here?"

Rupert shrugged. "Storing something, I suppose."

"When we are done here, go to the office and rent a space. There is your alibi. Of course, why in the world would someone like you, who does not live here in Maine, whose family has plenty of acreage, want to rent storage space? Quick, think."

"I am refurbishing a boat for my father as a surprise. The craftsmen will do the work here until it is finished; then I will have it delivered."

"Well, well." Forrest smiled and flipped an object in his palm. "Perhaps I underestimated you. Continue."

Rupert described the comings and goings at the cottage. "So, I discovered that the men have a poker game every Thursday night. Servants from other cottages come and join them in our servants' quarters, on our property. My mother has no idea, I am sure. She would certainly put a stop to it if she knew they were gambling up there. I had to listen in on quite a number of conversations to find out myself. But if we move swiftly during that party, my parents will probably point the finger at the strangers entering the property. Take the suspicion away from us."

"Thursday," Forrest said, his eyeteeth shining.

"This coming Thursday, correct?" Rupert asked. "I really do have to get back to my office soon. I cannot extend my vacation indefinitely."

"We could arrange that."

"Good," Rupert said, swallowing.

"Let's talk about the stones. Is the key still in the desk drawer?"

"Yes."

"How many gems would you say there are?" Forrest asked.

"I didn't count. Four or five hundred, maybe."

"What's their value?"

"Together? Tens of thousands. I do not know exactly."

The men went over how many trays there were, their relative weight, where the servants generally stayed in the house, and a handful of other details, Forrest grilling Rupert like a schoolmaster. The air in the room grew stale and thin with the lack of circulation. Someone pounded a nail in the far reaches of the building. An engine sprang to life.

"Anything else?" Forrest's beady eyes cut into Rupert like a switchblade.

"Not that I can think of."

"What about the pink diamond?"

Rupert started. How did he know? "What pink diamond?"

"Come now." Forrest held up a caliper he had been tossing in his hand, as if for display. "Did you think I would not ask about the crown jewel, the prize of your father's collection?"

"How did you know?"

Forrest shrugged his wiry shoulders, an annoying, dismissive gesture. "He's not exactly quiet about his acquisitions. People talk."

Rupert felt he absolutely must sit down. All his excitement and bravado drained. He found the stepstool in the corner, brushed the sawdust from its surface, and sat. "What about it?"

"Is it in the library as well?"

"No." Rupert did not look at Forrest as he lied, afraid his eyes would betray him. He did not know why he lied— though he wanted to teach his father a lesson, he felt suddenly that he did not want this scoundrel to come out the victor with such a grand prize.

"No?" Forrest asked incredulously. "That's not what I heard."

Rupert spoke quietly. "It is in the bank. In the vault."

"So," Forrest said wryly, "he did not use that special stone safe made for him?"

"I do not know what you are talking about," Rupert snapped.

"The one shaped like a plant stand? In the corner, by the window?"

Rupert was quiet, his mind flashing back to the night of the party when Forrest had joined him to look at his father's gem collection. He must have seen it then. How did he know what was in there? The stone mason? Was everyone in on it?

"Rupert, Rupert," Forrest paced as he talked. "I am disappointed. I really was starting to think I could trust you. Maybe we should call it off. Maybe you do not have the guts after all."

Rupert hung his head. "You may be right," he mumbled.

Forrest continued pacing the floor, his breath coming in heavy streams, exiting through his nose in loud snorts.

"Could I please have the emerald back?" Rupert asked.

"You want it back?" Forrest asked loudly, his face reddening. "I am sorry, Rupert. You cannot have it back. You want to know why? Because I have spent a good lot of time trying to help you with this. And now you want to quit? I should have known you do not have the balls for this. I think I deserve at least something for my time."

Rupert stood. "How am I going to explain its absence?"

"I do not care," Forrest said.

"You promised me."

"And you promised *me* that we were in on this. Looks like we both are going back on our promises."

Rupert felt suddenly invigorated. "I did no such thing. I never promised you a thing."

"I disagree."

"Give the emerald to me," Rupert said, knowing he sounded like a petulant child.

"No."

"I mean it." Rupert's heart pounded in his throat. "You have got no right to take what is not yours. You have no right."

"I did not take it, Rupert." Forrest swung the forceps menacingly. "If you remember, you gave it to me. The bartender saw it, thanks to your lack of discretion. So, I have a witness. Do you want to explain to your father why you gave me one of his stones, or do you want to let it go, pretending you know nothing about where it has gone? It is your call. If you implicate me, you are taking the fall, too. Do not doubt me there."

Forrest had always been a bully. It had been a mistake to get involved with him in any way. He should have said 'no' at the party when Forrest wanted to look at the collection. Brave? He had never even wanted to be the type of man who was considered brave. In his world, he was smart and skilled and respected—until he came home, until his father was once again in the picture, trying to make him into a different kind of man than he was. A rage boiled up inside him, borne of frustration and futility.

Suddenly, Rupert lunged at Forrest, knocking him off balance, and the two of them fell to the concrete floor, intertwining limbs, wrestling and pushing against each other's clothing, skin, and hair. Forrest cried out on the way down when the back of his head hit a metal vise clamped to the bench. Blood trickled from the wound and puddled on the floor below them as they thrashed about.

"Give it," Rupert demanded in short breaths.

Though Forrest was certainly the more experienced fighter, he had been taken by surprise. When his head made impact with the vise, a shiver ran down the length of his body as if his sight had gone blurry. He looked as though he was about to pass out, but new strength resurged as he struggled to fight Rupert off. Rupert was no match for Forrest's wiry muscles, but he was full of fury from a lifetime of putting up with bullies, of being beaten up. Forrest's pupils dilated and he bared his teeth like a snarling dog. His blond hair seemed to stand straight up out of the follicles, like a cartoon. Rupert fairly clawed at Forrest's pockets for the emerald.

"I do not have it here," Forrest panted. "I did not bring it."

Rupert stopped his frantic scramble, and Forrest wiggled out from under him, scooting back far enough so that he could stand. Rupert whimpered, still lying on the ground, face down, his cheek at the edge of the pool of Forrest's blood. Outside the door, the laborers wheeled a cart down the pathway, still cajoling each other. The pungent odor of cigarettes wafted under the door. Rupert stared at the sliver of light making its way under the door, unwilling to stand up from his defeat once again. What had he hoped to accomplish by attacking Forrest?

"Here." Forrest extended his hand. "Get up."

Rupert did not move.

"Do not be stupid. You are lying in blood, for Christ's sake."

Still, Rupert refused to look at his foe, though he did manage to push himself up off the floor, onto all fours. He stared down at the blood and touched his palm to his cheek, wiping the few drops that had touched his skin.

Forrest grabbed a rag off the bench and held it to the back of his head, wincing when fabric touched skin. Blood soaked the rag instantly, warm liquid spreading across his palm. Forrest released the rag briefly to check the amount of blood, holding it up to his face. Rupert watched, aghast. Blood gushed from Forest's wound as he moved his head to and fro, as if to shake off the injury; color drained from his skin. Suddenly, his pupils went cross-eyed, and as if a light were put out, Forrest crumpled to the floor.

Anger and shame at losing the wrestling match still flushed Rupert's skin. The crook's faint took him by surprise. Rupert stood over him, staring. Blood was everywhere, including on his own clothes and his hands. He grabbed another rag off the counter and wiped at his shirt, knowing instantly that his life would never be the same. No matter what he did right now. He knew he should help Forrest, put pressure on the wound—that much he knew from reading stories of war. He should go get the car, put him in it, and deliver Forrest to the doctor, explaining that they were hunting or boating or hiking and that Forrest had tripped over a root, on the deck of a boat, or some such tale. But Rupert also knew, in that same instant, that he would do none of those things.

The man's eyes were closed, and his face looked like a peacefully sleeping child's. Forrest had never looked so innocent, even when they were children. His pale hair soaked up the blood so that the tips near his ears were rimmed with red. Rupert reached down and patted Forrest's coat, a cheap canvas jacket with a jumble of pockets. He methodically unbuttoned the coat, surprised by his own calm. Forrest didn't stir. Rupert checked each of the pockets, and in a small, almost hidden pouch inside the lining, he found what he was looking for.

Before he left, Rupert checked Forrest's pulse. It was weak but still there. He knew if he left the man alone, he might die. But worse yet, what if he woke up and came after Rupert? He looked around at the tools in the small, airless room and wondered whether he had the guts to finish him off.

Chapter 20
You Servants

Willie finished letting the horses in from the corral, settling them all back into their stalls. He picked Faith's bridle up from the hook and was set to clean the brittle leather when Rebecca reappeared at the stables' door.

"Mrs. Hunt wants to talk to you, Willie," Rebecca shouted across the length of the room.

A stallion lifted his tail and defecated near the front of his stall. Rebecca, witnessing this, cried out and stepped further out of the doorway.

"Willie," she shouted again.

George and Theo watched, though they didn't tease him, like they might have a week ago, knowing how Willie might be in real trouble this time from the accident with the dog.

"I don't know how you all live with those animals making messes like that in their own rooms," Rebecca commented as they walked back to the house together.

"We don't live with it," Willie said. "We clean it up."

"Ew," Rebecca said.

Willie couldn't understand some women. Particularly certain white women, if he was honest. He felt a twang of disloyalty to Mabel for even thinking this, but no negro woman he knew would be put off by waste—animal or human. It was part of life. A big part, as far as he could see. "We don't pick it up with our hands."

"Don't be disgusting."

They didn't talk the rest of the way to the kitchen door where the servants entered. *Just once,* Willie thought, *I'd like to walk through the front door.* He wanted to step on the clean white marble of the entranceway without having to wipe his feet. He wanted to walk into the parlor and pour himself a drink the way he heard Mr. Hunt did each evening. Willie had seen his shadow in the library, in the parlor, glass in hand, neat suit, all crisp lines. He suddenly understood Mabel's desire to become a part of that world. It was not Mr. Hunt that Mabel loved; it was what the man stood for. All that cleanliness. All that freedom.

Before he stepped into the kitchen, Willie swiped at the hay sticking to his clothing. He imagined that Mrs. Hunt wanted to talk to him about the dog. There would be no other explanation for why she'd call on a stable boy. He stopped to wash his hands in the sink, Rebecca fussing behind him, telling him that Mrs. Hunt wouldn't want to wait. Willie had never thought very much about the state of his hygiene, but as he considered talking with Mrs. Hunt, or Mabel, or women in general, it was with different standards than with men. Mr. Hunt's cleanliness was admirable, but the women and their perfumes, their white bonnets, made Willie self-conscious.

"I think I should change my clothes," he told Rebecca.

"No time," she said, heading up the back stairs, "though you do smell something awful."

"Oh no," Willie said, stopping in his tracks.

"Nothing new, Willie," she said, now half a flight ahead of him. "All you stable boys smell."

Willie thought of his moment on the rocks with Mabel when he sat close to her and proposed. No wonder she had said no.

"Dear, come in," Mrs. Hunt spoke from the chair in the far corner of her anteroom.

Willie stood in the center of the room on an Oriental rug. He looked down at his boots, afraid he would leave tracks of manure. He shifted from foot to foot, trying to make himself lighter, smaller. Rebecca stood in the doorway.

"Rebecca," Mrs. Hunt said without looking at her maid, "leave us alone for a few minutes. But stay close so I may ring for you."

Rebecca closed the door reluctantly.

"Now, Willie, is it?"

"Yes, ma'am."

"Come, have a seat." Mrs. Hunt gestured to the cushion on a bench not ten feet from her chair.

"Yes, ma'am," Willie said and inched forward.

"Come on," Mrs. Hunt said, the edge of irritation in her voice finely veiled.

"I'm afraid I haven't bathed, ma'am."

"Nonsense," Mrs. Hunt said, rising from her chair. "Here," she said, walking into her bedchamber and grabbing an atomizer. "Close your eyes."

Mrs. Hunt sprayed Willie from head to toe with lavender eau de cologne. He leaped when the light, cold spray hit his skin, like the mist off the ocean at the cliff's edge. He had stood at the top of those rocks and felt the same light sensation; this mist smelled of plants, though, rather than of the sea.

"That's better," Mrs. Hunt said and sat again in the chair. "Now you know my secret."

Willie smiled.

"I think it is time you told me your secret, too, Willie."

"My secret?"

"Is there something you know that you have not told me? About Mr. Hunt?"

"Mr. Hunt?" Willie started.

"Yes, Mr. Hunt. What can you tell me about his activities?"

Willie looked from floor to ceiling, eyeing the striped wallpaper, the ornate cornices. "Excuse me, Ma'am, but why ask me?"

"Because I think you know something."

Willie rolled the possibilities around in his mind. What secret did he know about Mr. Hunt? Only the truth about the master and Mabel. Could that be what she meant? He cleared his throat. "I found out just yesterday myself, for sure, when I asked Mabel to marry me." Willie spoke quietly, as if he could further conceal the truth by whispering. "I know it is silly—well, I know people wouldn't like the idea of a negro marrying a white girl, but I didn't even care that she was in the state she was in, not when I thought that Mr. Hunt had... well, I didn't know she wanted to do it. She said 'no' to me because you all want her to marry Gardener, but I would've married her. I would have—"

Mrs. Hunt sat silently, looking out the window. Willie waited for her to respond, unsure whether he should get up, whether she was done with him or not. The scent of the lavender was overpowering, making his head spin as he looked at the finery in Mrs. Hunt's room. He had never seen such a place, the gold vanity with the mirror he spied through the open door of the bedchamber, so clean and sharp, the brushes and bins, the fine mahogany of the dresser, the double door that must have led to a closet, the shiny metal of the doorknobs on the entrances to two other rooms. Willie had heard that each bedroom in this house had its own indoor bathroom, with running hot water that came through pipes from somewhere downstairs. The curtains behind him looked thick and velvety, heavy enough to make him want to curl up in their dark burgundy fabric. Willie suddenly felt overwhelmed with sleepiness.

"What are you telling me, Willie?" Mrs. Hunt's shrill voice startled him awake.

"Ma'am?"

"Are you telling me that everyone at the cottage knows my family's business? That you *servants*,"—she hissed the word—"are gossiping about what goes on with the master of this cottage? That you have the right to assume, to know, to judge what any of the Ainsworth-Hunts are up to?"

"No, ma'am." Willie regretted every word he had whispered.

"I want you to tell me what you know about my husband running over Chou Chou. *That* is why I brought you here. *That* is the one thing we need to discuss—that you need ever think about regarding my family." Mrs. Hunt's voice began to calm the longer she talked. "So, tell me, Willie—and simply answer the questions I ask of you, please. I implore you to forget everything else—did my husband tell you to run over my dog?"

Willie felt a nervous laugh arise, but he morphed the sound into a cough. "No, ma'am."

"Did he have anything to do with it?"

"No, ma'am. Only he wanted me to show you that night."

Mrs. Hunt looked startled. "Why?"

Willie hadn't looked at Mrs. Hunt since she scolded him. He was afraid to answer this question, afraid to speculate. But then again, Mr. Hunt had behaved poorly. There was nothing Willie could do to reprimand him, to make him pay for what he had done to Mabel. It might be true that Mabel was a willing participant, but she was young and foolish. She couldn't be blamed for being duped by such an old man. Clearly, Mr. Hunt was at fault. Willie felt his head brimming with ideas, with chances, with opportunities. A boy like him could rarely hope to affect the future of someone like Mr. Hunt. Willie felt like one of the ants he had seen on the bluff; he was nothing bigger than a worker ant, blindly following the pack. But Mrs. Hunt, on the other hand, could punish her husband. Here was his one chance to make a difference. He swallowed. "He seemed happy, ma'am, that I had run over the dog."

"Go on," she said.

"I really didn't mean to hurt him, ma'am. He ran under the car as I was driving." Willie took a deep breath. "The dog was still alive when I got out of the car and carried him to the barn."

Mrs. Hunt looked on the verge of tears, biting her lips so that the skin around her mouth looked pale and smooth until she spoke. "Then what happened?"

"Mr. Hunt came into the barn and saw Chou Chou, your sweet little dog, lying on the hay." The words poured out of him. The lie became the truth. "I asked him if we could get a doctor, and Mr. Hunt, well, Mr. Hunt…"

Mrs. Hunt leaned over and put her hand on his knee, giving it a squeeze.

Willie looked up and into her face, puckered like a coin purse. "Mr. Hunt kicked the dog."

Mrs. Hunt let out a yelp.

"He kicked Chou Chou, ma'am until the poor little thing stopped breathing altogether." Willie had a flash, remembering how still and stiff the dog had been even before he had carried the body into the barn, how Mr. Hunt had stood and looked at the body, no kicking, just grinning.

Mrs. Hunt fainted back into her chair, wiping her brow with a handkerchief. "Evil," she moaned. "Evil."

"Then he made me carry him in my arms to show you." Willie bit his lip, glad his story had the desired effect. "I didn't want to, ma'am, but he made me. Mr. Hunt was laughing."

"Enough," Mrs. Hunt said and waved Willie away. "Go."

He crossed the room quickly, noticing that he had indeed left little smears of manure on the rug. His heart pounded from the rush of what he had done. He had never lied in his life. But then again, he had never loved someone like he loved Mabel. Hand on the doorknob, he froze, marveling at this revelation. He would have done anything to make Mr. Hunt pay for using her.

"Send in my maid," Mrs. Hunt said from her faint. He put his hand on the shiny brass handle and heard Mrs. Hunt say, "I will not forget this, Willie."

He couldn't tell if that was a good thing.

Chapter 21
A Menace

Rupert stood over the body of Forrest Wicks. Forrest had been an appalling child who had grown into a despicable adult, not worth all this trouble. A menace, really. But what could Rupert do? Smash him over the head again? Smother Forrest with a rag? Both acts would constitute premeditated murder. As it stood, if Forrest died and Rupert was found out (perhaps witnessed by the bootleggers who came by), he could plead self-defense. He leaned over and felt Forrest's pulse again. It was possible the man would bleed to death. The blow had been hard, making a resounding crack as his head hit the vice. Forrest was strong, though, and had fought him for a few minutes. Maybe he would make it. But the blood—the blood kept draining.

Down the dark hallway, Rupert found a dingy storage closet. A water pump inside emptied into a basin ringed with black soot. The walls were covered with cobwebs, and the floor looked like it had not been cleaned in a decade. He had never seen such filth. A can of lye sat under the basin; a mop and a bucket leaned nearby. Rupert pumped water onto his hands and dipped his fingers into the lye, letting the chemical burn his skin, scouring off the blood. His eyes watered, and he rinsed his chapped, reddened hands.

He felt his way back along the dim hallway without looking back into Forrest's space. If that was his space—heaven knew who owned it. Rupert stuck his head out the door. The truck with the laborers had reached the main road. Rupert hurried through the parking lot, emerald in his pocket. The air itself felt as dry as his mouth, hung with clouds of dirt kicked up by thick tire treads. The Oldsmobile was covered with a fine, tan silt. Rupert wiped his hands through the handle's dust and climbed into the car. His hands upon the steering wheel shook uncontrollably. Rupert slapped them together, as if he might shock his limbs into mobility. Out of the corner of his eye, he saw a car turn off the main route and head down Gilbert Farm Road towards the warehouses. He cranked the engine and peeled out of the parking lot, sure to keep his head down when he passed the other vehicle.

The cottage was quiet when Rupert returned. He slapped his clothes clean the best he could before entering through the kitchen. His wife, the butler told him, was out shopping with Madam, driven to town by Josiah over an hour ago in the Winton, as Master Rupert had taken the Oldsmobile. The young missus, he said, had been looking for Rupert before she left, but the butler had not known what to tell her. "It is best, really, if I am informed when guests are coming and going," the butler scolded, looking Rupert's clothes up and down.

Rupert listened to the wiry man, younger than the night butler but equally as thin. Both wore spectacles and had thinning hair, as if the second butler were a warning to the younger man, the ghost of his future self. Rupert did not at all appreciate being corrected by a servant, but his guilt was nearly palpable, looming heavily over his shoulders, that he dared not complain.

"Technically, it is my house too, butler," he could not help saying. "I am not really a guest."

"That is true, sir," the butler said and held out his hand for Rupert's coat and hat.

Rupert stuttered, "I will keep them." He started up the stairs, his coat wrapped tightly. "Where's my father?" he turned and asked.

"Like you, sir," the butler said, "he is hard to keep track of."

"Then you do not know?" Rupert asked testily.

The butler did not react, answering in a monotone. "I cannot say for sure. But I would imagine you should check the rose garden."

"Thank you," Rupert said and climbed the stairs to the guest room, to the shower.

His father was not in the rose garden. He saw the hulking form of the gardener entering his shed beyond the trellis and the hanging roses. When Rupert was a child, the shack had been bare, mere clapboard with a couple of windows and a rickety door. Perfect for a child's curiosity—well, his sister's anyway. Sarah had not been afraid of the gardener. Rupert was still amazed that such a fearsome, large man could grow such beautiful flowers. Rupert scanned the garden, scrutinizing the roses for perhaps the first time. All his life, the garden was there, a part of the greater estate, an aggregate of many features, many angles, and spaces.

The gardens on Serabelle had always seemed to Rupert to be too colorful, too stimulating, too complex, like the feeling one has in an Asian market. He had been to Siam once with his father when he was small, a disaster of a trip where he had become ill and had to stay in the hotel, watched over by a nanny. But he remembered that initial feeling, that inability to wrest out individual details from the whole.

In stark comparison, his house in New York was clean and open, with no bric-à-brac. Hardwood floors ran the length of the two-thousand-square-foot apartment. The walls were white and the furniture unadorned—wooden with velvet pillows—no patterns, no stripes. There were paintings on the wall of bucolic landscapes. A portrait that he and his wife had sat for hung over the mantle. Two silver candlestick holders with white tapers stood on either side of the painting. In the painting, his wife wore a green velvet dress with a white lace collar and a matching ribbon in her hair. The artist had perfectly captured her acquiescing smile, her demure look. He had also captured Rupert's pudgy hands, which he did not appreciate and almost did not pay the man over. Melinda had talked him into keeping the painting, kissing his hands, saying she loved his thick fingers.

Rupert wandered past the gardens, trying to locate his father before sneaking back into the library to return the emerald. The whole thing had been a big mistake, getting involved with Forrest. Of course, he could see that now. He didn't need an adventure to feel good about himself. Look at what he had. Rupert stood on the bluff, past the back gate where his father had taken a fall, looking out over the ocean. He would inherit all this someday. His father was getting older—he drank too much, everybody knew, and he took too many risks. The heist was something more like what Alistair would attempt—why had he thought he should be more like his father? A caper was not in Rupert's nature. He needed to go home, get back to the office, and resume his life in the city. Life was comfortable there, with the sound of occasional cars and pedestrians walking back and forth, the collective sound of their soles hitting the ground. Muffled chatter rose to his third-floor office, and the sound lulled him, made him comfortable in the knowledge that things were moving, that people were making progress.

Out here in the wilderness, time seemed to stop—other than the roses climbing over the tops of the trellises; other than the explosive growth of the ivy and the other green plants, time stood still out here. The house, though slightly worn by the salt and the wind, stood solid. The rocks in place forever. Perhaps millimeters smaller by the effects of erosion, but to the naked eye, ever the same. Waves pounded in a constant rhythm—loud when you were close, a constant crashing drone from the house. Waves and wind, that was all you could hear at the cottage. Nature, not people. Other than the nights when Alistair hosted parties, there was little sound and barely a sign of life.

Boats moved silently in the distance, and Rupert imagined they were peopled by fishermen, but there was no evidence of any living person, only boats bobbing with the waves. Seagulls screeched overhead, diving for fish. Behind him, servants skulked around the grounds as if they had secret lives of their own, as if they were the ones who owned the land, who possessed the big empty house. Why this massive house for a few people? Rupert wondered if, when his parents had built the cottage, they had pictured a large brood of children and grandchildren wandering the gardens, filling the myriad rooms. Had his mother and father imagined a lively, hopping estate filled with love and merriment? Or had they thought of the future at all?

Rupert couldn't imagine his parents as a unit, a pair with harmonious plans. For as long as he could remember, he thought of them individually, as having separate lives and interests, as he and Melinda did. Come to think of it, Rupert had no idea what his wife did all day, how she filled her time when he wasn't home. They had had no luck with having children themselves, and he couldn't say the lack bothered him.

His father was nowhere on the grounds that he could see. Rupert trudged back to the house wrapped in a sudden heavy gust, a wind that felt as if it was weighing him down, pressing on his skin. He sank in towards himself, trying to hold his body together, out of the prying breeze that felt as if it might loosen his very skin from his body. Rupert looked to the sky to discover where that force had come from, as if he might divine the source. Up above, cirrus clouds strung out thin like yarn being spun, almost breaking apart at the horizon.

Rupert entered the house through wide French doors off the casual dining room, startling the young maid as he entered. She looked up, wide-eyed, from where she sat polishing silver, as if she had done something wrong. Rupert scrutinized her briefly before turning away. He almost made it out of the room before a thought occurred to him. He stopped and turned toward the girl. "How long have you been here?" he demanded.

She had turned her attention back to the silver and barely mumbled to Rupert. "Sir?"

"I am speaking to you, girl. Look at me when I address you."

Mabel looked up. "Yes, sir," she said, but her tone was haughty.

"Stand up."

Mabel pushed her chair out slowly and threw down her polishing rag, clearly belligerent.

Rupert circled to the other side of the dining room, keeping his eyes on the maid. Her cheeks were ruddy, and she had a certain plumpness that didn't sit well with her frame.

He had a flash of insight, of which he did not know the source. Perhaps all that staring at the sky had brought him something after all. "You are with child; are you not?" The maid hung her head, properly chastised. He was right. Rupert fairly barked at her. "Does my mother know?"

"I believe so," she answered.

"You are not married, are you?"

Mabel bit her lip. "I am engaged."

Rupert let out a derisive laugh. "Jumped the gun a little, I would say, on this one; did you not?"

"Yes, sir."

Rupert continued pacing, trying to figure out why this should concern him. Why bother with the maid's business? What was wrong here? Something nagged at him. The maid was exactly the type his father liked. Rupert thought he had heard his father mention the girl when they arrived for the summer. How young she was, how enthusiastic she seemed. Usually, Rupert ignored those kinds of remarks from his father—delivered over the telephone in a rambling, nonsensical, often drunken speech. Now it was coming back to him.

"Who are you marrying?" he asked.

"The gardener, sir."

"That big redheaded fellow?"

Mabel's voice was weak, with no sense of haughtiness now. "Yes, sir."

"Is he the father?"

Mabel didn't answer. She barely jerked her head, but the movement was indecisive. The answer could have been a yes or a no.

"Look at me when I talk to you. How well do you know my father?"

Mabel looked up and bore her dark brown eyes into his lighter hazel irises. There was fear there, yes, but behind that, he noticed a stand of bravery.

"Tell me the truth now," he sneered. "Is my father responsible for your condition?"

Wind rattled at the doors, and Mabel walked over to secure the lock. "I should take down the umbrellas on the patio," she breathed. "The laundry needs to come off the line."

Rupert ignored her avoidance tactic. "I know my father. He would like you."

Mabel spun around, surprising him. "Yes."

"Yes, the child is my father's?"

"Yes."

Rupert wavered and caught himself on the high back of a chair before lowering himself down into the seat. He rested his elbows on the table before him and shook his head. He hadn't expected her to tell him the truth. Did he want the truth? What could he do with this information?

"My mother…" he uttered.

Rupert caught his reflection in the silver water pitcher in front of him. The maid hadn't finished wiping the piece, and white stripes of polish blurred parts of his face on the vessel's surface. He looked like some child's drawing of a circus freak, of a madman. The maid stood at the door, her petite back to him, as if she regretted her last words. He pictured his father attacking the girl from behind. He didn't suppose that his father had been kind in any way, that he had given her a choice in the matter.

"My mother cannot find out about this," he snapped. "Did you hear what I said?"

"Yes."

"I will give you money. You can go away, get this taken care of."

"It's too late," Mabel whispered.

Rupert stood and crossed near the girl. Yes, he supposed it was too late for that, judging from the fact that he could tell she was pregnant. "No matter. You can still go."

"How much?" Mabel asked.

Rupert reached into his pocket. He had two hundred dollars in bills and some loose change, which he handed to Mabel.

"That's not enough," she said.

He had the emerald. Rupert rubbed it between his fingers, inside his trouser pocket. He could give it to her now; they would assume the girl stole it after she had gone. What risk was he taking? None, really. The girl wouldn't be stupid enough to refuse him. She would never get another offer like this. The emerald was worth thousands, more than she would see in a lifetime.

He lifted the gem out into the open, holding it up into the dusky light descending through the glass. "I am going to give you this emerald, and you will be gone by this evening," he whispered.

Mabel kept her hands by her side, mesmerized by the sparkling gem.

"Do you understand?" he asked. "Do you?"

Chapter 22
Slight Little Splashes in the Vast Ocean

Julia Ainsworth had not entertained many suitors, though she had pined, moon-eyed, over a certain soldier from the time she hit adolescence—a neighbor boy in Worcester, a good five years her senior. Ryan Stafford was an officer, his uniform blue and tidy. His white gloves made her swoon. He was tall and slim, dark-haired with a slippery smile, the kind that made her stomach turn, his lips a shade lighter than maroon. Before Ryan was in the military, his hair had flopped nonchalantly over his forehead, giving him a rakish, devil-may-care look. Still, that attitude was gone when he returned home, replaced by a formal, rigid authority that impressed young Julia—and scared her. He was so mature.

Her dealings with Ryan Stafford were few and became more limited as the years passed. The last interaction she recalled with him was right before her sixteenth birthday. He was visiting his parents when Julia was sent over to ask Mrs. Stafford for a certain color of embroidery thread her mother needed to finish a piece.

"Why do you not send the maid?" Julia had complained. She had settled by the fire to read her novel, the type of light romance she often enjoyed back then.

"It is more personal, dear, if you go," Julia's mother insisted.

"If it is more personal, then perhaps you should go?"

Julia's mother looked hard at her, enough to let Julia know she had gone a step too far. Julia wore a plain, straight-bodiced tan dress, one she often wore on Saturdays inside the house. Unaware that Ryan was home, she didn't think to change before going next door. Julia would always believe that this choice—or lack of choice—had decided her future.

The Staffords' maid answered the door. The woman clucked and ushered Julia through the door, then left her standing in the foyer. Julia swung her hands idly and studied the portraits in the hallway. Unlike her own homely ancestors, all the Staffords seemed to be good-looking. The men and women on the wall had olive skin, shocking blue eyes, and dark wavy hair. How could one family produce so many strikingly beautiful people? How was it that her own family, on both sides, seemed to produce nothing but uncomfortably arranged faces? Nothing hideous, but not what would be conceived of as beauty. She had heard her mother whisper something vulgar and insulting concerning the Staffords' skin tone. Even young Julia could sense a veiled hint of jealousy in her mother's words.

"Who is this standing in my foyer?" Julia turned at the rich, stirring voice. "Could this be little Julia Ainsworth? Impossible."

Ryan Stafford, out of uniform but equally handsome, stood, hands on his hips, surveying Julia in her plain dress, without her finery or makeup.

"You have grown up." He laughed.

"Yes," was all she could manage.

Mrs. Stafford, mysteriously, exotically attractive, joined them. "Julia, dear, my maid tells me you are here. Is there something wrong? Is your mother well?"

"Oh, no. I mean, yes, Mother is fine," she stammered.

"You remember Ryan?"

Julia had done some foolish, half-curtsy motion. "Yes, ma'am."

"So polite, she is, the dear." Mrs. Stafford spoke to her son. "Julia's, what, sixteen now?"

"Almost," Julia answered.

"You all flower so fast."

"She's grown; that's for sure." Ryan smiled, and Julia's stomach felt as though it fell to her knees. "But I do not think she's quite flowered yet." He laughed. "Good to see you again, Miss Julia. Now, I must be going. I will return early this evening, Mother." Ryan planted a kiss on his mother's cheek and patted Julia on the head like a child. Like a dog, she thought.

That comment. It had stayed with her all these years. That crushing comment about her not flowering. She had pictured herself as a wilted bud, brown and plain, for years afterward, so when the proposal came from Alistair, clear and forceful, not at all romantic— "I think you should be my wife. It would make my mother happy"—Julia didn't hesitate. She worried that might be the sole offer, despite her family's riches. There had been others interested, but less wealthy boys, social climbers she could never trust. She believed that no man would love her for normal womanly traits. Her body was not soft or curvaceous. She might be called genteel but never beautiful.

Over the years, Julia had certainly wondered if she had made a mistake. Perhaps one of those other boys had loved her. A young one—the slim spectacled son of the apothecary—had sent her love notes when she was seventeen (the only such notes she had ever received), but she could not, in good conscience, take them seriously. Her parents would never have approved of such an affair. She had kept those notes. They were in her jewelry box still, under the bottom tray, though she had not read them in years.

The courtship between her and Alistair had been brief and formal. They had shared no more than a kiss before they married, and Alistair had barely looked into her eyes; even during the wedding ceremony, he was cool and distant with her. Julia assumed that to be the way husbands and wives interacted, not the way those scandalous novels portrayed love, those novels she put aside after she was a married woman. After all, did not all the adults she knew secretly despise their spouses? She had heard as much in the parlors of nearly all society women.

Julia had endured their perfunctory lovemaking those first few years. But after the birth of Rupert, the second child, the son, Alistair had not approached her again. He had his son; what more did he need of her? The distance suited her just fine. There was not a stitch of desire in her, certainly not for Alistair.

Julia wrapped a stole around her aging body, her feet cold and wrinkled atop the carpet, before finding her slippers. She stared out the front window where frost lay lightly on the pane, the first of such portents of winter. It was time they packed the house up and headed to Boston. The fall would be cold, she could tell, and she had no wish to stay and develop a sickness.

At the end of each restless, tear-filled day following her dog's death, Julia sat at her vanity with an ever-growing conviction that Alistair should pay for what he had done to Chou Chou—for what he had done to her. No man should be allowed to act so treacherously.

Apparently, it had not been enough punishment for Alistair to make an ass of himself at the party. The man thrived on public displays of idiocy. Even her efforts with the Temperance Union, her lectures on decency and pride, had done nothing to slow his pace. How could she humble him, hit him in the gut the way he had done to her, take away the one thing that meant something to him? What did he love the most?

His stones.

Julia quickly wiped at her makeup, letting her gray hair down from its tight bun, a low knot she wore on days when she didn't intend to entertain. Unless Alistair surprised her, Julia would not expect to see anyone tonight. She would take her supper in her room.

"Rebecca!" she yelled. No response. Julia checked the clock near the door. Two forty P.M. She wanted nothing more than to go to bed, even at this hour, to forget everything happening at the cottage. "Rebecca," she tried again.

She would have to trust her maid, the one servant at the cottage who kept Julia's interests in mind. And if the girl wanted to keep her job, she would do as Julia instructed. There would be some planning to do, she knew, to make it look as if the gems had been stolen by an intruder. Or should she walk the gems to the cliff's edge and dump them into the ocean, letting powerful waves reclaim the minerals?

Julia pictured the jewels tumbling from the tray, sunlight catching the edges, reflecting a rainbow of colors before the rocks plummeted into the water, slight little splashes in the vast ocean, barely making a dent on the surface. One by one, she would turn over the velvet trays, cascading the jewels down into the brilliant air—she wanted to plan for sunlight for the correct effect. She would wear a black velvet dress, with long black-satin gloves contrasting with the sparkling gems. She would cradle certain gems in her hand before she chucked them out into the water. Alistair must witness the act—she would somehow make sure he was incapacitated up in the east wing. She would want to discard the jewels herself, showcasing the damage the same way Chou Chou had been carried in, amid a party, no less. How could she possibly top that?

Julia sighed. She might have fantasies of equal revenge, but she knew as soon as her imaginings ended that she would not be so foolish as to throw away such a valuable collection. What else could she do? Could she sell them? The rocks were the only thing that Alistair truly cared about. It *had* to be the rocks.

"Rebecca."

This time, the girl answered, stepping timidly into the room.

"I have a plan," Mrs. Hunt turned from the vanity. "Part of a plan, anyway, and I need your help."

"Of course, ma'am."

"But I need your complete vow of allegiance. No matter what I ask of you, you must do it." Julia crossed the room with a heavy sadness in her chest. She flicked open the curtains. Normally, she preferred the soft yellow of the gas lamps, but she wanted to see Rebecca's face clearly in the remaining daylight. She wanted to make certain that there were no secrets between them. "Do you agree?"

Rebecca stood wide-eyed. "Ma'am, what do you need?"

"I will tell you in a minute," Julia said, waffling now about trusting her. "This is the first test I have ever put you to in all these years, Rebecca. I have never questioned whether you would do as you were told. But now, I want you to swear an oath."

"To what, ma'am?" Rebecca's voice trembled with the severity of the idea.

"Loyalty."

Rebecca nodded solemnly. "I will, ma'am; you know I will."

Julia paced, suddenly invigorated and anxious to put her plan into action. Echoes of the house going about the business of the day resounded through the floor: a fire being stoked, the scrape of plates and wine glasses taken from shelves in the pantry. And then the swing of the outer gate and the putputput of an automobile entering the drive. Julia crossed to her window to see what Alistair might be up to this afternoon. The auto pulled up in front of the door, engine killed. A chauffeur walked around the car and opened the rear door of the Locomobile to escort Mrs. Bates to the door. Whatever could she want?

Chapter 23
If She Still Existed

"Does she understand what?" Alistair barked from the doorway of the dining room.

They flinched simultaneously—Rupert stuffing the emerald quickly into his pocket while Mabel scurried back to the silver on the dining table. Alistair strode into the room the best he could on crutches.

"My son," he said. "Do not tell me that's one of my stones you have got there? Or have you taken a sudden interest in gemology after all these years? And do tell—if that's true—why you have chosen to discuss such a topic with the maid."

"Father, I—" Rupert flushed and turned away, eyes flickering back and forth, clearly gathering his thoughts. Alistair waited. Rupert squared his shoulders, as if remembering a brave act. "This girl had stolen one of your emeralds. Here." Rupert held it out to his father. "I was telling her I would have her fired."

"That's not true!" Mabel burst out.

"Hush," Alistair said softly to Mabel in the same voice he once used with her when they were alone.

Alistair took the gem from his son. "You expect me to believe that this little girl found my key and rifled through my rocks—the collection I showed you not three days ago—and chose a valuable stone such as this?

Just one? And then returned to polish the silver? Come now, Rupert; you are a lawyer. Certainly, you can do better than that."

"It is true."

"No, it's not," Mabel protested.

Alistair turned to Mabel. "What did I say?"

Mabel stepped back behind the men, her hands on her hips, her eyes wild from the excitement of being addressed—tenderly, no less—by Mr. Hunt, from being acknowledged and dismissed simultaneously.

"Rupert, my son, I do not believe you. But that does not matter." He draped his arm around Rupert and released the lock on the patio doors with the other. He threw the doors open, letting in a full blast of cool fall air that smelled of burning leaves. "What a night," he yelled over the wind.

"Father, I—" Rupert repeated.

"Do not tell me. I do not want to know what you had in mind. But I do want to know this: What were you scheming with my maid?" He gestured back at Mabel. "She is *my* maid, in case you forgot. I cannot imagine what business you might have with her, other than to fetch your coat."

"Are you jealous, Father?" Rupert asked angrily.

"Ridiculous," Alistair said. "*You* are the guilty party here, if I remember correctly. *You* are the one who's up to something."

"I am worried about mother," Rupert said.

The smile left Alistair's face in an instant. "Do not be."

"I think you should get rid of this girl," Rupert said.

Mabel held her breath, hoping the dismissal would not come and change her life forever, but Mr. Hunt turned and held her gaze. "I will not," he said. Three words that kept her hope alive.

"For mother's sake."

Alistair stepped onto the patio, dragging his son with him, though Mabel still heard their conversation. She still heard how Mr. Hunt defended her. "I do not owe your mother a goddamn thing. Do not drag this poor girl into our fight."

"You are the one who dragged her into it, I do believe."

Alistair slapped his hands on his trousers. "You all will think the worst of me. I might as well live up to my reputation."

"Are you telling me you have nothing to do with her condition?"

Alistair glanced quickly back at Mabel. The night fell heavily and fast around them, devoid of moonlight or stars.

"Listen," Alistair finally said. "There is no sense in stirring things up around here. We have had a wild summer; everyone is tired. Is it not time you went back to New York?"

"I suppose it is," Rupert admitted. "I had some ideas, but they were not great ones."

Alistair let out one of his great guffaws. "It is hard to come up with great ideas, son. Believe me, I know."

Mabel watched from inside as the men stood on the patio, the wind blowing hard around them. Her future discussed and tossed about by these men as if her existence were nothing but a fable, not a real thing with real consequences. She was not even allowed to speak in defense of her own life. Mabel fumbled for her pocket. She still had the two hundred dollars. But not the emerald. She would have left the cottage for the emerald. She would have figured something out.

Mabel gathered the silver, still half-polished, and stacked it on a tray, placing the group on the sideboard and rushing from the room unnoticed. Too distracted to do chores, she shook at the idea of the money and the possibility of leaving—and because Mr. Hunt had defended her, had wanted her to stay, even at the risk of his son knowing their secret. Mr. Hunt must love her, she thought, even a bit, if he did not want to lose her altogether.

Mabel shut the door to her room and took the money out of her pocket, her hand shaking. She had not released her grip on the bundle since she ran from the dining room, past the butler and the cook, down the dirt path from the back of the main house to the servants' quarters. Each step she took resounded louder than the last, the grinding of gravel underfoot, the thud on the wooden steps to her room. As if the world announced her escape, as if nature itself were in cahoots with those who would try to stop her. Who would try to stop her, though? Mabel's heart still thudded in her chest, even though she realized that the only person who knew she had the money was Rupert. Would he come after her? Not if she left the cottage.

She sat on her bed and thumbed through the bills. Ones and fives and tens and twenties, even a fifty-dollar bill. Never had she seen this much money. Her salary was less than three dollars a week. Mabel was not strong at math, but she knew she would never see this much, even if she saved every penny for the whole year. But it still didn't seem enough to live on indefinitely. Could she pack up and go right now and not have another thought about how she would live? Where would she go? A woman with no pedigree—she thought of herself as a woman ever since her affair with Mr. Hunt—a woman who was carrying an illegitimate child.

Mabel spread the money across her white bedspread. She had a wild thought: What if she asked Willie to go with her? Of course, she didn't think of him as a lover, but she thought she could trust him, like a brother. They would have to live as if he was her servant, in an apartment in a city, and he could get another job, eventually. He would be easily employable. They could make up a story about how her husband had died and how Willie had been asked on the man's deathbed to take care of his wife. But Mabel knew that a single, pregnant woman traveling and living with a negro male would draw attention.

Or maybe the women she had listened to at the suffrage meeting. The constable had said they were staying at the Breakwater. Were they still here? Would they help her?

Under her bed, Mabel reached for the small valise she had arrived with not a year ago. Already, dust had covered the surface, and she wiped at it, leaving streaks of dirt on her palm. The fabric was paisley—pink and green embroidered. Mabel remembered her mother carrying the bag when they stepped from the boat onto American soil. She was a child then, still holding her mother's hand. She remembered the fog and the crowds—so many people, moving like a flock of sheep down the gangplank—and she remembered the dark outline of her father's back as he disappeared through the throngs. Mabel felt like that was the day she had lost her father to America, as if he had never returned from that cacophony, though she was sure he must have. In all her memories, her father was no more than a shadow, a man she knew was disappointed to have a daughter, a man who had lost his son the day he had been born. This was before, in Scotland, before Mabel was alive. But her mother had brought flowers to Ian's—the stillborn's—grave each spring before they came to America. The boy's name was not mentioned in her household, but Mabel remembered it, as she knew her mother did, as she guessed her father did.

Mabel heard footsteps ascending the stairs, and she quickly thrust all the money into the valise, shoving it under her bed again right before Rebecca came trudging into the room. She cried out when she saw Mabel on her knees by the bed.

"What are you doing up here?" Rebecca squealed.

"I was cold. I came to get a wrap."

"You never seem to be working these days," Rebecca accused. "Every time I look, you're off doing something other than what you should be doing. You think because of your—I must say—your *sin*, that excuses you from doing work? Do you expect me to do extra because of your lack of virtue? If you think—"

"Rebecca, please," Mabel said, weary.

"I don't think it is fair, your wandering about doing whatever you please while I'm scrubbing and cleaning."

Mabel shrugged. "Well, what are *you* doing here?"

"I am, well, I am—" Rebecca suddenly burst into tears. "I can't tell you," she said through racking sobs.

Mabel stood and put her arm awkwardly around the girl. She was never very good at consoling, but she thought she should try. "Now, now," she said.

"I can't tell what's supposed to be my job and where I'm supposed to be a good Christian. I know I should follow Jesus, but I'm also supposed to honor my superiors. Correct? I wouldn't know what to do if I didn't work for the Hunts. I've always worked for the Hunts."

Mabel led Rebecca to the edge of her bed, and they sat, Rebecca crying into her hands, Mabel's eyes straying to the valise under her bed.

"Follow your heart; is that not what they always say?" Mabel asked.

"But if I do, I might lose my job."

"You will *not* lose your job, Rebecca. If anyone's going to get fired, it'll be me. We both know that."

Rebecca looked up, tears streaming down her chubby cheeks. "Mrs. Hunt asked me to do something awful, and I don't think I can do it."

"Then don't do it, Rebecca. The Hunts don't own us. We're not puppets that they can dance around to amuse themselves."

"What do you mean?" Rebecca asked.

"We *are* their servants; we're supposed to work for them, but that's it. They can't ask us to do more than what we were hired for: cleaning and cooking or gardening, those types of things. They don't own us. We're not slaves."

Rebecca looked at the door, her skin red and puffy. "But we have nothing without them."

"Look, if I wanted to, I could walk away right now, today. I could start a life somewhere else. I don't owe anything to these people. Lord, Mrs. Hunt would probably be happy to get rid of me." Mabel walked to the window and stared out as she spoke, talking to the whole of Serabelle and Mother Nature herself, trying to get to the core of what she actually believed. "I don't want to be a servant anymore, Rebecca. What if I had the chance to be something else; do you not think I should take it? Do you not think that a person deserves more out of life—every person, not just the owners of the cottages—than to spend your days on your knees, beating the laundry, washing the dishes, making the beds?"

"I don't know," Rebecca said nervously, as if the thought had never occurred to her.

"Of course, you don't. That's because you've never tasted what it might be like to live another way. Let me tell you. When Mr. Hunt danced with me, when he held me like he did…"

"Stop, stop. I don't want to—"

Mabel turned and looked at Rebecca. She seemed truly frightened, her eyes wide and her brow knit. "Tell me what Mrs. Hunt wants."

"I can't."

Mabel shook her head slowly, trying to shift her thoughts to Rebecca. "Without knowing what has been asked of you, all I can say is: do not do something you will regret. Look at me. Once you have done certain things, you can't take them back."

A wood thrush, active late in the day, flew to the bedroom window and stared in at Rebecca and Mabel. The bird tapped its tiny brown beak against the pane, looking for food, for shelter. Mabel flashed a smile at the little bird, so innocent. Over their own silence, the girls heard a commotion downstairs. They looked at each other, frightened that the noise had something to do with them. It was three o'clock, an odd hour for anyone to be in the servants' quarters, other than the second butler, who would be sound asleep. Beverly's voice rose shrilly over a deeper, male tone. The man's voice was calm and authoritative. Mabel knew who it was: Rupert. Coming to fetch the money.

✦   ✦   ✦

Rupert stood awkwardly in the main doorway to the servants' quarters.

"Where is that little maid?" he barked.

Beverly spoke evenly, calmly, as she did to all the Hunts. "Excuse me, sir?"

"The young maid, she has something of mine," he said. "Where is she?"

"Mabel?" Beverly guessed.

Rupert nodded sharply.

She sighed and set down the list she had been working on. "Well, I'm not certain. I can try to find her if you would like. What is it you think she has?"

"None of your business," Rupert said and crossed to the stairway. "Where is her room? Upstairs?"

Beverly instinctively threw her arms across the entrance to the stairs, blocking Rupert's entry. "Sir, you cannot come barging in here, demanding to enter a young lady's room. It's not proper. I'll see if she is up there."

"Do I have to remind you that my parents own this house? That we have the right to go anywhere we want on the grounds, including a maid's room?" Rupert stopped, hands on his hips, a wry smile on his face. "Besides, I think we both know she is no lady."

"Master Rupert!" Beverly scolded. "My goodness, what a thing to say."

Rupert slowly removed Beverly's arm from the wall and moved around her, up the stairs. "You might as well tell me which room it is," he said over his shoulder, "or I will try them all. God knows what I will find here."

Beverly followed him reluctantly up the stairs and pointed to the girls' room. "Mabel, are you in there?" she asked as a warning before Rupert flung open the door.

Mabel and Rebecca stood by the window, their backs to the door, but their faces twisted around toward the intruders. Rebecca's eyes were wet and reddened. Clearly, she had been crying. Mabel largely looked tired.

"Rebecca," Beverly said, "you too? What in the world is wrong with you now? Lord, am I the one person working today?"

Rebecca sprang over to Beverly, pleading with her to understand, but Beverly had already turned her attention to Mabel, who stood with her head hung down, as if trying to block out their presence.

"Leave us," Rupert said to Beverly.

"Go, Rebecca." Beverly shoved her out into the hallway. "We'll talk later." She closed the door behind her. "Master Rupert, whatever it is you have to say to Mabel, I would like to be a witness. The girl has had enough trials. She is fragile, you understand."

"Fragile?" Rupert chortled. "Hardly. And *no*, you may not stay. This is between her and me."

Beverly wavered by the door. "Mabel?"

"It's okay," Mabel said under her breath, still not looking up.

"I'll be right downstairs. You holler if you need something."

"Where is it?" Rupert demanded after he had heard Beverly's steps descending.

Mabel pointed under the bed across the room.

"You did not actually think I was going to let you keep it, did you?"

Mabel gave a little laugh, nervous and high. "I thought maybe you wanted me gone badly enough. I might have gone, you know, given enough time to form a plan."

Rupert knelt and opened the suitcase. money scattered across the satin lining. He gathered it up and made neat piles of the same denomination, taking his time, chatting with the girl as he stacked. "I am going to check that it is all here; do not worry about that. If you have hidden any somewhere else, I will know. I know exactly how much I had in my pocket."

"I'm sure you do," Mabel said under her breath.

"It seems my father does not want to get rid of you. Imagine that—the master of the house defending a lowly maid. Does not add up, does it? Why should my father care what happens to you?"

Mabel looked up defiantly. "Because he loves me."

Rupert jumped from his crouch by the bed and dove across the room, grabbing at the back of Mabel's hair through her bonnet. "Filthy harlot." Rupert put his face close to hers, his breath spreading hot and putrid across her cheek, making her eyes water. "Never presume that you have the right to speak of my father, in any manner. You are not worthy of my father's love. You do not exist as far as this family goes."

Before Rupert released his grip, he ground his mouth into hers, more of an attack than a kiss, drawing blood from her lower lip. He slipped his hand over her bosom and squeezed hard until she flinched. Then he threw her back across the bed.

"You do not exist," he said once more before he gathered the bills without counting and shoved them in his pocket.

Mabel turned her head away, shutting her eyes tight.

✦　✦　✦

Mabel tried to ignore Beverly's question. She thought in that moment that if she were standing on the ledge of the window or at the edge of the cliff, she could easily throw herself over, damn the consequences. But she was not standing on the edge of a cliff; she was lying on the bed, still, where Rupert had left her, tears soaking the bed cloth, blood drying on her lip.

"Did you hear me, girl?" Beverly insisted.

Mabel sat up and focused on the woman in front of her. Beverly didn't look angry, as Mabel had imagined she might. Her brow was knit, and her tone was firm, but not angry.

"Did he hurt you?"

"No," Mabel shook her head slowly. "He just scared me."

"What did he want?" Beverly asked.

"I think he knows about Mr. Hunt and me, and he's upset; that's all. He tried to threaten me. He *did* threaten me."

Beverly stormed across the room and back, hands on her hips. "Oh, those men. I don't usually get my dander up—I think you know that—but when they act that way, well, I cannot abide."

"Why are you being so nice to me?" Mabel asked.

Beverly stopped her pacing and cocked her head, considering. "No one knows this, not even my husband, so don't go repeating it." She sat down next to Mabel on the bed. "When I was about your age, I was working for a family in Nashua, where my folks are from, and the master of that estate—oh, how Mr. Hunt reminds me of that old man—he took a liking to me too." Beverly laughed. "Believe it or not, I wasn't a bad-looking girl— if not striking like you—at least what some would call handsome. That man chased me ah-round the house; scared the daylights out of me. Finally, my mother permitted me to quit my post and found me another job before anything dreadful happened. I never forgot that feeling of constantly looking over my shoulder. It's not right. The good Lord certainly cannot have meant for women to live this way."

Mabel smiled, rubbing her arms to ward off the chill that settled after the sun sank over the trees. "Did you ever want to do something else?"

"What do you mean?" Beverly asked.

"In life, other than being somebody's maid."

Beverly shook her head. "I don't think about that."

"Ever?"

"Mabel, one thing you learn when you get older is that you have to accept life as it is, not how you'd like it to be. I came from a family of servants. How would I ever have been anything else?" Beverly patted Mabel's knee before she stood. "Besides, I'm not purely someone's maid— I run a household—and a very special one at that. Rumor has it that the Ainsworth-Hunts are one of the ten wealthiest families in New England. I believe it. Look at what a place we have here—our own house, where I might add, you can run to your room during the middle of the day and cry, if need be. Things are not so bad when we look at it that way, are they?

Some people don't even have a job; they are begging on the street in the cities—I have seen them."

Beverly walked to the door.

"Besides, that young Mr. Hunt—Rupert—he'll be gone in a day or two—and the rest of the family will be on their way to Boston very shortly afterward. We'll have the place to ourselves this winter, provided they won't want you to travel with them. We can assume Mrs. Hunt wouldn't have that." She turned before she left the room, pausing momentarily. "I'm sorry this happened, but it all could have been avoided if you had thought to come to me first, before Mr. Hunt laid his hands on you, before you got in trouble. You could have trusted me, Mabel." Beverly sighed again, this time deeply and with finality. "That's another thing, I suppose, that comes with age—an ability to discern who is trustworthy. Life will teach you. Have no fear. I suspect you're going to learn quickly."

Mabel waited until she heard Beverly's steps in the kitchen, then walked over to the suitcase that Rupert had kicked back under her bed, hoping he had left a bill or two. She knelt and pulled the case toward her. Still open, it rocked on the hinge as she touched the side, running her hand through the bottom and inside the pocket. No. There was nothing; even the coins were gone. The smooth fabric remained, billowing and empty. She had been so close to escaping. Close, maybe, but not quick enough. She bet Willie would have gone with her. Maybe he still would. Did he have any money saved? If he did, would he be willing to spend his savings, running away with her? She would ask. She *had* to ask. The idea of freedom had been so near; she almost believed she had a choice. She wasn't ready to give up the dream. If Rupert was right, if she didn't exist to this family, then maybe she really shouldn't be at Serabelle. If only he hadn't taken the money back. Mabel sat back on her haunches.

Rupert took the money because he said Mr. Hunt didn't want Mabel to go. Did that mean that Mr. Hunt would take care of her? That he had had a change of heart? It warranted a discussion, at least, before she took off. She would ask him herself—if he cared that she still remained.

Chapter 24
Left for Dead

The cold of the cement floor had crept into his skin, numbing his blood and freezing his extremities. His head ached as if a steel-toed boot was resting on his face, forcing him down. Forrest turned his neck with difficulty. Light no longer leaked under the garage door, and there was no sound in the small cell, no smell other than the empty, oily scent of a garage and the salty odor of blood. Forrest raised his arm and felt the back of his head, his fingers immediately coated by the sticky, coagulating blood. His head cleared, and Forrest remembered his struggle with Rupert. He laughed, incredulous that the pudgy, pasty man had bested him. Forrest wiggled his toes, then his legs, making sure they had feeling before he attempted to arise.

He sat up, feeling lightheaded, still chilled and achy, but in one piece. His whole body smarted, and when he moved, he felt as if a pendulum swung back and forth inside his head, a small silver ball knocking at the sides of his skull.

"Well, well, Mr. Rupert," he said into the dark of the garage, "you have surprised me after all." His voice felt husky and thick in the heavy air, and Forrest wondered if he needed to get stitches. There was a lot of blood on the floor behind him, on his clothing, matted in his hair.

Forrest dragged himself up with the aid of the bench, leaning on its solid wood, his hand resting lightly on the vise that had taken him down.

He patted it thoughtfully, then shuffled a few items on the bench: a canister of saltpeter and a firecracker that he had been packing before Rupert arrived. Then Forrest remembered the emerald. He checked his pockets. Three times he checked, dubious that Rupert was smart enough to find the jewel. Nothing.

Well, the rich boy was clearly slicker than he had anticipated. But why had Rupert not finished him off, just to make sure? Surely, he knew that if Forrest lived, he would not forget what had happened. Or had Rupert left him for dead?

Regardless, the man had to pay. There was no doubt about that.

Chapter 25
Theodore

When Mr. Hunt came stumbling home a few days later, Theo was reclining on a bale of hay, reading his book—a copy of *Gulliver's Travels* he had picked up in town that day, as he always tried to have a new book on hand on Thursday nights. The poker games could go on for hours, and ever since his conflict with Gardener, Theo had stayed clear of both the poker room and Gardener. He didn't know how Willie forgave the brute, but he had— in fact, Theo had seen the two of them palling around the night before, joking after supper on the back stoop. Theo, on the other hand, had kept his head down, eyes averted whenever Gardener was around. He didn't want to be thrown down the stairs.

His book tucked tightly under his arm, Theo watched from the stables as Mr. Hunt pounded at the door to the main house. In his peripheral vision, his eye caught a movement in the woods beyond the hedges. Mr. Hunt was making an awful racket, but there was no response from inside the house. Finally, Theo made his way around to the servants' entrance and walked into the kitchen. The second butler sat with his back to the door, one hand on the table next to an overturned teacup.

"Mr. Wilson," Theo said.

"Wha?" The man turned sluggishly and looked at the boy.

"Mr. Wilson, do you not hear Mr. Hunt pounding at the front door?"

The second butler's speech was slurred. "Who was it?"

"Mr. Hunt. Listen." Theo came around to the front of the table. "Sir, are you drunk?"

The butler merely blinked. Theo shook his head, walking through the parlor towards the front entrance. Though he had looked through the windows of the cottage before, the splendor of the rooms, the sheer size of them could not be grasped without standing inside. Theo had a twinge of longing—if not for riches, at least for the comfort of more than a hay bale. Was it so much to ask that he should have a couch to sit upon while reading his books? Was it so much to hope for?

Once again, Mr. Hunt hit at the door, spewing profanities now, though with less gusto. Theo walked through the dim foyer and turned the lock on the front door, stepping aside as Mr. Hunt lurched in, grabbing at what would have been Mr. Wilson's lapel, but was, in fact, the rough fabric of Theo's canvas riding jacket, the same coat he wore day after day in the stables—the one coat he had besides his Sunday best, worn for church and for the occasional local dance or festival. Theo had only worn his suit—a relic from his days as a jockey, days before his father had died, leaving his mother with debts she had no way of settling—twice this summer, other than to church: once on the Fourth of July and once to the blueberry festival in August where he had danced with a pretty little blond-haired washer girl from the south end of the island.

Now, Theo tried to move out of the doorway enough to shut the door, but Mr. Hunt's weight leaned heavy against his chest in startling contrast to the memory of the young washer maid.

"You are not Mr. Wilson," Alistair said, still leaning in. "What are you doing in my house?"

"I heard you knocking. I was afraid you would wake up the household," Theo said.

"Did you lock the door?"

"No, sir," Theo protested. "I *unlocked* the door."

"Lock, unlock—you are not supposed to be in here, stable boy."

Theo shook himself free of Mr. Hunt with his whiskey breath. Unlike Willie, Theo was not good at kowtowing to the Hunts. He stayed out of their way, kept his head down, and did not engage. But Theo had a hard time bowing down to people he once thought, if not his equal, at least within close social circles. When he was a jockey, all wealthy families—particularly the patriarchs—would natter with Theo before a race. Even Mr. Hunt had spoken to him before, though now that Theo was a servant, Mr. Hunt acted as if he did not remember. The wealthy patrons came down to the stables, checking out the various horses slated to race, and inevitably, some man or another would plead with Theo to be lucky for them that day, to win the race—which he often did. He became somewhat of a celebrity in the racing circles. And now look at him, being chastised for helping out. Theo did not take kindly at all to Mr. Hunt's tone.

"Excuse me," Theo said with his chin held high, and he walked out the front, slamming the door behind him.

Upstairs, with her anteroom door cracked, Julia listened to their exchange. The words were nothing more than muffled chatter from that distance, but Julia could tell that her husband was drunk. *All the better,* she thought, for the shock he was about to discover. Rebecca had come to her earlier that evening, whimpering and crying that she couldn't do as she was asked, couldn't perform that type of sin, any sin really in the eyes of God. She was a pious girl, she said.

"I am ordering you to do this, you ingrate," Julia had demanded.

"I am sorry, ma'am. Please do not ask me such things. I feel that the devil himself has thrown this temptation at my feet, and I must resist."

Julia had been so irate, she had stomped down the stairs, grabbed an unstuffed pillowcase—one of her embroidery projects—and marched straight into the library, Rebecca trailing behind. The cook had already rung the dinner bell, so Rupert, Melinda, and Alistair would be at the table in the dining room. Julia barked at Rebecca: "Tell them to start without me. Say that I am finishing up a letter."

Julia locked the library door behind her, pulled the blinds, and dumped the trays, one by one, into the pillowcase. On the outside of the case, a half-finished Lord's Prayer had been immaculately stitched, the embroidery needle still swinging from a periwinkle thread. When she finished all the trays, the case was full to bursting, a compact two-foot by two-foot square, lumpy and hard with stones. Julia leaned against the edge of the desk and quickly stitched up the open end of the fabric, enclosing the package of gems. She neatly placed the trays back into the cabinet, locked the door to the hutch, and replaced the key. Julia thought she could not have planned it better. This was the perfect timing, with everyone at dinner, in the waning daylight, right under his nose.

Julia returned to the parlor where she had grabbed her embroidery and placed the packet of gems in her knitting bag. She threw the empty frame on top, as well as another piece of fabric—the makings of her next pillow. The tan canvas already had the sketch of Psalms 3:3 sketched in the center: "Oh Lord, You bestow glory on me and lift up my head." Julia stepped back and checked all the angles, ensuring the bundle was not obvious. Rebecca stood in the entrance to the parlor, wringing her hands, her lips trembling.

"I told them, ma'am," Rebecca said.

Julia blinked, checking the bundle again out of the corner of her eye. "You told them what?"

"What you said, that you would be right in."

With a quick pat of the knitting basket, Julia made her way out of the parlor and into the dining room where her family awaited, a nearly imperceptible smile at the corners of her mouth.

When she heard her husband in the foyer, Julia was sorely tempted to creep down the stairs to watch his reaction, should he find the gems to be missing, but she fought the temptation. She decided to wait out the night, feigning sleep until she heard his call. Julia lay on her bed thinking of the collection, sewn up tight into her embroidery pillow, lying right there where he would never think to look. She smiled at her own deviousness, a side of herself never before exposed. There was a chance Alistair might not discover the theft until morning, so she would have to be patient. The wait would be worth it. She glanced over to where Chou Chou's body still lay on the pink pillow. The body was starting to smell, even on ice, but she couldn't bring herself to part with him, not yet. She wanted Chou Chou to be a reminder of Alistair, a reminder of the day he went too far.

Chapter 26
Skip Greenfield

The Thursday night Rupert stood outside and spied on staff entering the yellow house, the men kept it down in the poker room. One of the neighbor groundskeepers had seen Rupert wobbling there in the dusk, hiding behind a tree, and when the men reached the third floor, they talked in hushed tones about what he could be doing, what he wanted from the servants. They couldn't imagine, but they hoped it wasn't to bust up their card game. The weekly poker night was nearly the most fun they had on the quiet little island. Every other night of the week, the stable boys and butlers, the drivers and gardeners were expected to be at the beck and call of their bosses—not every household had a second butler. Over the weekend, their households would have any number of guests and parties, so typically, Thursday was a quiet night, a night they stopped work early.

It was the next Thursday that Forrest decided to strike. He didn't want to delay any longer, couldn't wait until Rupert had left town, as he now wanted to ensure that Rupert was implicated. Normally, Forrest would have scoped the cottage out himself at least once before breaking and entering, but there was no time for that. Most families left Maine shortly after Labor Day, and the holiday was several weeks past.

Forrest's head was still tender, and he wore a bandage wrapped around the wound underneath his dark cap. He had not bothered with stitches, though he would get a nasty scar. He nearly fainted from the pain when he cleaned the wound at home, his mother knocking at the bathroom door when she heard him cry out in agony. Luckily, she hadn't seen him enter the house, all covered in blood and dirt. He wrapped his clothing in an old towel from the bottom of the linen closet and threw the bundle in the garbage bin. He kept a hat on, even in the house, so his doddery parents wouldn't ask about his injury. Forrest's parents were older than most of his peers' mothers and fathers: his father had been a ridiculous fifty years old when Forrest was born. His mother had been thirty-eight. Most women who were pregnant at that age didn't make it past childbirth. But somehow, Forrest's parents had lived on to fuss over him his whole life, never with any proper authority, more like grandparents who had already lived full lives before he came along.

Forrest parked his parents' car, a Sears Autobuggy, at the cemetery where his grandparents were buried, halfway between his parents' house and the Hunts'. He even put the perfunctory carnations on his grandparents' graves before he walked through the cloak of dusk to Serabelle. He loved that name, had always felt a jealous longing that his parents' house did not have such a sonorous title. Their little brick and white-columned house was called Crow's Nest. What kind of name was that? A pauper's name—that's what, something a pirate would think of.

He kept to the side of the road, flattening a sack against his shoulder, walking close to the oak trees that lined the street. He wouldn't want to be seen anywhere near the cottage this evening. Forrest was careful in his thieveries, enough so that if there was one witness, one person who saw him enter the grounds, he would abort his plans. He didn't need the money as much as he wanted revenge—not in the least for what Rupert had done to his head, but for something larger—for all the rich boys at school who had reminded him he was on scholarship.

Evening arrived earlier with each passing day. Forrest had waited until dusk to drive to the cemetery, and by the time he walked the two and a half miles to the cottage, dark had descended around him. He could barely make out the white skin of his hands and the gray edges of the larger rocks on the road. Moonlight was shrouded by wispy clouds, diffused and dispersed like the low, even flame from a fire viewed at a distance. Forrest craned his neck, but he couldn't find the moon.

He was adept at sneaking up on people, on houses. Forrest had not done a lot of burglaries himself—a handful of summer homes that had been locked up over the winter (his parents and he were one of the few families who stayed on Mt. Desert year-round). He had started the break-ins while still in school and had never been caught. In fact, he rarely stole more than a piece of silver, a watch, or a bit of cash he found. Again, the point wasn't the money. The point was that he was smarter than the people he stole from—slyer, craftier. Getting one over on the staff, though, that became the hiccup over the winters. He soon realized that if he didn't steal large amounts or make it look like a break-in, the servants would be blamed.

The revelation came to him his senior year at Exeter, two winters after he began the break-ins. One of the wealthiest boys in his class, Skip Greenfield, had complained that his parents thought their maid was stealing from them. A family heirloom, a gold pocket watch, had been missing for months. His father couldn't remember the last time he had worn it, but knew he always kept it on his dresser. One day, it was gone. Nothing else was missing; the staff hadn't noticed anything unusual. The obvious conclusion was that one of the servants must have stolen it, so the maid who cleaned the room was fired. Listening to Skip, Forrest realized what his petty thievery had likely done, and for that, he had a twinge of remorse—not enough to stop him altogether, but enough to give him pause.

In the distance, a lantern swung in a regular rhythm, drawing close to Serabelle's gate. His senses heightened, Forrest heard footsteps a good distance behind him, and he stepped up onto the embankment behind the solid oaks. He moved lightly and quietly until he made out the forms of two men, each holding a lantern, their sonorous voices chiding each other through the frosty air. A chill had come quickly with the night, making Forrest's hands stiff and unwieldy. He shoved his hands into his pockets, holding the sack with his elbow until the two had passed.

In this manner, Forrest made it to the outer wall of the cottage, taking his time and making sure to remain invisible and silent. The uneven rock wall that bordered the road surrounding the grounds was four feet high at the outer edges. The section near the front gate loomed tall, over eight feet, cresting like a wave in front of the drive. Forrest easily hopped the wall on the southern end of the cottage, wondering exactly who or what this wall was supposed to keep out. Even a determined deer could manage to clear the rocks.

Forrest pulled a few items from the sack as he crept over the pine needle floor of the sparse copse of trees. He stopped and rubbed his face with the residue of a piece of charcoal, wrapping the remainder in a rag and placing it back in the bag. Then he donned a pair of black gloves. Through the trees, he saw lights from the main house; a few were illuminated, in what looked to be—from what he had understood from Rupert—the front parlor, and then an upper bedroom. A lantern burned in the stable, and on the other side of the grounds, a glow arose behind the tall shrubs from the servants' quarters.

Forrest circled the house at a distance, moving around the stables and through the gardens. He watched Alistair Hunt climb into his Winton and drive off. Forrest wondered why he didn't take his driver with him. Forrest waited and watched with necessary patience, forcing himself not to shiver in the frigid night air. What had felt brisk at first now settled into his bones, a deep chill he knew would take hours to work out of his system. He had no choice now but to keep still and let the cold roll over his body.

One by one, lights were put out at the cottage. The night butler, a rambling old man Rupert had warned him about, came to the front window of the parlor several times, looking out into the night as if he suspected Forrest's presence. From where he sat in the bushes at the edge of the lawn, the night looked as if it had taken on an otherworldly quality, a stillness like in photographs that Forrest had seen. Suddenly, he had the urge to view the ocean. He heard its constant pull and crash upon the shore beyond the grounds, at the edges of the solid earth. And he knew that out there, the sea was not still like a photograph; there, on the ocean, life was in constant motion, and it called to Forrest for the first time in his life. He had never longed to be out on the water—fishing and lobstering honestly looked like too hard of a life—but right then, sitting still in the bushes, wanting a cigarette, not moving, he understood the pull of the sea, the resistance to the static life on land.

Forrest turned his attention back to the cottage. He knew the only way he'd be able to get in, now that he didn't have Rupert's help, was through the back servants' entrance. And it was likely that the second butler would be sitting back in the kitchen, sipping his tea, listening to the sounds of the night. He would have to create a distraction.

An owl hooted insistently in the distance. The haunting call echoed out into the darkness, like a warning. Forrest shivered and pulled a box of matches and the bundle of firecrackers out of his sack. He flexed his fingers and shook his limbs, trying to move some blood back to his extremities. He'd have to hurry if the timing was to work. There was no time for sluggishness.

Muffled laughter from the servants' quarters drifted under the occasional hoot of the owl. Rupert stood in the dark, listening and watching until he finally felt it was the right moment—that the card players were sufficiently occupied, that Rupert and his wife and his mother had all retired. No one else was near to witness him throw the firecrackers and run around to the servants' entrance.

He lit the fuses.

The bundle bounced twice on the soft green lawn underneath the parlor windows. Forrest didn't stay to witness the ignition but hustled around to the back of the house. As he ran, the moon crept out from behind the haze of clouds, as if it meant to light his path, a beam landing dead on the stoop of the back entrance. He had not quite reached the landing when he heard the firecrackers' pop, pop, crash. The blast boomed out into the night. Forrest recognized the scrape of a chair pushing back, and he lifted his head to peer through the kitchen window. As expected, the firecrackers had aroused the butler, who hustled out into the dining room.

Forrest quickly and lightly ran up the steps, let himself in, and deftly emptied a packet in his right hand into the cup of tea sitting on the kitchen table. He stirred the tea with a spoon that leaned on the saucer, then slipped out the door leading to the small, informal dining room opposite the main dining hall. Forrest had studied the hand-drawn map that Rupert brought with him to their second meeting. He knew the butler would be preoccupied in the front of the house, and he could work his way along the east side, holing up quietly in the hall closet beside the library until he knew the butler had returned to the kitchen. But he also knew he couldn't wait too long, that Alistair Hunt could return at any moment and might be up all night. He was the wild card here, he and the second butler.

The closet was completely dark and smelled of bleach and rye. Forrest had just clicked the knob shut when he heard footsteps on the main stairway, then Rupert's voice, shouting down to the butler.

"Yes, sir, what is it?" The second butler hustled around the corner from the parlor.

"What is that racket?" Rupert asked.

"I cannot tell, sir, but I was about to go over to the yellow house and peruse the grounds."

"See that you do so." Rupert started back up the steps. "And butler," he said, "make sure you lock up behind you. Keep all the doors and windows locked. We do not want any trouble."

The second butler scanned Rupert's face before answering, as if trying to decipher a mystery. "Of course," he finally said.

Forrest waited in the closet until he was sure that Rupert had returned upstairs and then slipped easily into the library. The room was pitch black—shades drawn tight over the window, so even the scarce moonlight didn't penetrate the richness of the dark. Even with his eyes adjusted, he couldn't see a thing, but Forrest didn't want to risk the second butler seeing a light in the library from outside. If he needed light, he'd have to wait until the old man returned to the main house.

He moved slowly and silently across the wood planks, testing his footing before stepping across the throw rug. The house creaked and groaned around him, and he froze several times at the slightest noise. It seemed to take him an hour to cross to the desk, moving as a cat might if stalking prey, one muscle at a time. The control he exerted gave him a thrill, even with his pounding head and the chill that had reached his bones.

Finally, his thigh touched the corner of the desk. Forrest inched his way around as he heard the front door slam shut. He crouched down behind the desk and listened to the butler's footsteps in the hallway, the steps halting outside the door to the library. Forrest dared not take a breath until the steps moved on, and even then, he stayed in his crouch for a full three minutes before he dared to stand.

Overhead, footsteps thudded, and he heard Rupert's muffled call to the butler, probably from the top of the stairs. He couldn't make out their words, but the exchange was brief, and then the butler walked away, presumably to the kitchen once again.

Forrest listened carefully for the steps to recede before he softly pulled out the desk drawer to retrieve the hutch key, right there as expected. Forrest held the key in his palm. He thought perhaps he had never experienced a darkness so black, so pure, as existed in that room. Forrest reached out his other hand and felt for the glass of the cabinet, stepping gingerly, his feet working toe, heel, toe, heel. The glass was cold on his fingertips as he found the keyhole. The hinge creaked open, and Forrest hesitated. With any luck, the butler would be asleep at the table by now, cold tea on his lips.

He put his hand inside the cabinet and felt for the gems. Forrest lifted the first tray off the stack and placed it gently on the desk. Then he lightly placed his sack on the ground, the piece of coal and a wonderlite making a small thud as they landed. Forrest's eyes flickered up toward the door and back again. He lifted the lid off the tray—a soft, velvet-coated lid with straps that he had to fumble around to find. He ran his hands across the tray contents, surprised to find no rocks, at least not in this first box. His fingers traced a satiny smooth surface. Forrest quickly turned and felt for the next tray, still stacked inside the cabinet. That, too, was smooth. And the next tray, and the next. There were no gems.

Forrest's chest heaved in a half-cry, half-silent laugh. Had Rupert outfoxed him? Had he moved the gems? Told his father? It seemed impossible that the man was that sly and forward-thinking. After all, had Rupert not left him for dead? Forrest wiped at his brow and pulled up the shade. Damn the consequences.

The moon had gone back behind its cover of clouds and mist, but even the dispersed light was enough for Forrest to discover that he had not been mistaken. The gems were, in fact, gone. He leaned with both hands on the wide window ledge, a chill moving up his spine. It was hard for him to accept defeat in this manner. Twice in a week, Rupert had gotten the better of him—this man who had everything—all the money he needed, a career, a beautiful wife, a cottage he would inherit. Surely there was a way he could still defeat this scared, spoiled man.

Forrest turned his gaze to the plant stand. The pink diamond. Hopefully, the gem was still there, inside the special safe. Forrest placed the plant on the floor—an ugly, common ivy that had turned brown for lack of care—and removed the top of the stand. A combination lock was inset. He didn't have the tools to deal with a safe, and that wasn't his type of expertise. His original idea was for Rupert to get the combination and keep the pink diamond. Forrest cursed himself for rushing into this break-in. He had not completely decided to steal the pink diamond because it would be nearly impossible to fence. The diamond was the only thing left now, though; he would have to take it with him. Forrest bent and tested the weight of the stand. Not bad, but almost impossible to carry for several miles—at least as quickly as he would need to. But he refused to leave empty-handed. He couldn't let Rupert win.

While he thought about his options, Forrest deftly re-stacked the empty trays to buy himself more time. He certainly couldn't carry the plaster stand back through the kitchen, even on the chance that the butler was asleep. The bulky stand would inhibit his movement, his ability to duck if someone stirred. Forrest checked the windows. His last hope.

The library was on the far south end of the main house, closest to the stables, the windows masked at the lower quarter by the perfectly trimmed hydrangea bushes. The windows cranked open on a hinge centered horizontally, the panes coming just short of parallel with the ground. Forrest unlocked and opened the window closest to the plant stand, slowly, inch by inch, until the pane reached its fullest extent. The night air hit him with a full, saline breath. Suddenly, he felt as if he needed to be outside, as if the cottage's walls were about to squeeze in on him. Forrest picked up the plaster stand, his tendons stretching with the effort, all his lean muscles tense. He turned the pillar sideways and ducked under the pane, leaning fully out the window, his body doubled over until he could place the stand upright in the bushes. He was making more noise than was wise, but given the circumstances, he had no choice.

Forrest hesitated for a minute, considering whether he should hop out the window or crank it closed and return through the kitchen. Who would notice that the window was open? No one but Alistair Hunt, upon returning, might see. Forrest counted on Alistair being drunk—his reputation preceded him—and not noticing until morning. By then, it would be too late.

Forrest picked up the plant and the lid to the stand and placed them outside the window as well. He cranked the window as tight as possible while still leaving space enough for him to slip through before placing the key in the desk drawer and then closing the blinds, once again darkening the room. Forrest slid under the blinds and through the window, his slim form moving like a worm through the dirt. He landed next to the pillar, behind the bushes, his hand squashing the plant. He sat watching the sky, catching his breath. The clouds didn't move, once again painting the landscape like a photograph. Even the trees in the distance refused to rustle.

Across the lawn, at the entrance to the cottage, lights approached. Forrest thought it could be the servants leaving, but the lights swung full and bright down the driveway, and he heard the hum of a car engine. Alistair. He would have to move quickly. Forrest waited until the lights moved past him, the car careening noisily towards the stables. He risked discovery if he tried to cut straight across the driveway to the copse of trees as he had arrived. Instead, Forrest grabbed the pillar under his arm and stayed low behind the bushes, hugging the cottage wall, moving north— farther away from where his car was parked but towards the protective cover of trees. He dashed in a crouch from the bushes to behind one of the great figures guarding the entrance, then behind the wall of bushes on the north end of the grounds, ducking finally behind the wall that hid the servants' path to their quarters. Alistair slammed the door of his car after he killed the engine. As Forrest ducked into the woods behind the yellow house, he heard Alistair's steps on the gravel drive.

On the third floor, in the poker room, lights still burned, music still played, though lower and quieter since the second butler had come over to scold the men. They had heard the loud bang, too. Gardener teased that they had thought old Mr. Wilson was having his own party.

Behind him, farther away each minute, Forrest heard Alistair cursing and pounding at the front door. The length of time this went on suggested that the butler had, in fact, drunk the tea. Time, of course, was of the essence in this situation. The men who had come to play cards were getting ready to leave from the yellow house, a good thirty yards away from the sparse woods surrounding the cottage. They relit their lanterns at the gate, talking jovially. Forrest stood still and listened, trying to make out the features of the men, seeing if he recognized any of them. He dared not move until they had left the grounds. And then, he knew, it would take a good while for the men to meander back down the road, as they were all on foot. This was a holdup he had not counted on.

Forrest held his breath, listening for sounds from the main house, but it seemed Alistair had either been allowed in or had fallen asleep on the stoop. No alarms had been raised, no servants questioned or accused that he could tell. Forrest waited until the lanterns had faded a good distance towards the horizon and then dashed, pillar under his arm, across the main road, and into the denser pine thicket. His muscles shook under the weight; he would find a hidden place here in the woods to mask the pillar, then come back with the car. His footsteps seemed too loud, crunching against dead sticks and brown pine needles, but he felt he must keep moving, keep putting distance between himself and Serabelle.

Chapter 27
I Will Find You

It was Rupert who discovered the jewels were missing. He had heard his father pound at the door. It seemed impossible that anyone might sleep through the racket, but Melinda continued exhaling lightly beside him. She was amazing in her capacity to sleep. He watched her lids flutter slightly when he got up off the bed, her nightgown twisted uncomfortably around her neck, but Melinda slept on, blue fabric shrouding her, blond hair mussed and tossed. She was a rough sleeper, deep in some other world, where she lost all inhibition, laid aside that tight sense of herself, perfectly groomed, perfectly ladylike. Rupert smiled as he watched a stream of drool trickle from Melinda's mouth and work its way towards the white satin of the pillowcase. He knew it would devastate her if she realized how she looked in sleep. Marriage was good for stripping away the facades of daytime. Who was *this* Melinda, who had never shown herself, even to him, her husband? This Melinda didn't appear in their lovemaking—in those matters, she was demure—nor in the few times they had become inebriated together. Even her dancing was controlled, proper, practiced. Rupert determined, then and there, that he would try to bring out the untamed side of his wife.

Perhaps this was what he longed for all along, in this business with the gems: some excitement, some abandon. Staying at Serabelle with his parents twisted his feelings and took them off track; his discontent had been misdirected toward his father. There was no purpose in trying to hurt the man; the best strategy was the one he usually employed: distance. Rupert determined he would not return to Serabelle the next summer. He and Melinda would take a trip somewhere else, the two of them, alone. Maybe they would sunbathe in the nude in Germany—that was all the rage this year. Rupert tried to imagine Melinda baring her pale, round breasts to the world. He laughed aloud and glanced to see if she had stirred, but his wife slept on, open-mouthed and uninhibited.

As he sat on the bed, Rupert listened to his father pound the door. He couldn't make himself go downstairs, wasn't interested in whatever the drunkard had to say. His old man had gotten worse over the years: his drinking, his carousing. And now this business with the maid. There had been others over the years, Rupert suspected, but his father wouldn't let this girl go. He couldn't understand why she was worth upsetting the household. By next spring, a bastard would be running around the grounds—his half-sibling. Rupert shuddered. How was a maid to care for a child and the household? How would the upstart act around the family? Would he know his place? What about Rupert's mother? Let Alistair wait out in the cold. His father was disgraceful.

Just as Rupert thought he could take the incessant pounding no more, the front door opened. Rupert jumped up, dashed into the hallway, and listened to his father talk to someone—a voice he didn't recognize. Rupert caught the back of what looked to be one of the servant boys marching out the front door. But would a servant go out the front? He thought his father had made a mistake in being too friendly with the staff, letting them believe that somehow they had rights, some claim to the cottage—and this one who walked out the front door proved it, as if the situation with the little Scottish maid wasn't proof enough.

Rupert waited at the top of the stairs while his father stumbled into the front parlor. What had happened to the butler? He heard his father repeatedly calling for the man. Maybe he went outside again to search for the source of the noise. Rupert felt something was awry, and he guessed the cottage staff was involved. If it were up to him, he'd fire the whole lot of them and start over. At his house in New York, his wife let the servants in each morning and locked the door behind them at night.

Rupert walked along the north corridor, past the room where his father had been recovering while his leg healed, into the small dining room, and through to the kitchen where he found the second butler, fast asleep. Rupert's anger rose, reddening his face until the thought flashed that maybe the man was dead. He rushed over and felt for a pulse on the man's neck. The flesh was wrinkled and rough as a reptile's, but it was still warm. Rupert slapped the man's shoulder, but he didn't stir. A deep groan came from the man's throat, and Rupert's body suddenly went cold. He felt the life drain from his limbs as if he were being bled. Weak-kneed, he sniffed the tea that sat at the man's right arm. A slightly bitter smell arose, and he didn't know whether it was from the tea or something more sinister. He wasn't sure, but looking at the butler's flaccid body, he guessed that Forrest was alive.

Rupert flew down the hallway as fast as his rubbery legs would take him and entered the library, half expecting to see Forrest standing there, grinning. A blast of cold night air hit him in the face, and Rupert felt like he had awoken from a dream. He struck a match and lit the oil lamp on the desk, looking at the cabinet. His father was still mumbling in the parlor, likely too drunk to cause a problem at this moment; in the morning, his father's wrath would, no doubt, arise.

The blind flapped lightly against the open window, making a fluttering tap. The room was ice cold, and Rupert pictured, ridiculously, blocks of ice he had seen in a storehouse once in Brooklyn. Why had he been there? He wondered, but couldn't recall. With the library door ajar, he crossed the room and lifted the blind, intending to close the window. The plant that was supposed to be on the stand was outside on the ground. With a sinking feeling, Rupert's eyes moved from the plant to the corner where the pillar had stood. The pink diamond. His mind had been on the smaller gems in the cabinet. Only Forrest would dare to take—or would even know about—the pink diamond. He had a fleeting moment of relief that he hadn't killed the man, that there was no murder on his conscience, but the feeling passed quickly into regret that he hadn't rid the world of such a man. And now Rupert would have to deal with his father, with knowing and explaining what had happened. Or did he have to? Could he pull off pretending he had no idea? Could he be a successful liar (as his father had already accused him) on top of an accomplice to a theft? Or *was* he? Technically, he had nothing to do with the crime. He had entertained a plot. You couldn't be tried for considering an act, he knew. His conscience, of course, would have to be mollified or beat into submission.

Forrest couldn't have gotten far, Rupert realized. How long had it been since the explosion? Twenty, thirty minutes? Of course, the sound must have been Forrest. He should've known when he heard the noise. It all might have been avoided—he might have said no from the get-go. And the poison. They had never discussed drugging anyone. Maybe there was time to catch him, Rupert thought. Get the gems back, start over. But would he have to kill Forrest in actuality this time? Was there any way to recover the gems otherwise? Rupert paced, considering, his dressing gown clinging tightly over his pajamas.

✦ ✦ ✦

Theo watched Rupert's silhouette through the window. He had lingered out in the driveway, unwilling to go back to the yellow house to deal with Beverly's displeasure—and too worked up to go back to reading. Little puffs of breath fumed, hanging in the night air. He was insulted and frustrated at his position. But Theo knew that he'd have to come to terms with the fact that his riding days were over. When he first took the job on Serabelle, he had harbored thoughts of someday returning to racing, reluctant to admit that this situation was permanent.

He wasn't alone in his irritated state; young Mr. Hunt looked troubled as well, his shoulders hunched and his fists clenched. Theo wanted no part in their familial drama, but he had made the mistake of trying to help, and now, he might get in trouble for it. He had better talk to Beverly. She might be mad at him, but at least she'd have an answer. Beverly always had a firm opinion and an order to give.

✦ ✦ ✦

Finally, Rupert ran upstairs to change. He'd track Forrest down, retrieve the gems, and hopefully talk the man into staying away from his family for good, one way or another. What a mess the entire trip had been. Melinda didn't stir, even with his rustling around for clothing. He took whatever was closest—the clothes he had worn yesterday were folded on a chair near the bed. He fumbled for his coat and found instead a thick sweater he had packed in case the ocean brought a cold fall wind. This time of year, you couldn't trust the Atlantic.

Rupert rushed down the stairs and past the stables to where the autos were parked. It took him three tries to start the engine of the Olds, but it finally kicked to life, and Rupert crept with the car out of the driveway, without his lights on, driving by the pale light of the moon until he had swung left, pointing away from the main house. As he passed, Rupert noted that the yellow house had grown quiet now, that the party must have broken up. He had a lantern and an iron from the fireplace set, which he was determined to use, if pushed. He could claim self-defense if he hurt the man this time.

Outside the gate, Rupert stopped the car. He left the engine running and climbed out with his tools, stepping to the edge of the woods and running the light to and fro, looking for any sign of Forrest. The night was still dark and offered nothing unusual to his eyes. Every twig snap, every groan of a tree in the breeze made him twitch. He felt his shoulders rise up around his ears, and he tried to calm himself. Confidence and strength were in order. He should be able to dominate a little skinny man like Forrest. Rupert remembered how he had controlled the situation with the maid and felt better.

"I know you are there, Forrest," he hissed into the woods. "I will find you."

An owl answered him, disturbingly close, chilling his blood. He hesitated, not wanting to give in to his fear, but finally stepped back into the car's protection. He drove thirty yards and climbed out again, repeating his sweep of the woods. The third time, past the cottage wall, he also checked the east side of the road. Rupert halted behind the automobile to stay out of the beams of the headlights. He wanted to see Forrest before the man saw him. He wanted to have control. *Keep* control.

Time was running out, Rupert knew. He was about to give up when his light flashed on a bright surface on the west side of the road, about two hundred yards from the cottage, a stone's throw from the ditch. He thought at first the light was the bark of a white birch, so he stepped closer to the edge of the woods and swung his light back and forth, leaning one way, then the other. There was most definitely the edge of something there, behind a large pine tree.

"Forrest," Rupert barked, his voice louder now that he was away from the cottage. The closest neighbor was at least a mile from where he stood. "I see you."

In the distance, a dog barked.

"Come out, you coward," he insisted.

The dog alone resounded, echoed by the ocean. A rustle of branches and leaves rose with a sudden breeze.

"What, are you scared?" Rupert taunted. "You should be," he said and tightened the grip on the fire iron, not quite believing his own threat.

Forced to make the first move, Rupert stepped across the shallow ditch on the side of the road. He kept his eyes on the bright corner of what he guessed to be the pillar, but might be Forrest's knee or an elbow. The leaves crunched noisily under his feet, and he knew there was no hope of sneaking up on the man, so he made what he thought sounded like threatening, guttural noises as he approached, like a snarling dog warning its enemy. Rupert raised the poker with one hand and held the lantern with the other. Ready to swing at the man's head, he leaned around the large pine to find, as suspected, the plaster safe. But the pillar stood alone.

Rupert looked around wildly, as if he were about to be attacked. He swung the lantern about, searching the ground, the trees, the canopy, thinking Forrest might plan to jump him from above. Rupert gave a short laugh. Could he be this lucky? Oh, what a surprise Forrest would have when he came back to gather his booty. Rupert quickly inspected the pillar. It seemed intact. But where were the other gems? He poked at the dirt and leaves, wondering if Forrest had buried them. He found no sign of the gems, no ground disturbance, no package.

The auto continued to idle on the road, and Rupert hurried to load the pillar, guessing that Forrest would be back soon. He at least had the most valuable item. Rupert sat in the idling car and considered his options. He could lie in wait, hoping to gather all the gems, hoping that he'd win a physical struggle between the two of them once again, or he could return with the pink diamond, making Forrest suffer the way he had, putting two and two together, guessing, but not knowing for sure that his rival had gotten the better of him. He decided it was better that way, accepting the loss of the smaller gems yet still winning against Forrest. Ultimately, it was about winning.

Rupert turned the car around and reentered the cottage grounds, his clothing heavy with the sweat of fear, his stomach settling at the thought of at least having found the pink diamond. He parked the auto back in its spot and tucked the pillar under his arm, practically strangling the plaster. The safe felt heavier than he had noticed before, and about halfway across the drive, Rupert shifted, holding the pillar in both arms like a groom carrying a bride across the threshold. He climbed the front steps, jumping back when the door flew open. His father stood in the foyer.

Chapter 28
Her Own Brand of Justice

Alistair awoke blurry-eyed and fuzzy-headed. He had heard the front door slam and the car pull out of the driveway a half hour ago. Slowly, painfully, his head already making him pay for last night at the lodge, a hint of regret settled over his shoulders, but he shook it off. Alistair wandered back to the bar, remembering that he had been calling the butler for ice before passing out. He turned his head with some effort and saw the upturned glass on the carpet next to where he had been lying. He picked the glass up, wiped the rim, and poured himself another.

Alistair shot the liquid back into his throat and felt instantly better. He shuffled again to the front door but couldn't see anything other than the stiff tips of grass catching the moonlight, the rounded bushes gathering dew. He heard the car, still idling on the road, past the cottage wall, but he wasn't about to meander on foot. What in the world was going on in the house tonight? After a minute, Alistair slammed the door against the cold and called again for the butler. He stood in the foyer and waited. Could Mr. Wilson have taken the car? Did the old man even know how to drive? And where would he be going? Would he even dare?

Alistair stumbled through to the kitchen. Mr. Wilson's forehead lay against the tabletop, but his hand had slipped from beside the teacup and now hung loose and lifeless next to his body. Alistair cried out and backed out of the room. Thoughts of how Mr. Wilson might now never manage to dig in a mine flashed through his head, and a brief sadness overtook him. He came forward and held two fingers to Mr. Wilson's neck, finding a faint pulse.

"I will make arrangements today, Mr. Wilson," Alistair said aloud. "I have not forgotten. We are headed to Nevada. We will find you an opal."

Alistair looked into his glass in hand and spun back to the icebox on the far side of the kitchen, where he found a large block of ice the size of a lunchpail. With the door to the icebox flung wide and glass in hand, Alistair finally found a knife in the drawer and chipped away at the block, trying to catch the flying pieces of ice as they shot out, some landing on his face and hands, melting upon impact. One or two chunks finally landed in his glass, and winded from the effort, Alistair gave up his attack.

He slammed the icebox shut and heard a groan from the butler. "Ah, good, you are rousing." Alistair slapped the butler on the back. "Did the promise of a dig bring you back?"

The man didn't move but made another grunting noise.

"Very well, then," Alistair said. "Sleep it off. I know how you are feeling."

Alistair returned to the main room and poured himself another whiskey over the remaining ice chips. He thought he still heard the low rumble of an auto engine through the window. He stepped back outside the front door and listened. Yes, there it was: the distinct sound of a gas engine. Again, he scanned the property, his eyes halting when he saw the open window of the library. He stared, unblinking, but even in his stupor, Alistair knew. He never would've left that window open. *Stupid servants*, he thought, then dropped his whiskey with a sense of foreboding. Glass shattered on the stoop, sharp pricks nicking his skin, tinkling on the concrete. Alistair ran to the library and stared into the dark room. He didn't need light to know that the gems were gone. He didn't have to blink to know his precious pink diamond had been stolen.

Upstairs, Julia lay on top of her bedcovers, listening to the sound she had been waiting for—her husband howling when he discovered his loss. Her eyes flickered to the corner where her precious Chou Chou lay. Now, finally, her own brand of justice delivered, she could feel some relief.

◆   ◆   ◆

Rupert stopped mid-track on the stoop when his father opened the door. All his well-thought-out explanations escaped him. Rupert's hastily donned shirt hung over his pants, and his disheveled hair heightened his frenzied air. He hadn't bargained on his father seeing this part of the operation and didn't have an excuse ready for being caught in the act. Rupert stepped into the foyer, his feet crunching over broken glass, and handed the pillar to his father without a word.

The men marched into the library while Alistair silently spun the dial to the combination lock. He lifted off the top and reached down, cradling the glass case in his palm. Alistair congratulated himself that he had had the pillar lined with fabric: the case was unbroken with a small nick in the corner. He took a moment to inspect the gem, opening the case and holding the diamond to the light. Exhaling what sounded to Rupert like a heavy sob, Alistair brought the diamond to his lips. Neither spoke until he had placed the diamond back into its case.

"Where is the rest of the collection?" Alistair asked, sitting down in his leather swivel chair at the desk.

"I do not know," Rupert answered.

"Are you going to tell me what is going on here?"

"Someone broke in."

"Someone?" Alistair roared.

Rupert crossed his arms petulantly. "Yes."

"And how is it that you ended up with the diamond?"

"I made chase."

Alistair laughed aloud at his son. "You expect me to believe that you chased down a criminal and wrestled back the goods he stole? Come now. You can do better than that."

Rupert stomped on the floor like a frustrated child. "Why is it so hard to believe I could do something right?"

"It is not a matter of right or wrong, Rupert. It is a matter of strength and cunning. Now, I realize that you are good at your job and are sly in the matters of the law—truth and justice and all that—but strangely enough, you are not a talented liar. Has anyone ever told you that? It is why I suspect you do best *outside* the courtroom. Anyone looking at your face could tell the truth. Look at how you stand when you lie, with your shoulders all hunched up like that and your gaze up to the ceiling. So, tell me what happened, and give me back my gems." Alistair pounded on the blotter in front of him. "I imagine you think you are teaching me some sort of lesson, but it obviously backfired."

Rupert, oddly, found himself warming, his heart catching on the few words of praise his father had managed to squeeze in between the insults— that he thought Rupert was good at his job. His father had never before been so complimentary.

"What I said is true, Father," he said. "I heard a noise and came downstairs. When I saw the window open in the library, I realized the thief could not have gotten too far, so I went searching. Is that so hard to believe?"

"Yes," Alistair said.

"Well, I did. I found the safe in the woods south of the cottage," Rupert said. "The thief must have dropped it when he heard me in pursuit."

Alistair nodded, knowing his son was not telling the truth, but powerless to make him confess. "Well, I will need to know where the gems are, so see if you can track them down too."

"I am afraid he got away, Father. There is nothing I can do."

Sobriety hitting him like the cold air of the night, Alistair slammed his hands down hard, flat against the desk, his palms stinging from the impact. "Impossible!" he yelled. "I want those gems back."

"What is going on?" Julia stood in the doorway, wrapped in a blue silk dressing gown. Alistair swore he saw a smirk on her face.

"Gather the servants," he said.

"It is the middle of the night, Alistair." Julia sighed. "They are sleeping."

Alistair stood. "Wake them."

"I will not."

"Rupert, you do it." He turned to his son. "Bring them to the front parlor. We are going to have an inquisition. And you better hope there are some answers for me."

"You are drunk," Julia said with disgust. Turning to Rupert, she insisted he not wake anyone at this hour.

"I am the master of this house." Alistair leaned ominously across the desk. "And you will do as I say, both of you."

"Or?" Julia asked.

"Or you will regret the day you ever laid eyes on me, so help me, God," Alistair shouted.

"I already do," she said and strolled back up to her quarters. Though she presented a stern face in front of Alistair and her son, tears welled up in her throat and behind her eyes before reaching her anteroom door. He was an awful man, and she was glad she had done what she had done. She would ensure the gems never made it back into his hands.

Chapter 29
It is Fine. Leave it.

Forrest had set the pillar down when he was well away from the cottage, his arms trembling with sustained effort. The poker players were off the road, lanterns fading into the dark of night by the time he placed the pillar on wet leaves. He ensured it was hidden behind a large pine, not that anyone would come along the deserted roadway. Most of the families along this stretch had headed home in the last few days; usually, the Ainsworth-Hunt party meant the end of season. He considered trying to smash the pillar but he thought the noise would be too loud and might alert the household. As he backed away from the pillar, Forrest whispered, "It is fine. Leave it. It is fine."

He took off in a trot along the dirt road, feeling confident now that he could stay out of the trees. Though the night was dark, his eyes were accustomed to the moonlit glow. Twice, he tripped, though he easily caught his balance. He continued his hustle and felt a burning sensation in his lungs but enjoyed the slight pain. A rush of excitement flushed his body at the idea that he had pulled off the heist, had gotten one over on Rupert Hunt. As he ran, he heard an engine far behind him. His heart thudded as he caught the flash of distant lights before they turned in the opposite direction. The engine faded, and Forrest was once again alone on the road. He was up the grassy slope and at his vehicle within fifteen minutes, cranking up the engine.

His headlights lit the row of graves on either side of the green path. Old headstones tilted slightly, having sunk into the earth. Newer gravestones reflected his headlights; the polish on the poor's granite and the wealthy's marble glared side by side, family by family, silent in the night. Forrest quickly gazed at the stones before circling around and out of the graveyard.

He felt confident about where he had left the pillar, halfway between Serabelle and the Gantrys'. The tree he chose was the largest in the copse of pines and maples, and he had leaned a dead branch from a white birch up against the trunk, to make sure that he'd recognize it from the road. As he puttered by, he easily saw his marker, but he saw no edge of the pillar and congratulated himself on his abilities. Forrest turned the car around in the middle of the road and kept the engine idling, though he cut the headlights, just in case. He hopped lightly from the driver's seat and closed his eyes for a moment until he felt he could see once again in the dark. Overhead, clouds moved north in a constant wispy motion, dispersing the moon's glow in a flickering pattern, occasionally allowing the full force of a beam through the haze. The light gave the night an eerie pallor as Forrest walked into the trees to retrieve his prize.

Chapter 30
The Inquest

Sleepy-eyed and bedraggled, the servants lined up in the parlor, all having hastily changed from their night clothes to their uniforms or daywear. The men who had played cards all night smelled of ale. Only Mabel was wide-eyed, having not slept for even a moment that night. She had lain on top of her covers, fully dressed, waiting to speak to Mr. Hunt, pondering the idea that she might depart, even without the money that Rupert had ripped away so brutally. Each fantasy of leaving, though, was squashed under the weight of knowing she would not. Leaving would mean certain death out here in the remote wilderness with winter coming on and a baby growing in her belly, not even enough saved to pay for a train ticket. Now, standing in the room where Mr. Hunt had danced her around the carpet not six months ago, Mabel allowed herself to imagine, briefly, that he was about to announce his love for her, that he had brought them all there to confess to the servants that she was pregnant with his child.

Mabel smiled at the fantasy, and as Alistair walked into the room, the smile took him off guard. The little girl was radiant, standing in the middle of the night amongst the rag-tag group of servants, like a Madonna in a Botticelli painting. He found his tight fists relaxing with her downcast gaze and hint of a smile, her wispy hair that refused to stay confined under her less-than-white bonnet.

"I want some answers," Alistair said, recovering from his brief trance.

"Yes, sir," the first butler said. "Where is Mr. Wilson?" he asked, though no one answered.

"I know you have parties on Thursday nights." Alistair waved his hand to ward off any protests. "Do not deny it. I hear you up there, doing god knows what, and not one of us has ever tried to stop you, have we?"

"No, sir," the butler replied.

None of the stable boys dared gaze on Mr. Hunt, relieved that the butler was speaking for them. Gardener, still drunk, looked brazenly up and forward, smirking dangerously. Alistair was not watching Gardener, however, who stood in the back amid the shuffling stable boys. Josiah cleared his throat and threw quick glances at Mr. Hunt. Of all the servants, he perhaps knew the master of the house the best, recognized this mood—drunk and ornery, and he knew not to make eye contact, not to speak.

Beverly stood erect, ready to answer Mr. Hunt, but the butler had beaten her to it. Mr. Hunt addressed his questions to the men, but Beverly kept an eye on the women, ensuring they did not appear disgruntled or haughty. She worried that the cook seemed put out, but again, Mr. Hunt didn't seem to notice. He spoke to the men who had gathered towards one side of the room, segregated from the women. The two groups faced off like armies about to battle: men to the east, the women past the couch on the west, nearer the windows.

Mr. Hunt paced between groups, his face and neck bent, his head craning up every so often to watch the group of male servants. When he entered the room, Mr. Hunt had stared at the women—too long, Beverly thought, to hide the fact that he was staring at Mabel—but then he had turned sharply and addressed the men, not once turning back around during the speech.

"Tonight." Alistair stopped pacing and faced the men square on. "Tonight, I have come to regret that I let you have your way. Obviously, I should have stopped strangers from coming onto my property without my knowledge. You should be my first defense when you are on *my* property, eating *my* food, drinking *my* liquor—and it *is* my liquor since it was bought with money that I gave you. And now, you ingrates, it seems you do not deserve a thing I have so generously given."

The men shuffled their feet and bit their lips. Gardener's face twisted from a sardonic smile to furious anger as if he might pounce any moment at Mr. Hunt. Everyone in the room knew it was possible, even probable, that Gardener would win—at least that one fight, if never another.

"I will give you thirty seconds to come up with an answer to my question. If I do not get an answer, every single one of you will pay." Alistair let the weight of his words settle on the staff before he asked the question: "Where. Are. My. Gems?"

He turned, sidling close to the women, scanning their faces. If anyone in the room knew a thing, he would find out. But the women all had blank, confounded stares. Alistair stopped in front of Mabel, and she felt his breath on her face, hot and slightly rancid with alcohol. He lifted his hand and ran a finger down her nose. He felt a stirring that belied his anger—or perhaps intensified the emotion. His body was agitated, and he thought he might pick her up and storm out of the room at that moment. Without looking Mabel in the eye, he continued to stand in front of her, breathing heavily until he heard a noise in the wide doorway. His son Rupert and his wife stood watching with identical glares. Alistair grinned at them and spun back to the male servants.

"I was gracious enough to give you time to find me an answer. Tell me. Who stole my gems?" he shouted.

Even the butler remained mute.

"Come now. Somebody saw something. Or maybe you are all in on it. Getting one over on your employer—is that it?"

"No, sir. I do not know anything about what you mean," the butler said. "I was sleeping, as I do every evening, in order to serve early morning."

Alistair looked at the butler with disgust. "Driver," he said, as if he would not deign to use Josiah's name. "What do you know?"

Josiah stepped forward. "We heard a loud noise, like a shot. I sent George to look for Theo, but he couldn't find him. Nobody knew what the sound was."

"Theo?" Alistair barked. "You let me in the house, did you not?"

Theo stepped forward. "Yes, sir."

Alistair moved up close to Theo, standing over him by a good two inches, a rare event for the short estate owner. "What were you doing in here?"

Theo still had not recovered from Mr. Hunt's previous insults. "Sir, I have explained earlier about Mr. Wilson."

Mrs. Hunt, who had not yet spoken, suddenly walked into the room. "Where is Mr. Wilson? Why is he not here?"

Theo turned to her, already resigned to the idea that he would lose his job. He knew right then that they would blame him for whatever had happened. "Mr. Wilson is in the kitchen, passed out. Something has happened to him—not that anyone here cares. He might be dead by now, for all we know."

Beverly burst out of line and ran through the side door, through the dining room, and into the kitchen. The staff heard her scream from the front room, but no one dared move as Mr. and Mrs. Hunt both glared. Finally, Beverly returned to the parlor. "Call the doctor," she panted. "Mr. Wilson is very ill."

"We will do no such thing," Mrs. Hunt said. "For all we know, he is probably drunk."

"Theo," Mr. Hunt said. "I am going to ask you *one* time." Alistair walked up close to the boy and knocked the riding cap off his head. The boy did not try to pick it up. "Did you steal my gems?"

"Sir, I don't know what gems you are talking about."

"That is not what I asked you," Alistair growled.

"No, I did not steal your gems."

Alistair searched Theo's face, thinking he was most likely telling the truth, but he did not like the boy's air. "Rupert!" he screamed, without looking over at his son. Theo flinched. "Do you think this boy's telling the truth?"

Rupert crossed the room and flopped his body on the couch, now that the heat was off him. "I do not see why we should believe him."

"And what do you suggest?" Alistair asked his son.

"Send him packing."

Alistair shook his head and resumed his pacing. "I could do that, of course, but the problem, my dear son, is this: that does not get my gems back. Say this ruffian did steal the collection; I am sure he would be happy to leave here with his booty. You see my dilemma?"

"When you put it that way."

Beverly stayed near the door to the dining room, incredulous that they had not attended the second butler. "Theo would not steal your gems, sir," she said from behind the group of men.

Alistair looked up, surprised. "What was that?"

"Theo, sir, he is the gentlest among us. I would bet my life he wouldn't steal from you. He is of good breeding, sir, and more interested in reading books than playing poker. The sole reason Theo entered the house, sir— he told me as much earlier this evening—was to help you. Please do not punish him for being a kind soul."

Mr. Hunt's face turned a bright red, the same hue, Mabel noticed, that the skin of his chest and neck flushed in the heat of passion. He stopped in his tracks and pointed with his full arm at Beverly. "You dare? You dare tell me what I can or cannot do? You suggest that my judgment is not sound? I will tell you what, I'm going to teach you all a lesson. Beverly—I am firing *you*. You are through." Alistair spun and addressed his son. "Guess why I can fire her? Because I am sure she does *not* have the gems." He lifted his head and addressed the entire room, gesturing wildly. "In fact, until I get them back, I am going to fire one person a day, someone unlikely to have stolen from me, though I can see through your rat eyes that I cannot trust…"

"You will do no such thing," Julia said over his rampage.

"Excuse me?"

"You will not fire my servants. They are too hard to find up here, too hard to train." She stepped into the room and sat next to her son. "I have become used to this group. Besides, Alistair, we are leaving next week. Why bother?"

"You would let this group of swindlers stay up here alone without us all winter? Maybe they are all in on it," Alistair raged.

"Be reasonable, Alistair. They stay here every year—someone must care for Serabelle, or it will fall to ruin by next summer. I trust Beverly to keep them under control."

Alistair glared at his wife as if he might throttle her. "And my gems? Should no one pay for the crime? Should I not be entitled to find my collection?" His voice rose high over their heads and seemed to echo a booming, threatening sound through the room. The servants all cringed—all except Gardener. He still managed to stare boldly at Mr. Hunt.

"Eventually, every soul loses something they care for, Alistair. I suppose we all have to learn to live with the loss," Julia said. "Is that not right, Rupert?"

"Yes, Mum," he said wearily.

"I will tell you what. If you are so keen on firing someone, do as I suggested before and get rid of that little maid you like so much. Her, I will allow you to fire."

The room went silent as a church vestibule. Mabel stared with wide eyes at Mr. Hunt. Would he do it? Would he abandon her at his wife's insistence? Her limbs trembled, and she clasped her fists tight, hoping to stop the tremors, but the movement was uncontrollable. Her whole body shook.

Alistair's face drained of the intense color his anger had brought on. He walked over and poured himself another whiskey. "Butler," he said, "go get me some ice."

"Yes, sir," the butler said quietly, though he did not move.

"Now!" Alistair snapped.

No one else in the room moved or spoke. Rebecca felt Mabel trembling next to her and thought about putting her arm around Mabel, but did not dare. Tears had formed in her own eyes at the thought that she might be fired herself, and she allowed them to brim over and roll down her cheeks without attempting to wipe them. Concentrating on the feeling of the cold, slow tracks allowed Rebecca to keep her mind off the frightening form of Mr. Hunt.

"Well," Alistair boomed. "Isn't this sweet? My wife. My *wife* is trying to make a fool of me in front of the servants. Everyone in this room is interested in making a fool of the man who provides for them, keeps them safe, and makes it possible for them to live. Is that what is happening?"

"You do not provide for me, Alistair," Julia said sharply.

Alistair lifted his arm and threw his whiskey glass against the far wall. The sound echoed in the room. "No, of course, I do not. Why the hell would anyone want to provide for a woman like you?"

Rupert leaped up at his father's insult. "That is enough!" he said. "What is wrong with you two, having this fight in front of the servants? We are in a crisis here. We should stand united. Figure out solutions, not blame each other."

"Quite right, dear," Julia said through clenched teeth. "Your father is simply upset about losing his gems. He is not thinking clearly."

"Where are they?" Alistair screamed. "Who has my gems?"

"Charming," Julia muttered.

◆   ◆   ◆

Beverly followed the butler back to the kitchen and worked at chipping off ice shavings while the butler attended to Mr. Wilson, still passed out at the table. The second butler was still breathing and did not smell of alcohol, but he did not awaken, even with a slap to the face.

"I think he might have been poisoned," the first butler said. "We really should call the police."

"They will never allow it," Beverly said.

"Perhaps the doctor then," the butler suggested.

"You know as well as I do that the Ainsworth-Hunts don't want their dirty laundry aired in town. Obviously, they'll do whatever it takes to keep their affairs private."

"Then what do you suppose this is about?"

Beverly stopped carving away at the ice block. "A private feud. Between the two of them."

"And the gems?"

"I don't know." Beverly lowered her voice to a whisper. "But wherever they are, I can almost guarantee that Master Rupert is somehow involved."

The butler stood from his bend. "Rupert?"

"What is he still doing here, this time of year? Tell me that."

The butler took the tray of ice from Beverly, shaking his head. "Maybe you should stay here with Mr. Wilson—put a compress on his head, at least. Try to revive him."

Beverly silently agreed.

◆ ◆ ◆

Rebecca continued to cry, unsure of what she should confess. If she listened to her heart, to what the lessons of Jesus had taught her, she should tell the truth—that Mrs. Hunt had asked her to steal the gems. Her loyalty alone to Mrs. Hunt would be rewarded, she knew. Mrs. Hunt had given her the warning stare when she walked in the room, a look that Rebecca had never seen on her Mistress before, but she knew immediately what the look meant: "Do not say a word." When Mr. Hunt yelled, Rebecca had let out a whimper that caught his eye, but he did not question her.

"Somebody tell me something," Alistair growled.

Finally, Theo spoke. "I saw Mr. Rupert in the library."

Rupert jumped up off the couch where he had resettled back down next to his mother. "You little..."

Alistair stepped between them. "What is this now, Theo?" He threw his arm around the boy and pushed his son back toward the couch. "Tell me more."

"After I let you in, I waited outside, and I saw him in the library, pacing back and forth."

"I heard a noise," Rupert whined.

Alistair ignored his son. "What else did you see, Theo?"

"I saw him open the blinds and look outside, leaving in a hurry. Afterward, I went back to the yellow house to talk to Beverly. She can attest to that. I heard the car start up after that, and a while later, after I had gone to bed, I heard the car return. That's all I know."

"That is not much, Theo," Alistair said, frowning. "Did you not see anything else in the house?"

"Mr. Wilson, sir," Theo said.

"What about him?"

"There was something wrong with him."

"Yes, we have seen that." Alistair sighed. "Drunk, is he?"

Beverly stepped out of the kitchen with the ice. "He is not drunk, I am afraid." Everyone in the room turned to Beverly. She crossed to Mr. Hunt and placed two shavings of ice in his glass. "I believe someone drugged him," she said. "Mr. Wilson would not drink on the job. I am sure ah that. And he is out cold."

"So, we have my son pacing in the library, and the butler has been poisoned," Alistair said with a sneer. "Any other pieces of wisdom?"

Mabel watched with fascination as Mr. Hunt paced, every bit the figure of authority. The fact that he could make this many people sweat—even his own son—was impressive. What would it be like to have that much power? To have any power? Beyond the thick stone walls, Mabel heard the pound of the ocean, too muted to perceive unless you blocked out Mr. Hunt's footsteps and Rebecca's whimpering. So constant and rhythmic that the crash could be lost in the symphony of everyday sounds: the settling house, wind against the panes. But there it was, underneath every melody, almost as if the ocean itself was calling Mabel out to the rocks, tempting her, begging for her to join the ebb of the waves.

Suddenly, Willie stepped forward. "I saw someone."

"Willie," Mr. Hunt said joyfully. "I knew I could count on you, my boy."

Willie smiled at Mr. Hunt. He had been weighing his options, trying to decide where his loyalties fell. No one on this estate had stood by him, had lived up to his ideals of honor and goodness. In his mind, they all deserved to pay for how they behaved.

"Tell us, Willie. What did you see?" Mr. Hunt prompted.

"I saw several things tonight. Every one of them is suspicious if you ask me." Willie followed Mr. Hunt's example and began pacing the floor. From across the room, Mabel smiled at Willie's imitation. Her smile faded when he began to talk. "Master Rupert came to the yellow house this afternoon."

Rupert struggled to stand, but his mother threw an arm across his chest, preventing him.

"Willie," Beverly warned, but the boy continued.

"I had gone back to the house for my gloves—I had forgotten them and hadn't needed them all morning, as I had been brushing Faith, and I don't use gloves when I'm brushing, just when I'm baling hay or other such work. So, I was up in my room on the third floor when I heard Master Rupert storm in. I heard Beverly's voice, and then they were up on the second floor. I crept to the staircase so I could overhear. It was Mabel's room he was in. He threatened her; I heard it."

"And what did he say?" Mr. Hunt prompted. Around the room, grim faces were set, glaring at Willie as if he had made the threat. He thought he heard a low snarl coming from Gardener, but he didn't dare look in his direction.

"I must insist that we stop this at once," Rupert said.

"Go on, Willie," Alistair said.

"I didn't hear his exact words," Willie said, "as I was a floor away. But I heard his tone, alright. He was definitely threatening her."

Rupert flailed his arms about. "Are you really going to listen to the accusations of a stable boy, father? A *negro*?"

Alistair looked at his son. "Did you pay a visit to Mabel today, Rupert?"

"I most certainly did not."

"What does this have to do with the gems?" Julia burst out. "Really, let us move on."

"Hold on," Alistair said and moved up close to Mabel. "I want to hear what you have to say, dear. Did my son bother you today?"

Mabel's eyes flickered from Mr. Hunt to Beverly, from Master Rupert to his mother. She didn't know how to answer, but Mr. Hunt's tone was soft, like he could be sometimes, like he was earlier in the summer, with just the two of them. She nodded slightly, enough that he could discern that she was agreeing.

"What did he want? You can tell me."

She found she couldn't speak with everyone staring at her. Her throat was dry, and her eyes felt like she hadn't blinked in a week. Mabel felt her skin turn crimson and knew she would be marred with patches of rash after her emotions had cooled.

"Are you embarrassed?" Mr. Hunt asked.

Mabel could only nod her head, thinking she might faint.

"I will not make you tell me now," he murmured. "You can tell me later."

On the couch, Mrs. Hunt's face was stony, as if there were no emotion whatsoever behind her glassy eyes. How could she sit there, Mabel wondered, and listen to her husband? Did she care nothing for him? Mabel dared not hold her gaze. She felt everyone stare, accusing her, judging her. She wished Mr. Hunt would stop, but she also desired him to continue, to stay close so she could feel his warmth, a comfort she thought was lost to her forever. And now here he was, trusting her, loving her over his own family. She nodded her head, making him a silent promise.

"What else do you know, Willie?" Alistair prodded.

Willie fumed, watching Mr. Hunt speak to Mabel in such an intimate manner. This household was insane. Why did Mrs. Hunt just sit there? Why did Gardener not speak? Was he also cowed by the great and mighty Mr. Hunt? Willie was thrilled at the possibility that he might also now be able to pay back Gardener for bullying him, for treating everyone else as if they were inferior, solely because they lacked physical strength. What Willie said next was for Mabel, Theo, and everyone who had been bullied.

"I saw a man jump out the window of the library."

Rebecca gasped.

"Who? When?" Mr. Hunt asked, his words slurring and running over each other so they sounded like "Howwen."

"After the card game had broken up, as you arrived back at the cottage, Mr. Hunt. We heard your car, and George came up and warned us that Beverly said we needed to call it a night." Willie continued to pace, now thoroughly enjoying his moment. "I was staring out the window of the pok... a room on the third floor, when I saw a movement at the front of the house. Mr. Hunt, you parked the car, and I swear, I saw somebody jump out of that front window."

"What did he look like?" Rupert asked, suddenly interested.

"I saw him run across the front of the main house and into the woods north of the cottage." Willie stopped pacing and held his head high. He took one sly glance at Gardener and said, "He was a large man. He had red hair."

"Why you—" Gardener growled and then stopped when Rupert hopped up. "Are you sure he was not blond?" Rupert asked.

Alistair looked quizzically at his son and then turned back to Willie. "Red hair, you say? There are not too many men with red hair, I would guess, in these parts."

"No, sir. There are not." Willie stood his ground.

"The gardener has red hair."

"Yes, he does." Willie did not dare look toward Gardener but could feel the man's eyes boring into his skin, heating up the places where his gaze fell. Willie was sure that if it was possible to hurt someone with a stare, Gardener would have maimed him, at the very least. "It could have been him."

Gardener could take the insinuation no longer and charged at Willie, easily crossing the twenty feet between them. He grabbed Willie's throat, encircling it with his large hands. Willie stumbled back, knocked off balance with the force. His eyes grew large as his windpipe closed under the pressure of Gardener's brutish thumbs.

Rebecca screamed, and Beverly called out to Gardener while Josiah and the butler grabbed at Gardener's shoulders, trying to peel him off the boy. Theo and the other stable boys hung back, shouting at Gardener to let go, though they did not dare touch him.

The Hunts stood in horror, unsure how to handle the clashing servants. Alistair, though taken aback, was amused by the display of passion. In his mind, there was nothing better than a good tavern brawl— of course, they were not in a tavern, but he thought these men were the types one might find fighting in a barroom.

Rupert stood with his arms crossed over his chest, stepping out of the way of the struggling group, hoping they would fire the lot of them.

On the other hand, his mother was horrified at the brutality, though there was a grain of pleasure inside her as well, a speck of glee that she had created this chaos through her cleverness. Why was Willie making up this story? Why did he blame Gardener? It occurred to her that these servants—these people—had lives beyond their duties to the family. There were stories and intrigues on the grounds that she knew nothing about and likely never would. Julia was frightened to realize they might at any time be over at the yellow house scheming and planning—possibly plotting against her.

Willie's eyes went from surprise to fear to real panic before Josiah wedged his body between them. He pried Gardener's powerful arms apart with his shoulders and stood face to face with him, Gardener standing half a foot taller than even Josiah. Willie stumbled back and rubbed his neck, taking great gasping breaths. Mabel and Beverly ran to him and pulled him close, stroking his hair.

Alistair clapped his hands together and let out a big, hearty guffaw. "Well, now that is some excitement. Tell me, Willie, now, did you make all that up, or did you see a man with red hair jumping out the window?"

"I saw a man," he choked.

"Was it Gardener? Did Gardener steal my jewels?" Alistair held a hand toward Gardener, ordering him to restrain himself, though Gardner was already being held on one side by Josiah and on the other by the butler.

"I do not know," Willie admitted.

"How could I steal the jewels?" Gardener yelled. "I was in the poker room with you, Willie, you imbecile."

"Is that true?" Mr. Hunt asked.

"He had been," Willie said. "But by the time I saw the man jump out the window, everyone had left the room. I don't know where Gardener was."

"Did you see Gardener go into the main house?"

"No."

"How much time between when Gardener left the *poker room*," Alistair said the words emphatically but did not stop to comment, "and when the man jumped out the window?"

Willie wiped at the corners of his eyes. "A few minutes, I guess."

"Be precise. How many minutes?"

Willie seemed to have caught his breath. "Maybe ten."

"Is that enough time for him to walk around to the servant's entrance, steal all my gems—putting the trays back into the cabinet all nicely, by the way—and jump out the front window?"

"Probably not." Willie sighed. He had not thought of that.

Alistair turned to his son. "What was that you said about a blond?"

"That was nothing," Rupert said nervously. "Just an idea."

"What kind of idea?"

Rupert figured he might as well plant the seed about Forrest. "I simply wondered, Father, because the night of the gala, I found someone in your study. Someone I suspected was up to no good."

Alistair strode up to his son. "Who?"

"Remember Forrest Wicks? The lad I went to school with? The son of the poor couple down the road at the Crow's Nest? It was him. I saw him in the library."

Rebecca's eyes grew wide. She recalled seeing both Master Rupert and this yellow-haired gentleman in the library, all right; they had seemed in cahoots. But she knew better than to say anything. She was keeping well out of this investigation. Her head spun from all the factors, all the people involved. She wished she could kneel down right this moment by the foot of her bed and pray for comfort, for this all to go away, and for life to resume as normal on Serabelle.

"Do tell," Alistair said.

"I am not sure who invited Forrest to the gala, but he was never the type I would associate with. He was always into trouble—not at all our sort of person. He recognized me immediately, of course, and tried to engage me in a conversation. Father, I believe he even referenced your gems. Yes, now that I think of it, he mentioned he had heard of your collection. I, of course, never having felt comfortable with the man, made my excuses and got out of the chat. Later that evening, I happened upon him in the library and asked what he was doing there. He said he was looking for the washroom, of all things."

"And I suppose he is a blond? This is your idea, that Forrest Wicks stole my gems?"

"Do you have a better theory?" Rupert said.

"And when you went off chasing this Forrest, did you happen to see him? When you mysteriously found the diamond in the woods, was there no trace of this man?"

"Diamond in the woods?" Julia looked puzzled. "What are you talking about?"

Alistair poured himself another drink. "Do you not know? Your son tried to be a hero and chase down the thief. This is what he tells me, anyway. He came back to the cottage carrying the pillar with the diamond."

"Impossible," Julia burst out.

"That is what I thought. We both know our son's no hero."

Julia looked closely at her son. What was he playing with? Did he know that Julia had the gems? Was he covering for her? Unlikely. Then what? Were they both trying to make a fool of her, toying with her when they knew all along it was she? Had Rebecca confessed?

Julia turned to her servant. "Rebecca, come with me." The two of them stepped out of the parlor and into the foyer.

Rupert watched his mother go and then turned to Alistair. "That is what I get for trying to help you, father. I should have left it out there for the thief to come and gather. That is what you deserve." Rupert followed his mother out.

Watching his family leave the room one by one, with nothing resolved, without being any closer to recovering his gem collection, Alistair lost control once again. The servants stood motionless; even Gardener's anger quelled at watching the master of the house in his infantile rage.

"I want my gems back!" he shouted, stomping his feet. "I want them back right now!"

Mabel jumped with his great roar and fought the temptation to comfort Mr. Hunt. This room, with its velvet curtains, its long settee, the phonograph, would always be, to her, the real place their affair began—when he pulled her into his lap at the party. He was, she saw in this moment, nothing but a child. He was a perpetual teenager, playing at love, playing at war, drinking and fornicating and blaspheming. And a teenager would have trouble accepting the reality of her pregnancy, wouldn't acknowledge his responsibility in the matter. If Mr. Hunt hadn't grown up yet, he never would. But Mabel would *have* to grow up. She would *have* to take responsibility within a few months, regardless of his reaction.

Mabel looked over at Gardener, at his barely satiated anger, and thought that he, if loutish and uncontrollable, was at least wholly adult. But Willie—Willie with his scrawny body nearly the same size as hers, with his strange stories and bravado, his ridiculous accusation that it was Gardener who stole the gems. What was he up to? Willie was also a child, in years and maturity. His innocence was endearing.

✦   ✦   ✦

In the foyer, morning sun passed through the glass, falling a foot short of where Mrs. Hunt whispered to Rebecca. The sun lay at their feet as if even the light awaited permission from the Hunts to rise.

"Did you tell Rupert anything?"

Rebecca's hands shook. "No, ma'am."

"What is he talking about, with the pillar?"

"I don't know, ma'am."

They lifted their heads when they heard Mr. Hunt scream. "One moment," Julia said and walked back to the entrance to the parlor. "Alistair, stop your tantrum," she ordered. "In front of the staff." Rebecca stayed put, wishing she were anywhere but inside the cottage. Master Rupert started past her on the stairs when his mother stopped him, yelling from the entrance to the parlor. "Where do you think you are going?"

"Bed," he said, his back to his mother, his hand on the mahogany knob of the balustrade.

"Rupert," Julia ordered. "Get down here and tell me what in the good Lord's name you are up to."

"Whatever do you mean, Mother?"

She joined him at the foot of the stairs and spoke in a tone so low even Rebecca couldn't make out exactly what she said. "Rupert, what is this nonsense about you finding the diamond in the woods?"

"Exactly what I told you, Mother. I heard a noise and followed the thief to the road where I found the pillar. I did not find the other gems. He must have gotten away."

"Indeed," Julia said. "Why did you take the car? If you heard a noise, why did you not follow on foot? The path through the woods where Willie said he saw the thief go?"

"I relied on instinct."

"I know you are lying." Julia eyed her son through narrow slits. "A mother knows these things. I cannot, for the life of me, figure out why you would take that pillar with you. What were you thinking?"

"I did not take the pillar, Mother. I returned it—not that father deserves it."

"No, I do not suppose he does."

For a moment, they smiled at each other. In the center of the foyer, Rebecca stood watching, suddenly bathed in light as the morning approached. She looked wholesome, standing in her white uniform, bright bonnet, rosy, blushed cheeks, and round limbs. Watching her, Julia knew that though she could count on the girl's loyalty in matters of servitude, she could not count on her intelligence or wit—and she could never count on discretion from Rebecca. She would break in an instant if questioned. Julia needed another ally, someone whom she could confide in—and, most importantly, someone to keep the jewels as she hid them from her husband. Julia briefly thought of confessing to her son, but held back, remembering when he was a child.

Years ago, Julia had done something quite out of character once: In Boston, where they lived over the winter, she had received an invitation to a neighbor's house. Mr. Pimrose, a middle-aged bachelor, invited her. She had been out shopping—Rupert was four or five. She did not remember why her daughter Sarah was not with them, but she must have been with her tutor. Mr. Pimrose had been friendly with the Ainsworth-Hunts, but they did not know him well. That day, he ran into Julia in Jordan Marsh and asked her to join him for lunch—he was testing out a new cook and needed a woman's opinion. Please, please, would she come for a bite? She could bring the boy.

Julia still remembered why she had said 'yes' that day: Alistair had another lodge banquet over the weekend when she had wanted him to come to the symphony with her. He was always off doing something without her, and so she decided to have an adventure of her own.

Mr. Pimrose was nothing but a gentleman that day at his house—Julia was not the type of woman that men tried to take advantage of. And though she had sworn her son to secrecy, Rupert had not spared a moment in telling his father about the whole ordeal, as if his little body had been bursting with the information. He had blathered on about the fun they had, how his mother drank champagne in the middle of the day. Alistair did not blow up in a rage, like she thought—maybe even hoped he might. He laughed and said, "Good for you."

No, she could not trust her son. There was someone, though, whom she knew she could control. Julia left her son on the stairs and returned to the parlor. Her husband sat on the couch, having thrown yet another glass at the fireplace.

Julia spoke to the butler as the rest of the staff listened. "I think it is time we all called it a night. Get everyone back to bed."

"Yes, ma'am," he said, relieved that the questioning was over.

Julia continued with orders as the staff shuffled out. "I will expect you all at your posts in four hours. My husband needs to sober up before we continue."

"Ma'am, what about Mr. Wilson?" Beverly asked.

"Get the men to take him to your quarters," Mrs. Hunt said. "Let me know after a sleep if he does not rouse. And Beverly…" She waved the head servant over and murmured. "First thing in the morning—I suppose it will be nearly ten o'clock by then—send that other maid up to my quarters. I want to talk to her."

"Mabel?"

"Yes, that one."

Chapter 31
You and I Will Be Bound

Still, Mabel couldn't sleep. She stared at the ceiling, afraid to get up and wake the rest of the house, worried about disturbing their few hours of rest. How could they all sleep after such a night? She needed to use the bathroom but hated to make the trek into the cold morning air. Before they had crawled into their beds, Rebecca had confessed that she was frightened. She had kneeled at the foot of her bed and prayed loudly to God, asking for clarity, purity, and guidance during these difficult days. For a moment, Mabel had envied Rebecca's faith that God could take over her mind and give answers—as if life were that simple. Then Rebecca pulled the covers over her and was instantly asleep.

Time seemed to continue indefinitely, never moving or stretching; the hours became unbearable, Mabel's eyes unblinking. Rebecca didn't stir from where she had flopped down on the mattress, mouth open to the ceiling, arms stiff by her side. She made a light puffing sound with every other breath, as if she were an engine refusing to turn over.

Outside the yellow house, the world awoke to the day—robins pecked at the ground hoping to beat the frost, gulls circled over the water looking for an early breakfast of herring or mackerel. Even a late moth flittered past the window as easily as leaves that fell from the great oaks surrounding the cottage. The joyousness of the robins' song contradicted the dark mood of Serabelle. The cottage would never be the same quiet, complacent establishment that Mabel had joined less than a year ago. She was about to have a child who would belong as much to the cottage as Master Rupert did. And by default, like a mother who birthed a child in a foreign country, she would also belong. What would happen here? Would she spend the rest of her life trying to explain to her child where he or she was from, or would the child grow up on the grounds? And what about Gardener? She had answered 'yes' to his marriage proposal. Could she take it back now?

Beverly came for them early, knocking lightly at the door before she entered. "Rebecca," she said, her eyebrows drawn wearily together, "I want you to get the laundry stahted today, while Mabel goes up to see Mrs. Hunt."

Rebecca sat straight up. "What?"

"You heard what I said. Mabel, Mrs. Hunt has asked to see you."

"Is she mad at me?" Rebecca asked, fearful.

"I don't know." Beverly sighed. "Now, we've all had a rough night. I want everyone on their best behavior until next week—until the Hunts leave fah the winter."

"I'll still be going with them, won't I? To Boston?" Rebecca leaped out of bed, her feet cold on the bare wood floor.

"Do as you're told." Beverly headed down the stairs to start the tea kettle. The men stirred on the floor above, boards creaking with their weight, their voices a low rumble.

"Oh no," Rebecca muttered, "I hope I haven't made a mistake. I have to go to Boston. I always go to Boston." She rushed over and knelt at Mabel's bedside, taking Mabel's hands in hers. "You must tell Mrs. Hunt for me that I promise to obey her, that I won't disappoint her, that I'll do whatever she asks. Tell her it is important that I go with her to Boston, that I'll never let her down."

Mabel shook off Rebecca's hands and got dressed. There was nothing else to do. She was anxious, in fact, to get the day over with—to know what her future held, one way or the other, no matter if it held a punishment or—and it was more than she could hope for—a reward. Mabel didn't stop for tea after she used the outhouse. The morning hit her eyes like a revelation. The days would go on, cold and bright and crisp, or dreary and sad. None of it relied upon her happiness or her failures.

✦   ✦   ✦

Mrs. Hunt was standing over the dead dog's body when Mabel entered. The room smelled of decay and dog hair, but Mabel thought Mrs. Hunt would not have noticed. She stood with her head down, staring at the corpse, not speaking to Mabel for a full minute. The ice under the dog bed had melted to a shallow pool inside the metal basin that the butler had delivered to the room. He had kept the ice refreshed all week but failed to deliver more ice this morning with the complications of the last twenty-four hours.

"I have something I want you to do for me," Julia said.

"Yes, ma'am," Mabel said without a hint of her usual derision. She was too exhausted.

"I want you to take the body of Chou Chou and bury him for me."

Mabel didn't answer. She did not know if she could do such a thing.

"Did you hear what I said, girl?"

"Yes, ma'am," Mabel whispered. "Right now?"

"Of course, you stupid girl. Can you not smell him? Can you not see that he has to be buried?"

"Yes, ma'am."

Julia stepped aside as Mabel bent to pick up the stiffened body of the animal. To avoid touching the cold fur, she thought taking the dog bed with her would be best. As she drew near, the stench became overwhelming, and Mabel gagged. She held her breath and turned her face away from the animal's open mouth, the dried blood matted in its fur. Bile rose from her stomach, but she swallowed it down. The bottom of the dog bed was sopping from the melted ice, and the water soaked through her apron.

When she reached the door, she realized she couldn't manage the handle while still holding the cushion. "Ma'am," she tried, hoping Mrs. Hunt would be sensible enough to realize her dilemma. "Ma'am," she said again.

Julia turned away, walking to the windows and opening the curtains wide.

Mabel placed the dog back on the floor and opened the door. Before retrieving the bloated body, she spoke again. "Where would you like me to bury him, ma'am?" she asked.

Mrs. Hunt turned towards Mabel, but still, her gaze floated somewhere above the maid's head. "In the garden," she said, "under a rose bush. Have the gardener make a headstone for Chou Chou."

"Yes, ma'am."

"And when you are done, come back up here. We have other matters to discuss."

✦   ✦   ✦

Mabel made it to the garden before she vomited, but her heaves were dry and empty, as she hadn't even managed a glass of water this morning. Rebecca saw her rush out the back door of the dining room and watched with horror as the stiff corpse tumbled out when Mabel chucked the bed aside and doubled over. Chou Chou's body landed in a bush, front feet straight up in the air, back paws and tire-crushed hips matted and bloody. Rebecca rushed to her side.

"You dropped the dog," Rebecca said.

"I know that," Mabel mumbled, wiping the spittle that hung from the corner of her mouth.

"What did the Mrs. want from you? Why did she ask for you?"

"She wants to punish me, Rebecca. She made me carry her dead, smelly dog and told me to bury it."

"You best do the job, then," Rebecca said. "Don't let her see you dropped him, or she'll have your head."

✦   ✦   ✦

Mabel knocked lightly on Gardener's shack, though she guessed he was not about yet. She knocked again before entering the dark shed. The room smelled of must and cobwebs, and Mabel smiled for the first time that day when she remembered vomiting upon his proposal. Mabel searched for a shovel, and as she laid her hand on the wooden handle, she heard footsteps on the garden path.

"What're you doing in there?" he barked.

"Getting a shovel," she said without turning around. She was glad she had laid her hand on something that could be used as a weapon, just in case. Judging from what she knew from last night and all the stories she had heard about Gardener, he could be dangerous.

"This is *my* shed. You need to ask permission."

Mabel swung around. "I certainly do not. This is not your shed. This is the Hunts' shed. Lest you forget: everything," she said, stepping out with the shovel in hand, "*everybody* on this cottage belongs to them."

"Not forever," he growled, close to her ear as she passed.

"What does that mean?"

"Someday, Mr. Hunt will die. He cannot own me in death, can he?"

"Do you not know?" Mabel said, almost sadly, underneath her vehemence. "People like us will always be owned by somebody. Maybe not Mr. Hunt, but somebody."

✦   ✦   ✦

A light rain had begun as Gardener and Mabel finished burying the dog. Gardener had followed along behind Mabel, speechless for once, in a stupor from too little sleep and too much alcohol. He had taken the shovel from her hand and dug the hole, and for a moment, Mabel had softened toward him. What made him act so frightening? Underneath all that rage and bravado, could it be that he had a gentleman's spirit? Gardner grumbled, telling her to go find a stone, pointing to a pile of neatly sorted granite rocks he used for landscaping. They worked easily together.

Mrs. Hunt had dressed by the time Mabel returned. She wore a tan blouse with a high collar and a linen skirt. Only her hands and face were visible, the ghostly white of a woman who spent her days indoors. The room still held the deathly odor, though Mrs. Hunt had opened the window.

"Is Chou Chou gone?" Mrs. Hunt asked.

"Yes, ma'am."

"Did you make his grave pretty?"

"Yes, ma'am, with flowers and a stone."

"Very good." Mrs. Hunt gestured towards one of the Chippendale chairs near the window while she paced. "I want you to listen. Listen and do not speak until I command you."

Mabel nodded. Was this it? Would she finally be let go? Maybe that would be a relief from her constant worry, to know she was free—and destitute.

"You may think I do not know what is happening in this house. But I do. Godlessness. That is what has taken over this whole cottage. And my husband is at the center of it all. I am not an ignorant woman. I see what is going on. Even my son has somehow gotten wrapped up in the spell you have cast over my husband."

Mabel's eyes grew wide at the accusation, but she held her tongue, gripping onto the striped fabric of the chair.

"I am privy to everything that happens here. It is my house, after all. *My* house." Julia stopped and looked coldly at the maid, though still above the level of her eyes. "I know what child you are carrying. And I know you have been to that suffrage meeting. You are a troublemaker in every sense of the word."

As if on cue, rain hit harder at the windows, hammering out Mrs. Hunt's disgust.

"I am sure you realize that any other pious, righteous matron would not put up with having such a sinner amongst her staff, and I certainly have considered getting rid of you, at the very least. Everyone here knows that is what you deserve."

Mrs. Hunt took a deep, fortifying breath.

"I am willing to make a deal with you. Here is the offer—I will make it once: You can leave the cottage today and never return. I will not give you money or support you in any way. I will make it impossible for you to get a job anywhere around here—and believe me, I can make that happen. You will have to leave New England altogether. Or—"

Julia wrung her hands as she paced, letting forth her words in a rush, before she changed her mind, before she gave up her whole ruse.

"You can stay here and raise your bastard child on one condition. Marry that Gardener as planned—yes, I know about that arrangement—and this is the important part: you will do one thing for me without question, without protest. You will keep a secret for me. I will not tell you what this secret is until you choose. But once you have chosen, you cannot go back on your promise. You and I will be bound from that moment. I will keep you employed and sheltered with a home for the rest of your days."

Julia stopped with her hands on the back of the chair across from Mabel and looked the girl in the eye, searching for truth, for honesty.

"Speak now," Julia demanded.

Mabel bit her lip.

"Tell me your decision."

"Ma'am, must I marry Gardener? I am not sure—"

"Without question. I cannot have a harlot living under my roof."

"If I leave… you have given me a choice between life and death." Mabel cried. "Neither option is—"

Julia gripped the arms of the chair. "It is still a choice. You must make it."

Mabel shook her head, knowing that she chose life that day on the window ledge when she couldn't make herself jump. Some force kept her going despite the hopelessness of the situation. Was it love for her unborn child, or did she possess eternal optimism?

"I will keep your secret," she choked out.

Julia held her gaze. Mabel stared straight back at her with a look of iron determination, her green eyes trying to pierce. A jolt seemed to go through Julia's body, as if she understood for a moment why her husband had fallen for Mabel.

Julia broke the stare first. "Very well," she said, hesitating for a second. "Take this." Julia picked up a wicker basket from the table between the chairs. "Downstairs, in my sewing basket in the parlor, there is a half-embroidered pillow. It is stuffed and heavy. I want you to put it in this basket and bring it upstairs here, to me. After that, I will tell you the secret that will bind us." Julia thrust the basket at Mabel. "Go." When Mabel reached the door, Julia added, "And do not speak to anyone, particularly not Rebecca. Do not tell anyone what you are doing or what we have discussed."

Mabel nodded and left the room. She was tired of thinking, of questioning. It was good to have finally come to a decision. There was no possible way for her to leave. In her exhaustion, she understood that all those thoughts had been nothing but daydreams. Rupert's money? A fantasy. The idea she would be with Mr. Hunt? A fairy tale.

Mabel managed to walk to the parlor without running into anyone. The whole house was quiet, the servants going delicately about their business after the disturbing inquest. No one wanted to wake Mr. Hunt or agitate Master Rupert. In their estimation, the son was worse than the father, and the household would be glad when he and his wife departed.

Immediately, Mabel divined the contents of the pillow. Though padding softened the edges, only a simpleton wouldn't guess. She put the jewels inside the basket as planned and covered the bundle with another bit of stitching and a spool of thread. When she was nearly at the top of the stairs, Beverly called, asking about her activities. She replied with a brief, "I will be down soon." Beverly clucked in disapproval and then went back to her polishing.

Mabel's voice carried down the hall, alerting Rupert, who rushed out of his bedroom at the far end, but he was too late. Mabel moved safely inside the room with the basket of jewels, holding the steady gaze of Mrs. Ainsworth-Hunt.

The older woman's stare broke at a swift knock on the door.

"What is it?" Julia answered sharply.

"Oh, Mother. I saw the girl," Rupert said. "I wanted to make sure she was not… I wanted to make sure you are all right."

"Everything is fine."

Rupert hesitated outside the door. Finally, they heard his footsteps recede.

Mabel placed the basket between them, back onto the table. Mrs. Hunt now sat in her high-backed chair and gestured for Mabel to sit across from her. "You know what is inside the pillow?" Mrs. Hunt asked.

"Yes."

"I have good reason to deceive my husband, as I suspect you do, as well. He has dishonored us both. And now, together, you and I shall pay him back. As you know, we are leaving for Boston within the week. I cannot take the pillow with me. We are in close quarters while traveling, and I cannot trust Rebecca to take care of this for me. I am also not ready to return them to Mr. Hunt. I may never—I have not decided."

Mabel listened to the rain outside, feeling for a moment that everything would work out, enjoying a moment of solidarity with her lover's wife. She tried to imagine what Mrs. Hunt felt, acknowledging the woman her husband had impregnated. It struck Mabel that Mrs. Hunt's shame might be even greater than her own. She felt a moment of compassion for the woman, though Mrs. Hunt had never been anything but rude and condescending toward Mabel—barely treating her as if she were a human. She had treated her dog with more respect.

But now, they looked straight at each other. They understood, Mabel felt, what it might be like to be in each other's shoes. Mabel had a flash of the night she had traipsed across this very floor in Mrs. Hunt's slippers, and she smiled to herself, remembering her own naïveté.

"This is no laughing matter," Julia said harshly.

Mabel's smile faded. "No, ma'am."

Mrs. Hunt stood and went to her closet, pulling out a wooden box with exotic carvings. The wood was dark and solid, the carvings on top of tropical leaves and jungle animals. It reminded Mabel of the letter opener she had used to carve her initials in the chair. A pang of heartache arced through her body.

"Put the pillow in here," Mrs. Hunt ordered.

Mabel did as she was told. Mrs. Hunt shoved the packet flat so that the lid could close and then produced a key. The tiny lock clicked shut. Mrs. Hunt held onto the key and thrust the box toward Mabel.

"You are to hold onto this for me."

"Me?" Mabel stuttered.

"There is no one else. I have spent the night considering my options. I had wanted Rebecca to do so, but she is too weak." Julia turned to the window and spoke as if looking for strength as she surveyed her property. "I watched you last night. You believe yourself to be in love with my husband. I know that feeling, and I know firsthand the disappointment that comes following his disenchantment. And though he may now and again deign to notice you, I hope you will remember how it felt when he refused you entry to his room—yes, I know all about you trying to see him after the fall. As I said, I know what happens in my own house. Do not be fooled by his fleeting interest. He is fickle."

Mabel stared at her hands while Mrs. Hunt talked, not wanting to hear this truth but knowing she must give up the illusion that Mr. Hunt cared for her if she was to survive.

"What I am offering you is permanent protection. Unlike my errant husband, I can be trusted. And I am counting on the fact I can also trust you. Am I correct?" Julia did not wait for Mabel's response. "You and I, we will have a bond. We will keep each other's secrets. Now, I have not yet decided whether we will return the gems to Alistair. That depends on his behavior over the winter. I realize you may consider running off with the whole package, but do not imagine that you would ever get away with that. The police would find you, and you would go to jail—forever, without your child, without anyone to care about what happened to you. I suggest you leave off any idea of running away. But that is up to you. It will hurt you alone in the end—no one would believe I had anything to do with the theft."

Downstairs, the cook rang the bell for breakfast service. Footsteps trod down the stairs. The light clanging of dishes and pans rang out from the dining room each time the door swung open.

"I had the idea," Mrs. Hunt went on, "that you and Rebecca would trade positions, but obviously, with that child in your stomach, you cannot travel with us. You are to stay here, have the bastard, and await our return. Remember where your loyalty lies. You are to take this box with you, under the laundry." Julia gestured toward the basket in the corner of the room.

"Where you keep it, I do not need to know. But make sure, whatever you do, that no one else finds it. If the box is discovered, I will deny knowledge of the theft. Our bond is tightest when it is silent. You will have no better protection than mine in this household. If you betray me, you will not find a worse enemy. Do not confide in anyone but me. Do not even tell," Julia turned and looked meaningfully at Mabel, "your husband, Gardener, about our arrangement. Understood?"

"Yes."

"And one more thing. No more meetings. No drawing any attention to the household. Now go. And take the box with you."

Mabel carried the basket with her down to the laundry room. Rupert watched the girl descend the stairs, her bird-like fingers twittering along the edges of the basket and her green eyes darting back and forth around the foyer. His wife, Melinda, stood beside him with their bags. They were, at her insistence, traveling home to New York. Rupert would have liked to stay and sort out exactly where Forrest Wicks had made off with the gem collection. He hated to let the ruffian have even that much, but Melinda was impatient and didn't understand why they had lingered so long. She wanted to be out from under the pecking gaze of her mother-in-law.

As much as Rupert hated to let Forrest get away with thievery, he enjoyed seeing his father squirm. Perhaps the seed he had planted about Wicks might send his father after the man. That would be interesting to watch, but he did have work to get back to—a life beyond his parents' world—a whole adult, respectable life wherein he did not regress into childish behaviors. Rupert wondered if all progeny behaved as such—used the same familiar behavior patterns they had relied upon in childhood— each time they visited their parents. He had easily fallen into old mannerisms.

His father had always thought Rupert weak, incapable, and stiff, so he became such around the man. During this visit, his resentments were so large, he had wanted retribution. He did not behave this way in New York. He was not childlike in his normal, everyday activities. Two weeks here on Serabelle, and he was infantile again, with all his insecurities and indignation rising to the surface. As if the place had cast a spell on him—

this big, half-empty, cold house made of stone. He was ready to go home and break the spell.

✦ ✦ ✦

Mabel watched over her shoulder as she transferred Mrs. Hunt's dirty clothes into the larger basket in the laundry room. The wooden box lay uncovered for a second until she placed fresh sheets and pillowcases on top. She took a moment to reflect on what had happened. She was stuck now; that was clear. Her face burned at the thought that Mrs. Hunt knew about her affair. That she had been instructed not to attend suffrage meetings. An anger grew from her belly. This woman was trying to control every aspect of her life. But she also knew she was safe. She and her child would have a home here on Serabelle. To someone with no money, no real friends or family up here, safety was everything. And did she not now have some minor power with the jewels and Mr. Hunt's child? She was unsure exactly how she might wield that power, but maybe someday she would need it, the leverage she had over Mrs. Hunt.

She needed simply to make it through the halls without being discovered. Beverly was in the kitchen ordering the cook to start lunch. Beverly's voice carried like no one else's. The laundry room, down at the far end of the west hallway, was at least four rooms past the kitchen, but somehow, Beverly's voice, the timbre high and piercing, made it through walls, around corners, echoing into empty rooms on the main floor. She always knew where Beverly was in the house.

Rebecca too—her steps noisy, almost clumsy in her daily bustle. Rebecca couldn't sneak up on you. Mabel counted the other servants who might be in the house. The first butler rarely came into the laundry, and his quick, proper heels always click-clacked on the wood floors as he approached. But the second butler—he was another type altogether. Mabel felt glad that the man was sleeping. Not that she wished him ill—she was sorry he was poisoned or sick, or whatever had happened to him—she was, however, glad he wasn't in the house.

Mabel paused with her hand over the clean sheets. If Mrs. Hunt had stolen the jewels—and clearly she had—then what had happened to the second butler? What was the business about Rupert and the pillar? Who was in the car? Who did Willie see jumping out of the library window? Did he make that up? First, she would stash the jewels and then have a conversation with Willie. And she knew the perfect hiding place, somewhere neither Beverly nor Rebecca ever trod.

♦   ♦   ♦

Mabel had not entered the room in the east wing since the day she had considered jumping to her death. She was supposed to change the sheets weekly, but no one had known the difference. During the last month, Mabel had entered every other bedroom, changed sheet after sheet, and dusted surface after surface in the empty rooms. She had scrubbed the floors and pounded the rugs, but somehow, she couldn't make herself enter what she thought of as her and Mr. Hunt's room.

Now Mabel pushed the door open and smelled the slight dankness of the untouched, unoccupied space. A shaft of morning light bled through the bay window, showing dust on the bureau, on the bedposts. Otherwise, the room looked exactly as she had left it. The chair—her velvet chair stood staunch and regal in the corner, as if proud of what it had seen all those months ago. Mabel closed the door behind her without consideration of the rules. How she had changed in the last six months, she thought. The affair with Mr. Hunt had truly made a woman of her. She was no longer scared of what Beverly might think. With this pact she had made with Mrs. Hunt, Mabel knew now that she had a special place in this household. She would truly belong to Serabelle. And part of the estate—particularly this room—would belong to her.

Mabel set the basket down in the center of the floor and surveyed the room. She pulled out the dresser drawers one by one. Two lace doilies were folded in neat squares and sat lonely inside the top drawer. Fragrance from a pine sachet wafted up from each of the successive drawers, combating the dank odor of the closed room. Mabel knew she could easily leave the box here, and no one would check—not unless they had guests, and that wouldn't happen for at least another six months. She lifted the jewels from under the sheets, tracing the carved surface. The mass of gems inside weighed heavily on her left hand as she ran her right across the designs, the wood cold and hard under her fingertips. Mabel bent her nose to inhale the soft scent of polish and hardwood. Iconic figures on the box were perfectly rendered, a jungle of leaves and tropical flowers, a parrot and a woman's profile with a flower in her cascading hair—no bonnet—and even though Mabel was alone in the room, even though she was looking at a simple carving, she was awed by this woman's beauty and exotic air.

The box was too splendid, Mabel decided, to be concealed in a drawer. She thought it perfectly matched the letter opener that lay atop the dresser. Mabel placed the box at her feet and pulled out the dust rag she kept tucked in her waist, wiping the surface of the bureau. She picked up the letter opener and turned it around inside the rag, cradling it like a sacred object, as if made of glass rather than wood and metal. Briefly, she contemplated picking the tiny lock with the tip of the opener. Was it possible? Could she take one gem, one valuable stone that would be enough for her and her child to live on for the rest of their lives? How would anyone know if she took one? Mabel thought about all the possibilities, the threats that Mrs. Hunt and Rupert had made, and she knew it wasn't worth the risk. They would find her; she was convinced of that. Life here at the cottage was a sure bet for her child. And he would be near his father. Mabel smiled, realizing this was the first time she had called her baby a 'he.' She wondered if her instincts were true, if she could know such a thing.

Mabel carefully placed the box on top of the dresser. She stepped back and studied the room. The box looked as if it belonged there. She crossed to the window, threw open the panes, letting in the salty air, and then turned her attention to the bed, stripping off the sheets, working quickly and mindlessly until the rest of the room was orderly, free of old dirt and must. She ran her hand across the back of the chair, feeling for her carved initials. From the corner of her eye, Mabel saw a shadow break the light of the morning sky, but when she turned, though still raining lightly, the sky was a bright, solid white.

She finished plumping the pillows and smoothed the wrinkles out of the newly made bed, thinking briefly of her mother, wondering if her life was the same, if anything had changed. A letter from her mother came several months ago. She still lived in the same household in New Jersey, writing with very little news. Nothing of interest ever happened to her mother personally; all information concerned the family she worked for.

Mabel had yet to tell her mother she was pregnant. She had not known how to bring that up—particularly in a letter. The last few months had passed so quickly, her path so unstable, that every time she took out her stationery to write, she was unsure what to say. But now, so far along, so profoundly into the family's machinations, there was almost no way to explain. Once she knew for sure that Gardener was going to marry her, then she would write. Her mother would figure out the rest, Mabel thought, from the timing of the birth. Whether she would ever confess to the true father of her child remained to be seen. She couldn't imagine hiding the fact from her mother forever—they had always been so close—but that seemed the sort of information she should give face to face, not in a letter. Would they ever be face to face again?

Mabel crossed to close the window and glanced down at the rocky shore below. She reached out for the knob of the window, about to yank the pane shut, when she noticed a figure on the rocks. Mabel leaned out, squinting against the rain that still hit the sides of the house, the glass, the skin of her face. A small cry escaped her lips. The figure wasn't moving. On the rocks below, a dark body lay immobile, crushed.

Chapter 32
Throwing Shoes

Gardener made it to the body first. Four hours of sleep hadn't been sufficient to energize his limbs, so he sat in his shack in the rose garden for a half hour after he helped Mabel bury the dog. Most of the staff was slow to move that day, everyone treading lightly, afraid to be noticed, holding their breath until the Hunts left for Boston. Despite the grudges he held, Gardener intended to lay low, to stay out of Mr. Hunt's sight. Impending marriage be damned, as long as he still had his job. He had to remember what the cottage was like in winter—the freedoms he retained. Gardener took great pride in his work and didn't slack off when the Ainsworth-Hunts were gone, as people might expect. In fact, he probably worked harder, protecting the plants from frost, from storms that would ravage their fragile limbs. But he was freed from taking orders. If he kept the coming months in mind, he found it easier to accept his servitude now.

Gardener had been kneeling at the newly formed grave of the dog, wiping dirt from the granite, when he heard a sharp cry and saw a flash out of the corner of his eye. He looked up, imagining a bird had swooped past his peripheral vision. The sound wasn't recognizable as human or animal. He scanned the horizon, the sky, and the tree line, but saw no evidence of what would have been a massive bird—possibly an eagle or a hawk. Gardener even had the fleeting thought that maybe he was still drunk, or at least affected enough to see visions, to hear noises.

He wiped the rain from his eyes and brushed aside his wet bangs. These people paid more attention to a dead dog, he thought, than to an ailing servant. The family's behavior the evening before, their refusing to call a doctor for Mr. Wilson, enraged Gardener. But he was powerless to change who they were.

A second female cry startled him out of his reverie. He trotted out of the rose garden through the path that led to the back lawn. Mabel was leaning out the same window where he had seen her throwing shoes. The memory almost made him laugh until he saw her face, her features twisted in shock and her finger pointing down to the rocks below.

He followed her directive and ran across the lawn to the stairway carved into the rocks. From the top of the cliff, Gardener could just see the outline of what Mabel pointed at: a body, twisted and smashed on the rocks below. Though the face was turned away as if looking out over the vast ocean, he could tell whose body it was.

Gardener flew down the steps and over the pebbly beach until he climbed atop the massive granite boulders, the cliff behind him rising sharply up to the path along the waterfront that edged the back lawn. He started at the sight of Willie, distorted and bloodied—gone. His head had shattered upon impact, his skull broken and oozing out what looked like brain matter in red and gray lumps. Gardener gagged as he saw that Willie's eye had popped from his head and hung from a single bloody cord, melding with the rest of the flesh that had torn and burst with the pressure of bones and guts inside him. Gardener was glad that the boy had been dressed, as he didn't want to imagine what parts and pieces were poking through the skin of the rest of his body. The ocean pounded at the rocks, spraying saltwater across his face. The mist and the rain soaked Willie's body, washing blood down into the rocks, back into the earth.

Gardener himself was soaked through to his skin. He looked out towards the horizon and took a few deep breaths. A flash of the moment he found Sarah's doll on the rocks all those years ago arose. He knew Rupert was responsible—he had always been a selfish, destructive child. Gardener repaired the doll, taking it to his shack and gluing it back together. He had only wanted to protect the girl, to make her smile.

Instantly, he felt the same for Mabel, the urge to shield her from the bloody mess. But he needed a moment to compose himself before he went to her.

What happened here? The movement he saw out of the corner of his eye had obviously been Willie falling. He must have been on the house's upper floors, possibly on the roof. But the fall. It had been so silent. Just that one unearthly cry. Had he jumped? Was he pushed? Suddenly, Gardener wondered if he himself had any responsibility for this death. He hadn't really disliked the boy. Why had he acted so brutally with him? Would they blame him?

Gardener looked down once again to the body, searching for a clue, for some sort of sign that would tell him what happened. He inched closer, avoiding Willie's mangled face. He checked his hands, thinking perhaps there would be a note, but his hands were splayed, fingers bent unnaturally, skin snapped in places like the burst casing of a sausage. Gardener patted Willie's jacket, looking for anything, some object that might give an answer. His body felt warm and wet under the jacket, jelly-like. Gardener straightened and sniffed, holding back tears, which were rare for him, but threatened now. He had liked the kid; truly, he had.

◆   ◆   ◆

Mabel stumbled at the top of the stairway, crying out when she saw Willie. With great shoving motions, she tried to push past Gardener, but his bulk held her fast.

"Do *not* look," he said. "It's horrible."

Mabel stopped struggling and cried into Gardener's shoulder, massive sobs that shook her body. At that moment, she felt so tiny, so fragile, like a glass figurine he had seen in a shop window downtown.

Mabel's scream had been harrowing and pierced through the cold stone walls of the cottage, reverberating. Even Mr. Hunt stirred in his sleep. Beverly bustled to calm Mrs. Hunt, telling her she would look into the noise. The servants all met in the foyer and then moved as a group out onto the back patio, where they saw Gardener and Mabel huddling together.

"Maybe he scared her," Rebecca said. "He *is* scary."

Beverly nodded, unsure. "Butler, please go investigate."

The butler huffed out a short breath and walked toward the couple, clearly rankled that Beverly had given him an order. But even he was unprepared to put up a fight this day, too intrigued or exhausted to argue.

Gardener watched the butler approach and nodded down to the rocks, turning Mabel's back to the devastating scene. The night's events had seemed a grim tale, a story told in the night to scare children—possible poisoning of Mr. Wilson, figures skulking, Mr. Hunt's behavior in front of his wife, his family, and the rest of them. Willie making up stories. And now this?

The butler faltered when he saw Willie, nearly falling over the edge himself as he stared down. He waved his arms at the rocks as if to erase the vision. He stumbled back up the lawn and told the others what he had seen.

Rebecca screamed nearly as loudly as Mabel until she was dispatched to tell Mrs. Hunt what had happened. Beverly gathered Mabel back from the cliff edge and ordered Gardener to tell the rest of the staff—her husband Josiah and the stable boys—what had happened. And he was to find out what the stable master knew. Gardener, unusually quiet, simply nodded and walked off after murmuring in Mabel's ear. Beverly blinked briefly at this strange display of tenderness and then hugged the girl herself.

"Did you see Willie fall?" When Mabel didn't answer, Beverly pulled away, raising Mabel's chin. "What happened here, Mabel? What do you know?"

Mabel kept her eyes lowered. "I was cleaning in the east wing. I saw him on the rocks… from the window."

"Do you think he jumped?"

"Maybe. He said he loved me, Beverly." Mabel sobbed into her hands. "He wanted to marry me… and I laughed at him. I laughed."

Beverly stood without speaking, looking at the gray of the sky above them. "Was that enough to make him want to take his own life?"

Mabel didn't look up.

"Answer me."

"I don't know. But I think I saw him… well… I didn't see him, but I felt him… a shadow, from a room in the east wing, on the third floor. He must have been on the roof. How did he get on the roof?"

✦   ✦   ✦

Gardener found the ladder propped against the eaves on the south side of the cottage. Willie must have found the ladder inside the utility shed. He pictured the boy crawling from the utility room's second-story roof onto the house's main wing. The ceramic tiles slick in the misty rain would have been dangerous. Gardener walked around to the rose garden. He looked up at the roof, picturing Willie standing there, able to see Gardener kneeling, ridiculously grooming the dead dog's grave while Willie contemplated his own death. Why had the boy done it? He had seemed, of everyone here, content enough to work with his horses, to be living at the cottage. Gardener shook his head and trudged to the stables.

Inside the damp barn that reeked of hay and manure, boys moved in a steady rhythm. They brushed and shoveled while horses whinnied, demanding oats, hay, or attention. No one spoke as they went about their chores, but both Theo and George looked startled that Gardener had entered the barn, making a beeline for the stable master's office. They both came running when they heard the old man's voice raise in distress.

"No, it is not possible."

"I saw his body myself," Gardener said ruefully.

"I sent him out fah the old pitchfork in the shed." The stable master stood, gesturing towards a broken tool on the ground. "Snapped right in two. The handle were weak. Never seen the like."

"He found a ladder in the utility room," Gardener explained. "He jumped from the roof."

The boys came tearing around the corner, stopping short of bumping into Gardener, when they realized it was Willie the men talked about. George had teased Willie not an hour ago about breaking the pitchfork, about not knowing his own strength, about Willie's scrawny body. He wished he had not said that.

"He wouldn't have jumped. I know it," Theo cried.

Gardener cast a sidelong glance at the boy and then addressed the stable master. "Any reason he should have been up on that roof?"

"I cannot imagine." The old man sighed. "I cannot imagine."

◆　◆　◆

Alistair ambled out of the house in his slippers and robe. The staff was huddled on the porch even though the rain continued to mist down, casting a shimmering glaze over their skin and clothes. They all stared towards the sound of the waves, and Alistair thought perhaps they, too, thought the noise deafening.

"I rang," he shouted.

The butler crossed to the doorway. "Excuse me, sir, but Willie…"

"Willie?" he roared. "What is it with you servants? Do you not remember why you are here at Serabelle? I will give you a reminder: you are here to serve. Me."

"Willie has died, sir."

Alistair closed his mouth, halted his voice that had been poised to continue threatening. His body felt as if he had slammed against a wall at a full trot. He looked from the group to the ocean beyond and suddenly took off across the slick grass. His cast lent him the appearance of an amputee balancing on a wooden leg. The butler hurried behind as Alistair skidded and hobbled across the lawn, righting himself just short of toppling from the cliff. Images of his missing jewels flashed back to him as he hustled to the edge of the cliff, wondering how the collection and Willie were related. Below, a white spray splashed onto Willie's body, residue from the full waves that crashed onto the rocks below. Alistair turned his head from the bloody mess. His head reeled, and he released a noise, not unlike the cry of an animal caught in a trap. The butler grabbed Mr. Hunt's shoulders as he crumbled to the ground with a thump.

"Willie?" he said questioningly as if he were addressing the boy directly.

The butler answered for him. "Yes, Willie."

"Why?"

"We do not know, sir. We may never know."

Chapter 33
Sebago Lake

Willie had intended to fetch the pitchfork and head back to the stables straight away. He pulled up his collar and huddled down against the salty air as he walked the short distance from the stables. The morning was misty and cool, the type of weather he liked to ride in, but he knew he wouldn't be allowed. He could do nothing but chores. They watched you like a hawk at the cottage, someone always aware of where you were, what you were doing, who you talked to. Willie wondered what it would be like to live all alone in a cabin in the woods, hunting for food, chopping wood for his own use, foraging, and making his own tools. He would learn to smith to make his horse's shoes. He would take a wife.

A sharp pang pierced Willie's stomach as he thought of Mabel. She would never be his, he knew. But surely there was another woman out there somewhere—a woman who was like him, his equal, who would love him, scrawny body and all, lack of money or importance or learning. Was it possible that he could be loved? Who knew? He didn't think that anyone other than his parents had ever loved him, and he hadn't seen them in years now. He might never see them again.

Willie opened the shed door and searched for the pitchfork, but the room was dark. He felt blindly with his hand stretched out in front of him, and his fingers became entangled in a spider's web. He brushed his hand against his trousers and waited for his eyes to adjust to the dark. As he stood quietly in the dusty shed, he heard a peeping sound. He cocked his head to the side and listened again. There it was, the chirping of a tiny bird—at least it sounded tiny, its voice meek and barely audible.

When he could finally see, Willie searched the shed for the source of the noise, thinking there might be a nest, but he couldn't find one in the dark room. Willie stepped outside and listened. The noise grew louder, and he stretched his neck back to eye the eaves of the shed, but again, he could see nothing. The cries surged, as if the bird was in distress, and Willie wondered if it were not a bird at all, but maybe some other sort of animal that needed his help. Quickly, Willie grabbed the ladder he had seen inside the shed, leaning it against the eave about halfway up the roofline. He shuffled up the rungs in an instant and inspected underneath the eaves, looking for a nest as the noise grew louder and what seemed to him more frantic.

Willie looked at the chimney above on the main roof. He climbed to the tip of the ladder and grabbed for the peak of the lower roof, pulling himself up onto the tiles. They were wet, and he straddled the top, resting for a moment, feeling the damp soak through the seat of his pants. What was he doing? The stable master would be mad at him, he knew, if he was much longer. Willie considered climbing back down, going back to work, but the view from even up on this second story was magnificent. It reminded him of when he was a boy, and he and his parents had visited relatives in New Paltz. There was a tree in his cousin's yard—a big old oak that he had climbed to the highest branch. He had seen the whole city from that tree and had thought that if he could be a lumberjack, he would be happy. Or maybe someone who worked on those high beams he had seen as a little boy in the city. Willie had always liked heights.

He pulled himself up and shuffled to where the shed's roof met the main roof, peeking out over the top, though he knew he was unlikely to see the ocean from where he stood. The noise of the bird had softened, though he could still hear a muffled peep. Willie hopped up onto the main roof and crawled up to the chimney. The household rarely used the fireplace in the south end, as the wing was used for guests, and most came in the late summer months when the warm weather rendered a fire unnecessary.

Willie stood with his ear to the brick chimney and listened. He was sure now that the peeping sound was a baby bird. Either it had resigned itself to its fate, or it sensed his presence. Willie was not tall enough to look inside the chimney or even reach the top of the stack, so he leaned against the brick and looked out across the expanse. He couldn't see the shore, but he could see the straight, hopeful line of the horizon.

Willie imagined living on a boat, fishing, and sailing, maybe, though he had no idea what that entailed. He recalled that trip with his father again, fishing out on Sebago Lake. But a boy like him, he knew, working in the stables, would never own a boat, not the kind he could go sailing in. Now that he had run over the dog, he probably would never learn to drive automobiles properly. There was little chance of his becoming a chauffeur, especially on Serabelle.

Even on this misty day, boats floated out on the water. They seemed a million miles away, like toys. Willie loved the view from up here. He couldn't imagine going back to the stables right now, under the rueful eye of the stable master. Willie stretched his arms out wide and balanced on the inverted V of the rooftop. It had been such a strange night, and his body was stiff, his head bleary from what he had said and done. He didn't know why he had tried to blame Gardener for the theft. Spite, he assumed, but it was unlike him. He had felt so crazy lately when it came to Mabel, and the way the Hunts treated her, treated everyone at the cottage. Life seemed so unfair. What was wrong with wanting something for yourself, wanting a different position, a different angle?

Willie walked gingerly across the top of the roofline, heading out towards the stripe of blue horizon. He looked back at the stables, ensuring the old man wasn't searching for him. Free and adventurous for a few moments, he felt rebellious. Willie watched as a bird swooped down past him and towards the chimney. A starling, he knew, the mother arriving with some sort of food for her baby. As Willie turned quickly to watch the path of the dark bird, he lost his footing. He felt his shoe slip on the wet roof, and he threw his arms out to steady himself, his right leg swinging out for balance until his left shoe caught on a dry piece of tile. Willie stumbled a few inches, circling his arms wildly. And then he caught himself, tapping into the same inner balance he used when horseback riding.

He crouched into a squat, shaken, both hands flat on the roof as he caught his breath, keeping his eyes on the path of the starling as it entered the chimney. The baby was quiet now, having the comfort of its mother near, knowing that its next meal was imminent. He remembered that same consolation when his mother came home from her long hours in the dress shop where she worked, knowing she would take care of him. Now, he had no such security. He had not saved anything, as he usually lost his meager wages in the poker games. He was dependent on the cottage.

Willie unfolded from his crouch and scanned the horizon once again. Would it ever be possible to have a different life? The idea Mabel had brought up, her notion about some people not mattering, suddenly struck Willie as the truth. He was probably—most definitely—one of those people. If Mabel, the one friend, the focus of all his affections, didn't care for him, then who would? Thinking of her, the pangs he had felt earlier were gone; his stomach was calm, and he felt resigned to his aloneness, to the fact that she would never return the fire he had felt. The acceptance made his body numb for the first time, sensationless, empty. Willie moved toward the roof's edge, looking out over the back lawn, down the path where he and Mr. Hunt often rode. He surveyed the shore below and the ocean beyond. Waves pounded violently onto the rocks, making a thunderous sound, and he closed his eyes, taking in all of nature's odors and noises. The misty air was thick with salt, and even from the rooftop, he smelled the dank, fetid seaweed, the rotting fishy smell of the tidal pools that grew among the rocks. Willie longed to be down on the shore, peering into the shallow water filled with barnacles and anemones. When he first moved here, he loved finding snails and jellyfish in the murky water. And in late summer, when he was lucky, he had searched and found a bevy of sand dollars.

Willie opened his eyes and took in the gray vista, the dramatic shoreline here in Maine. He watched as gulls squawked out over the water, dropping mollusks on the rocks to break their shells. The birds dove sharply down to the rocks, sucking up the gooey innards. Watching the birds, Willie had a desire to fly with them, to feel the air beneath him holding, cradling his body, floating him down like a feather, into the ocean, into the great beyond. He had swum in the cold Atlantic a handful of times, on hot Indian summer days last year after the Hunts had left for Boston, but right now, he thought he would like to feel any sensation, no matter how cold, no matter that the chill would enter his skin and soak into his bones. He poked at the skin of his arm, wondering if he had lost all sensitivity, as if he had been sedated from the inside out.

Below, in the garden, off to his right, Gardener's wide back was bent over a pile of dirt. He had never despised anyone the way he had Gardener in the past few weeks. But now, as he watched the hulking form below, he felt nothing like hate. He felt detached, as if he were watching his life from afar, watching someone else's story unfold. He couldn't imagine going back to the stables now, couldn't picture ever coming off this roof—as if having climbed this far, he should keep climbing, reaching for some new life, some new way to be. Willie breathed heavily of the salt air. He circled his head and felt crunching inside his neck. Would he grow old here, on this estate, all alone like Mr. Wilson, quiet nights in the kitchen, fetching things for these ungrateful people? Or would he move from household to household, never having a true home of his own, always a slave to another man, bitter like Gardener, crotchety like the stable master? It all seemed pointless now. Why live if it was in service to another? Willie had no desire to spend his life watching other men—men like Mr. Hunt—enjoy themselves. What did he care?

He didn't care, he thought, though a tear traced a path down his cheek. He swiped at it, as if the tear itself had betrayed the idea of his emotionless self. Willie took one last look at the horizon before returning to the peak. He knew he'd have to go back down and face the stable master and eventually the Hunts. As he turned, the starling swept from behind him, crossing within two feet of his head. Surprised, Willie wobbled at the edge of the roof. His knees felt rubbery, and he struggled to regain balance. He lifted his right leg to widen his stance but missed the roofline. His foot punched through the empty air, and his whole body lurched. The wrenching surge of fear flew up his throat, and he released a sharp yelp. Willie felt his weight being pulled down, and he tumbled into the wind.

Chapter 34
Amen

Alistair felt Willie's death was a personal insult. He clung to his grief and hid away, locking himself in the library, staring at his empty trays, wondering if he had done something wrong, if he had contributed to Willie's death. This shock, this sweet boy's death, shook him to the core—to the point of trembling limbs. He had felt genuine affection for Willie; he had almost loved him.

In his library, Alistair went so far as to pull paper and an ink pen out of the desk; to what end, he could not say. To write his feelings? Perhaps. He attempted a few scribbles, uneven lines that did not add up to a word in any language. He knew he had made a mess of things, but where to go from here? Back to Boston, yes, but would life ever be the same after this summer at Serabelle?

He scratched at the notepad, drawing a semblance of an automobile, a childlike rendering from someone with little artistic talent. He had loved his autos and had fought so hard to bring them to the island, but maybe he had been mistaken. Maybe they should have left the Olds and the Winton in Boston. First the dog, then the gems. He believed that his own flesh and blood, Rupert, driving the auto in the middle of the night had something to do with the theft, though he could prove nothing. It was heart-breaking that Rupert could steal from his own father and then return to New York without even a goodbye. What had he done to deserve such treatment? Had he been such an awful father?

These questions and others about the maid became overwhelming and muddled his brain. Mabel. Saying her name gave his heart a little ache in the center. He had made such a mess of it, he knew, but he could not bear to part with her. She had brought him joy, that tiny, fiery girl. Such surprise. The very essence of what he had always loved about people: the surprises they could bring, the amazing answers to his questions. But now, at over fifty years old, he finally understood those surprises were not always good. Sometimes people robbed you blind.

All talk of the gems' theft ceased. In fact, nearly all conversation came to a halt between the walls of Serabelle. The servants moved as ghosts between the houses. They left it to Gardener and Josiah to help the coroner. The stable master constructed a simple pine box, and Josiah used the wagon team to cart Willie's body to the graveyard. The servants walked quietly behind, every member present—including both butlers. Not even Beverly mentioned a word that the Ainsworth-Hunts were without a servant for a few hours. The cook and the stable boys, the chauffeur, and the maids would grieve in their own ways. Ultimately, each person was left alone with their misery.

Beverly kept her arm around Mabel on the walk. Mabel had tried to refuse to come with them, her face blank and wan after she had finished crying. But Beverly wouldn't allow it. "You need to be beside the grave," she said somberly. "You have got to see your friend buried. Remember how fragile life really is. Everyone would do well to remember how this day feels."

The leaves of the oaks along the road were at the height of fall color: yellow ochres and reds spreading across the veins, wiping out summer's brilliant green, as if nature itself were in tune with the somberness of the day.

Mabel had a knot in her stomach, a twist as if someone had grabbed her insides and wrung all the moisture from her body like a piece of laundry. Even her tears had finally dried. The name 'Willie' remained on her lips, halfway out of her mouth, a name she thought she would never forget, never cleanse from her tongue. Not twenty-four hours ago, Mabel had imagined the two of them running away together, and she could not come to terms with Willie not living—his vitality had been so hopeful, so overwhelming, she had almost allowed herself to believe in a future filled with happiness. It seemed impossible that the joyful, optimistic boy would no longer be gracing the grounds of Serabelle. He had seemed to embody hope itself at times, and Mabel could not visualize life at the cottage without him.

Low clouds were slung across the sky like lace. The servants gathered around the open gap in the earth while a reverend spoke in a monotone voice: "By the sweat of your brow, you will eat your food, until you return to the ground, since from it, you were taken; for dust you are, and to dust, you will return."

The stable master spoke briefly of his fondness for Willie before his eyes brimmed over with tears. Men lowered the coffin into the ground with thick hemp ropes that they pulled out from under the box once the weight had settled into the dirt. The stable boys had brought the cottage's shovels to save the expense of a gravedigger—they had spent the morning hollowing out the hole they had put their friend into. The lone funeral cost had been paying for the reverend and the plot itself. Beverly wrangled the sum from the drunken Mr. Hunt, though she had not mentioned the burial. She knew enough not to upset Mr. Hunt further and insisted she needed the money for new tapers in the parlor. He would not remember, she knew, that there was already a set of candles in the supply closet off the kitchen. Mr. Hunt had grumbled for a moment before he threw the money at her, telling her not to bother him with such trivialities.

Mrs. Hunt had not made a comment on Willie but simply ordered Rebecca to continue packing her things. They would leave in three days for Boston. The boy's death overshadowed her glory in stealing her husband's gems. A gloom had set over the cottage; Julia wondered, satisfyingly, if they all felt as she had at Chou Chou's tragic end.

As Julia packed her jewelry in her travel case—a task she did not entrust to Rebecca—she hoped she had made the right choice in enlisting Mabel's help with the gems. But what else could she have done? Hidden them herself and then taken the chance of a staff member running across them? Thrown them in the ocean as she had dreamed? No, it was better this way, to have them safe, looked after while she watched her husband suffer. Julia stopped with a necklace of pearls hanging between her fingers. Had her life come to this—her biggest pleasure in seeing her husband, the man she had pledged her life to, unhappy? Julia pushed the small bench under her and let her knees fall to the rug below. She dropped the necklace on the vanity and clasped her hands together, praying to God for forgiveness.

"Please, Lord," she whispered. "Please take this bitterness from me. Guide me on the righteous path. Let my husband show me one single sign of affection. Let him remember the woman he married. Let him gaze upon me once more with the eyes of a true husband, and I swear, I will confess my sin. I will give him back all that he loves if he will but once see me as the woman I was."

Julia's eyes flickered open, and she saw the old, lined face gazing back at her in the mirror, and she knew, thinking of the beautiful young maid, that her prayer would not be answered.

"And let me believe," she continued on, averting her gaze, "that we could once again be happy here on Serabelle, that my husband will not be a laughing stock, that my son will respect both his mother and his father, and that he will give us grandchildren who will love us."

Julia heard a stirring at the door and saw Rebecca standing, waiting.

"Here, come pray with me," Julia said, and the girl shuffled over and knelt beside her. "Dear Lord," Mrs. Hunt continued, "We wish to take the righteous path, though those unworthy among us have led us to death and destruction, into the devil's arms. But let us cry no more. Let us know your mercy once again. Amen."

"Amen," Rebecca repeated.

Chapter 35
No Other Protection

Mabel and Gardener were married in the Eden Congregational Church on October15th, 1913. Mabel would have chosen city hall, given the option, but she wasn't asked her preference. Since Willie's death, she went about her days in a trance—doing her chores, eating enough to stay alive, lying in bed throughout the night, though she didn't often sleep. Beverly made all the arrangements for the ceremony, altering her own wedding dress—kept stowed away in a cedar trunk at the foot of her bed—for Mabel. Even after taking in the sides and hemming up the lace, the dress dragged lifelessly on the floor behind the bride.

Beverly had asked if Mabel would like to invite her parents to the celebration, but she shook her head, ashamed at the thought of her mother seeing her in such a state. Though Mabel didn't believe in sin, her mother, a strong Catholic, did. She said she would write a letter after the wedding, perhaps blurring the timeline, but she thought she might stop writing her mother altogether.

The Serabelle employees sat on uncomfortable pine pews, running their fingers over hymn books and pawing at thin red cushions. A handful of Beverly's friends from a neighboring house were present, as well as some fellows who traipsed through the yellow house every week up to the room on the third floor. The sight of the women cheered Mabel—she recognized two from the suffrage meeting, and she wondered if she might someday have the courage to attend another while the Hunts were away. How would they know? And even if Mrs. Hunt found out, what could she do but admonish her?

Even with these guests, only the first three pews were populated. Beverly had ordered two vases of lilies—everyone in the household had contributed—and she had made a white cake that was in the icebox back at the house.

Mabel kept her eyes pinned to the blue cassock of the minister. She dared not meet Gardener's—or Patrick Raymond Mahoney's—eyes. He was loud and boisterous throughout, calling upon his friends to congratulate him, grabbing at her borrowed wedding dress when the minister allowed them to kiss. His lips were rough and sunburned.

Gardener picked her up and sauntered down the aisle with her legs dangling over his muscular forearm. Mabel buried her face in her hands. This man was her future. The Ainsworth-Hunts had left for Boston the previous week. As she watched Mr. Hunt climb into the Olds without so much as a glance in her direction, Mabel finally understood her fate. She would have to learn to be comfortable with Gardener.

As they threw open the doors to the church, the sea air hit their faces. They would hold the wedding celebration in the yellow house at Serabelle. Rebecca and the cook had gone with the Hunts to Boston, but the rest of them remained, awaiting the next summer, keeping the house in order. They would battle against the destructive elements of the ocean, brushing and polishing away salt deposits. Day after day, the servants would do their jobs.

As her belly swelled, Mabel occasionally sat in the velvet chair in the corner of the room in the east wing. With her eyes on the carved box atop the dresser, she imagined how things might have been different, how they might yet be. Mabel would then stand, crossing to the window. She would throw open the panes, letting the salty air caress her skin. Mabel would take a deep breath and look to the horizon, gathering the courage to turn her gaze down to the rocks below.

Author's Note

I feel the need to make a statement about some of the language in this book. I deliberated over including some derogatory phrases, particularly regarding the Black character, Willie. As *Serabelle* is a piece of historical fiction, I also felt it was necessary to portray an accurate rendition of local attitudes and speech during that era. My use of words such as "darkie" and "boy", were meant to show the ignorance of the characters saying those words, rather than condoning the use. If I have insulted anyone with these terms, I deeply apologize.

Acknowledgements

My family's history informs this novel greatly. My great-grandmother Mimi worked as a cook on Sonogee, the Atwater-Kent estate in Bar Harbor. When I was a child, my family would sneak onto the grounds of what was at that time a nursing home. We played on the rocks with my grandmother, Grace, and gathered shells for hours every summer, instilling in me a fascination for the landscape.

I was handed down a piece of jewelry, a pin with sapphire and moonstone that was said to be gifted to my great-grandmother by Mrs. Kent herself. When my mother spoke of Sonogee, it was with pride, as if our family, too, belonged to that cottage. Throughout the novel, I explore what ownership and dignity mean to all facets of life on the estate.

To the readers of this manuscript early and late—my Lesley University professors and critique groups, the MISers, Kimberly Coughlan, and my Vashon writer's group—my deepest gratitude. Alice Bloch, may you always be my best editor. Ture Brusletten and Matthew Chasan, I'm sure you'll find those last two typos.

Christine Junge, I miss our work on The Personal Element—mostly, I miss being in constant contact. I wish you time and healing my friend.

To my sister Vickie Black-Vigue, whom I chased across the rocks with seaweed, and my brother-in-law Tom Vigue, who has always believed in this book, all my love. Thank you to my mother, Bobbie Black, for sharing your love of books. And to my father, Russ Black, a true Mainer, solid as they come.

A.J. Verdelle, I hear your voice with every draft, reminding me that clarity is non-negotiable.

To the Easy Like Sunday Morning Runners who didn't get a mention in my first book, I'm going to name you here. Not because you read the book, but because you kept my lazy butt energized enough to keep going: Susan Swan, Jenny Nordling Wegley, Ginger Hamilton, Katie Simpson, and Kristen Cohen, thank you. You're the only reason I get up early on Sunday mornings.

A huge thank you to Maizy Smallidge of the Bar Harbor Historical Society for taking the time to comb through photos for me. What a treasure to see Sonogee in its heyday.

I am honored to be part of the Black Rose Writing family. Thank you for welcoming me in so thoroughly.

And as always, to Dorsey and Zelda Davis, I love you. Now stop talking so I can work.

✦   ✦   ✦

For news about giveaways and events, sign up on my website
www.taviblack.com

Follow me on Bookbub, Instagram, Goodreads, and Pinterest:
@Tavitaylorblack

Sources

Vandenberg, Lydia Bodman & Shettleworth, Earle G. Jr, (2009) *Opulence to Ashes: Bar Harbor's Gilded Century 1850-1950*, Downeast Books

Lee, Maureen Elgersmand, (2005) *Black Bangor: African Americans in a Maine Community 1880-1950*, University of New Hampshire Press

Brechlin, Earl, (2002) *Bygone Bar Harbor, A Postcard Tour of Mount Desert Island & Acadia National Park*, Downeast Books

About the Author

Tavi Taylor Black lives on an island near Seattle where she designs sets for the Vashon Dance Academy and was the founding director of the Dove Project, an anti-domestic violence non-profit organization. Before earning an MFA from Lesley University, Tavi spent 14 years touring with rock bands.

She has a writing podcast, *The Personal Element*, with co-host Christine Junge. Her debut novel, *Where Are We Tomorrow?*, was the winner of the 2022 Nancy Pearl Award and was a finalist in the NYC Big Book Award and the National Indie Excellence Awards.

Note from Tavi Taylor Black

Word-of-mouth is crucial for any author to succeed. If you enjoyed *Serabelle*, please leave a review online—anywhere you are able. Even if it's just a sentence or two. It would make all the difference and would be very much appreciated.

Thanks!
Tavi Taylor Black

We hope you enjoyed reading this title from:

www.blackrosewriting.com

Subscribe to our mailing list – *The Rosevine* – and receive **FREE** books, daily deals, and stay current with news about upcoming releases and our hottest authors.
Scan the QR code below to sign up.

Already a subscriber? Please accept a sincere thank you for being a fan of Black Rose Writing authors.

View other Black Rose Writing titles at
www.blackrosewriting.com/books and use promo code
PRINT to receive a **20% discount** when purchasing.

Made in United States
North Haven, CT
14 August 2024

56070069R00169